FEAR of DRIVING

FEAR
of DRIVING

Daniella Brodsky

BERKLEY BOOKS, NEW YORK

THE BERKLEY PUBLISHING GROUP
Published by the Penguin Group
Penguin Group (USA) Inc.
375 Hudson Street, New York, New York 10014, USA
Penguin Group (Canada), 90 Eglinton Avenue East, Suite 700, Toronto, Ontario M4P 2Y3, Canada
(a division of Pearson Penguin Canada Inc.)
Penguin Books Ltd., 80 Strand, London WC2R 0RL, England
Penguin Group Ireland, 25 St. Stephen's Green, Dublin 2, Ireland (a division of Penguin Books Ltd.)
Penguin Group (Australia), 250 Camberwell Road, Camberwell, Victoria 3124, Australia
(a division of Pearson Australia Group Pty. Ltd.)
Penguin Books India Pvt. Ltd., 11 Community Centre, Panchsheel Park, New Delhi—110 017, India
Penguin Group (NZ), 67 Apollo Drive, Mairangi Bay, Auckland 1311, New Zealand
(a division of Pearson New Zealand Ltd.)
Penguin Books (South Africa) (Pty.) Ltd., 24 Sturdee Avenue, Rosebank, Johannesburg 2196, South Africa

Penguin Books Ltd., Registered Offices: 80 Strand, London WC2R 0RL, England

This book is an original publication of The Berkley Publishing Group.

This is a work of fiction. Names, characters, places, and incidents either are the product of the author's imagination or are used fictitiously, and any resemblance to actual persons, living or dead, business establishments, events, or locales is entirely coincidental. The publisher does not have any control over and does not assume any responsibility for author or third-party websites or their content.

FEAR OF DRIVING

Copyright © 2007 by Daniella Brodsky
Cover art by Ali Smith
Cover design by George Long
Text design by Kristin del Rosario

Excerpts from the *Connecticut Department of Motor Vehicles Driver's Manual* used with permission.

First edition: April 2007

Berkley trade paperback ISBN: 978-0-425-21080-2

An application to register this book for cataloging has been submitted to the Library of Congress.

PRINTED IN THE UNITED STATES OF AMERICA

10 9 8 7 6 5 4 3 2 1

This book is dedicated to friends: all the really wonderful friends who are there when it really counts, in the nitty gritty way most of us have no clue how to be. It's for the ones who can make you breathe right, carry a garbage bag of memories the size of a truck down to the incinerator, incite giggles in the absolute worst of circumstances. It's for the ones who tell it like it is, put your makeup on and force you to get it together, extend the most generous gestures without ever caring to let you know, the ones who simply claim, "that's who I am; that's what I do," the ones who fly across the country (or continent) and back, the ones who cry because you're crying and that really hurts them, and the ones who make you laugh so hard you piss your pants. It's for the ones who masquerade as sisters and aunts and cousins and husbands. It's also for the ones who are with you way, way after they aren't.

Author's Note

Special thanks to the very talented and very chic jewelry designer Jules Kim, whose in-depth information about her work breathed life into this book.

To err is human, to forgive divine.

—*Alexander Pope*

The philosophy of existence reminds us, once more, of what all great philosophy has tried to teach us: that there are views of reality which cannot be completely reduced to scientific formulations.

—*Jean Wahl*

One

───

This book helps you to learn how to drive in a number of difficult and challenging situations.

—Connecticut Department of Motor Vehicles Driver's Manual

Ruby Reynolds met Ed Robbins at a wedding of all places—far away from her home in New York City—in the small Connecticut town of Middleville. Knowing the way her momma felt about weddings, in fact about marriage in general, Ruby should have taken this as a sign. But she was never much for signs; she'd passed too many by in beat-up passenger seats, with her gangly bare feet tossed up on the dashboard, to be discerning about them anyway.

She really shouldn't have been at the wedding at all.

Really, it all started on a Saturday afternoon in late spring, which she'd begun in the normal way, with a long, leisurely cup of cheap Mexican coffee out on her fire-escape-turned-balcony. She'd upended two milk crates and draped them with a towel to create a decent lounge chair. Ruby was nothing if not resourceful. In fact, she'd once made a headboard out of four cardboard packing boxes. And everyone said it looked great (everyone being Dina and the elderly woman down the hall who'd knocked to complain about the banging when Ruby was constructing it), until there was a leak from 4P right above and the thing sogged up and sank to the floor.

She pretended to read the paper, but really she was looking out at Elizabeth Street, where her apartment was tucked into the third floor of number 223, looking across at the sad-looking cemetery monument shop with its morbid "sample lawn," the brick buildings alongside that, and down at all the stylish people who had normal jobs and were off today doing things like seeing their families, or having sex (not that she could actually see that), or eating three-egg omelets woven with greasy onions and peppers.

If she had one complaint about this neighborhood it was that the people were too stylish in the kind of way that made her feel absolutely unstylish, which she was not. Not really anyhow, not anymore. Of course she was unstylish just then, in old, droopy cotton shorts that had been cut from droopy cotton pants and a threadbare tank top with uneven straps she'd picked up at a street fair years ago—something only brand-new Manhattanites would get swindled into buying: a tank top with the words *New York* silk-screened in graffiti style, with a brick wall background and a cheap-looking Statue of Liberty drawn with inaccurate proportions on the back.

She did love the expensive coffee shops and the restaurants that dotted her street, but not to actually eat in, only to look at their charming menus from the sidewalk. Her tight hold on the purse strings was a holdover from her poverty days. Ruby squirreled her money away for the most part, assuming there'd be a time when she'd again have nothing.

Her friend Dina called her cheap sometimes. But she always defended herself. "We prefer the term 'cost conscious,'" she'd say.

The one thing she wouldn't do this morning was feel lonely. She would do anything to avoid that. First she balanced her checkbook, which took up about five seconds, since it was flawless, and then she straightened her T-shirts in the pile in her closet, made her bed, took everything off and made it again in a different way, and then sat on it, feeling the soft chenille in her hands and wondering what she'd do for the next four hours until she was going to meet Dina.

She didn't want to work. That was for sure. She'd had enough of staring at those tiny scraps of metal meant to be made into a stencil for a necklace pendant, imagining the hole she punched through the middle of it was a mouth, and that the mouth would say, "Do you really think that *this time* you're going to make something that's going to get you a comeback?"

She looked at her little workbench, which for a while had been her best friend—the place where she'd created the Endangered Animals collection, the pills and tablets pieces, and the food charms she was perhaps best known for; the pieces she'd run over to the caster with and sat there and watched him make them into little wax castings, and make the mold from that; and then finally he'd poured the melted metal into it to make the necklace pendants. The caster was a hairy Harley Davidson guy named Leonard who so patiently carved these delicate things out of wax. He told her, "People don't normally sit here and watch us you know."

"I know," she said, though she hadn't really. She'd only taken one jewelry course in college, not a very formal education to say the least. At Kingsborough Community College—where she'd wound up because she had no money and no grades, and because the woman who let her share an apartment when she first arrived in New York had gone there—they only had one jewelry course. She'd spent her days traveling an hour and a half by subway and bus—one of the faceless thousands—to the commuter school, studying philosophy until the idea of "nothingness" began to consume her, until she wasn't sure she was even alive anymore. She happened to land on the catalog page for jewelry making when she was registering for her junior year, and after that semester she'd left school to pursue her career, which at first had seemed to be the anti-"nothingness" she'd been after in the first place. Here she was creating something from nothing, something that would be duplicated and weave itself within society and out to all these other people, even if Ruby herself couldn't manage to accomplish something like that.

Even if she had been acquainted with caster's etiquette, the thing was, she hadn't had anywhere else to go, no one else she knew here except this Harley guy named Leonard, with his long, wispy pony-tail and his leather vest, who liked to eat peanut butter and banana sandwiches.

So, she'd sat, watching him attach the sprue, which she imagined as a tiny umbilical cord, to the soft wax mold, fit it all in the steel tube, stick the rubber stopper in the end, melt the tenpenny weights of silver grains, shoot them in the negative space, and voila . . . there was her piece.

When he pulled the cooled, final piece out, it was never as good as she'd imagined it would be. In the beginning, this had been the disappointing part. But she began to notice that the other people didn't see it that way; they hadn't seen the vision in her head that hadn't turned out exactly right. She'd force herself—feeling like a phony—to walk to the boutiques on her block, introduce herself as their neighbor; refining her spiel so she stopped saying, "Yeah, I live across from the gravestones," working nights at a local restaurant devoid of patrons to pay Leonard. And they bought it. And she was actually making good money. She quit the depressing restaurant to spend depressing days alone staring at the workbench and the mouthy sheets of metal.

But lately her luck had waned.

Ruby decided to go back to sleep on that Saturday, and when she woke up she had just enough time to dress in an acceptable way: a form-fitting black blouse and skinny jeans with heels. She dried her red hair, which was getting very long, almost to the middle of her back, and pulled it back in a ponytail.

Pastis was bustling, as it always was on a weekend. Dina had turned her onto the expensive, glamorous brasserie, and they loved to dine on the beautiful steak frites which Dina often ate for free since she was a restaurant reviewer. Lucky for Ruby, her friend was currently a single restaurant reviewer. When Dina had dates, Ruby ate at Burger Heaven.

"Oh my God," she moaned as she wiped her hands on the paper napkin, the meatpacking district abuzz with shoppers outside the window. The fries were perfectly crisp, hot, salty.

Dina was slick, straight lines to Ruby's moving dust cloud. She'd just had her hair cropped into a slim bob with angled bangs that Ruby would never be able to pull off.

The waitress filled their water glasses, removed an empty bread plate on which they'd left exactly two microscopic crumbs, and when she turned away, Dina cleared her throat. "Okay, I've got a proposition," she said to Ruby. The acoustics of the open room with the high ceiling were such that the words echoed a little bit, lending them magnitude, or at least that's how Ruby remembered it.

"I'm not that kind of girl," Ruby said.

"Ha ha . . . I happen to know you are; however, this is not the kind of proposition I have in mind."

Ruby raised a faint, red brow—a couple of shades lighter than her hair—and said, "Continue."

Dina's cousin Sestina was marrying the heir of a golf-ball fortune from West Hartford, Connecticut. "It's none of the big brands you would know," Dina said, as if Ruby would have known even a single golf-ball brand. Jeweler's saw brands, brands of bandages, of garlic pickles, Ruby would know . . . but not golf brands. "But the thing is, I can't bear going alone and getting all the *questions.*" She put her entire face into her wineglass when she took a long sip, but Ruby knew she was hiding, getting ready to ask something that was really difficult for her.

Dina had been left by the love of her life in college. His name was Troy, and even now there wasn't a man in the world she could muster an ounce of feeling toward because none of them compared to Troy. Ruby sometimes joked that it was unfortunate Dina's heart had been broken by someone with such a high school romance-novel name, but she could only be that light about it sometimes, when Dina was in a Troy-bashing mood (often after two dirty martinis and old episodes of *Party of Five*, which for some reason riled her up) because for the most part, this loss still weighed heavily on Dina.

"My real question is, how do *you* know someone who is going to be an heiress?" That doesn't seem very . . . us." Ruby lightened up the tone so that Dina would feel comfortable enough to ask her whatever it was she wanted to ask.

"Always a hair ass, never an heiress," Dina declared, licking her lips lightly.

Ruby knew there must be a man walking directly behind her, because Dina liked men to see her lick her lips. She once told this to Ruby (again, the two-dirty-martini rule) and later denied it. But these were the types of mortifying things they shared with each other; it was what bound them. "So what's the proposition?" Ruby asked. Whatever it was, she'd do it—the joy of being connected to a friend who actually knew you!

"Can you go through your pretty little address book and see if there is anyone in there you can set me up with to bring to the wedding?"

"No problem," she sang. There had to be someone in there, right? Ruby pulled out her worn leather address book with the endangered animal clasp she'd designed for Filofax—the income she was living off of while her jewelry business suffered a "down phase." She flipped through each page, and began, "Oh . . . Jacob Aigner! No, no things hadn't ended well with him . . . Rodney Billington . . . but, no forget him . . . Chris Connersly . . . oh, that was . . . nevermind . . ." She started to flush; the curse of the red-headed, the great flush that told all, that betrayed you over and over. From A to Z, each man was off-limits. There wasn't one she hadn't run off from because he'd looked too long in her eyes or too long in the waitress's eyes or neglected to laugh at her joke. She could pick up a runner's scent a mile away. And the second she did she was off.

No question's asked. She'd made it her life's goal never to be left. If anyone was going to leave it was going to be her.

"Don't tell me there isn't one." Dina shook her head as Ruby smacked the back flap shut. "Maybe if you actually stuck around long enough with one of these guys, there'd be a single friend for *me*! Why don't you put your damaged childhood issues aside long enough to think about *my* love life . . . When you were breaking it off with at least one of those guys, you could have stopped for one second and said, 'You know, one day Dina's cousin might be getting married and she could possibly need Randy Zimmerman for a blind date,' and then waited until it mutually fizzled out. Then we wouldn't be in this situation, would we?" She crossed her arms and threw herself facedown over them. "If only I could just fall in love with you, Rube. We understand each other so well. Now if you're as good in the sack as I think you are, we'd be perfect together."

Ruby rubbed her friend's arm, thinking that even the worst thing about best friends—that they always tell the brutal truth—is still a wonderful thing. It was true that Ruby had never gotten over her father's running out on Ruby and her mother before Ruby was old enough to have even a fleeting memory of him. And now, if Ruby thought there was even a slight chance a man might consider leaving her, she'd run like the wind. Unlike her momma, Ruby wasn't anti-marriage, she was just scared shitless of it. "Sorry my emotional health is getting in the way of your sex life. I really am." She stuck her tongue out when Dina picked her head up again.

Sure, she could make light of it with Dina, but she could feel her issues catching up with her. Lately, she'd been dreaming about a huge boulder gaining speed behind her. At a rocky beach, it would loosen from a cliff behind where she was lounging, reading an old Nancy Drew mystery she'd been holding on to all these years, and relentlessly chase her down a huge hill. In the dream, she was always wearing galoshes, like her momma liked to wear in the winter.

"All right. I accept your apology. But there *is* one way you could make it up to me." Dina batted her eyes like an innocent—which she absolutely was not. For kicks she would order pizzas and not answer the door when the deliveryman arrived, or have a salesgirl help her for two hours with absolutely no intention of buying. She said it was her way of balancing out the universe for all the people who'd treated *her* like that.

"Oh God. What? What is it?" Ruby and Dina had met five years back at a boutique opening. Their encounter had occurred just as Ruby was growing bored of avoiding interaction by trying to look like a piece of sculpture, which on par with past experience had only served to sustain her for about twenty minutes. They'd been inseparable ever since. She would do anything for Dina. Dina was family, outrageous behavior and all—and besides her momma, who was the kind of family you tried not to think about, Dina was the only family she had. Dina always made a big deal over birthdays, and on random days picked up gifts that reminded her of Ruby for no occasion at all.

"I want you to come as my same-sex date."

Ruby laughed a bit of cabernet out of her mouth. Two women in slinky tanks and jeans turned to shoot her dirty looks.

"Ignore them. They're jealous of your figure. Hear me out before you say no. If they all think I'm a lesbian, they'll be too stunned to ask me anything. My cousin Rourke has been wearing his mother's housecoats and filing the neighbors' nails into perfect half moons since he was *five*. And *no one's* talked to him for three decades."

What did Ruby care? She sawed at her steak with a knife. "As long as you drive, it would be nice to take a little road trip for the weekend." Ruby didn't drive. Period. It scared the crap out of her. In all the places they'd moved to in their lives—Florida, Jersey, California, Nevada—her momma had done all the driving. And she didn't care to be anything like her momma. When her momma left, she packed up everything and headed out of town. Ruby merely chose not to return phone calls. Which was completely different. Eventually

Ruby would find the right person, settle down, and get started on having a real family. She wasn't going to run away from that.

The wedding was one of those manicured estate jobs that are always in the magazines. Wherever possible, there was a perfect white lily, stems so straight they seemed to be patronizing Ruby's slouchy persona. Even in the bathroom there was a white lily sprouting from the toilet tank, on top of the hand towels and next to a box of complimentary tampons—so you could be sure to have one in your face in every compromising position. At the reception, Ruby smiled in a way that Dina had coached her to do—seductively, but not slutty—and put her arm around Dina's shoulder whenever she thought it was appropriate for a lesbian lover. Sometimes for a joke, she pinched Dina on the butt. Dina seemed to enjoy the tears she brought to her mother's face, exponentially so when she threw her face down on the table and asked, "God what have I done to deserve a lesbian daughter?"

During the father and daughter dance, Rod Stewart's "Have I Told You Lately that I Love You?," Ruby plastered on a wax smile and hoped that Dina would buy it.

"Don't give me that stupid smile," Dina said. "You can't trick your lesbian lover." And then, tenderly, she draped her arm around Ruby and whispered in her ear, "*Pssst!* Weddings suck, pass it down."

It wasn't until after the new couple's first dance that she was introduced to Ed.

"This is my lesbian lover, Ruby," Dina said to him, swishing down a red wine in one hand and a white in the other. They'd just finished the salad course and had already run out of polite things to say to the three couples at their table.

"God, why do I always miss out on the best tables?" He had a half-goofy smile and the kind of longish nose Ruby tended to go for. Ruby couldn't be sure if he was reacting to the guys-love-lesbians thing or to Ruby alone, but she hoped it was the latter.

He asked her to dance. They danced to Ella Fitzgerald's "When a Woman Loves a Man" and stared at each other. Every once in a while one of them broke a smile. Partially this was out of the awkwardness of the immediate attraction, and partially because Dina kept yelling, "Ruby, nobody's gonna believe we're lesbian lovers if you keep acting all googly-eyed with Ed!"

But it was too late. She liked the way his brown eyes were flecked with tiny light spots and the angle of his lashes. At the end of the dance, he'd already brought his plate over and smooshed in between the two of them. "I hate to ruin a good lesbian lover plot, but I'd like to sit here. Rolls?" He brought three over to the table as a peace offering.

"I might as well. If my mouth's full, at least I can't answer any damn questions!" Just as Dina stuffed a huge piece in her mouth, her aunt appeared, as if from nowhere, and asked, "So, Dina, has your lesbian lover left you for Suzanne's boy, Ed?" And then, "Oh, hi, Ed!" The conga had just started and a couple of band members were passing out maracas.

"C'mon!" Ed said, pulling her toward the conga line.

"You're kidding, right?" Ruby said. She was more into melding into the woodwork.

"Nope!" It was too late. He had her up there. She was giggling with nervousness. This was so not her!

Dina rolled her eyes to say, "Do you believe this loser?"

But despite herself, she was enjoying it, the way Ed could get silly and shake his maracas at the senior citizens and get them blushing like it was nothing. Her hips shook slightly, the minimum. But she was drawn to him, smiling uncontrollably beneath all that fancy scrollwork, beyond the intimidating brass band, even through the intricate web of how these people were all related. When he turned back to her, he wove his hand around her waist, looked at her seriously, and then lifted her maracas and gave it a shake. "You know you can't control yourself any longer," he deadpanned.

The pair had lots of time to get to know each other in between the surf and turf and the Venetian hour, sharing a laugh when the bride's Aunt Edna slipped on the Ferrara marble after her second glass of pink champagne, chatting about topics that should have been disastrous, but weren't—how big cats can interbreed across species to create "ligers" and "tigons," and what a huge headache someone must have gotten discovering the mil, the measurement equaling one thousandth of an inch—as everyone in Dina's family came over one by one, asking her what happened with her lesbian lover and offering their condolences on how Ruby had dumped her for Ed. Also, as luck would have it, they were all spending the night at the same hotel.

"Come over here, my little lesbian!" Ed said to her, when they met outside at the hotel's pool later that night. It was still a little cold for swimming, and there were only a few chairs. They basked in the mystery of new acquaintance.

"I'm not little," Ruby joked, feeling even then that despite all the running away she'd done, this time she was going to stay. It might have been the way he sighed after a laugh or the way his hair stuck up the tiniest bit on one side; she couldn't put her finger on the exact reason, but the fact remained.

They sat forever with their feet in that not-so-new pool, their toes full of raisin wrinkles, lips chapped from kissing, constantly kissing. He was casual with her, easily forking over information—he was a claims rep for American Insurance Corp, LLC, in Hartford, which meant he tried to cheat people out of their due, ha ha, no really, it wasn't that bad but it would be if it weren't for Edna Binzer's bottomless bowl of candy—that sort of thing.

She shared, but much less so: she liked bananas, which, did he know, were grown mostly in Brazil and take twelve to fifteen months to reach their full size at five to thirty feet? Did he also know that they originated in Malaysia approximately 4,000 years ago? But that was Ruby. She never knew what it was that made her dad leave her and her momma all those years ago and so she didn't risk inspiring a repeat performance by giving a bad impression.

They laughed (Ed snorted twice, which made her like him immensely) and at times stared awkwardly in the silence of new emotions at dismembered leaf segments floating on the pool's surface. Dina's cousin Stephen took up residence on a chaise longue across the way with the tallest of the bridesmaids. It was pretty clear what was going on under all that chartreuse silk chiffon.

Later, the odd couple—the one just over five feet and the bridesmaid just a hair under six—came over to chat with a bottle of cabernet sauvignon, and Ruby was posed the question, What do *you* do?

"I'm a jewelry designer," she said, looking down and partially covering her mouth. She was prone to shyness. She always felt the word "designer" had a pretentious connotation that didn't truly reflect who she was.

"Oh! That is so cool!" the bridesmaid exclaimed. "Did you make that necklace you're wearing?"

It was an old piece—one of her favorites—a very ironic, rich-looking thing like she used to love. It was a pretty diamond set in a yellow gold string bean.

Ed looked over at her proudly, squeezed her in a little tighter, as if he were connected to her in such a way that he could take some credit for her profession.

She warmed quickly to it. Who knew the wonders of watching someone glow with pride on your behalf?

"Yes, she did. Isn't it beautiful?" Ed pinched the string bean away from her neck between his two bony fingers and stared at her all the while. "It's a beautiful string bean."

Later, after Stephen and his date left, Ed said, "It takes a special girl to find the beauty in a green vegetable."

"Well, they are pretty miraculous; they grow in half the time it takes for most beans to mature. These little guys aren't even nearly ready when they're tossed out into the world for consumption." She was only talking about beans here, but already she worried she'd said too much. The thing was, though she looked for signs to the contrary, Ed—giving her that glowing look still—appeared to like it.

She came to know that look very well over the following year. And other things about him, too: when Ed said, "I'll call you tomorrow," he actually meant it. When he said, "Why don't we see a movie?" he didn't mean it as an abstract, some far-off-day possibility. He meant the following Wednesday, and he'd even take a personal day to see it with her. She learned that Ed preferred Kettle Baked Chips (the kind she always referred to as "the expensive kind") and that he had a brother and a sister, and that he'd been "the problem child" of the three. After once coming to school and hooting the sounds of a hyena instead of talking like a human being, he'd required monthly trips to the school counselor in an orange cinder block room with three depressing wood chairs and a scratched metal table. He'd thought it was funny, but realized after that it marked the end of his dreams of becoming a comedian, was how he explained it. She learned lots of things like that about him, while he looked at her, propped on one elbow, in her little bedroom where all the furniture nearly touched all the other furniture, her lace-edged sheet over his bare chest. She learned it over takeout of all varieties: Hungarian and Mexican, Thai and kosher deli, Cuban and southern barbecue— the little containers over her coffee table, happily populating the often empty space. Sometimes, when she was alone and Ed was tucked away at his office in Connecticut, wearing his alarmingly bad ties, she'd notice a tiny drip of sauce and smile that all that living had been going on here.

Summer to fall, and then winter into spring and summer again— now nearly ending. They'd done it all in that year—Central Park picnics with pungent cheeses that Ed wouldn't touch, and forsook for a hotdog with too much ketchup. He would get right in her face, right up into her breath and her vision, where you could feel the heat off someone's skin and the little fuzz, too. And she liked that. Boy, did she like that. In fact, when she looked at them together, in those silly picture booth strips, with fingers in her ears, or in bunny ears over Ed's head, she saw herself as that person you always hope you'll be—that far off me that you never quite are. She hadn't run away, and this was a huge step. She considered herself cured.

They did laugh/cry off-Broadway comedies about young relationships. They walked the promenades on both sides of the city from top to bottom. They bought silly plastic souvenirs to commemorate this day or that one—a miniature Miss Liberty or an "I ❤ NY." They ate so many times over small, cramped tables with a little candle glowing between them. Ed did a wonderful impression of a demon, with that candle making his face glow wickedly. "And are *you* afraid of the dark, Miss Ruby Reynolds? Hooooooo hooooo haaaaaaa haaaaaa haaaaaaaa," he'd ask. He could easily lift one eyebrow and lower the other. And then he could switch. Always, they laughed.

Once, after a mediocre off-off Broadway sketch comedy about such things as a neurosurgery that had gone awry and magic glasses that made people look like goldfish, he asked, "Tell me what happened with your family, Ruby." They were strolling by Twenty-eighth Street and Ninth Avenue, where nothing looks all that great.

She made light of it, rather than reveal her fears. "My dad left right after I was born." She shrugged as if she'd just announced they were out of milk. "My mother had a lot of boyfriends, but none of them were husband material, I guess, so we tended to move around a lot when it didn't work out." She didn't mention Jeff in Lake Okeechobee, Florida, and how she'd longed for him to become her father, how he'd once so gently soothed her during a lightning storm. She didn't mention that he'd folded his tall, spindly body under the table where she hid and said, in just the voice you'd want a father to have, "I brought you a Mountain Dew. I heard they haven't got a lot of beverages 'down under.'" And she didn't say that although she'd wanted to like anything, she hadn't grabbed onto Jeff when he mimed bunny rabbit quotes with his fingers, because she'd always known he would never be anything more than a dot along the route of Ruby and Momma on a torn Texaco map. And she couldn't bear to miss someone else like that.

Instead, she changed the subject sloppily. "And what's your stand on Disney World?" What was the use of dredging up the past? "We went there once when we lived in Florida, and I loved the 'It's a small world after all' ride. When people say they don't like Disney World, I think they are forgetting about 'It's a small world after all.'"

In the country around Middleville, they spotted a copperhead snake (Ruby squeezed her nails into Ed's left hand, although a five-year-old boy was standing over the snake and pointing it out to them where they stood, seven full feet away). They consumed many flavors of ice cream sitting on a peeling red patio bench. Ed and Ruby spent time with some of Ed's old high school buddies who would laugh and say things like, "You two are really nauseating, you know?" and "Do you have to look so fucking *happy*?" Ed wouldn't say anything, just look at Ruby and flatten a palm against her hair, following it down to the ends, or look at her like none of these other people were anything. Sometimes he'd whisper, but really just to her, "Yeah, I do."

TWo

We do not follow specific routes nor must we exclude any roadways (including limited access highways) during the course of a driving test.

—Connecticut Department of Motor Vehicles Driver's Manual

On an Indian summer evening, Ruby was just getting ready to leave her small but—she thought—elegant apartment. She hated to leave all the little perfect things she'd arranged just so behind as much as she had been. Ten years ago, she'd wanted this place and she got it. *No, not 1,251 dollars! 1,250 dollars and that's my final offer!* She'd yelled that, like a contestant on *The Price Is Right*. She'd slammed her palm on the desk to show she meant it, too. She'd signed the lease and left her mother's crazy lifestyle behind her—no more roommate; no more moving. She'd been free to be normal. Free to jump on the bed with fruit punch in her mouth, gurgling the Star Spangled Banner. Free to stay inside for three days and eat only delivered pork lo mein. And she'd created a very safe, know-where-your-coffee-cup-is-in-the-morning kind of place that she loved.

But truth be told, now she was actually starting to enjoy the open space she had for jewelry making over at Ed's. Rather than a cramped corner of her living room, at Ed's she could spread out in an entire room that was otherwise empty, save for a cigar store Indian, and even that was growing on her. It kept her company. And served as a good hanger for finished necklaces.

She took one last moment to admire the fluffy bleach-white towels on the little iron scroll rack she'd just refurbished with a bit of sanding, paint, and crackle finish. "You have to work quickly with it." That's what the salesman at the paint store had said, his glasses shifting up and down with each syllable, the movement adding an extra level of seriousness. All the while she'd rushed through the various coats, she'd experienced a sense of gloom at the possibility of not finishing quite quickly enough.

She took a breath and hurled herself out into the city.

It was a fabulous day. Of course, you couldn't see much of the day in New York City. Instead you *felt* it. You felt it in the way people lingered outside on the street chatting, the way the sidewalk seating would fill up at cafes and parks. It was evident in the lines for blended fruit drinks and iced coffees that would snake past vendors.

You learned these things about New York City after a little while. It hit you in waves that you wouldn't notice all at once. But before you realize it, you're cozied up to this place that doesn't really *seem* cozy at all. You become immune to the display window beneath the neon PINK PUSSYCAT sign, the metal-spiked thong and Day-Glo vibrator cluster assembled like aquatic dancers in an old movie. One day you pass it by as if it's simply a pharmacy artfully displaying school supplies.

Ruby walked to the Spring Street station just as planned, and checked her watch. *One minute, thirty-five seconds.* She descended the staircase where she was blasted with a rush of air from the train she'd successfully willed to arrive, felt around in her jacket for her Metrocard, swiped it, and just as the doors of the 6 train opened, she slipped between them, and the train whisked her past all the local stops toward Grand Central Station. *Ladies and Gentlemen, if you notice any suspicious packages, tell someone immediately. If you see something, say something. A message from your local MTA.*

She was used to the unpredictable nature of Manhattan travel. In fact, she considered herself a New Yorker, period. She was never leaving. She wouldn't be one of those ladies who lunched—no. She'd live downtown, send her kids to relaxed schools that emphasized self-expression, take them to art classes at the Guggenheim, and on the weekends to ride the Cyclone and eat Nathan's franks in Coney Island.

Everything made sense here. And that was just the way she liked it. Before the Big Apple (*Now what's* that *about?* she liked to ask people. *What's the deal with the apple?*) there was New Jersey, which she'd been too young to remember. And Florida, which was real nice, on account of the constant sunshine and warmth and the way you could eat dinner anywhere you wanted at 4:30 in the afternoon on a whim—that is, if you didn't mind the glare of the setting sun off the surrounding silver hair. And then New Orleans, Louisiana, where at age five she tasted her first pink hurricane cocktail served in a novelty cup with an alligator for a stirrer and then a small Massachusetts town. After that, Ruby and her momma lived in Orange County, California, then Las Vegas, Nevada, then backtracked up to the lesser known wine country north of Sonoma where all the locals go for the best marijuana. They did a short stint in North Carolina, over by Winston-Salem, then another small town in Massachusetts just about one hour from Boston. In between the canned descriptions there were a lot of rushed good-byes and awkward hellos and wearing the wrong sneakers and the wrong hairstyle and sitting in the corner where people might not notice her.

But she was surely past all that now. And as far as the pitiful search for a father—well she was over that, too. Her mother wouldn't tell. The hospital didn't have a father listed. When her grandmother had been alive, she could only remember two years during the McCarthy era, and, mysteriously, every piece of jewelry cataloged in the Princess Diana auction at Sotheby's.

When the train platformed at Grand Central Station, Ruby

checked her watch. *Seven minutes, forty-six seconds.* Her system was running, no pun intended, she thought as she shimmied her sleeve back down over the watch, just like clockwork. Once she was safely inside Grand Central Station, with absolutely no risk of missing her train, she bought a sweet vanilla chai latte at Oren's. Then she took her time browsing at the Hudson News shop, through all the inviting magazines with their soft focus take on life. She purchased three with which to busy herself on the one-and-a-half hour train ride to Connecticut. She read them to funnel it all in and spit it out as inspiration for her jewelry collection. And sometimes to know how Jennifer Aniston's hair was being styled.

Ruby treated herself to a big, round naan bread and a disproportionately small plastic container of mint chutney from the Indian stand in the food court, although it was only 10:30 in the morning. She never understood why certain foods were meant for the morning and others for afternoon and still others strictly for evening. Ruby had heard the Japanese eat rice for breakfast, and liked the idea of that. She sat next to an elderly wooly-smelling woman on one of the slippery leather chairs in the waiting area to eat the soft cushion of naan. She felt inside her bag for the little Miss Liberty statue she now carried with her everywhere, so that she could run her fingers over the nicely grooved torch.

From the corner of her eye, she noticed a tiny pouch slip from the old woman's pocket and onto the tile floor. Before she could say anything, a young man about Ruby's own age reached down and scooped it up.

"Ma'am," he addressed the woman politely.

"What!" she screamed.

The young helper tried not to look discomforted by her sour breath. "Your purse, ma'am." He refrained from screaming back, perhaps not wanting to appear insensitive to the over-sixty group, but she posed a challenge. Instead he said sweetly, maybe a little louder this time, "Your purse, ma'am," and dangled it in front of her.

"What!" she yelled again, grabbing onto the chair arms angrily.

He again gently repeated, "Your purse, ma'am!"

This went on and on until the old woman called a policeman over.

When it became clear to the balding policeman—who very courteously, Ruby thought, removed his hat in front of the woman—that the man was not trying to steal her purse, the ordeal was over, and Ruby's train was announced. She stood and brushed the naan crumbs off her shirt and lap distractedly, listening for the track number, spraying a few flakes into the air and a couple onto the old woman. She considered bringing the woman's attention to the matter, but thought better of it and headed to track 21 without mentioning the crumbs.

Her own fingers were greasy from all the butter, and she felt them as she settled into a seat on the train. She tried to tell herself the urine smell in the car would fade as the journey got going. In the past this had proven true. She could walk and walk through each car sniffing like a police dog, but they each smelled that way. The trick was not to wonder why.

One of the magazines she'd bought was an industry title, *Accessories*. It was something you had to do: keep up with the trends in your industry, even when you were experiencing a "downturn" in business, as she was. She'd started out on a good run, it was true. But the past two seasons she'd been panned as a wash-up. The orders had been slim, and the returns disastrous. She'd had to dodge phone calls, answering as Ruby's secretary, with an ineffective Russian accent.

Ruby flipped to the jewelry spreads—styled pages of models dramatically displaying the newest pieces. She'd had a couple of calls from the magazine and silently prayed now that her pieces had made it in. This could mean a comeback. There was always another chance to win back the public.

She flipped and flipped and soon she was through with that section and on to monogrammed luggage. There was still another chance. She returned to the front of the magazine, where tiny articles about different collections or materials or events were mentioned. And on page three her name jumped out at her.

Ruby Reynolds' newest collection, CITY, was, unfortunately, as uninspired as her last two collections. Though we've seen her style and craft grow increasingly refined over the years, it seems there's no sense of self, no substance to her. On a lighter note, Carolyn Hughes has wowed us with her reinvention of opal settings . . .

Criticism was one thing, but no sense of self? For Ruby, who'd pushed her personal problems as far down as she could, started an entirely new life, succeeded in her career, found a best friend, and now a wonderful boyfriend, this was a complete smack in the face. She was sure this collection would be different. With all the experiences she'd shared with Ed, how could she possibly still be uninspired?

She'd done an entire line of foods he liked, as interpreted through the eyes of love. There was the Kettle Baked Chips piece, with the tinkly hanging chips with the difficult edges that she'd snapped two blades on and the one dangling heart, and the fusilli pasta charm with the heart, which she was particularly proud of.

She'd taken all those critical words to heart; she'd tried to get to know herself, to express herself in this collection as part of a couple, rather than a woman who slept with her shoes on, just in case. She read books with titles like *Step Inside . . . Yourself* and *Adventures of the Lost Soul, Found.*

She smacked the magazine closed and turned her attention to the window. Despite the bushy trees, the open fields of waving grasses, and the birds overhead, Ruby felt she was still in New York until the doors of the train opened and she stepped out onto the platform in Milford. But now, with the last green burst of summer, she looked at it differently. This wasn't New York at all. There were no five-dollar pashminas for sale on the corner, no four-star chefs with burger vendors in the park. There was only one New York, and this wasn't it. She closed her fist around her Takashamya paper shopping bag—something that underlined her identity. She knew who she was! She was a New Yorker! And she wasn't going to have that taken away from her now. Identity! Ha! How was she expected to retain a sense of self when she had to see herself described that way?

She felt inside her bag again for the Miss Liberty statue that had become her talisman. But after pulling out her book, a couple of necklace clasps, an old wax mold, a broken saw blade, her wallet, and three Band-Aids, it became clear: she'd left it on that seat. She'd been so concerned over that old woman, she'd simply left her Miss Liberty statue standing on that pretty leather seat all by herself, holding a torch for Ruby though it wouldn't do a thing to bring her back. Again, there was a sign Ruby should have paid attention to, but didn't.

She was in a mood, but she promised herself she wouldn't show it. The train pulled into Milford—Middleville was so far out in the boondocks that it didn't have its own train station. She recognized the tiny red-planked station house alongside the track, and the daisies in the planters by the door that she had discovered were in fact silk.

She zippered her jacket up and tossed a light summer scarf over her shoulder; surely she trumped the locals in sophistication, with their imitation Vuitton and shapeless rayon blazers. She was a New Yorker among Nutmeggers. It didn't matter one bit what that woman wrote in *Accessories*. She knew exactly who she was. Every artist suffered a down period. She would snap back and that would be all.

The sight of Ed, sitting cross-legged on the hood of his old brown truck, struck her tenderly. She knew the three steps down from the platform now, and negotiated them without a glance at her heeled sandals. He smelled of oranges, as if he'd just eaten one in the car. Arriving was a wonderful, wonderful thing.

He drove them to dinner zipping in and out of traffic. Every so often he looked in his rearview mirror.

Ruby caught his eye in there. "Where we going?" she asked. It didn't matter much. The food was a universal disappointment around here. She'd once happened upon a Zagat's guide for the region. It was so slim they'd appended a section on the not-so-nearby Berkshires.

"A little Italian spot." He smiled again, found her hand. Rubbed it into her jeans with his palm. From inside that car, the world looked unrecognizable. Everything was colored with Ruby and Ed.

Roasted Red's was a lofty place, consisting of two floors done in Spanish tile and sponge-painted mustard walls hung with orange-framed puffy chef prints. By the bar, a lounge singer was doing a throaty version of "Sister Christian." They were seated on the main floor in a room toward the back. They scanned the plastic-coated menus, waited for the waiter to come by, and ordered.

"Watch this," Ruby said while they waited for their food—pasta, pasta, with a side of bread and garlic bread and bruschetta bread. Little did these people know that in New York, bread was on the NYPD's most wanted list. She snapped the napkin from her lap and introduced it with her free palm. She raised her eyebrows. She grabbed her salad fork and jabbed it down into the center of the napkin. "Ooh! Look over there!" She pointed well beyond their table.

Ed shook his head, smiling, but pretended to be distracted all the same. "Oh, yes, I see. He does. He does look like a young Roseanne Barr. You're absolutely right." When his glance returned to Ruby, she'd already removed the fork and stuck it in his water glass.

"My god, that is an awful trick." Ed said it, but his eyes danced.

"Waiter," he said, when the lanky college boy with the messy hair and the bored smirk walked by. "There's a fork in my water."

As if this happened every night, the waiter said, "Oh, I'm sorry. I'll get you another one."

"Now that's a good trick," Ed said. His face turned solemn. "Seriously, though. I want to ask you something."

There was a great pause, during which Ruby had lost her breath somewhere in her chest. Could it be?

He smiled grandly. "Ruby, I want you to move in with me."

Her life flashed before her eyes like a person drowning, because after all she was in over her head, and finally treading water wasn't going to do it. Ruby had seen this coming. Truly, she had known they must be headed in this direction. It was getting ridiculous, the way they spent so much time together and then all that time apart.

Still, she hadn't allowed herself to explore all it might mean because she'd been waiting for that time when she'd let Ed really know her. First she'd started with telling herself she'd talk to him more seriously next Tuesday, which turned into the following Friday, and then a week from next Monday, and eventually she'd stopped marking it in her calendar, the inability to cross the item off starting to weigh on her.

But now she saw that time had caught up with her. Could she— a Reynolds woman—actually handle living with a man? She'd been proud of herself for sticking it out thus far with Ed, but not running away was one thing; committing herself to the implied shared future this kind of thing represented . . . that was something completely different! In the seconds since he'd posed the question, she'd already become annoyed by the way he'd scattered crumbs on the tablecloth. She didn't want to become that kind of person.

All the same, she felt this was what she wanted, too, terrifying as it seemed. Her smile was too big as she said, "That would be wonderful." She wasn't sure what moved her to smack her hands together the way she did. Where was her identity in *that*? Still, she could probably fit his dresser in the nook under her window, and they could call in a closet organizer to make room for his stuff. If she looked at it in the right light, maybe she could convince herself this wasn't all that different from what they were doing now.

"Aw, Rube, I'm so glad. I can't tell you how glad I am." He squeezed her hand tight and looked at her funny.

She narrowed her eyes, ruffled her brow. "What's going on?" she asked, smiling in a confounded way.

All of a sudden, his free hand was balancing a black velvet box, hinged open to reveal a diamond engagement ring, as if she were a character in a romantic comedy. "Make me the happiest guy in the world, Rube. Marry me."

The chatter went quiet. Ruby's lips felt puffy and clumsy. She could see Ed, but he appeared watery, strange. Why did she have such a problem with this? She loved Ed, had already dreamed of marrying him, felt it was the natural thing for them. It was obvious Ed was not her father. And she was not her mother. "I'd love to," she said. And when the words came out, she knew they were the right ones. Whether she could live up to them was another story altogether.

Ed slipped the ring—a great big emerald-cut thing with two green stones on either side shaped like perfect stars—from its satiny slot and threaded her finger through it. At the knuckle, it got stuck. Panicked, she looked up. Again with the signs.

"It's nothing! I guessed the size and I was wrong. We'll fix it tomorrow."

Ruby tried to make light of it. "Definitely. Tomorrow. It's beautiful. It really is." This was the kind of ring that required a consideration of all the pieces she made, all the things she spoke of and wore; it was a risky, unique piece that was for the right sort of woman. Ruby realized this, though she didn't know how to express it, as she leaned over and kissed Ed softly. "I love you," she said. It was true. And she hoped, with everything running in her genes, that it was enough. Meanwhile, she tried desperately but unsuccessfully to shove the ring over her knuckle. For now, she'd have to believe that the hope of their success was a nice enough thing. Hopefully, nice enough to keep them together. Whatever she did, she wasn't going to stay up worrying what the improperly sized ring meant. Because that would be dumb. And she told herself again . . . she was never much for signs.

"I love you, too." He kissed her in a crazy way, on her nose and cheek and ear, and then stood up. "Everyone, put down your pasta!" he proclaimed to the restaurant at large—a couple of large groups and a handful of couples.

Ruby was both mortified and thrilled. She turned purple when he said, "Stand up, Rube." When she didn't move, he egged her on, motioning for her to rise. "This is Ruby Reynolds from New York City, by way of New Orleans, by way of Florida, by way of Mendicino, California, or something like that."

Ruby grabbed for her wine and gulped it. It wasn't very smooth and she puckered, nearly choking. She wanted to hate the attention. Ruby was always saying how much she hated attention. But the truth was, it felt great, the way he singled her out, showed everyone here what she was all about, according to him. Those were just the sort of things that had made her stay this long, she knew that much.

"We're getting married!" When he announced that, everyone applauded. One guy cat-called. Another hooted, "Good job! She's a hottie!"

There was such a mix of emotion whirling around inside of her, she could hardly hear him now. Fear threatened to freeze over her body in stages, but there was a giant smile on her face and she couldn't help but feel thrilled in spite of it. She was getting married to the man she loved!

They settled back down at their table.

"My place in Nolita will be a great location if you work on Wall Street. That's where you would probably work, I assume?"

The waiter placed a large bowl of corkscrew pasta in a pesto sauce in front of her. He scooted around to Ed and set a huge square of lasagna down. In between, he plunked down two sides of bread and some more garlic bread. He left the bruschetta bread in case they still wanted to pick at it. Ruby thought she couldn't be further from the Meatpacking District if she tried.

"Thanks," Ed said.

The waiter retreated to the kitchen.

They both tasted their pasta.

"Rube, that all sounds great. It really does. But . . ."

"Yes?" She sucked a corkscrew between her lips. Maybe they'd need a bigger place. It was a point. With two salaries to pay the rent, they could probably afford something larger. Maybe with a doorman?

When Ed was thinking exactly how to say something, he would scrunch up his whole face, like the harder he did that, the less area he'd have to search for what he was looking for in there. "Rube, Ruby Baby, I was actually thinking maybe, possibly, you might consider moving *here*?"

The waiter returned. "Is everything okay?" he asked with an aloof smile, like he was really just there to pay for his course books and wanted them to know it.

She forked a load of corkscrews into her mouth. "Here," she garbled, shaking her head up and down wildly. A bit of burnt garlic lodged in her throat and she started to wheeze. "Water," she choked. "I need some water."

Three

Prior to entering the test vehicle, observe nearby parked cars, people, or objects that could affect your ability to safely put the car in motion.

—Connecticut Department of Motor Vehicles Driver's Manual

Probably if Ed had seen her kissing her floorboards good-bye he'd have called the whole thing off. But this was her *home*. She could eat off those floorboards. Ruby scrubbed them with her own hands each Sunday. Her momma was never much for keeping house. She would let the trash heap up into a stinking mountain. They always ran out of toilet paper . . . and clean underwear. But not Ruby. She prided herself on that.

She'd made herself someone else here, far from that new girl at the Cimarron Memorial High School in Las Vegas in the mortifyingly fake Champion sweatshirt that read "Champ!" whom everyone called "Fooby" because she'd garbled her own name in front of the lip-glossed blondes—their hair shining so much in the light you could be blinded in a room full of those kids.

But, here she was . . . moving again! And it scared the bejesus out of her! She knew the hard work required to build a real home for herself. Would she be able to do it again? She thought of Ed, and planning a wedding and then a family, and buying a real home—not just a tiny apartment she pretended was a castle. It would be worth it.

Manhattan had been a change from the coolness of long, empty lunchroom benches. Those metal grooves, long and too cold against bare thighs, followed her from school to school, it seemed. People often said there was a dignity in doing things alone, in being able to hold your head up while you shoved a past-its-expiration-date turkey breast sandwich in your mouth. Those people had obviously been squished in, ten to a side, on a lunchroom table, consuming sweet-smelling Fruit Roll-Ups instead of bruised bananas, and hadn't noticed how undignified Ruby looked in her terry one-piece dress with the hem coming undone in the back.

Ruby's doorbell rang. She pressed the intercom button and sang, "Who is it?"

"It's your best friend who's gonna miss you like hell. Now let me up, bitch."

Ruby smiled. How would she make it without Dina? She was the only real friend she'd ever had.

Ruby hated to leave a place behind, but worse than that were the people. Sure, she hadn't had friends, but there were her mother's friends—quiet, solicitous people who needed a loudmouth to lead them around, to say outrageous things they'd never heard before. People often flocked around her momma, like they do the man in tinfoil who plays the saw in Union Square station, only they didn't throw pennies at her; they escorted her to thrift stores and asked for her recipe for squash soup to hear her say, "First you squash the squash," and laugh like this was somehow hysterical. "Don't you have to *cook* it?" Ruby would say, behind her momma's shoulder, trying to show them she wasn't as funny as they thought, maybe get her to yell at Ruby so they'd see she wasn't nice, either, that the squash soup wasn't even good.

She'd also grown heavyhearted to leave the couple of teachers who seemed to recognize something different in her. Their "great job!" and "well done!" so heartwarming, never to be seen again. She went cold with it when she hugged Dina in front of her door, which soon would belong to someone named Olaf who'd come to see the place and kept saying, "Good, good," his words punches in the air.

In the elevator, they bumped toward the first floor and she didn't let herself cry.

"Where do you want to eat?" Ruby asked.

"Where else?" Dina asked.

They walked in the direction of Burger Heaven. It would be a good twenty-five-minute walk. But they both preferred walking when they had the time. When they reached Houston, Ruby looked up at the big DKNY mural and wondered if she would miss something like that—something she hadn't paid much attention to.

"Getting used to the rock yet?" Dina asked. She was a big fan of the unique style of it. She'd described it in at least ten different adjectives: retro-modern, glamorous, lighthearted, chic, understated, and on and on. For a cynic, Dina sure had a thing for romance. She'd asked Ruby to repeat the engagement story five times.

"It's strange—some days I wake up and find myself shocked to see it there. Other times it seems like the most natural thing in the world." She'd had it resized by her caster, Leonard.

"No charge," he'd said, as if being engaged were punishment enough.

"What is that supposed to mean?" she'd asked, despite her suspicions.

"Nothing at all," Leonard replied, in the kind of dismissive tone she didn't care for.

"I'll tell you what's not natural," Dina said. "Moving out of the city. There's no going back from here. There are country people and city people. And you, Ruby, are city people."

Ruby hoped this was not true. She was scared enough. She tried to think of herself as Annie Oakley, a gun-slinging frontierswoman, but that vision didn't stick. She had grown used to the trees and the quiet over at Ed's, but what if that grew tiresome? "Oh, come on! Lots of people move out to the country and love it!"

A couple in black studded leather with matching chin piercings that connected to eyebrow piercings with heavy chains passed by, and this helped Ruby to think maybe she didn't fit in here anymore. She ignored as much as she could the belted raincoats and loafers crowd that might disprove her theory.

"Okay, name one."

"Candace Bushnell." It was true. She'd just read about it in *Bazaar*. Wasn't she the absolute Queen of New York City? She'd literally invented *Sex and the City*!

"Yeah, but she kept an apartment here."

"Okay, I'm officially creeped. Happy?"

"Ecstatic," Dina said. She weaved her arm through Ruby's and kissed her on the cheek. It was clear she was broken up about Ruby's leaving.

After lunch they headed to Saks Fifth Avenue to look at the registry items. "This is the one time in your life you should treat yourself to the best there is." Dina was insistent. They'd spent many hours over the past few years window shopping on Fifth Avenue. Sometimes Dina splurged, but Ruby mostly drooled and then headed to Fourteenth Street for bargains.

"Can I help you?" the saleswoman asked, her swinging eyeglass chain brushing her shoulders.

There was a faint smell of something pretentious, like fig or bergamot, which Ruby couldn't place exactly, but it reinforced the fact that she was out of her element. She looked to Dina, who didn't mind acting like the kind of person who could afford these things; thrived on it, actually. Dina shook her head, encouraged Ruby.

"Yes," Ruby said finally. "I'd like some help picking out a china pattern." Ruby's momma hated china. So she wanted to make sure she had one picked out straightaway. Once she'd said the words out loud, she smiled a bit, enjoyment of the prospect trickling over her.

"You've just been engaged? That is so exciting! Let's see the ring," the woman said. There it was, that raw attention she'd been garnering ever since she'd had the ring sized so it would fit her. Ruby felt like *someone* the way everyone was fussing over her. The woman walked them over to a glass case housing a shelf of white plates, cups, saucers, and bowls with gold rims. "This is on the simpler, more traditional side," she said, unlocking the case and removing the plate for Ruby to touch.

The plate was smooth, substantial. She ran her finger over the raised gold line. "It's beautiful," Ruby said.

"Awesome," Dina agreed.

The woman replaced the plate, locked the case, and walked them over to another. Here, she removed a wild, modern square collection with an amorphous multicolor print all over the surface.

Ruby held it far away. "No, I don't like this one at all," she said, shaking her head.

"Ghastly," Dina agreed.

"Then there's everything in between," the woman said. She led them to a desk, pulled out a stack of catalogs and brought them out some tea in dainty china cups. Ruby and Dina leafed through the books one at a time for hours. They were transformed into professional china connoisseurs, offering comments about each plate's good and negative qualities, "Too Queen of England" or "Too South Shore, Long Island." That was where Dina was from and she described it as having a unique brand of mass-marketed ostentation. There was no end to the items she could associate with the area she'd been reared in. "That guy" could be "so South Shore, Long Island," but so could "that outfit" or "that movie" and even "that word." Ruby could think she had the meaning down when Dina would go and blow her mind by describing something such as a

meal as being "so South Shore, Long Island." One thing she knew
was that Dina never meant it in a good way.

"Ooh, this is it!" Ruby exclaimed at a Tiffany-style collection,
with a delicate weave of gold around the rim.

"Gorgeous!" Dina said. "That is it, definitely."

Of course Ruby couldn't go and sign up for it without Ed's
looking at it first, although he'd already said she could do what she
liked with the china. She was sent off with a color photocopy, all the
information, and the satisfaction that she'd found the perfect china
pattern. This done, she felt she'd accomplished something. It hadn't
been that difficult! What had she been so worried about? China! It
felt real now.

She was hit with an image of Ed and herself, calmly looking
through the wedding magazines, choosing chef's knives and salad
spinners on his patio. Leaving Manhattan didn't seem to be so bad
when she considered that. What did it matter *where* you were when
you were in love? Why had she always made this out to be so complicated? Honestly, she was easing through it all with flying colors.

Four

[You should] recognize any warning lights that may be displayed on your instrument panel.

—Connecticut Department of Motor Vehicles Driver's Manual

"Grab the salad tongs!" Ruby was passing herself awkwardly through the sliding glass doors onto her wooden patio to eat dinner with her live-in fiancé. She was desperately trying not to care about the mosquitoes.

"What?! Our salad wears a thong?" He was nothing if not sarcastic. Ed could keep a straight face like nobody's business. "Seriously, though, I don't see them."

Whenever she couldn't find anything, Ruby tensed up. She became a Rubycicle, realizing whatever it was, it was most likely in one of those boxes. And as fearful as she'd been of looking at them once they were packed up—well, she was even more afraid of unpacking them. It was as if she was pushing off the finality of it, pushing off the last phase, where everything she had would be woven—inseparably—in with everything Ed had. "I left New York for Middleville!" No, it still didn't quite fit comfortably. She'd been washing out the same two pairs of underwear for a week. She wasn't going to think about the graying bra underneath her shirt. She'd unpack tomorrow.

"All right. Just grab a big fork and spoon!" she screamed to him, her back to the kitchen doors, her face to the sun setting over the mountains. You didn't see a thing like that in New York. It was haunting and hilarious and exhilarating all at once and it happened every single day. You could count on that.

"You don't have to scream. I'm right here." He was whispering in her ear, his hands around her waist, a bunch of cutlery in one hand, a wad of napkins in the other. Napkins! Ed was a maniac for napkins. To Ruby, who'd relied on dining out or dining in out of a takeout box, napkins had never been on her shopping list. What did you need them for when you could just use a scrap of paper towel, a kitchen towel, or even a tissue if one was available? Still, it was cute, the way Ed liked to use napkins, the ones with little farm animals on them.

"Moooo," he'd say and raise the paper square over to her face. When she didn't react he'd shake himself out and do it all again, as if she simply hadn't gotten it the first time. When Ruby would slap her palm on the table, hold her stomach as if he were just hilarious, and then roll her eyes, he'd nod his head up and down and smile, wink. He could make her laugh. She'd give him that.

"Would you like a napkin?" he asked her when they sat down. He folded one on the diagonal ceremoniously and slid it underneath her lime green plate. She'd just bought the plates at Kmart, where you could get anything you wanted for cheap. It was the complete opposite of the City, where you could get nothing for cheap. In her experience, you'd go out always imagining you could, thinking maybe this time. And that would make the whole thing even more frustrating—that you thought there was a chance. Wasn't that just the way with everything, though? That you never learned from the past? That you always wiped your slate clean of experience so you could screw up in exactly the same way each and every time? She was overwhelmed with the sensation that all of this—the patio, the

Kmart bargains, the cow napkins, the idea of his socks swimming around with hers in the wash would slip away through her fingers, before she had a chance to get comfortable.

She reminded herself that beside the couch stood a respectable stack of bridal magazines with dog-eared pages. Surely this had to represent some kind of progress on her part.

The matching cups were striped—pink and lime. *Preppy,* Ruby thought. The look was marinating in her mind. She thought perhaps tomorrow she might work on something in those colors— quaint, choker style, a few strands, maybe with tiny gold beads somewhere in the pattern. The hamburgers sizzled on the grill.

"Duty calls," Ed said, grabbed his industrial-size spatula, and raised his eyebrows twice before turning to tend to the burgers. When the grill top was hinged open, a warm gust wafted over her way. The smell was intoxicating. "Watch this," Ed said, readjusting his backward baseball cap. He drew a theatrical breath. In one movement, he slid the industrial size spatula underneath the burger and flipped it up. And up it went. Up. Up. Up. And over the patio ledge, and with a light *whoosh!* onto the grass one story below.

Finally, they caught their breath. "I give the somersault of that fine burger a 9.0!" exclaimed Ed.

"I say a 9.6!" Ruby wiped a tear of laughter from her eye. "The form! It was spectacular."

They watched one happy dog discover and devour it in two bites, his tongue stretching up over his nose in search of crumbs.

Up on the patio, the rest of the burgers were topped with bright cheddar cheese slices and ready for buns.

Ruby brought out a stack of recipes she'd torn out of magazines.

"Why don't you look through these while we eat and tell me if any of them sound attractive?" she asked. She doled out a plentiful mound of salad to both Ed and herself, piled her own burger with tomato, onion, shredded lettuce, and a couple of pickle slices and some ketchup.

He didn't say a thing about the recipes, didn't even give them a glance. But when she looked up at Ed he was staring her down. And all the while he was slowly pulling something from his right front jeans pocket.

"Whatcha got there, buddy?"

"Oh, you mean *this* mustard bottle?"

"But, but you said you don't, you don't *use* mustard!" It was on their third date. She took Ed to Burger Heaven. She told him she was contemplating the western burger—the one with sautéed onions and barbecue sauce, though normally she was a purist. "Speaking of which"—she'd looked up from her enormous menu—"you don't like mustard on your burger, do you? Cause I've got a strict no-mustard policy with boyfriends. I probably should have told you that on our first date, but I liked you a lot and frankly, I was afraid you sort of had that mustard look about you."

"You must have gotten that 'mustard look' mistaken with my 'custard look.' I get that a lot. I'm a fool for custard," he'd said.

And she'd really liked the way he said that.

But what did this mean, if he hadn't been telling the truth about it?

"Oh honey, now we're living together, all the dirty little secrets come out!"

Was that true? Was Ed going to see the real Ruby? The one who back in L.A. spent her days sitting on a rusty lounge chair in the backyard, picking at the torn plastic straps that held her two inches from the concrete below while she drew the one palm tree in their backyard over and over again? She hoped not. Because she didn't want anything to do with that Ruby whatsoever. Was this all too difficult? Was it silly that she even *try* to make a life here? Had she bitten off more than she could chew?

She must have looked devastated. Ed began slowly lifting his hands up over his head in surrender. "Fine, fine, if it means that much to you, I can forgo the mustard."

"Really?"

"Nope." He squirted a squiggly circle of it on top of his hamburger. "Sorry, I just can't do it."

That night they watched the DVD of *Ray*. After, Ruby was filled with the energy it captured—she thought she could do anything . . . and would. Of course she could have this, make this new life. The past was the past. She turned the television off and headed to the bathroom to get ready for bed. Each step seemed to deflate that energy just a little bit more than the previous one.

At her own apartment, she'd followed the Clinique three-step cleansing regimen. But she just couldn't bring herself to remove all of her makeup yet where Ed was involved. She couldn't yet bear his eyeballing the red marks where she'd picked at her pimples, the tiny sprinkles of dark pores over her nose and cheeks, the greenish tint to her skin. She'd just take it off in the morning and let her skin breathe then. She brushed her teeth halfheartedly, shut the light and crawled into bed.

"Goodnight, John Boy," he joked before reaching for her, kissing her in that way that had convinced her to leave the familiar for this.

As a hamburger connoisseur, Ruby took it upon herself to explore the various hamburger operations in the area. Was it that she was really a hamburger connoisseur, or that she was afraid to discover the area had no offerings in the other things she loved, like sushi, tapas, Middle Eastern cuisine, Korean noodle shops? Could she live in such a place? Should she? She searched via the Internet and then presented Ed with the findings when he returned home in the evening.

"Oh, Jones's? Sure, I know that spot," he said. "Been around forever. Let's go."

The place had a silver camper look to it, like you could just drive it off and park it somewhere else. There was a small overhang above a handful of outdoor tables. The burgers were served on doubled paper plates with ridged perimeters. The fries came waffled and dumped right on top of the burger, so they spilled out over the plate. Ruby thought it looked pretty that way, like the main character surrounded

by the supporting cast. *I'd like to thank all the small fries . . .* She
squirted her ketchup in dots every few inches around.

"You've got character, that's for sure." Ed was now all mustard,
all the time. He squished a puddle of it on his burger patty. Her
stomach turned. Sure it was just mustard, but now it made Ruby
think of all the things that might come out, even the things that
might be wrong with Ed.

"And you've got an unattractive, unhealthy attachment to mustard. But I love you anyhow." They were sitting on the same side,
and she fanned her hand over his back, leaned in to kiss him.

After, they headed to Neiman Marcus to officially register for the
china. The mall was a half hour away. Ruby wasn't sure she'd get
used to the idea that she was located a good half hour from any real
shopping. Back in the city, she loved to pop into the tiny boutiques
on her way home and see what was new, check out the competition,
how her own designs were selling. And then she'd run into Dina
sometimes and they'd grab a French coffee or split a slice of chocolate cake. She definitely missed Dina.

The registry department was a swanky affair with white pearly
wallpaper, soft lights, and lots of shined-up gold. "*Congratula*tions
on your en*gagement*." The woman spoke in grand sweeps, her voice
a good four octaves higher than Ruby's own. She embraced Ruby
heartily, like a grandmother might, and then shook hands with Ed.

"Thank you," Ruby said. Despite herself, she had to admit this
was sort of fun. She felt like she was Madonna or Gwen Stefani for
one second and everyone wanted to treat her the best way they
could.

"I'm Rene Anderson, and I am going to make sure that all of
your registry dreams come *true*."

A modern-day fairy godmother! Ruby found herself swept away
on Rene's wonderful voice. She stood up a little straighter.

"Let's see the ring," Rene sang.

It was obvious from Ed's smile that he'd bought the best ring he
could, that he liked the idea of Ruby walking around wearing it.

They'd been close before the ring, but something about it drew them in further. They were going to be a family. That was the important thing.

She looked over to him and they shared that thought. It wasn't the china that was important, it was the two of them, together.

Rene asked if they would like some champagne, and they both declined. "We already know what we want, so we should be in and out," Ruby explained.

"Okay," Rene said. "What did you have in mind?"

Ruby handed Rene the photocopy of the china design she wanted.

"Elegant, classic. An excellent choice. Now are you *sure* you don't want to look a little bit more before we set this up?"

Ruby answered, "No." But to her surprise, Ed had a different idea.

He answered, "Well, let's look." He shook his head in deep consideration.

"I thought you weren't interested in the china," Ruby said. She'd shown him the pattern and he'd said, disinterestedly, fully engrossed in a History Channel show on steel, "It's very nice," just as the saleswoman at Saks had predicted.

"Well, we're *here*. If I'm only gonna do this once, I might as well experience it."

"Okay, sure." Ruby said. She couldn't see a problem with that, she guessed.

"Excellent," Rene said, standing and leading them towards the glass cases. She started with some designs in the same family as Ruby's pattern.

"So far I'd say yours is the best," he said to Ruby. "She's a jewelry designer, you know. So she's got fabulous taste," he said to Rene.

"Well, how about something on the other end of the spectrum?" Rene suggested. "Just so you have an idea what some of the young people are after. Not everyone has the timeless taste of Ruby."

Yes, Ruby could definitely get used to being a bride.

They followed Rene way across the showroom floor to a little nook peppered with bean-shaped vases and statues, a giant Miro on the wall. Rene pulled out the very same square plate with the crazy color swirls that Ruby and Dina had laughed like crazy over. Ruby was ready to recall something Dina had said about it being called "the morning after a lot of tequila."

"Now, this! This is something I could really see for myself!" Ed held it up, twisting it this way and that.

"Ha ha," Ruby said. "Very funny." Then she turned to Rene. "He loves to play devil's advocate like that. If I say let's eat early, he'll say we should eat late. It's a little game of ours."

"I see." Rene smoothed the front of her blouse. "I'll just leave you two to talk it over." Ruby didn't like the way Rene acted like she'd seen this before. They weren't like other people! They were going to be a family!

"Ruby, really, I like this plate a lot. I didn't think I'd care about china, but this plate is super cool. It makes me want to care about china . . . and everything else."

Just her luck! The one guy who cares about china! "Rene!" she called at her back. "I will have some of that champagne after all! Make it a double!"

She turned back to Ed. "Ed, ummm . . . look, I love you. You know I love you very much. But I absolutely hate that plate. I don't think I could live with a plate like that." When she'd left her momma for New York on that rainy day, she swore she'd make her own decisions for the rest of her life. Oh, how she missed her terry towels folded perfectly on the towel rack! She was going to unpack those the second she got home. Or better yet, maybe she could just not unpack anything, go back where she belonged; maybe Olaf would be nice about it if she could help him find something else, bigger or newer.

"All right, well then, I think what we need is a compromise."

Ruby saw the beautiful, elegant china pattern weave of her dreams slip between her fingers. Was anything ever what you'd expected?

Rene explained to them about all the different types of plates, the entire speech she'd heard already in New York. "Bone china is the gold standard, of course: thin, light catching, and durable. And then you have the porcelain place settings, which are a bit less durable, but still very light and delicate looking. The high heat it's fired at keeps it resistant enough to use daily. And then you've got stoneware, which is tough stuff—can go in the oven, be used every single day however you like. The heaviest of them all is earthenware; it's also the most casual." She said all of this as if it were a set of laws each citizen should live by.

She encouraged them to register for a service for twelve and then left Ruby and Ed with all those catalogs again, pulled out samples when she had them. She brought a plate of chocolates, like she knew they'd be there awhile. Ruby was starting to dislike Rene.

Each time Ed yelled, "What about *this*?" Ruby was afraid to look. In the end, they wound up with bright yellow dishes rimmed with bands of dark orange and an Asian-looking branch painted in the part where food would go. They'd made so many compromises to get there, Ruby couldn't even recall how they'd come to this one. The silverware pattern was heavy (Ruby's wish), and the handle was carved to look like bamboo (Ed's wish). It occurred to Ruby that compromise sucked. They'd save Bed, Bath and Beyond for another night.

"Can I do this?" Ruby asked Dina after she related the china incident. Ed was at the store renting another movie for them to watch. She wasn't sure what the heck he was going to find there. It was unbelievable how much they stayed in, living out here. They changed into jogging pants and ratty old T-shirts, wrapped themselves in throw blankets, and settled in at 5:30 p.m. Could she possibly be the same girl who'd knocked the secret code at the door of after hours clubs at 5 a.m.?

"Was it at least good champagne?" Dina wanted to know.

"What the hell has that got to do with anything?" She scraped her hair back from her forehead and leaned back in Ed's fuzzy, ugly Barcalounger. She was surprised by the backwards rocking and stuck her feet out straight to steady herself.

"It's got everything to do with the fact that china patterns are complete bullshit."

Nothing could look great from a Barcalounger. She said as much to Dina.

"Yeah, well I miss you and all, but I don't want you coming back here and being pathetic with me—two overaged single girls eating a pint of Only 8 yogurt and watching reruns of *Sex and the City* because they can't get past their screwed-up pasts. Suck it up, okay?"

Maybe Dina was right. They were both crap at relationships—the trusting and the open-mindedness and the giving people a chance on the off possibility that they could be different. Dina had a date the following week with some guy from her building. Who knew, maybe it would go somewhere and then Dina could come and move out there with her. And then they could do all the quaint country things that New Yorkers did when they moved to quaint, country places. They could bake gourmet cupcakes or open a country quilting store or arrange holly sprigs and berries into gigantic, expensive wreaths for the holidays.

That night, before bed, she brushed her teeth, flossed (falling amongst the portion of the population who must floss every night, or else! was always disheartening to her), rinsed with Listerine, and inspected her face. So far, she'd not noticed any negative results from removing the makeup in the morning. But she had been a fool to think it might last. The very next morning, right there on the tip of her nose, it was there, bright as her own little sun—a monstrous pimple!

"Good morning, Rudolph! Today's the day we get you a car!"

Ruby clapped a hand over her nose and pouted. She had never been a fan of the morning, but this was unbearable. And not even a Starbucks in sight. And, mind you, with that bulb on the end of her nose, she could see a long, long way.

Five

When driving a vehicle in Connecticut, you will be expected to know [your warning lights].

—Connecticut Department of Motor Vehicles Driver's Manual

Ruby was thankful for cover-up. She had a great tube, but mostly she was thankful it hadn't been in one of those boxes. It was right under their sink, with the rest of her makeup. With the cover-up, two layers of foundation, and a bucket of powder she looked a tad like a circus member, but in most lights sort of like a porcelain doll with perfect skin except for the outrageous bump on her nose. At least she'd gotten the red covered.

They looked at Mitsubishis and then Toyotas. On the way to the Honda dealership Ed explained a bunch of car buying stuff to her. "The guy's gonna wanna take you on a test drive right away, before you get any of the details out on the table. This way, they think, they'll get you hooked, maybe you won't even get to the numbers and then you'll give a deposit, come back, and then when you find out how much the car *really* costs, you're already signed up on a payment plan at nine percent with the keys in your pocket." Ed was driving, and she could tell he was getting hyped up about this. He negotiated in his job—*we'll pay this part of your claim, because of this, that, and the other.* He knew the importance of having the facts, picking a number and sticking with it. He spoke to Ruby in a hushed, strategizing tone.

When they arrived at the dealership, the pair were peeking though the window of a black shiny model when a big voice boomed behind them. They were just off the highway and the sound of the traffic whizzing by was startling; they were all going so fast, too fast.

"You like the Civic?" the salesman asked.

Ruby knocked her head into the glass with surprise. "You break it, you bought it," the voice said from behind a long face, chapped sort of lips. He wore a black suit with a black shirt and black tie, like a Halloween costume of night.

Ruby and Ed were unsure whether this was meant as a joke. Nobody laughed.

"Just kidding with ya!" the salesman said after a couple of awkward seconds.

"I'm Ed," the salesman said.

Ruby and her own Ed looked to each other. "I'm Ed, too," Ed said.

"Ed Too? That's a funny kind of name. What is that, Italian?" Salesman Ed patted Ed's back with a rich, "Ha ha! Ha ha!" Maybe it was more a costume of the grim reaper.

Ruby and Ed tried to stretch their mouths into smiles, slit their eyes as if they were amused. "This is Ruby," Ed said. "The car's for her."

"Why don't we take it for a test drive?"

She thought the car was cute . . . for a death trap. She didn't know why, but Ruby didn't want to get into her fears with Ed. She felt this was something she needed to do on her own. The whole driving thing was so loaded for her—leading her to memories she'd rather forget.

Just seeing all these cars lined up, she could picture her mother at the wheel now, mirrored drugstore sunglasses at her nose, driving barefoot with her left leg up on the seat, a loose ponytail threatening to come undone at any moment. When they'd left Las Vegas, Ruby's mother packed their breakable things in newspaper serenely, as if people did this every day, and casually announced, "We're moving on." She drove and drove and she never looked back. That day at school, Ruby's Spanish teacher had pulled her over and said, "You did beautifully on that test." Ruby had enjoyed that statement so much. While they drove, Ruby thought how she'd never see that woman again. She knew she shouldn't have allowed herself to feel the glow of pride, but she had.

In the car, leaving another home behind, Ruby had tried to get a sense of what had gone wrong. Always she wanted to know, peeking around in dusty corners and under mattresses, what had happened here? Ruby had studied in the rearview the way her bedroom window looked from the passenger seat until her momma opened the driver's side door, and pulled the rearview mirror right from the windshield. "Ruby Booby, you've gotta stop looking back. Ain't no good looking back." How many times since had Ruby found herself sneaking out from a boyfriend's bed in the middle of the night and telling herself just that?

She had come so far here with Ed, and she was not going to give in, despite the china incident. She considered herself past that now. But when she'd tried to tell Ed, the words didn't come out as she'd planned. Instead they came out, "Wanna rent a movie?"

She was a strong girl, though! She already had a license! She could have passed the test before she was old enough to see over the dashboard. They spent so much time in the car her momma used to tell people, "It was so funny, Ruby's first word was 'Chevy.'" But Ruby never saw the humor. She drove to one party in Las Vegas, one party that she wasn't invited to, on the off chance she could walk in without being noticed, just to do something, to be somewhere. But they'd laughed her away from the door. She drove back home and cried into her momma's back, wetting a large spot onto her purple top. There wasn't the freedom to driving that she had assumed there would be. It had occurred to her after the party that she could get on the highway and run away. She thought of those kids being sorry, maybe being so screwed up from her being a missing person because they'd laughed at her. She'd smiled at that, and at the vision of her momma crying into her Prince of Wales tea. But in the end, she realized she sounded just like her momma. She'd been given the freedom, but she didn't know what to do with it. She'd always said before, "I'm running away from you when I'm old enough!" But she didn't say that again after that night. She wasn't running. Not in a car, anyhow.

Once she got behind the wheel now, surely things would come together. She was a different person, miles away from her momma, and she wasn't running away from anything. She wasn't a runner. Cars whizzed by the dealership and the heavy beating pattern in her chest seemed silly. She wasn't any different than they were! There wasn't a reason in the world she couldn't slide into any one of these cars and drive home, where she belonged.

"Why don't we go inside and talk about the details first and then if everything sounds good, we'll do the test drive." Ed was cool and his gaze didn't once waver.

"Oh, I'm sure the little miss is dying to get behind the wheel." Salesman Ed looked right at Ruby when he said this, possibly for the first time.

Ruby couldn't help but compare these two Eds. Salesman Ed had nothing on her Ed. How come she loved and trusted him so much that she'd left the safety of New York behind to face all of this? Was this finding her identity, or having an identity crisis?

"Actually, we'd really like to go over the details first."

Salesman Ed looked to Ed and then to Ruby once more and then shrugged his shoulders. "All right, Monty. Let's make a deal," he said.

As Ruby and Ed followed Salesman Ed into the showroom, Ed winked at Ruby and squeezed her hand. Their magic number was telepathically confirmed between them.

The showroom was shiny. Every surface seemed to reflect off

every other surface and the overall effect was somewhat disorienting. Plus the air-conditioning was turned up to turbo. Each time Ed wrote a number on a piece of paper, Salesman Ed laughed, said the sticker price was final. Then he shook his head, cradled his banana chin in his thumb and forefinger, and disappeared inside the manager's office for negotiations.

Ruby knew from the car prep that she wasn't supposed to say anything during this time. This was all part of the game. So she poked Ed, smiling with anticipation. He poked her back. She mouthed, "Owwwwww," and rubbed at her arm.

After three times around, Salesman Ed was looking a little peaked, but Ed held firm. This time the manager's door opened to spill both Salesman Ed and the manager himself out. The manager's skin was tanned to a leathery brown except in half moons beneath his eyes.

"This is the absolute lowest price we ever sold a Civic for," the manager said. "I'm leaving my office now to go tell my wife there's no college for our daughter, so this is the ultimate last offer, okay?"

"Okay." Ed shook his head with resignation as if he hadn't got just what he wanted.

"Shall we go for that test drive now?" Salesman Ed wanted to know, dangling what would soon be Ruby's keys in front of Ruby.

She looked at the keys. They swung back and forth, back and forth as if he were hypnotizing her. She wasn't ready. She needed to buy herself just a few more minutes. "Ed, you should drive, because that way you can make sure everything feels right. I'll have plenty of time to drive." She tossed her palm around and spoke in a dramatic tone that the situation didn't call for. But she was worried. Buying the car was a big enough step. Surely she didn't have to drive it in the same day?

Ed looked strangely at her, but they were good like that. They didn't air their personal issues in front of other people. It was something Ruby had expressed the importance of many times. In her memory burned so many mortifying moments. "Ruby has a yeast infection," her mother had told an acquaintance they'd run into at a

supermarket once. "Ruby is afraid of the dark," she told the unfortunate student forced to sit with them for lunch on a class trip. She'd
squeezed her face even further down into the depths of her crinkled
paper lunch sack.

"That's a good idea," he said.

She would learn to love their china. She would learn to drive
this car. If it killed her. Which, she considered, it very well might.

It seemed, just as she was relaxing into the safety of putting off
the drive, she was handed the keys once again to follow Ed home
from the dealership in her new car. They were cold, too cold for it
being only the end of summer. What was she doing here? How was
this going to work, exactly? Her temperature gauge must have been
broken because now her palms began to sweat precisely as chills ran
up her back. She was hearing everything as if it were coming to her
through a long, hollow tube.

He looked at her before leaving her in the driver's seat. "You're
okay, you know . . . up for this, right?"

What was she supposed to say to that? She'd just spent over
twelve thousand dollars on this car! Was she supposed to admit she
couldn't drive it? Stronger than her desire to live (rather than die in
a car crash), was her desire to live with Ed. Ruby wasn't going to be
punched through with holes like a Swiss cheese Ruby right before
Ed's eyes—not before they got a chance to live . . . happily ever after! "Of course!" She said this too dramatically, her eyes open too
big, her smile too wide. She sprung a few drops of spittle on his face
pronouncing the hard "c."

Salesman Ed came running out of the dealership. "Hey, get in the
car! I'm gonna take a Polaroid so you can always remember this moment!" He tossed a Honda cap on her head, screwed it down tight
until her eyes were barely visible.

"Perfect!" Ruby said, frantic, her hands gripping onto the wheel.

"Okay, now smile big," Salesman Ed coerced.

Ed made a funny face behind Salesman Ed and the camera so
Ruby would smile, as people did for infants who couldn't focus.

Click!

Salesman Ed waved the Polaroid around, blew on it. When it was dry he took a look. "Fabulous! You look great!" He handed it to Ruby. Ed walked over to her open window and looked with her. Ruby was surprised. She looked very happy. She looked up at Ed and he smiled big. It was shocking to her, the way she'd learned to cover things up, toss them into closets and shove the door closed with her back.

"I love you," he said. Ed leaned down and kissed her. "Congratulations, baby." How could she live with herself, keeping all these things from him with the patience and kindness he showed her?

There was no choice now. She squeezed the key tightly and, her throat tightening, turned the ignition until the confident whir of machine sounds chided her with its automatic response.

She worked the toylike gearshift into drive and Ed walked over to his own car, pulled in front of her, and winked in his rearview mirror.

She did fine until the turnout of the parking lot, which she couldn't bring herself to make. Ed pulled out when there'd be enough room for the two of them to merge into the traffic, but she'd hesitated too long and now a car was coming and she'd have to wait. Ruby tried to concentrate on locating his car—it was a big honker of a truck and so this shouldn't have been as difficult as it was. But she had to keep watching for her opening to pull out into the traffic, too. She kept watching and watching for his car, and then for an opening to merge on the wide four lane street, but she'd lost him and on top of that, none of the spaces seemed like the right one. Finally, with no other choice, she hoped the cars would make room for her and stepped on the gas—a little too hard, so that the car screeched wildly on the turn. She reacted by slamming on the brakes. The person behind came very close and then honked at her mistake, waving a fist at her. When she looked up, Ed was nowhere in sight. Nothing looked familiar. There was a golf ball lodged in her throat. Could this possibly have been a good choice?

As if answering her question, Ed pulled out from the McDonald's parking lot a few feet ahead, waving proudly as he pulled in front of her.

It turned out that thanks to a back roads route, the dealership was little more than around the corner from where they lived, and so Ruby was home sooner than she had suspected she might be. She pulled into a spot and cut the engine. She'd just driven home! That was huge. Still, she was in no rush to get back on that road. Her breath began to come more normally; the feel of her skin grew more familiar. She closed the door behind her with a bang; Ed showed her how to do the remote control lock by pressing the keychain button twice.

"That was awesome, champ," Ed said, leading her back upstairs to their apartment.

"Thanks. You weren't so bad yourself, Mr. Negotiator," she said.

"If you want, I can take you around driving until you get used to it again," he offered. "It's been so long since you were on the road."

"Oh, no. That's not necessary." She was a terrible actress, but she did her best, tried to think of a confident sort of actor and mimic that. She settled on Jack Nicholson. And did her best to keep up the act without looking too much like The Joker. She tried to cover up the tensions that had settled upon her once she'd climbed behind the wheel. She wasn't about to show him that having a car was something Ruby had avoided all her life because of this one fact: she was terrified of where she would go.

They were upstairs and she didn't know if it was the adrenaline or the fear of leaving it all, but she lost herself in the planes and curves of him, the gentle whisper and touch of him, and it was already dark by the time they dressed. In the way he slipped his head through the hole of his sweatshirt, she thought she saw that everything would be just fine.

Six

Driving is a skill and how well you have developed this skill will be the deter-mining factor when the inspector evaluates your driving test.

—Connecticut Department of Motor Vehicles Driver's Manual

Ed was long gone for work by the time Ruby rolled out of bed a couple of days later, on a Wednesday, wearing a pair of Ed's boxer shorts and a long-sleeved Kingsborough College T-shirt.

She was often split about the merits of this lifestyle. Sure, you could sleep in. But if you did you were directly impacting your income. You could sell a necklace for five hundred dollars, but that wasn't a lot of money if you really thought about the amount of time that five hundred dollars would be covering. If you woke up earlier, you made more necklaces, had the opportunity to sell more necklaces; more necklaces equals more money. And that was a lot of pressure.

What if you just weren't in the mood? What if you worked for hours and the thing fell apart and you had to start all over again? What if it just sucked and then all that time had been wasted?

Despite all the what ifs and what they could do to her running through her head while she drank her morning coffee, Ruby had done pretty well until her recent slump. And she'd invested wisely—in low return, but guaranteed safe CDs—and so she'd been making money even when she wasn't really making money. She knew her fate was in her own hands. And so she was determined to wake up today and get started making those pieces she'd been inspired by since the move: the sun design and the preppy look.

Even after the pimple had sprouted, Ruby still slept in her makeup, telling herself she obviously couldn't show Ed how bad it *really* looked. And now, washing off the makeup that had been sitting on her skin for over twenty-four hours, Ruby felt less than clean. In fact, after washing, she exfoliated and then toned, and still she felt grayish and gritty. She applied a deep cleansing mask and sat down in front of the television for a few minutes before her shower.

The Food Channel was doing sushi. There were so many colors! And the crab looked out of this world, never mind the spicy tuna. The tiny slivers of cucumber and the mushy hunks of avocado! And that hot wasabi, disguised in a child's candy green! She was inspired—what a great color for a necklace—maybe she'd work with clay beads, or glass. But, she was also craving. Where was she going to get sushi around here? Ruby thought of her old local spot. She could just walk around the corner, and *voila*! There was a combination plate of six sashimi, one spicy tuna tempura roll right in front of her, with a complimentary bowl of edamame literally overflowing with happy-looking pods.

Had Ruby been hasty in her decision to leave all of that? From here, she could see her car parked outside. The sticker was still on, taunting her with its bright orange letters: SOLD! All she needed to do was get inside, buckle herself in, and drive herself to a local sushi place. Surely she could find one! But it seemed like such a massive undertaking.

Still she tried. The metal handle was hot, shining in the sun, so obviously unused in its absence of fingerprints. There were barely any other cars in the lot. Most everyone was working. She sat in her car, clutching her purse. *Enough!* She screamed the word and then it just faded to wherever it is such sounds go, in their tiny invisible waves. The plan was, try out the driving locally and then call an instructor.

Ruby placed her purse on the floor of the passenger side. She buckled her seatbelt. Raised the setting to accommodate her height. She used to be so tiny her mother had Ruby tuck the shoulder strap behind her back. And look at her now. Now she was tall. Did that mean anything? You could be tall, but not grown-up. And this sounded odd to Ruby just then.

Her thumb and forefinger squeezed the large head of the key, in its sleek black plastic, with its Honda logo molded in. This car was hers. And she wouldn't necessarily use it to escape. That was just stupid! She could drive. She had a license, for crying out loud. She'd gotten a perfect score on the road test! And well she should have, she could have driven when she was five years old. Her mother had sometimes had Ruby steer when her hands cramped up, balling them into fists and then over-extending the fingers as if they were made from rubber, while Ruby leaned in close, intoxicated by White Diamonds, which her mother would apply from tiny department store sample vials—drawing invisible lines on her neck, back and forth, back and forth. Ruby always held tight on either side of the wheel until her hands felt wet with sweat.

Here she was, terrified, her hands in that same position; now it was clear they were unable to shift the key the few inches it would require to start the ignition.

She peeled her fingers from the steering wheel. She dug through her huge black purse to unearth her cell phone and dialed.

"Dina, tell me not to eat sushi."

"I'm eating it right now!" Her phone was a little crackly.

Already, Ruby thought, their communication was weakening.

"But what about the bacteria that could kill you?"

"Oh, please. I've been eating this stuff at least three times a week for five years. Come and get me, bacteria!"

Oh! The irreverence in her voice! New Yorkers spoke in shades of sarcasm. She missed the sarcasm. "So, how are you Dina?" God! She didn't think it would be *this* hard! She just wanted to tell her friend to stay put, just wait a couple of hours and she'd be right there, stuffing spicy tuna rolls down her throat ungracefully. But she couldn't even turn her car on! She was stranded, trapped, shanghaied. How was she ever going to get out of this?

"Oh, you know. I'm living it up." She turned the dial on her radio, though it was off. It was her radio. At least she could work the radio.

She was grateful that Dina wasn't sugarcoating things. If those two ever started getting polite, that would be the end of things. "What's wrong, Deen?"

"Remember that guy from my building? The one with the thing?"

The "thing" was a slightly funny walk, as if one leg may have been shorter than the other. At least Ruby still knew which "thing" her friend was talking about. Whatever you did, you could never stop knowing the "thing." You could just forget it if you did. Surely nothing could be so bad if she were still intimately acquainted with someone else's "thing." "Yeah. What happened?"

"Ruby, he friggin' stood me up last night. I was sitting at MeKong and I must have shredded twenty-three napkins! I sat there, smelling that pad thai and waiting and waiting to order like a good girl should. But the guy just never showed up."

"No!"

"Yes! And even worse, I see him this morning in the elevator and he says, 'Oh, sorry about last night. I was just, well . . .' He didn't even bother to think of an excuse."

"Ew!"

"I know! I seriously give up!"

She didn't know what to say. It wasn't so long ago she was going through the same exact thing as Dina, thinking she'd never survive all those false starts, high hopes that never panned out. Turns out, though, once you've gotten past that, there are a whole slew of other atrocities you've got to endure. Who would have guessed?

Beyond her windshield was a view of the garbage facility. She watched a young man drag a toilet over to the white-sided building. If only it was that simple for Ruby to dispense of the crappy, old things that weighed her down.

"Aw, don't give up, Dina! What about online dating? I hear they have better match techniques now." It was so easy to give clear, take-charge advice to someone else.

"I met that guy online!"

"Oh." What else could she say? Still, sometimes there was nothing to say. If she'd learned one thing, it was that.

"When are you coming down here, Rube? I miss you. I need someone normal I can talk to."

"Speaking of that—and by 'that' I mean both coming down there and being normal—I am sitting in the driver's seat of my brand-new car and I am terrified to drive it!"

"But you don't drive!"

"I know!"

"Why don't you just have Mr. Lesbian Lover Stealer teach you?"

"I'd rather just handle it on my own. So I'm gonna hire a driving instructor. You know, I don't want to owe all that to Ed."

"Oh, no. That's yo momma speaking." Dina loved to make fun of the way Ruby addressed her momma. She also loved to point out the dysfunctional personality traits Ruby had inherited from her.

"It is not! It's just more practical. There's enough to fight about with the wedding planning, picking out your lavender taffeta dress and all." She could try to change the subject. But she knew Dina never bought into that sort of thing.

"Listen Ruby, from where I'm standing, your situation looks pretty damn good. You are miles away from yo momma, so don't let her influence you. There's nothing wrong with settling down and depending on someone. That's all I'm gonna say about that. And if you want me wearing lavender taffeta, you're gonna have to kill me first."

The line crackled so loudly Ruby had to hold the phone from her head.

The crackles grew louder until they seemed to rise up and over Dina's voice, swallow her whole while Ruby pieced together fragments of comments about Ed's single friends and matching them up in the wedding party.

"Dina? Dina!" Just like that they were disconnected and it resonated so much deeper than just a dead line. It smacked her in the face—she was stuck here in a gently used Honda and there was no yoga studio upstairs, no sushi around the corner, and nowhere to buy that naan bread she loved to eat so much on a whim. And this had all been her choice.

All in one instant, Ruby felt the ridiculousness of this. She was just growing up was all! She loved Ed and she loved it here! She could already see a couple of leaves turning, their new crispness rustling, and the idea of pumpkin picking and baking apple pies swam around in her mind. She turned the key, jammed into reverse, and let her foot ease off the brake. Ruby was going to face her demons, was what she was thinking.

She shifted into drive, looked left toward the street and then turned the opposite way into the mass of their development's parking lot instead. She drove around twice, pulled back into her spot, and went right back up to her apartment.

She was going to face her demons, she thought again. Just not today.

Inside her apartment, Ruby dropped her keys into a pretty Mexican carved bowl. At least she'd taken them out. At least she could hear their jingle-clink into the bowl. That had to count for something. It just had to.

Maybe she couldn't accomplish anything out there, but she could sure as hell accomplish something in here! It was a big place—a full one thousand two hundred square feet, in comparison to her four hundred-foot spot in New York—and, sure, she didn't know where a blasted thing might be located outside of it, but she could tell you where everything she owned was tucked away in her apartment, that was for sure! Unless, of course, it happened to be inside one of those boxes. She sure as hell wasn't ready for that. Their mass was taking up the whole front room. Ruby wished they'd stacked them some- where else. Somewhere she didn't have to squeeze by them each and every time she came and went. Depending on how you looked at them, they could look either very well structured or ready to tum- ble down at any second. All that cardboard and tape. The well- meaning content labeling in black marker: "Kitchen Stuff" and "Winter Coats" and "Cleaning Supplies." The clear, clean lettering seemed to say, this shouldn't be so hard! But it was. It just was.

Once she bypassed them, backward, arms out like she was scaling a wall, she could move onto something else. There were always the necklaces. Maybe she couldn't make them without the supplies she'd run out of, but she could *order* the supplies. At least she could freely navigate the Internet fearlessly. As if she were proving this to the world, Ruby surfed around the Internet for over four hours. The idea of it offered some solace; she could convince herself that "surfing" was more than just a metaphor for sitting and typing on a keyboard. She was discovering! She was adventure-seeking, traveling to the greatest corners of the World Wide Web! That is . . . if TheKnot.com was considered an adventure. She looked at the wedding reception venues in their area. She checked out invitations, photographers, tent rental companies. It was another world. That was for sure.

She lost herself for a couple of hours in floral arrangement options.

And then her phone rang.

"So? How's the new place, Rube?" Her momma always spoke too loudly on the telephone. It didn't help that Ruby's phone was crackling like mad. Now she saw the sounds growing, like an out of control weed, up and over, twisting their way into everything she was, through fingers and around legs, until they completely cut her off from the world.

When Ruby had first gone out on her own, she thought there'd be safety in feeling a distance between her momma and herself. But there wasn't. She hated her, but she loved her. She hated to think about it, but Ruby called her momma nearly every other day; and on the off days, she thought about calling her. She blamed her, and yet there was no one else who'd been there through all of that, who saw and knew maybe what she really was.

"It's great," she said. Her voice, so meek and low, surprised even herself, and the crackling didn't help matters. But her momma didn't seem to notice. She'd been putting off telling her momma about the engagement.

"Well, that's good, honey. Wish I could say the same for things here. That Louis is a real moron, I'm telling you. He just lost his job. Who ever heard of an engineer getting *fired*? Can't seem to do anything right. He must have been born with some kind of deficiency, I'm telling you." Her mother's voice went up and down, loud and low, words stretched and distorted in the bad connection.

Even with all the distractions, even with the miles between, she could feel that tingling in her feet, moving up, up, and that meant her momma was getting ready to move on. There was nothing worse to Ruby's momma than failure. What would she need with a failure?

"Well, I have some news," Ruby said.

"Well, what is it?" her momma wanted to know. She'd played this conversation out twenty different ways and none of them had fit her desires for the outcome. She had wanted her momma to be excited for her, despite the fact that she was opposed to marriage, and at the same time she wanted to piss her off slightly, while proving to her momma that Ruby wasn't like her in the least.

"Ed and I are engaged." Ruby channeled Meryl Streep in *Postcards from the Edge*. Ruby always saw the actress as so determined. She'd waited until she was safely moved to Connecticut to tell her momma under the pretense that she'd be less likely to be swayed once she'd taken the first major step. Still, it was more difficult than she'd even imagined.

Her momma was silent. Finally she said, "Engaged? You mean like, to be married?" To Ruby's momma, getting married was akin to joining a cult. She'd spoken twice with Ed on the telephone and both times had described him as sounding "cute." "Now he's cute, isn't he?" she'd said, like she wouldn't take him seriously.

"Yes, Momma. Ed and I are going to be married."

Momma harrumphed. "Ruby, don't you know men are useless? What do you need him for? You're much better off leaving it open, so that, when he disappoints you—WHICH HE WILL—you can just go, easy peasy."

She wasn't going to get sucked in. She hated the saying "easy peasy." "We are getting married, Momma. I'm an adult and that is my decision." Why was she still on the telephone? Why did she subject herself to this? Why did she feel like she was convincing *herself* that she was an adult?

"Ruby! I cannot believe, after *your* life, that you would ever subject yourself to that kind of thing."

Oh, her mother was pushing her! She'd begged and begged to know her father, but her momma said she couldn't remember, or she'd had an immaculate conception. She could never get a straight answer. She told herself she was older now and what was the point of trying to find out? What could a father do for her now anyway? She calmed herself, tried to unscrunch her face. She looked to the mountains beyond her window. They seemed solid, held a remote promise that they might ground her somehow.

"Momma, we are going to start looking at places to hold the wedding. Ed's mom is going to help us out with some of the decisions. She's lived here forever and she knows everyone."

Her momma cut her off. "*Ed's* mom? Well, *I* am your momma. I should be involved, too!"

Ruby wished she hadn't said anything about Ed's mom. Her momma was so competitive, there was no way she would let Ed's mom take care of everything, no matter her stance on weddings. "Yes, I'm going to check my calendar and then I'll come and help you ruin your life."

"I can't wait," Ruby huffed. Now it would loom—a day in the future when her momma would come, when she would be there. Ruby could just picture her momma telling everyone at the bridal shop that marriage was ridiculous, I'm telling you. And when a dress didn't look right she could tell them all how she called her Ruby Booby because she never had any boobies to speak of.

Ruby was exhausted after talking to her mother. And that crackling was still ringing in her ear. She probably should have called her cell phone company to complain. But sometimes these things just cleared themselves up, she thought. She'd just wait it out.

She started picking up—Ed's clothes, his dishes, his wet towels. What was with this? He threw everything on the floor! Had he been living in a zoo before they'd met? *Step up and see the world's most messy man! Hasn't picked up a thing since he was four years old! Oooooh . . . ahhhhh.*

How, when, had he become this . . . this disgusting!? The towel in her hand, heavy with water and the scent of strawberry shampoo, seemed just then to be intolerable. How could she be expected to live like this? If she was going to change her whole life, defy her mother and learn how to drive, surely he could pick up a damned towel? If she was going to force herself to get behind the wheel of death—grip it with her fingers and force herself to do everything she'd never done—well, then, surely he could pick up this one fucking towel?

She stared at it God knows how long, its formerly perfect white fluff now hardened with being left out over and over again, before she threw it in the washing machine, finally, with the rest of the light-colored items he'd left strewn on the floor, like wet pasta stuck to a wall, all the angles unnatural and dead looking.

When Ed got home he was full of pride, as if he were keeping a big secret. It was a welcome sight. Oh, the energy he could bring in with him! How did it fit through the door? It nearly overshadowed the dirty laundry frustration. Nearly.

He was all smiles, teeth everywhere. "How's my widdle baby waby?" They were in the baby talk stage.

"Wood." She'd meant to say "good," but it hadn't worked out properly. Ruby couldn't get a handle on baby talk, and she eagerly awaited the next stage of their relationship, whatever that might be. In the meanwhile, she tried to cover up her discomfort by playing with her wet hair.

"I'm wood, too. We're a coupla woody two shoes." He was pulling his tie off. Unbuttoning his shirt.

She started kissing his neck. She closed her eyes, getting into it. But when she opened them, Ed's shirt was on the floor. She was going to say something. "Woney?" she tried to approach on his level.

"Wes?" he asked, kissing her hand.

"Do you think you could put your dirty clothes right in the hamper from now on?"

"Oooh, baby, you sure know how to talk sexy." Ed turned to face her.

"Ha ha. If you like that, we can go into the laundry room and fold towels after this." She raised her eyebrows two times.

"After what?" he teased, now laying on top of her.

After, they both lay facing the ceiling. "Whaddyou wanna do for dinner?" she asked him, turning onto her side, propping her head up with an elbow. She pulled a stack of recipe tear-outs from a magazine that she'd piled on her bedside table earlier. "Hey, look through these and pick one you want," she said.

"Actually, I wanted to take you somewhere special," he said, putting the recipes back where they'd come from, not giving them a glance. "Somewhere special for my cutey wooty."

She smacked him with a pillow, hoping to end the baby talk quicker. "I'm no one's wooty—cutey or otherwise."

Ed took the pillow and proceeded to smother her with it, tickling with his one free hand. "Say you are my cutey wooty, or else!"

She couldn't breathe from laughing. The underarms were the most ticklish. "I won't do it!"

"Ruby Booby, say you are my cutey wooty!"

"Nooooohhhhhhhh!"

"Say it!"

"Fine, I'm your freakin' cutey wooty."

"Say it like you mean it." He was now tickling at her kneecap.

She roared with the sensation of it. She knew she never should have shown him how sensitive her kneecap was to tickling.

"*It* like you mean it."

"Ruby Reynolds, what *are* you?" He pulled the pillow away and looked at her so close she could see all the tiny speckles that made up his eyes.

It frightened her how much she loved him, how much she could feel, allow herself to feel now she'd come this far. If her mother knew Ed, she'd feel differently. Her eye glassed, threatening tears, but she choked them back. This was her wonderful life and she was lucky to have it. "I'm your cutey wootey." She said it sweetly, like she meant it.

Twenty minutes later, they were driving in Ed's old truck up a road she didn't recognize. It seemed to Ruby there were infinite roads. Not just here, but everywhere you turned. Their dulled, pocked blackness covered surfaces as far as the eye could see. *Life really is a highway*, she thought. She could follow them or not. They weren't all bad. She was starting to see that. She breathed in deep, and noticed something familiar in the air.

"What is that?" she asked.

"What's what?" Ed turned to her with a blank face.

"That smell. You must smell it. It's so familiar. What the hell is it?"

"I don't smell anything," Ed said in his nutty way, eyes dollar coins.

Up and up they drove until it seemed to Ruby they had reached the top of the world. The smell was all through her then, and its identity was right at the tip of her tongue. Ed jumped out of the truck, tilted his seat forward, and revealed an insulated bag tucked behind.

"Whatcha got there, cutey wooty? That's the smelly thing, isn't it?" Ruby asked with a smirk.

"Don't you worry your pretty little head over that." Ed snapped the chair back and came around to her side. He was always doing surprisingly gentlemanly things like that.

"Why, that's some rock you've got on your finger, Mrs. Robbins." He'd been calling her that lately. It was growing on her.

When the door was closed behind her, Ed turned Ruby around to see this place he was taking her to. It was a tiny little lake with a simple wooden bench and there wasn't another person around. There was one duck, making elegant ripples as it glided forward. It was a beautiful duck, white and long in the neck, and so it didn't make you sad to see it alone.

They walked over to the bench and sat down there. Ed unzipped the insulated bag and that familiar scent grew stronger. In Ruby's hand, Ed placed a stack of two tiny plastic cups. And in each, there was a small amount of soupy, deep green mint chutney. Two, because one, she'd once told Ed, was never enough for the great big naan bread you got in Grand Central Station.

She found out just then, though, that two was exactly right. And as she was ripping into the buttery bread, the duck raised her feathers and adjusted her head further backward. And out of nowhere another duck skidded across the water, and together they made their way around the pond.

Seven

You should follow your vehicle owner's manual for routine maintenance. Some you can do yourself; some must be done by a qualified mechanic. A few simple checks will help prevent trouble on the road.

—Connecticut Department of Motor Vehicles Driver's Manual

She wanted to try it one more time on her own before calling in a driving instructor. Ruby had always had a thing about doing things herself. All she had to do was think of all the things she hadn't wanted to do in her life, but was forced to, and the will would burn right up. It was there when she'd bought a car she didn't know how to drive, and it was here now, when she was trying to learn how to drive it. In the car, a million reasons not to turn the key ran through Ruby's head like an express train to Nowheresville. And then that girl in the wheelchair she'd seen the other day, coming from an apartment on the first floor, wheeled herself in the exact angle of Ruby's rearview mirror. She watched the girl turn three circles in her chair and then throw her hands up and let them fall with a *smack!* to her thighs, like the girl was monitoring Ruby and was disappointed in her efforts.

Ruby didn't care what that girl thought. She couldn't have been a day over seventeen! Still, she grabbed for the key. It seemed to weigh two thousand pounds. The effort required to twist it—ever so slightly—to life! *Vrroooooooommmmmm*. Again she traced that curve with the back of the car, yanked it into drive, and curved around the parking lot once, twice, like an airplane gaining speed for takeoff. And then she looked left, right, and took the turn onto the main road. The lines followed alongside—one yellow, the other a double white—and it was apparent she was going somewhere, really going somewhere today. It all *felt* different. Today she had a plan. She'd thought of somewhere she needed to go and that was exactly where she was headed.

The road curved right and then left, trees lining it and waving her on—a couple of leaves falling to the ground trailing behind her like applause. It was a silent victory, but when she pulled into a parking space in front of the Super Stop & Shop, Ruby knew she'd done something spectacular.

BUY ONE, GET ONE FREE! Ruby stopped her cart in front of the macaroni and cheese boxes. There were at least twenty varieties. She grabbed for a box with dinosaur-shaped pasta and one with fat-looking aliens. This place was huge! The Gristede's she'd frequented back in the city was just ten grody aisles, mostly with molding produce and rotisserie chickens. At the produce aisle here, she was overwhelmed with the vast selection. She squeezed grapefruits and oranges, scooped spicy olives into a container, perused fancy cheeses, and at the deli counter she ordered prosciutto de parma for only two dollars and fifty cents! In the city this would have cost ten times that. At the condiment aisle she found a jumbo-sized mustard for two fifty-nine and so she tossed that in for Ed. It could be funny if she set it right at the door, so that when he swung it open, the mustard would be staring back at him.

There was a special on chicken on the bone—twenty-nine cents a pound—and so she carefully considered, with absolutely no perspective with which to do so, how much would be suitable for Ed and herself.

She turned to ask the man in the white coat smeared with blood. His name tag read, "Hi, my name is Richard."

"Richard?" she ventured with too much volume. Three women alongside turned to see. But she'd lost the steam now. "Two people?" she asked like a riddle you had to figure out the sense of. She could be shy at the strangest times. Moving syndrome, she called it.

"You'll have to speak up, miss." He said it with barely a glance in her direction, stacking turkey drumsticks way back in the deep refrigerator. His T-shirt was coming untucked at his waist. Richard was wearing a paper hat.

She tried again, but this time only the beginning half of the question came out. "How much?"

"It's twenty-nine cents a pound," he said, pointing to the sign right in front of her face.

She'd just have to estimate how much to purchase. Ruby settled on four packages. It was a good sale, after all. And if she froze it, chicken could last right through the next century, couldn't it?

"Ed, I defrosted the chicken legs for dinner!" She could picture herself telling him this on his way out in the morning. That would be nice, wouldn't it?

Under the sign for BREADS, Ruby read carefully about the benefits of whole grains, shaking her head up and down at interesting points. She checked the grams of carbohydrates and the serving sizes before settling on some wholesome-looking wheat-colored loaf with an armored Roman on the package. There were onion pitas that also looked interesting, and so she dunked them into the carriage and headed back over to the other side of the store where she expected to find some garlic hummus. Maybe she could make some falafel, too. She'd done it once before and remembered it being relatively simple.

Ruby zigzagged the store like that until the ice cream in her cart looked sogged in on the sides, the wet of it all dripped off. She couldn't believe how much she'd missed shopping! Somewhere between the frozen corn niblets and the cans of crushed plum tomatoes, Ruby came across a mini Staples store—right there in the supermarket! She tossed in a few printable pamphlets she could use for marketing, some cute tags. When she turned the aisle, there was an entire book shop, filled with all the new releases, best sellers, magazines. She shopped and shopped and shopped and in the Hallmark card aisle she dropped a box of thank-yous and was struck with terror. It hit her. She was going to have to drive home.

She'd been here too long and lost her nerve. Still there was a mountain of items in her cart and something blue was starting to drip onto the floor. She rolled up to a patio furniture display at the end of the aisle, used the stuck-on straw to prick open one of the Capri Suns she'd loaded into the cart for nostalgia's sake, took a seat, and tried to figure out her next move.

She was just going to have to call Ed. Women were walking by, jingling their key rings like it was nothing. Panic rose in her like a giant Honolulu beach wave in a 1950s movie. *Mistake mistake mistake . . .* it was running through her brain like a ticker tape. She'd wanted not to tell Ed, it was true. But if she really thought logically about it, they were going to be a family. And she was going to have to learn to rely on him. And that was okay. She didn't have to do everything herself. Her mother didn't know it all. She was marrying him, after all!

Richard the butcher walked by, wheeling another cart of bloody animal parts to the freezer. He caught her eye and then raised his eyebrows in surprise. Just as quickly, his face wrinkled in tightly, the concern unmistakable.

How long had she been here? He must have packaged, stickered, and loaded all of those up into the cart since she'd last seen him. Hours must have past. She started to feel embarassed in a warm way at the pit of her belly. Ruby sucked the last bit of her Capri Sun through the straw with a slurping sound.

Richard was back, this time without the cart, in just a couple of minutes. "Are you homeless?" he asked, tugging his shirt down into his belt.

Ruby didn't answer, didn't know how to answer such a thing. Wasn't she wearing clean, if not necessarily stylish, clothing?

"Because," he said, his eyebrows raising his paper hat slightly, "we can't have homeless people just sitting here, piling food into a wagon, reading magazines, drinking Capri Suns because . . ." He didn't seem to know how to finish.

"I'm not homeless," she said with a guilty tone to her words. She'd felt homeless before, but not in the way this man meant. Sure, she hadn't been born here, but this was her home, just as much as it was his, wasn't it?

Still, he didn't leave. "You know, it's not right what some people do. A supermarket isn't meant to solve all the problems of the universe."

Ruby wished he would just stop talking. She didn't like the hopelessness in his voice, the crimson smudges on him, the dark pinheads of his facial hair ready to spring through.

Without saying anything she rose, paid the $235 grocery bill, called Ed, and made up some lame excuse. "I came to the supermarket, but I'm feeling dizzy all of a sudden and I don't think I should drive," she said.

He was quiet, then said, "I'll come get you."

She waited outside for him to come and pick her up, feeling like a liar, pushing him further away. She tried not to think about how long all that meat had been sitting out unrefrigerated.

Ed arrived in record time. He was in the passenger seat of his own truck with someone she didn't recognize. Ed waved the guy off, ran over to Ruby, and squeezed her like she was the last stubborn drop in a toothpaste tube.

She buried her face in the crook of his neck and tried to hide how stupid she felt. But it was already burning at her cheeks. And when they separated, he put his hand right there, to where her feelings shown out of her control.

A mother passed by, laughing wildly with her daughter who kept singing, "One, two, three . . . boo boo beeeeee." It was their secret joke and that touched Ruby. It was something to share yourself with another person like that; it was something to make it look so easy. Seeing that family seemed like a sign for Ruby. It was trying to tell her she was doing the right thing, even if it didn't seem so very easy just then.

Ed directed his coworker Jim to Ruby's car, loaded up the groceries, and drove them home in his truck, his hand rubbing down over her hair, smooth, smooth, like a wonderful dream. The friend followed in her car.

When they approached their own subdivision, Ruby saw that girl in the wheelchair again. This time, a woman was pushing her, hunched over like her back was breaking from the work of it, her long, flowered skirt flowing up on either side with each step of her feet so you could get a glimpse of her white canvas sneakers. She was talking, breathy, but Ruby couldn't tell what she was saying.

The girl didn't seem to be agreeing. She was shaking her head back and forth, back and forth, at great speed, her shoulder-length blond hair rising in long pins around her, giving her the overall appearance of a ringing bell.

Ruby knew the feeling and thought the woman wheeling must be this girl's mother. At this rate, the pair crossed from the bushes on one side of the subdivision entrance to the other, after Ed's truck drove through. Ed pulled into a crosshatched unloading space and again they came into view; the girl had ceased shaking her head, and had taken instead to looking down at the ground, her hands making a canopy at her lap. The mother was still talking, the general sound of it gruff in tone, but not unkind. Her white sneakers peeked through just the slightest bit now, as if she had slowed, was growing tired.

Again they disappeared behind the green leaves and the few remaining blossoms. Ruby and Ed loaded themselves up with as many plastic shopping bags as they could handle and left the rest for a second trip. When they returned again, the mother and daughter appeared, retracing their path. When they were just about to disappear again behind a rather lush branch, the girl looked up and caught Ruby's eye at the back of the truck's bed. She didn't smile or frown, just looked.

The mother changed direction, wheeled her daughter right over the grass toward Ruby's own building.

Ruby walked to the lawn to wait while Ed pulled the truck around and into his assigned parking spot. Ruby craned her head to see the mother and daughter return to their apartment. Though she wished she hadn't, she heard the wild commotion of it; she saw the mother wrench the girl up and over the hump in the doorway, smashing the armrests and then the footrests like a cacophony of mortification. She couldn't glimpse the girl's face, but she didn't have to. Sick was how the whole thing turned Ruby's stomach. It was wrong that her disability should be so loud, so full of banging and scraping, shouts of, "Pull your foot in!" that could be heard for miles around.

The deafening sounds ceased, or at least were closed behind their apartment door, and Ed was at her side.

"I feel bad for that girl," Ed said.

"Yeah, it doesn't seem like her mother knows what to do with her," Ruby said.

She playfully smacked his behind on the way up the stairs, trying to distract him from all the question marks surrounding his rescue mission.

"Ow!" he exclaimed, rubbing the area with his one free hand.

"That didn't hurt!" she was smiling, clucked her tongue, like a character in a bad play.

"I know. But I love to see that look on your face."

She shook her head at him as they turned with the stairwell, still playing the role. He shimmied his key in the lock and she couldn't help but be swept away in the relief. They were home.

Eight

The inspector will instruct you to follow certain directions or perform certain maneuvers in order to evaluate specific driving skills.

—Connecticut Department of Motor Vehicles Driver's Manual

"I told Louis to sign up for unemployment, but he's too haughty for that. *Noooooooh*, he wouldn't dare march himself to that place. He's just gonna wait it out. 'Engineers don't sign up for unemployment,'" her momma mocked Louis. It seemed the crackling had ceased. Ruby's mother's voice was so clear, it was as if she were sitting right there next to her, her oversize sweater shimmying with the power of each word. That's how she spoke—with movement. Everything she did, it seemed, was fluid.

It occurred to Ruby, as she leafed through the yellow pages on a hunt for "D," that her momma probably had no idea why Louis was against the idea of unemployment, that she probably hadn't bothered to ask. Ruby had only met Louis a couple of times. He wasn't a big impression-maker. That was Ruby's momma's job. But Louis had been courteous, had asked whether Ruby wouldn't like some Jasmine tea they'd picked up at a farmer's market the previous weekend? And he'd offered both artificial sweetener and sugar—the kind of thing someone did only if they made the effort to consider preferences dis-similar to their own—and she remembered that and wondered if this sensitivity didn't somehow play into his hesitation towards unem-ployment, towards the people it really might be meant for?

Driving Schools. She found the page, but didn't look directly at it yet. Instead she sank back in their sofa, felt the bones of corduroy soft one way and then spiky the other.

"I don't know about him, I just don't. I'm working all day, sell-ing books to all these tiny shops outside of Boston—to people who make their living the good old-fashioned way, no savings accounts, no 401(k), these people are good, honest people—and when I come home, there he is, lounging around like he's king of the world. And he says, 'Well, I made some calls,' like that should shut me up."

Ruby wondered why sometimes she didn't just look at the caller ID and decide not to pick up. In theory, it would be easy—you just let the phone ring until it stopped. She looked up at the height of her ceiling. It was angled and lofty and she tried to breathe in the full resource of oxygen in it.

"So, I'm gonna take you up on that invitation some time soon." Her mother didn't make plans. She didn't pick a day and time and confirm a couple of weeks before. She said something when she was feeling it, and then followed up on it if she ever happened to feel the same; if she never did feel that way again, then she never mentioned it. The result was a floaty, semi-transparent threat hanging there like a sour cloud that never quite dissipated 100 percent.

Ruby allowed her mother to talk and talk, knowing when she hung up she'd have to call the driving school. Before she did, her mother did inquire about that. "Did you get over your driving 'thing' yet?" Ruby admitted she hadn't. "Ruby, how many times have I told you to just never look back?" Things were simple to her mother; you either did or you didn't—whatever the topic might be. And that ad-vice was applied universally, with no special considerations. "I can't believe a daughter of mine is afraid of driving. The *idea*!"

If Ruby stayed on one minute longer, she was afraid her mother would decide *she* was a failure, too. And the only idea worse than her mother coming, was the idea that she'd never want to.

When finally she took in the yellow pages of the Yellow Pages, it was bent over the low coffee table, a magic marker in her mouth. She singled out the ad right away. Not because it was larger or more professional looking, but because of what it said.

DRIVE FOR LIFE
Jack Christianson

We specialize in "special cases."
(860) 555-5555

> *WHILE I was fearing it,*
> *it came,*
> *But came with less of fear,*
> *Because that fearing it so long*
> *Had almost made it dear.*
> —EMILY DICKINSON

It was some time before she picked up the telephone. And in that time, Ruby had pictured Jack Christianson . . . a romantic, poetic image in a long beard, but sharp as a scholar. Like a Jesus painting she'd once seen at a Greek Orthodox Church, with pronounced eyebrows that joined in a feathery union in the middle, and with kind eyes faintly calling out to the best parts of you to come forward. She pictured him with the same long hair that coiled around with hope—twisting, twisting to whatever might come next.

But the voice on the other end, the one that came after she'd waited to dial the last 5 for twelve and a half seconds, didn't sound very much like she'd pictured. In fact, it sounded a hell of a lot like someone hacking up a lung. "Excuse me," the voice said, in a tone striated with years—lots and lots of them. "Let me start again," he said. "This is Jack Christianson, and it would be my pleasure to escort you through the emotional journey of learning to drive."

It sounded good, but maybe a little gooey? Ruby considered, though, that perhaps gooey was exactly what she needed. She pushed the jaded New Yorker sensibility down, telling herself this was no time to consider what may or may not be cool. Her inability to drive herself home from the supermarket had certainly not been cool—except maybe in a David Sedaris–personal-essay–type of way, which certainly had no practical application in her current life. She tried not to sound condescending or sarcastic as she replied, "Well, Jack, I would be very interested in that type of escort." Only after she said it, did it sound like she might be a prank caller out for something too taboo to consider. "I mean, I really need to learn how to drive . . ." She thought of the ad, and added, "Drive, um, for life." She hated to sound like such a moron, and slapped her forehead with the heel of her palm.

Jack Christianson didn't seem to notice. And if he did, he didn't let on. "Well, let me take some preliminary information here." There was some shuffling of papers, a fair amount of drawer opening and closing, and then Jack asked, "Name?"

"Ruby Reynolds," she said, and then let the sound of it echo and contort in her head. She flipped the magic marker around between her fingers like a baton.

"Well, isn't that pretty?" he said, like he actually meant it. "Address?"

She rattled it off.

"Oh, do you know Terrence Reed?" he asked her. "He lives right over there, too . . . well, down the road a bit, but close enough."

Ruby didn't know Terrence Reed, but she liked the easy way of this guy. She took to the familiar tone in his voice and felt herself relax a little. Maybe this would be easy. "No, I don't," she said, and thought that came out in a negative way she hadn't meant it to.

"No matter!" He laughed a bit after he said it. "License plate number?" Ruby said she didn't have that handy, and Jack said that was no matter, either; he could grab it off of the car when they met up. "How about right now?" he offered.

This knocked Ruby into a straight line, her back a wooden board, her eyes pennies. At first, she thought, why not? She should! She should just meet him wherever it was they were going to meet and start learning. The ability to do so rose up, up, into her heart and through her neck and vocal chords, right up to her lips, where she could have used it to say yes. But then it kept rising, rising, right up to the top of her head, and floated up where she couldn't reach it, to the highest part of the ceiling. "I, I'd love to, but, I've got a . . . a lot of stuff to do today." Lies, lies. Something else rose in her, though, and before she could realize it was honesty—whether planted there from desperation or sheer will she didn't know—Ruby said, "No, no, really, it's not that. It's, well, I'm just scared to death of it, Jack. I tried to push myself but then I just froze up. It's like I'm paralyzed to go somewhere because I'm afraid where I'll go." It sounded crazy, and it didn't make any sense—even to her own ears.

But Jack just said, "I know just what you mean Ruby. And so, why don't you take a day and then I'll meet you down your block— at the parking lot of that park, if you know where I mean—and we'll tackle this thing together."

She hadn't asked his fee, but she didn't worry much over that. Whatever price she had to pay, it was a bargain compared to the price of never doing this.

Ruby spent a few hours trying to think how she could get out of this, researching various illnesses she could say she'd contracted (E. coli, the bird flu). She picked up the phone to cancel, hung it back up again, watched reruns of *The Cosby Show*, and thought how her life would be so much easier if she was in that family. But then she recalled the problems Lisa Bonet had gone through and the accusations against Bill Cosby a couple of years ago. She settled on "nobody has it easy," which she thought impressive, given her romantically depressed mood, and finally stepped into a much-needed shower.

"Well, *heyyyyyy* there." Ed tried to sound like a porn star, or an actor in a skit about a pick-up artist, when he surprised her in the shower right in the middle of soaping up her armpits. He pulled the curtain to one side to take her in.

Ruby had been thinking about the driving lesson, now with a mixture of dread and relief—that last moment before a monumental one that you've been anticipating far too long. It was a manic state, and so when they had sex—the spontaneous and exhilarating kind—it seemed appropriate, the soap dish driving a rectangular hole in the middle of her back. When it was over, Ed kissed her quick, but very tender, his hands absentmindedly catching in her wet hair.

"Boy, you have really big knots in there," Ed said. He proceeded to soap up his own hair into a white helmet of suds, which he then rinsed out easily, gently running his fingers through, before he proceeded to grab a towel and sidestep out of the tub.

It occurred to her to say something about the cheap shampoo he stocked up on, as it was ruining her hair, but she couldn't. She couldn't lead him to the why don't you's, and there's a store just down the road and maybe you could pick up some, but oh yeah last time you tried that I had to ask my friend to take me to get your car out of the Stop & Shop lot, blah-blah-blah and so on.

And so Ruby poured out a small amount in her palm despite the mess it was going to make—she'd been finding the less she used, the less she had to pull and pull at those knots. There was no conditioner to speak of at all, and it occurred to Ruby she could have picked some up at the Super Stop & Shop. But she hadn't. She'd been too busy cooing over raspberry Fruit Roll-Ups. However, tomorrow . . . tomorrow she should be able to. And maybe she would. In the meanwhile, she was pulling and pulling.

Ruby tried to remember then that it wasn't Ed's fault about those knots in her hair; she tried to remind herself over and over again that they were sarcastic—two freaking sarcastic people, who tended to pick up on obvious things and point them out as if they'd discovered the pull of gravity for the very first time. And this calmed her. It calmed her while she applied lotion—squishing the last bit

from the tube alongside the sink, and while she dabbed a bit of perfume onto her wrists and behind her knees.

But, when Ruby found herself in the living room and there were
three pairs of inside-out socks, puffed up like slightly deflated bal-
loons, in clusters—left with right, left with right, like a path to somewhere, but nowhere she could see—she screamed, "Aargh!" And it
became obvious this would have to be something they spoke about.
It would have to be something they spoke about once Ruby felt like
she could pull some weight, once she could scream, "Yeah! I will go
off and replace that AWFUL shampoo and I will pick up BLAH-
BLAH-BLAH on the way back! So shove it!" Then she might say, "I
drove around all day, getting shampoo, and blah-blah-blah, and I
don't need to come home to your socks turned inside out on the
floor like dead baby bunnies." They were depressing when she
thought of them like that, but she couldn't go back to deflated bal-
loons now, no matter how she tried, and she supposed when the time
came, maybe she shouldn't say it like that, so very harsh like that.

Under the tree, waiting for Jack the next day, Ruby felt like a spy, her
hat and sunglasses obscuring most of her face. She didn't want to be
recognized for some reason; she wanted to do this neatly and simply
and be done with it, one-two-three. And when it was over, Ruby
imagined herself getting on with her life—the imagined version of
it, with everything diamond eyed, and animals that could talk and
such. Ed was there, and at the end of it, they walked through a heart
that closed smaller and smaller around them, until they disappeared
into "happily ever after."

She didn't have to wait long until a car drove up into the otherwise empty parking lot. The car cancelled out her disguise with its
tented, lit-up sign over the roof, sending up dust in a faint cloud.
DRIVE FOR LIFE!!! the sign read on either side, with three exclamation
points. In case someone missed that, the words were painted across
the driver's side doors as well.

It should have felt more exciting, this meeting up secretly to save her relationship, herself really, but more than that it felt like a skit about someone meeting up secretly to save her relationship—especially when Jack emerged from the vehicle, opening the door, an act which served to separate the IVE FO from the remainder of the logo painted on his side of the car. He was wearing an oversize foam cap which was printed identically to the tented sign on top of the car and the driver's side doors. Ditto, his T-shirt.

Jack spoke with that unmistakable voice, feathery but not frail, raspy but not coarse, when he said, "You must be Ruby." He was older even than she'd supposed on the phone. His glasses were held together on the left side with red electrical tape, and this imperfection, this show that he was a misfit, maybe as misfit as herself, made her like him—the swingy skin and comb over of him, the mophead eyebrows and liver spots of him—immediately.

Two cars crossed in opposite directions; somewhere a ways off a dog barked and then howled.

She held her hand out of the window, and he took it. Then she realized she should have gotten out of her own car, should have stood face to face with him. Mid-handshake she awkwardly pushed the door against him with her free hand, nearly knocking him onto the ground. But he insisted against it. "No, no. Why don't you just stay put, Ruby. I think we should use your own car, so you feel more comfortable."

She fell into his instruction, thrilled she wouldn't have to ride in the embarrassing car with its advertisement of her fears. Ruby adhered to the authority of his decision. Jack took some time getting comfortable in her passenger seat—he pushed the seat back as far as it would go to accommodate his long legs in their suit pants. He fastened the seat belt with a confident click.

"You can start the car now," he said. And something about the permission of it made Ruby do it, made her turn the key, not think but just do.

He directed her onto the main road, and they passed by the

Shop & Stop when he instructed her to turn right, and then left, all the while looking straight ahead, never at Ruby. "At that light ahead, you'll turn right," he said.

She slowed to a stop without thinking of where she was going, without taking note of the signs, but looking instead at the cars she was alongside of, sprinkled in among, feeling the swell of accomplishment. She lowered her window slightly to feel the air she shared with them all. And before Ruby knew it, she was approaching the mother ship of driving feats—Interstate 91. Her breath caught in a gasp.

"What you'll do is continue to speed up," Jack said, slowly, deliberately, with authority, "and then you'll pick which spot—between which two cars—you're going to pull into and you'll speed up or slow down to get into it. Once you've picked, do not falter."

She did as he said, though she didn't know how it would work—weren't those people to her left going much faster? And she couldn't exactly see them all as she curved along the on-ramp, its merge sign so tauntingly simple looking.

When the time came, she didn't pick so much as happen coincidentally upon a place between a black SUV and a classic shimmery red Mustang. The movement was easy, smooth, a Latin dance step, the subtle slide and twist and then you've got the guy's hand around your waist. She shouldn't have been so surprised to feel like she was reacquainting with an old friend, a friend she shared a complicated relationship with.

Jack didn't speak for a while and Ruby realized her heart had been thump-thump-thumping at triple time, and now it was slowing, slowing inside her burning chest.

Ruby looked at her hand on the wheel and thought it looked so familiar—the way she'd grabbed onto the top with her right, allowed her thumb to tuck beneath, how she'd lightly wrapped her left hand way down at the bottom, so it was nearly resting on her lap.

And then she realized just what that looked like. Her own hand, the way it grabbed on, the lines of her knuckles stretched flat, the nails uneven and rounded, the skeletal angles of wrist to knuckle to knuckle to knuckle to fingertip—that was her mother's hand. *We're not like them, Ruby Booby.* But why? Why couldn't they just try to be? How many times had she seen her mother's hand positioned, talon-like, that very way? How many times had she stared at it? Wished it to just stop, stop!

On the way from New Orleans to Massachusetts, they'd stopped in Connecticut all those years ago. Somewhere along the shore they'd parked in a tiny little town called Madison—a sprinkle of expensive gift shops and a couple of galleries, two cafes. They'd eaten lunch—split a turkey sandwich with Russian dressing and a pickle spear broken across the middle. They even shared the Coke. Ruby's momma had spoken loudly, the way she often did, so others could overhear. "I think we'll go to Boston," she said. "Somewhere cosmopolitan, where we can get you into a really good school with some wonderful kids."

Ruby shouldn't have, after all the disappointments, but she believed her mother's speech. She pictured, while she watched her mother's hands on the steering wheel, all those nice kids in shiny button coats and the kind of muffler you stuck both hands through. She saw them welcome her, ask her to come over after school and play their fancy computer games. That hope, though unfounded—they'd not made it to Boston—had kept her company all the while. And she thought of it now, felt it well up again, so profound and tactile. These were the steep, very steep ups of the downs.

She started to panic. All of a sudden the things she'd been doing—holding the gas steady, tapping the brake when necessary, checking her mirrors—seemed impossible, clumsy things that couldn't be managed all at once. She felt herself veer a little into the shoulder from the right lane she was traveling in. Seeing a car speed up the on-ramp just ahead, she couldn't imagine how she'd do that dance with it now; she confused the gas and the brake. All at once, she felt her face burn, her blood thumping beneath.

"Ruby, you are okay. Don't worry. Everything is fine. Just tap the brake a tiny bit and that car will glide directly in front of you."

She shook her head quickly, afraid if she spoke the tears would come raining down uncontrollably. Ruby did just as Jack said, though she overthought it, was terrified for a second she'd mixed up the gas and brake, that she'd misjudged the amount of time it would require to slow down. When the moment had passed, Ruby wasn't calmed as she'd hoped she would be. Instead, the smallest maneuvers hovered before her as great impossibilities—passing a truck, switching lanes, tapping the brakes, speeding up. She would have to speak. She would have to say something to Jack, tell him this had all been a gigantic mistake and that she apologized for wasting his time.

Thankfully she didn't have to; Jack saved her.

"Now, at this next exit, I'd like you to get off, and then make a left turn." Jack was still looking ahead and she was glad because her hands felt like clown hands—like a spectacular show he wouldn't be able to keep his eyes off. She sure as hell couldn't.

When they made the left, Ruby realized where they were; she realized they were at Jones's Burgers.

Jack instructed her to pull in at the parking lot, which was really just packed dirt. She might have sat there forever, if Jack hadn't said, "Now, take the keys out of the ignition and engage the parking brake." She was here, and yet she was so far away, back on the road, the terrible wonder of it.

"You hungry?" Jack asked, turning to her for the first time.

"Two deluxe burgers with Cokes!" Their order boomed out from the window.

Once they'd walked up to retrieve the tray, Jack and Ruby took their double-layer paper plates, piled high with fries poured on top, over to the same table she'd sat at with Ed. When she thought of that, Ruby felt a little spike of dishonesty, like she was doing something wrong by being here secretly.

Ruby watched as Jack squirted ketchup on his burger and then closed the top back up again. She let out a sigh of relief. They sat in silence for a moment. Ruby squirted the little beads of ketchup around her plate's perimeter, something she now associated with Jones's.

"That's quite an intricate design for ketchup," Jack said, through a bite of burger. He had a circular kind of chew, like a horse.

There was a tinny radio on inside the kitchen and the volume spiked for a second.

"Yeah," she agreed, sitting way back on the bench, tempting gravity to pull her over while she considered it with a head shake. Ruby dipped a fry in from that angle and then sat up straight again.

"You did really well," Jack said after a few minutes.

"Thanks." She had done well, for the first half. But something had happened. For now, she didn't know what to think of it. For one second she didn't want to think about anything.

"You know, there are others like you."

Ruby could have taken that five million ways. She tried a short answer that might encourage him to change the subject. "Yeah, I know," she said, although she didn't, although this intrigued her much more than Jack could fathom.

"I mean, they can drive perfectly, but they don't think they can. When they think about it, that's when they get tripped up. If they jump right in and face things a little at a time, the anxieties tend to fade. It's the attempt to hide from it, to deny it and cover it up, that gives these fears life."

Ruby looked right at him, at the possibility he might tell her something she wanted to hear, something about her history that she'd been wanting someone to tell her for a long, long time. And then she realized she was sitting at a quilted RV eating a cheeseburger with her driving instructor. She crunched two fries at once, Dina-like. "Jack?" Ruby finally said. "What do you think about *mustard* on *hamburgers*?" There was just so much she wanted to face in a day.

"Would you mind driving back?" Ruby asked when they'd finished, tossed their paper plates and soda cups into the trash. She'd heard what he'd said back there, but she was too afraid to face it.

Over the trash can, Jack looked Ruby right in the face. He said, "I know this feels too hard. Believe me, I know. But I also know that you can do it. And if you let me drive you home now, you won't have a second lesson. You'll ignore my calls and sell your car and compromise your freedom. I have seen it happen before. So, as difficult as it is, you're going to do this, because first of all, I'm here with you"—he hesitated only a second before putting his hand, the skin so soft, on Ruby's hand, the one holding the keys—"and because if you don't, the alternative will be so much more difficult in the long run."

She flicked her eyes up to meet his for a couple of seconds—as long as she could hold them there—and allowed the caring, paternal attention to seep into her, savoring every last syllable, every last sensation of his hand and gaze on her. "Okay," she said.

They walked to the car, she unlocked the doors and slowly, very slowly, clicked her seat belt, turned the key, pulled her visor down against the sinking sun. On the way home they took a different route and Ruby felt lost, like she was in a video game she'd played as a child, one of her mother's boyfriend's games—Tommy or Alex or John—where you were stuck in a forest, but you couldn't see anything, you had to use your imagination to find a way to get out of there, typing in commands on a DOS screen like *Turn left, walk three miles.* She'd never been very good at it. And then they were in that parking lot, facing Jack's car, and Ruby thanked him and wrote out a check for seventy-five dollars and pulled away.

As she pulled into her parking space, her cell phone rang. "Ed," the little screen said.

"Hello?"

"Hey, where are you?" he asked.

"I'm ummm, home," she said, looking around, considering the truth of this.

"Oh, really, cause I called the home line and you didn't answer."

"Ah, you got me. I was sitting outside on the patio having a cup of tea." She could make up fantastical lies on command. *Yes, I'm very sick today,* she could say to the school secretary when she'd call. *I've got shingles.* She could say that, and then go back to watching *One Day at a Time,* wondering what kind of a father that Schneider might make. The thing was, when she came in the next day, healthy as a horse, she was always undone.

"Would you like to meet up for lunch?" Ed asked.

"Already ate," she said. "I'm sorry." But she wasn't sorry really. She was relieved because she couldn't drive over to meet him for lunch. She'd driven far enough for one day. She'd faced enough truths and she wasn't ready to tell Ed everything. Maybe soon, but today she'd had enough.

For the next three weeks, Ruby met Jack on Tuesdays and Fridays at 1:30 in the afternoon at the same parking lot. They went over truck safety and snow tips, how to best utilize the lower gears, and how to manage your way through a skid. The mechanics, she'd found, were easy. It was the way she had to quell the fears, and the deluge of memories that accompanied them, that made the undertaking seem so damned impossible. But even those, she found, became easier to coexist with each and every time she slid in behind the wheel, and with each intimate memory she shared with Jack, who for some reason, was so easy to talk to. Ruby was learning how to drive, despite the fact that it still scared the shit out of her.

Nine

You should know when and to whom you must yield the right-of-way and recognize when it is being yielded to you.

—Connecticut Department of Motor Vehicles Driver's Manual

Ruby drove them to IKEA. Lately she took to saying things like that as often as she could fit them into conversation. "I drove to IKEA today," she'd tell Dina on the telephone as if she'd mentioned trying a new toothpaste. "I drove to the gas station and filled up."

"Woooh," Dina would reply.

Still, it was a big difference compared to the way she used to get around. Sure, you could while away a train ride reading a book or the *New York Post*, but if New Yorkers wanted to go to IKEA they took a bus to New Jersey from Port Authority. You had to have anything large delivered. Ruby mentioned this to Ed.

"Well, good thing you've got a car now. Isn't this so much better?"

Ed preferred, like Ruby, to walk whenever they were in the city together. Wasn't that such a simple way to travel—one foot before the other? No questions, no steel anvil of demons pressing down on your back while you struggled to keep straight against the seat? But even back in Manhattan, she realized, she'd tripped, scraped her knee several times, cracked off heels. There were dangers regardless of your mode of transportation.

She thought of the one time she and Dina had gone to IKEA. They'd walked around the New Jersey store for an hour and a half, said how cute everything was but tossed nothing in the cart. Then they ate hotdogs, drank sodas, and scarfed down cinnamon buns for dessert, and finally went home on the bus feeling sick. "Yeah, it is."

They turned off the exit and stopped at a red light. Ed turned the radio off on "Tiny Dancer."

"Was it difficult for you?" Ed fiddled with the IKEA flyer they'd gotten in the mail.

Ruby hoped she wasn't as red as her internal temperature would have her think. "What?" she managed.

"Driving—you know, after being a walker for so long? I just read this article about it, in the *Times*. It said that after being a walker for a certain length of time, that sometimes it's a difficult transition back on the road. In fact, they said that after this new study came out, driving schools have been targeting this particular demographic with ads that say 'we want you back.'"

She gulped. For someone so terrible at lying, she'd been doing an awful lot of it lately. She thought of the way she'd opened up to Jack, the hours they'd spent talking about this very thing. She didn't know why, but she just couldn't do it now. She couldn't tell Ed about these fears of hers, all her hang-ups, the ugly things inside her.

The light turned green. She fumbled for the gas pedal, quelling any neuroses that told her she didn't know which one it was. "No. It was like getting on a bicycle again," she lied.

Ed rumpled his brow for a second, but Ruby told herself it was the sun in his eyes. The sun was in his eyes was all.

"I'm just glad you're not avoiding it, like some people might."

Her chest froze over. He couldn't know, could he? She became mortified, and then her mortification turned to fear and the fear turned to anger, something she could finally work with. "Oh, you mean like how you avoid picking up your underwear piled by your side of the bed?"

He pointed at her trigger-style with his one free hand, and clucked his tongue. "Touché. Maybe I should take a lesson from Martha Stewart."

It was their first nasty exchange. She could only hope it would be their last.

"Well, we're here," he said in a lighter tone a couple of minutes later, at the giant sign, the giant building, and the giant parking lot. In the midst of all this, Ruby hoped his tone meant he'd moved on; she prayed her worst fears weren't true—that he hadn't figured it all out before she had a chance to tell him herself. She hoped that inside the giant store with all its confusing verbiage and spot-lit displays of what life was supposed to look like, it wouldn't be difficult to lose track of the undertones of that conversation. She crossed her fingers and hoped.

They entered IKEA through a giant revolving door. The scent of cinnamon buns that Ruby suspected was pumped through a special venting system smacked them in the face. Up the escalator, voices echoed—families, they were everywhere. It was peaceful, the idea of those furniture vignettes with their televisions, knick-knacks, and hard-backed volumes of *Moby-Dick* and *Anne of Green Gables.* They were lives everyone wanted. She touched the book spines, moved her fingertip over the embossed titles. She wandered in and out of living room after living room and thought how these were lives people were making here. Was it really possible to *create* the life you wanted, the way she was trying to? In light of the tense possibilities evoked by the conversation in the car, the idea of it simultaneously thrilled and intimidated her. What sort of model had she to fashion herself after?

A girl rode a man's shoulders high up, at least six feet, into the cozy living room where Ruby was picking through the books. Her feet kicked up sporadically, but her father had her—his huge palms covered her shin bones entirely in that feathery way a dad could hold you secure, but not too tight. She was intimately acquainted with spotting that way from afar.

Ruby had transformed fathers into figures of mythical proportions. There wasn't a thing they couldn't do perfectly. *You should see them slice and dice!* Without one, a daughter was completely lost and doomed to roam the world deficiently, without the ability to hammer things properly or catch a curve ball. *You'll never believe you lived without one before! Call today and you'll also receive a handy-dandy confidence booster for absolutely no additional charge whatsoever.*

"Ruby, Rube." Ed was behind her now, his own hand feathery on her shoulder. He led her toward the only living room she hadn't liked—the black leather.

The ceiling spotlights suddenly felt hot now that they were shining down where she stood. The bony girl who'd been on her father's shoulders pulled at her coiled pigtails and squealed with delight over a life-size stuffed donkey in the opposite corner. Ruby was glad they weren't in the market for a sofa. She didn't think she could live with the black leather. Now the girl jumped on the donkey and started pulling at his leather reigns. "Whoa! Whoa!" she was screaming. Ruby squinted her eyes against it. She told herself this girl had nothing to do with her at all.

Ed plopped down in the sofa. "This is *ni-iice*," he whistled. He spread his arms out wide behind him, his hands hugging either end of the puffed back. He had no taste in furniture whatsoever, but he was cute.

Since they *were* only here for a coffee table, Ruby figured a white lie might be the best way to go. She sat next to him gingerly, only half of her actually sitting on the sofa. Despite her efforts, it was the best she could bring herself to do. "Very nice," she said. Ruby shook her head and raised her brows to feign that she truly meant it.

Ed readjusted the brim of his Yankees cap, and smooshed his lips from side to side. When he looked at Ruby, his head was cocked, his eyes sensitive. "You're a terrible liar. Absolutely the worst ever," he said.

She went cold again, the context of his earlier questions still hovering about.

"But I love you anyway," he whispered, kissed her quickly, and then pulled Ruby to her feet to find what they came for.

Everything would be fine, she assured herself, though it wasn't an idea she could grab onto wholly. When had this proven true before?

She caught sight of the side of them in a long, wide mirror. Her hair was in a ponytail, still rather dead-looking from the shampoo she'd done nothing about. She hated to think it reminded her of her mother's hair. She wore a fitted black sweater with a hood and jeans. Ed was taller, his hair getting a bit long at the sides and back now. Tiny sprigs of it hung over his ears. She liked the idea of the way they looked in that mirror, despite the tiny imperfections. For a moment, guilt stabbed at her vision of them. She wasn't being honest. There was no way they could know each other if she wasn't honest. There was no way they could know each other if she kept one foot on the ground.

Ruby tried her best to concentrate on coffee tables. There was a white one with two drawers that they'd placed in the "not bad" category. At a curly cast-iron model with a glass top, Ed proclaimed perfection. Ruby wasn't completely sold. Finally, they stumbled upon the Hazelbub in the very last living room. Its wood exterior was stained a deep chocolate, and the shelf beneath would be great for a couple of covered storage baskets. In a pinch, she could scoop up the socks Ed left all over the place and hide them inside one of those.

On the walk to grab a boxed up Hazelbub, Ruby pictured herself and Ed crossing their feet on top of it, watching old episodes of *L.A. Law*.

"Do you like *L.A. Law*?" she asked.

"Nah," he said, puffing his lips out.

"Me, neither," she lied, the pull of escapism growing greater and greater now.

At the inventory area, there wasn't a Hazelbub in sight. "Looks like the cast iron, baby," Ed smirked.

"Noooohhhhh!" Ruby feigned pain, crossed her arms over her chest like a wounded player in a Shakespeare production. But she couldn't stand to walk the store for one more moment. The sticky buns were making her sick now. The children had all started to wail at the same time. She'd been hit by a teenager's wagon back in Home Entertainment. The back of her heel had been scraped. The tissue she pressed against it to stop the blood kept falling out the back of her shoe.

"When we get the couch, you can pick it," Ed said. "Since I know you don't like black leather."

"Deal," Ruby said, wondering if all the lies in the world sometimes couldn't keep you from your fate.

At home, Ed had all the pieces torn out of their plastic baggies before she was out of the bathroom with a fresh Band-aid over her shopping wound. He was using an Allen key to tighten a screw into what might have been a leg. Or a side. Or a shelf base.

"Want some help?" she asked, sitting on the couch behind the carpet-based work station.

"Nah! This is baby stuff. I can do it with my eyes closed. You go paint your toenails or something and I'll call you when the man's work is done." He scratched his sides with his fingernails like an orangutan.

Ruby smiled. "Okay." She dragged the syllables out and grabbed a magazine from a stack on the end table and took it into the bedroom. She clicked the television on for sound, and propped the pillows up against the headboard. Shuffling through the channels, she landed on an old episode of *Our Country's History*, a show she sometimes liked to watch because of its inclusive name, which made her feel a part of something.

Ruby lay down, bent her knees, and rested the magazine on her thighs. She read the thing cover to cover, tore out a few inspiring pages—a plaid suit, a silky brocade dress, a lacy blouse with a Victorian neckline.

The sun fell beneath the hills. The show had ended, giving way to an infomercial for a food storage system that stacked up to save space. She padded into the living room to check in on Ed. He had every single light in the room on.

"How's it going?" she said as she made her way toward him. But she shouldn't have asked. There was sweat on his forehead. His jaw was set. The table didn't look very different than the way she'd left it an hour earlier.

"Is that some kind of dig? Because that's not very nice, you know."

She wasn't used to Ed being snippy. The tone sent her head back in a jolt.

Instead of responding, Ruby snatched up the instruction booklet. Maybe she could shed some light on things. "Ralingle," the front cover read. Beneath it, there was a line illustration of two carefree characters—with their feet crossed over it just the way she'd envisioned herself and Ed. "Step 1," it said, "read the instructions." There was a tiny star next to that entry, indicating a footnote. Ruby turned her attention down to the footnote at the page bottom. "Due to the specific nature of the Ralingle assembly, the instructions are particularly important."

Ruby looked up to Ed. Should she say something about the specific nature of the Ralingle assembly? Perhaps he wasn't aware. She'd heard about men and instructions.

She heard a *crack*!

"Fuck!" Ed yelled. He tossed the Allen key way into the bedroom. It thunked against the wall. They looked at each other blank-faced. What did it say that Ruby hadn't a clue how to talk to Ed when he was upset? What did it say that she'd never seen him upset before? She looked down to her ring, still sparkling but dulling a bit from wear.

"Hey, these instructions look pretty good!" she offered encouragingly, flying the booklet up over her head like a flag.

"Instructions are for pussies," Ed said, positioning a length of side molding.

"Oh, look at this funny guy they've got in the diagram!" she tried again.

"You know what would be really helpful?" Ed didn't look up. He was hopelessly trying to tighten the screw without the tool. "Find that stupid thing I just threw."

She got up to do it. In the bedroom, Ruby turned the light on. She pulled the bed away from the wall and looked for the key there. Although she rescued one book, two magazines, three paper clips and four socks, the tool was nowhere to be found. She looked behind the end tables and over by the window. She checked in back of the easy chair and even in the closet—although its door had been closed. You just never knew.

She came back into the living room apologetically. "Ed, I can't seem to find it." She really did feel terrible. Did she even know Ed at all? Here they were engaged to be married and she couldn't even figure out how to help him to feel better. Hadn't he tried so hard— in vain—to encourage her when she was down? Sure, but she hadn't given him much work with either. In fact, she realized with a pang that maybe they were perfect strangers.

Whatever the case may be, what she did say seemed to infuriate him. His face grew red in patches. His shirt hung with sweat. She walked over to him and sat down to rub his shoulders. She didn't want him to feel inadequate.

"Why don't we get a bite to eat and look over the instruction book leisurely and maybe see where we've gone wrong. And then we can come back and get a fresh eye on finding that tool and work on it together?" It sounded super logical to her. In fact, Ruby was proud of how *un*accusatory she sounded, how understanding.

"*We* haven't gone wrong," he mocked.

Ruby was taken aback. She'd never heard Ed speak that way before.

"*I've* gone wrong. I don't want to read the fucking instruction book because I'm a fucking moron dyslexic. There, I said it. Feel free to leave now. I don't want you staying with me because you feel bad and then losing your attraction over the years, only to have an affair with some reading whiz who'll sit and read Dante to you in bed."

Ruby didn't think she could hide her shock. That's why he didn't want to read the instructions! Or the recipes she was always piling for him to look through, to see if anything interested him! How could she have missed all the signs? As soon as she fit the pieces in, Ruby realized why she hadn't put it together before. She'd been entirely too wrapped up in her own phobias. They were two blind-folded people feeling around desperately just to survive. What were they so afraid of? How could it be that two people engaged to be married didn't know anything about each other?

"Ed!" she was crying now. It was so clear this was the perfect opportunity to say something about the driving, about her obses-sion with finding her father. But she didn't! There weren't words there at her tongue, ready to explain the unexplainable, ready to reveal the kinds of things she didn't want to share—or even admit to herself. "Oh, I am so glad you told me that!" Her heart swelled with love for Ed.

He began to explain. "It all started in the second grade. I couldn't spell for shit. When the teacher would call on me to read, I'd struggle sounding out the damn words. It was so embarrassing that eventually I started refusing to read. Then I'd get stupid home-work assignments back with notes that I confused my b's and d's. Did you know that even my messy clothing on the floor is an ex-pression of dyslexia? Honestly, it's because I feel like if I put it all away neatly I won't know what I've got."

Now his little socks were magically changed into adorable little bunnies, they weren't the dead ones she originally suspected them to be. Her heart nearly melted, her love for him was so great. Here was this sign all along and she'd misunderstood it, walked right past it without ever having a clue.

"You don't know how mortifying it was to get called out for my extra help. Everyone knew and they made fun of me like it was freaking hysterical."

She hugged him tight.

"I know, it's so lame," he said.

"No, It's the opposite of lame. It's something that makes you you, if you know what I mean."

"Do you have any questions about it?" he asked.

"Well, how do you work it at your job?" she asked.

He sighed. "Let's just say I have an amazing secretary, who makes magic happen. My boss doesn't even have a clue."

"I'm sure he wouldn't mind if he knew, as long as you're getting your job done."

Ed looked thoughtful. "Maybe, but it's just not something I want people to know about me."

Her instincts took over and her hand was at his hair, smoothing his back. His back shook with tears. It had been difficult to tell her. "I was afraid for you to know that," he said. "I've been tortured by the idea of telling you."

She knew what that was like. Her chance, she watched it grow and grow and raise up over her like a giant balloon on a string she couldn't reach no matter how she danced for it.

He pulled away, sniffling. "You know what I mean?" His face was kind, the blotches purplish now.

She did know! And now was the chance to say it!

"I know, I know," she repeated it, but nothing followed.

And her heart sank with the idea that it wasn't going to.

Instead, they found the key, Ruby read the instructions, step by step. And in less than an hour the thing was together. The two of them crossed their feet on top of it, just like she'd envisioned earlier. But she wasn't carefree, like she'd imagined. The weight of her secret was even heavier than it had been before. And the weight of smiling over it was unbearable.

They switched on HBO and covered themselves in a soft throw blanket. "You know, Ruby?" He looked tired from all that had passed. His lids were puffed. "I could do this for the rest of my life." His hand smoothed up and down inside the neck of her NYPD sweatshirt.

Now if only she could believe a thing like that.

★ ★ ★

Ruby had been excited in particular about the sushi necklace. She'd always done well with food and there was something about it that kept her coming back to the table again and again, so to speak. There was the detail of it—both the natural and the prepared varieties—and there was the challenge of presenting it without any of the color or smell, of somehow translating those qualities in gold or silver only and pouring significance on it. She sometimes imagined herself having something in common with United Nations translators in this highly specialized way of enabling people to understand things they wouldn't be able to without her. Of course, her dealings weren't that important, but in a way, they were more important, or personal perhaps, to the wearers who found themselves in her interpretation of things—or had someone who knew them well enough to find them in it—and therefore purchased her piece, feeling it between their fingers now and then to remind them of that point. Then again, sometimes she wondered if people didn't get it at all, if they just said, "Oh, that's cute—sushi" and bought the thing without ever thinking deeper.

She woke up, excited to call her caster. She'd FedExed the piece a few days ago and now looked forward to hearing how it had come out. The anticipation of seeing the finished pieces kept her going after all the painful work required to get it to that point. She loved the roundness of the sushi roll. All the delicate little things packed in perfectly also seemed to remind her of what she'd left behind in New York. She hoped she'd be able to wrap that all up in a pretty package, too; that she could go back there and say, this is what I left: a decent shrimp pad Thai and five-dollar Chinese slippers and a view of headstones. She hoped she could wave hello to it and come back feeling she'd done the right thing leaving it all for Ed, despite the difficulties.

So when Leonard called, she nearly jumped up and down at the thought of a shipment of pretty sushi charms coming her way.

"I've got a bit of bad news," he said instead.

"What?" she asked, smashing back down onto the sofa, where she'd been kneeling in anticipation.

"The piece you sent us got shattered in the mail." His voice faded out. Somehow she'd twisted up the idea of the sushi necklace with the idea that she'd done the right thing moving here, facing all of this, and now that it had been smashed to bits she felt the solid ground slip from beneath her. Her neat package of confirmation was smashed to bits. It would be so easy to go back there, to say, good-bye, Ed, I'm sorry but this is not for me, and step back into her old ways of comfortable avoidance that led to nothing.

"Can it be glued together to make the mold?"

"You know, it's so smashed up I wouldn't know where to start. Almost looks like an elephant stamped on it."

"Oh," Ruby said. But what she was thinking was, *Are there forensic jewelers?*

"Why don't you come and pick it up here, and bring your other stuff down in person? I remember you used to sit here and watch us all the time."

Ruby sat with this information for a long while. It was true. She was a runner. Things were getting tough now and she was looking for any excuse to run off in search of easier ground. She pulled her arms tighter around her legs as if this might ground her here. She wanted all of this—this set of Halloween glasses from Target and Ed's biographies piled unread on the coffee table, which for other reasons was dripping with its own memories. She didn't want to leave it. She told herself it was only a necklace that broke in the mail, that it had no bearing on her life whatsoever.

There was Ed's photo of the two of them on the fireplace mantel—a funny, off-center thing, with his head one quarter cut off, that he'd taken at the beach last fall. She loved him; the three quarters of his head she could see there tugged at her heart and she knew that for certain. But was that enough to drudge through all of this?

The idea of driving to Brooklyn seemed outrageous, beyond the scope of her abilities—both literally and emotionally. There was the Belt Parkway and there was the pull of her old, simple life right over the bridge that allowed her to say good-bye and never look back whenever she felt like it.

Without thinking too long, Ruby phoned Jack. "What do you think?" she asked after explaining the predicament. By then, she'd piled on a good amount of trust to his point of view.

"I think it's pretty clear you need to go," he said. "You need to hop in your car and go—without a second thought. You should go today, if at all possible. What is so different about driving to Brooklyn? Nothing. The only thing that's different is that this is an avenue of doubts you hadn't considered yet. You're always going to encounter them, whichever way you turn, so you'd better start learning to recognize them and drive right through them. Have you spoken with your fiancé about this?"

"Not yet, but I'm going to. I just thought since you were my driving instructor that you might have the most informed decision about this." What exactly was she saying? It didn't make an ounce of sense.

"Drive right through it, Ruby," Jack said. "I know you can do it." It was purely pathetic, what those words could do to her, but all the same, they steeled her, allowed her to imagine her emotional bleachers were occupied with her own cheering section.

Just that morning, Ruby had pulled her goggles down and set to work on a piece she called "The Last Leaf." It required quite a bit of piercing with her saw and three separate sheets of metal. But in the end, she thought it made a statement—a huge leaf, the last one, holding onto a brittle looking branch, holding out as long as possible after it had become very, very difficult to do so. She'd soldered the leaf onto the branch and as it cooled, she got the feeling this was something good she'd done. It had been so long since she'd felt that way.

So, should she pack the Last Leaf, get in her car, and go? The answer smacked her in the face, came around and pounded her in the ass: *yes*. She needed to go.

Her hands trembled as she turned the key in the ignition. She was going to cross a state line, she was going to retrace her steps—look back, something she'd grown up thinking to be a shameful, dangerous thing that she pondered only in the dark of her unfamiliar bedrooms at night, the ones she'd stopped decorating, stopped trying to make herself comfortable in.

Everything was familiar until she passed the Woodbridge/New Haven exit on the Merritt Parkway, and continued on. Her city life came back to her like a screaming train then. There was Jacob Aigner and Chris Connersby and Rodney Billington. Had it been so bad enjoying all the beginnings, the initial rush, and not having to deal with any more? She remembered some steamy memories, some barely-through-the-door moments which had made her feel alive, if only briefly.

Had she been crazy to think she could do something else—become a domesticated woman with a husband and maybe some kids of her own? Was this the kind of thing that only a certain kind of woman should attempt? A woman who was qualified in some way for this kind of thing?

It was undeniable that the air around her had changed now that she was alone, crossing the border into New York. She could act as neurotic and screwed up as she wanted and nobody was going to be sitting there, looking hurt because she hadn't shared. This was comfortable, something she could do with her eyes closed. Suddenly she found herself driving faster, more confidently, along ground she recognized.

Ruby parallel parked in front of the dingy looking warehouse building the caster studio was housed in. She cut the engine, pulled the little box containing the Last Leaf out of the glove compartment, grabbed her purse, and opened the car door. She paused for a moment, with one foot on the sidewalk, to look around. Now she was here, the air had changed once again. Memories struck her from every angle. So many times she'd descended the staircase of that subway, her head bowed, with nowhere to go and no one to see.

She'd always tried to push away the painful thoughts that edged in: the thought that this proved that it wasn't her momma's fault she was this alone, and even worse that she needed her momma. Of course, pushing these thoughts out had only led her to the gold ring of hope: that when she found her father, it would all make sense, she'd make sense, and her loneliness would disappear.

She stepped out of the car and made her way to the building. The worn brass doorknob felt familiar in her hand. As she climbed the wide, industrial steel steps, she saw herself walk that same path many, many times—her hair up sometimes, sometimes down, with bangs, with bangs grown out; wearing tank tops with long belled jeans, wearing sweatshirts with front zippers and hoods and bundled under a wool pea coat and scarf. In all those visions of herself, Ruby looked so lonely, it nearly broke her own heart. Had it been so bad? Now she took for granted that she had an audience for those comments she liked to make during television shows—*Oh give me a break! Like anyone would go down that dark alleyway all alone!* There were things she'd come to take for granted now. Yes, this was true.

Now Ruby wondered, had she come here to drop this necklace off, or had she come here to show herself she still had an out if she couldn't bring herself to open up to Ed? She climbed the last two stairs, steeled herself, and pushed the oversize studio door open.

"Leonard!" Ruby said.

"Hey Ruby, how are you?" he said, his ponytail frazzled-looking as ever. Today he was in full leather, his late fall regalia.

"I'm good," she said. "You?" She took her seat at that long table, and it was all coming back. She had just been wasting time, so much of it. How could she go back to this?

And she sat and watched Leonard, realizing that after all those years, she didn't know a thing about him. This was how she'd filled her time because she didn't know how else to do it. Watching him now, his gentle, beautiful movements, Ruby knew there was nothing here to go back to.

It hadn't been necessary for her to cross the Brooklyn Bridge into Manhattan, to park her car right in front of 223 Elizabeth Street and buzz Olaf in her old apartment. She didn't really need to hear him say, "No, I don't know Ruby, no." She didn't need to picture that he'd replaced all of her things with flashy red furnishings and lots of lacquer, but she had. She walked up to Burger Heaven and that sealed the deal. She felt pathetic as ever eating her burger all alone, no one to laugh at her ketchup pattern. She found herself longing for Jones's. The truth was, they made a better fry anyway. There was nothing here. She had spent all that time here building this life that was so different from the one her momma had dragged her along on, and it turned out the whole thing was empty. It was absolute crap. She felt like the Ghost of Christmas Past had escorted her to look back at her old, pathetic self.

The good thing, she guessed, was that she'd tasted enough of an actual life to see she'd been so empty before. The bad thing was that this escape hatch she thought had been open, waiting for her to run back to all this time, was closing up, losing its luster. Here was another sign flashing. And the sign said: "Ed will understand. Just go home and tell him everything before it's too late."

She took a taxi back downtown to her car after she finished eating, and Ruby realized the worst part of the whole thing: her momma had been right; there was nothing good to be found in looking back. She wasn't a New Yorker now, and she'd have to realize this, realize that there was no New York for her to run back to.

At the Connecticut border once again, Ruby dialed Ed.

"Hey, where were you?" he said.

"I had to go into Brooklyn to my caster," she said.

"How was that?" he asked. There was surprise in his voice, but neither of them addressed it.

"It was . . . interesting," she said. It wasn't a tell-all, but it was a start.

Ten

The road test is a behind-the-wheel evaluation of your skills.

—Connecticut Department of Motor Vehicles Driver's Manual

"Hello!" Ed's mother, Suzanne, had a 1950s aura about her, as if time had turned off for her somewhere in that decade. She still carried herself in the manner of Jackie Kennedy—the pillbox hat, the wool suit with the cropped jacket and wide lapels. Her dark hair flipped under dramatically at her chin.

The first time Ruby had dinner with them, she was struck with the sense that she'd seen the very same table spread in a Norman Rockwell painting. She felt she'd stepped into one of her dreams, and yet got the impression that she could only reach out so far into this dream, that there would be no grasping her fingers around it finally.

Now, she jumped out of her front door as if she'd just time-warped there—glossy smile and all.

"Hello, Mom," Ed said, hugging her.

"Hello," Ruby said warmly, awkwardly kissing a few inches from her face.

"Well, hello there, Sadie, Married Lady!" She'd been calling Ruby that since Ed proposed. It made Ruby blush now as it had before. She only hoped she'd stick it out long enough to prove the nickname true.

"All right, kids, pile into the Mercedes. We're going wedding shopping!"

When they arrived at the Hills Club, Suzanne said, "I've been to a couple of weddings here. It's very nice."

Ruby and Ed held hands as their guide Kathy showed them the Elegant, Wonderland, and Symphony rooms where they could hold their party. Each was very nice, just as Suzanne said. Each would work just fine. The bells and whistles were minimal. At the final stop, the Symphony room, the saleswoman said, "This is where you'll come out for your first entrance as husband and wife . . ."

Ruby felt everything grow mute. She could see Suzanne and Ed speaking, maybe laughing over something funny, but she couldn't make it out. She couldn't make any of it out. Husband and wife! She hadn't thought of it that way before. But it wasn't really all that different from saying, "We're getting married," the way she had dozens of times by now. Why should it hit her this way? But she knew why. She could hear her momma now. *Don't you know men are useless? What do you need him for? You're much better off leaving it open, so that when he disappoints you—WHICH HE WILL—you can just go, easy peasy . . . I'm just sayin', Ruby Booby.*

"Rube, Ruby . . . are you okay?"

"Easy peasy . . ." she babbled before thinking.

But everyone was in a light mood, the saleswoman included. And so they laughed. In the car they all put the Hills Club on the "maybe" list. Ruby hoped she could get herself off of that list and onto something a little more sturdy. Maybe she'd been wrong to assume she'd been over this mystery of her father's identity. Maybe, if she could find out the truth about that, then the idea of staying put would be a lot easier to stomach.

Connecticut Hotel offered only one banquet room and the mirror in the bridal suite made Ruby look fat and distorted, like a sideshow freak. Everyone laughed but Ruby, who thought that was just how she saw herself. She looked through the china, tablecloths, and hurricane glass centerpieces half-heartedly. When Steven, the flamboyant man who took them around, asked, "Have you chosen your wedding song yet?" Ruby and Ed looked at each other in that same way she recognized from Dina's cousin's wedding. Her head began to fill with all the details of them—the days at Central Park and the sunsets at the beach, tiny shells he'd pressed into her palm, and sugar packet fortunes they'd read.

On the way to the car, Ed whispered in her ear, "I love you." What a difference from the glimpse of her old life she'd seen in Brooklyn just days before! In response, her anxiety heightened, the pressure mounting now, time seeming to close in on her. Now she had everything to lose.

Their next stop was at a medieval-looking castle. Right from the parking lot, it had a heavenly look, as if everything should have a soft halo of light around it. Antique limousines lined the brick-paved circular drive. Flowers were colorful, plump, standing at attention. There were just the right number of weeping willows, evergreens, and tall, skinny Tuscan shrubs.

"Now kids," Suzanne said, looking intermittently over at Ruby in the passenger seat and back through her rearview at Ed, "this place is the tops—the absolute tops. I mean, I probably shouldn't be taking you here at all, but I just couldn't help myself. You know, Steven and I got married at the church over on Main Street and then had lasagna over at my mother's house. I've always wanted to make sure you all had the most beautiful weddings."

Ruby sensed another feeling break through the ambivalence. Her heart went out to Suzanne, a woman who truly wanted the best for her kids.

"Mom, you don't have to do anything for us," Ed said.

"That's just it. I know that. But I want to. If you kids love this place, which I know you will—especially Ruby, with her elegant artist's tastes—I want to pay for the whole thing. You kids just worry about the music, photos, and invitations."

"Suzanne, we . . . we couldn't."

"Ruby, you're my daughter now. It's not every day you get a new member in your family, and we've worked hard enough to spend money on a damn good celebration for it."

"Thanks," Ruby managed to say. She hadn't thought about it that way—that she was gaining a whole entire family marrying Ed, that she wasn't merely a visitor among them. This warm, wonderful mother now somehow belonged to her, too. *Was* it possible to create the life you always wanted? Ruby had tried to do that in New York City, but she'd failed; there was an essential part missing there. She didn't have someone to love like she did here, she didn't have the possibility of all of this. Sure it was terrifying, but wasn't the idea of this enough to get her through, to make her face everything?

"I . . . I couldn't have asked for a better family," Ruby said, wrapping her arms around Suzanne, trying to get her mind around the fact that somehow, in some way this woman was connected to her.

The castle's ballroom was fitted with everything a ballroom would have—crystal chandeliers with thousands of tinkling pieces and brocade curtains over floor-to-ceiling windows, murals painted on the walls like an Italian villa, and spectacular views of the river. Ruby slipped her hand over the back of an elegant bamboo-look gold chair.

"Did I tell you, or did I tell you?" Suzanne said, nudging her lightly.

"This place is amazing," Ruby said. It was the kind of place where she could really leave her old self behind for good. She thought of the exchange, of telling her old self, *Well, this is the end of the road.* But she couldn't convince herself. How could she believe that kind of thing could truly happen after all the years she'd had to convince herself to stop trying to believe that it could?

"I think it would be awesome here," Ed said. When the guide

left them to discuss amongst themselves, Ed said he'd like to go outside to the gazebo where they would have their wedding ceremony.
Suzanne stayed close to the castle, sitting in a shaded chair, her hand
shielding her eyes from the sun as Ed and Ruby walked the few
dozen feet to the gazebo at the river's edge, the same walk they
would make on the day of their wedding.

"Do you, Ed . . ." Ruby joked, grabbing both of his hands in
her own. Suddenly, she felt much lighter and easier. Actually being
here, feeling the velvet drapes, the cool of the chair, the river
breeze against her skin, all of this brought her to think of how far
she had come, how much she was trying to make this work—even
if there was no guarantee she'd be able to get through it all in the
end. He was worth it; she loved him, and here, now, this was very,
very clear.

"Ruby, I just wanted to say that I'm really happy. I don't know,
doing this today, going to these places, it feels so real, I just don't
know how we'll wait all that time now." They were considering
dates eight months from now—in May. But the to-do list was long
enough to require that sort of time frame, at the least.

She pulled him in for a tight hug. All this time, she'd been wondering how she would make it, too. But not for the same reasons.
Her heart swelled with the excitement of the day, the vision of a
white gown and a pretty veil sweeping the floor, Dina at her side, re-
arranging the dress train and beaming. She thought how very much
she loved him, and how she would do whatever it took to make it
through this. She'd beat down her issues once and for all. She promised herself that, and then she said, "Well, do you?"

"Yes, oh yes. I definitely do."

"Do *you*?" he asked after a couple of seconds.

"You bet your ass I do," she said and kissed him. A practice
kiss—long and sweet, soft and with a slight coffee taste—where in
eight months, God willing, they would marry.

★ ★ ★

A couple of nights later, Ruby kicked her flats onto the floor of Ed's truck, folding her legs in like a calf. It was an Indian summer evening—one of the few they'd had. One of the highlights of living in Middleville was the diversity—you could drive four blocks, right, left, right, and there was nothing—trees, trees, windy hills going up, up, and then a tiny farm with a shingle swinging back and forth, gently, that read FRESH STRAWBERRIES! NATIVE CORN! And then a couple of houses and then a left, right, right and a house from 1862 with twin wreaths on the red doors and matching shutters and a weathered plank barn, and then the university campus with its disheveled Colonial frat houses with hand-drawn signs on computer paper printed with PARTY FRIDAY NIGHT, $5 ALL YOU CAN DRINK.

They'd been so busy planning the wedding lately—tasting phyllo pastries and Crab Rangoon, listening to different renditions of "At Last," and deciding between engraving, thermography, or letterpress printing—that they'd missed the transition into fall.

They turned onto Main Street to find it was "Cruise Night." Banners were strung across from telephone pole to telephone pole explaining just that. There were Chevelles and Mustangs and Roadrunners and old fashioned kit cars. And their owners were draped over them, shining up a fender with the hem of a T-shirt or at the wheel, cruising slowly down the avenue. You could see them, like a scene from a small town movie, as far down as your eye could travel. There were mothers holding children at their sides like grocery sacks and guys in plaid work shirts and arty, intelligent types with grayer than gray hair pulled proudly into long, puffy ponytails, wrinkles of experience looking gorgeous.

Ruby was swept up with the idea that this was her home. It was her home if she chose to make it so. It was her home in the same way the city had been, and she could one day, ostensibly, be that gray ponytail wearer or the child-grocery-sack carrier. And she could know that man in the glasses and the one with his hands on a horse's reins and the one driving that Chevelle.

She recognized the possibility—the feeling had come to her often in new places, despite the harsh facts of the past. The fresh, unsullied prospects of somewhere new could make Ruby think anything was likely to happen. Of course she'd already done some things she'd rather forget—she thought of Richard and the supermarket incident, the lie she'd told to Ed that day.

"Wanna park somewhere?" Ed asked. He said it with a flick of his head, his mouth in a pucker, the whole of the gesture testing whether she liked the idea of it or whether it was somewhat hokey—which, in a way, it was. The New Yorker that had been seeded and watered inside Ruby always put up an initial defense against questionably hokey or "touristy" attractions—Disney, Broadway, Times Square, street fairs, chain restaurants, carnivals—but she'd always found, five minutes in, that she was snapping to the beat of Goofy's song and dance, requiring extra tissues on account of the trials of Jean Valjean in *Les Mis*. "Loser," Dina said when Ruby purchased a bamboo shoot from a street vendor—a sprightly shoot with but two tiny leaves stuck into a base of smooth stones in a clear glass cylinder. They'd laughed over the fact that Ruby could like something so obviously set out for newcomers to New York—college freshmen and visitors from Kalamazoo. "How's the loser bamboo?" became "How's the loose bamboo?" which became "How's the slut plant?" Ruby smiled at that. Her slut plant was on their windowsill now—right above the sink. And it was doing well.

"Let's do it," Ruby said, already feeling her initial defenses rising, everything transforming to silliness around her. But, when he came around to her side and pulled her out, and she straightened her skirt and stepped into her shoes, Ruby looked at Ed and realized this was something . . . something real. And she accepted his palm and touched the smoothness of it with the more calloused palm of her own—the cuts and burns and rough bits from her work always there. She felt inspired by the rush of emotion she was experiencing, but the fear was creeping around it like a caterpillar, circling, circling, creeping, creeping.

A half hour later, they turned off the main drag and onto a side street, where the far-off sound of music was floating like a concert you didn't have a ticket to. And as they walked it grew stronger and louder. On a whim, Ruby pulled Ed's arm in the direction of its source—the town's public library. And through the heavy, stained-glass doors, she saw another open door and it led them to a garden—a hole cut right in the middle of the building. And there, a woman so soulful the stuff was leaking out of her eyes, shooting from her deep mahogany, storytelling hands and swinging hips, was juggling notes up and down, up and down, and up and down—pulling out every bit of some indiscernible word, dismantling it to atoms and stringing it together again as something completely new. And after it flowed in and out of Ruby—who let her guard down and allowed her head to glide back and forth to the beat of it, allowed her foot to smack against the bricks in rhythm—she realized the word was "everything."

They took a seat along the brick wall that lined the garden and the singer caught Ruby's eye. At first she wanted to look away, to Ed, who was a safe touchstone for her, but that woman, her voice—the way she sang the word "child" like she meant it, like she really cared and knew what those people sitting there went through, like she'd gone through it and was here to tell it to you, show you a way to get through it all—kept Ruby's gaze firm.

In the end, Ed and Ruby stayed through the whole set—about six more songs—and they laughed at themselves when they realized they'd been grooving to Mustang Sally and singing the "naah, naah-na-na-naaaah's" at the top of their lungs along with the old woman in a bright orange jumpsuit and white plastic sunglasses, and the little boy in the striped T-shirt running the perimeter, clapping his hands out of beat, and a couple of young Hispanic girls with jumbo hoop earrings and high ponytails.

And the purple of the night grew more intimate—a little smaller and more manageable. Ed and Ruby both found themselves offering up a "wwwooooooooohhhh!" when the band said their farewells, and we'll be here and there next Friday and the following Thursday. Then they were in the truck again, the windows now closed against the gathering wind, which made the night feel chillier. That was when Ruby realized how good it all was, how genuinely wonderful her life could be. These moments had visited her before, though, her cynical side reminded, and they didn't ever prove themselves to last.

"Oooooohhhhh, sweet thing, don't you know you're my ev-e-ry-thiinnnnnng?" Ed sang the line—half seriously, half self-consciously, head bobbling, hands swirling—that the band had sung just a half-hour earlier, and he cut the engine and opened his door.

"Ed," she said, breathy, and all at once ready, then just as quickly unready to say what needed to be said. He'd just walked around the back of the car to her side, the door ajar between them.

"Yeah?" His look was expectant, his limbs frozen through the smudge of the window.

All the hopefulness, the passion that could make her hold onto this, it was strong in her, like a current running through. She would find a way to keep everything. "You know I had a funny childhood," was what she finally said to the poured blacktop, the smoothness of it, as she jumped down onto it, their street, in their town, where they lived.

"Yeah, I know that," he said.

"But I love you." She let out the breath she'd been holding in. She'd thought she had said a lot, but now she wondered if it was really anything at all—the story of her life. She prepared herself for what this might lead to, being left or leaving, to big empty beds and long, empty nights.

"Can I help you with anything?" he asked. "Whatever it is, Ruby, I'll do it." He put his hand on her side firmly. It was a kind, thoughtful way to act, with the very limited information he'd been given, but she read things into it anyway. Had his tone changed? Had he looked at her—even if fractionally—in a different, pitying, way?

"No. No, I've got it. I . . . I just wanted you to know. I just wanted to tell you so that we are closer and not further apart."

"All right," Ed said. He threw Ruby over his shoulder.

"My underwear is showing!" she yelled her head off as he carried her up the stairs like that. Either he'd sensed she'd said enough just then, or he really was a descendent of cave men.

Eleven

Bring the car up to driving speed in a reasonable amount of time.

—Connecticut Department of Motor Vehicles Driver's Manual

Fall was in full swing on the day Ruby started to unpack the boxes. The apartment had been empty all these months, bare walls and all, and she'd made allowances—like using Ed's hair comb and sometimes sleeping in his sweatshirt. She'd worn summer clothes way past the appropriate weather, and compensated with shawls and a jean jacket. Even Jack had asked if she was freezing during her last lesson, when they'd gone over the more intricate details of tractor-trailer safety. Without unpacking, her studio was still makeshift at best. The plastic cases she kept all her little clasps and chains and rings in were stacked on the floor rather than hung on shelves, and magazines were tossed about all over the place.

Ruby looked sideways at a box labeled "Books." She removed the random items that had found a home on her bookcase shelves during all these months, brushed it over with a feather duster, took a knife to the box's packing tape and pulled the flaps apart.

She'd never had the luxury of holding onto a lot of things.

Books were easy. Hers were mostly small, and often in cheap paperback. They could be tucked into the corners of bags and suitcases. They were friends and entertainment both, and since her mother sold and respected books she approved of making room for them when necessary.

Ruby's books were stamped with second-hand price tags atop the pages. She'd learned to like the way you could fan out all the musty pages, stretching out the price stamp until it looked as if nothing at all had been there, except maybe some dust, and then pull them all tight together and see right there the book cost a dime. She loved how the kids had marked their names inside the covers. Ruby always thought she knew what that urge was about, to put your mark on something, let the world know it was yours. The belonging grounded you and connected you to something else.

Ruby was glad to have her books. Now she stacked them with care—some lying down on their covers, others standing straight with their spines facing out. She pulled out the cast-iron hunting dog bookends she'd found at an antiques fair next to a rusted holiday cookie tin, and the few photos she liked to display with her books. One was of her estranged grandmother, years ago, before she'd even been sick at all. There was one of Ruby with Dina at a birthday party wearing matching "My Friend's Old" pins on their chests, and one picture Ruby could just look at and look at—it was of Ruby and her momma. They were sitting at a redwood picnic table and they had their chins resting on their elbows. The thing about that picture was, Ruby's momma looked so happy. But the very next day they had packed up their things and moved on. It reminded Ruby that things could change at a second's notice, and that getting comfy was one hell of a risk. She lined the three pictures in their cheap but pretty frames on the windowsill and thought, in some ways, this was the complete story of her life.

She piled up hard-backed books with pictures of fairies and others with all species of frogs, another of wild birds with kaleidoscope

feathers. She could look at a book of almost anything and funnel all
that color and silhouette and mass, or lack thereof, and come up
with something for her jewelry. Old books were better than new
ones for that. They were lived-in yellowed pages, late night cigarette
burn marks, pages curling at the corners. Those things leant a human
quality to all of the contents, and this personality was exactly the
kind of inspiration Ruby searched for. Maybe she wasn't the one
who'd lost her identity, maybe it was just that she'd never had one,
that she'd scrounged for other people's and now finally someone was
taking notice.

   Now, Ruby fanned out one of those books. It was a silly high
school romance she could barely remember the plot of now, or why
she'd even kept it, with its mildew-sweet smell and moisture-rippled
pages. She let the wind of it sweep over her face, and then squeezed
the covers together tight, and when she looked at the price, she
could barely read the faded smudge of it: five cents. Right then, the
idea of it, of a price that stood for nothing, an item you couldn't
value but did all the same, was something that brought her to ham-
mered silver and gold, forged into lots of tiny discs, with numbers
one could just barely make out—like change in your pocket that a
giant had stepped on, lending a softened shape—something to hold
onto when you need it. There was something about this piece. She
could never be quite sure, but she felt a renewed sense of satisfaction at feeling the tiny paper-thin discs, their curvy, pocked surfaces. Ruby slipped the bracelet template over her own wrist and
watched it slide up toward the widest part, all the coins hanging
down. As she worked over the next few days, she watched the way
it jingle-jangled with lightness and she was sure this was an important turning point for her.

   Ruby worked hard to unpack her pretty yellow colander and her
formal dresses. She found her good cooking knife and her salad
spinner. And when she emptied each box she found a new place for
its contents in her new home, in her new life. It had taken her a
while to get to the last box, but she thought she was ready to face it

now. This was her father's box. In the years and years of knowing
nothing about him, there were these things that she'd looked to for
some meaning and sense of self.

She'd not opened the box the entire time she'd been in Manhattan. That part of her life had been about letting go. But this part
seemed to be about coming back. Between the driving and the marriage, it had been impossible to ignore her past here. It came up and
smacked her in the face at every angle. Always it seemed to be saying, ha! As if you could just leave everything behind and have a normal life! It taunted her while she washed pots in the sink wearing
yellow rubber gloves that looked stuffed with hands even after she
pulled them off, and when she sat and watched the sunset with a
glass of sweet chardonnay. But she was determined to meet it with
everything she was worth.

And if she was going to do that, she'd have to face this, too.
She'd kept these things in a wooden box with a top Ruby and her
momma found in Mexico. If her momma had known she'd used it
this way she'd have flipped! Even after all these years, the idea of
pissing her mother off could make Ruby giggle.

The box was covered in bold flowers painted in hot colors. It
hinged open from the back and snapped shut in front with a gold
flap that fit snugly on a tiny peg. She lifted the flap now, pulled back
the top. She unearthed his pack of Marlboro cigarettes. Just as
they'd been the last night she'd looked at them—the night she'd
waved her mother off at the Boston train station, and boarded the
train to New York City. The packet still held four cigarettes. They
were stale smelling and hard when you felt them between your fingers.

Her mother had never known Ruby took the cigarette pack
from her. If she did, she hadn't asked. But when Ruby came across
them in her mother's closet, in the pocket of a pilled pinstripe suit
jacket her mother hadn't worn in some time, she had wanted to
know—why had her momma kept them all this time if she hated
Ruby's father so much? What was it that Ruby didn't know? Over

the years, they'd come to symbolize some kind of mystery, the thing that had brought her parents together, that possibly one day could bring Ruby back to her father. She replaced them in the box carefully, an archaeologist's artifact.

Also inside that box there was a torn corner of notebook paper—yellowed and softened where water had apparently been spilled—on which was penned a note to Ruby and her mother. Such a strange thing to see those words, frozen still! As if he'd be back in five minutes from now instead of years and years ago, when he'd returned only to leave them again—for real. *Beautiful Ladies, Gone out for milk. Be back soon. Love, Dad.*

Now, as she looked at it, Ruby couldn't help but be sucked back in. How could such a person up and disappear forever? Something didn't seem right! He'd referred to his family as "beautiful ladies." She could will that family into being now—her parents cooing over Ruby in a crib, so happy. But even if she could recapture their smiles, their peals of laughter, her father would be faceless. And she wasn't sure how his voice might sound, or what he'd be wearing.

But she was done with that search, with her chest pounding as she typed his name into the search bar on the Internet. She wasn't going to order the Yellow Pages from any county, city, or town, she wasn't going to let them pile up like a golden city of all the "no's" that never amounted to anything concrete. Sure, she'd lost time she'd never get back, scanning faces for similarities at rock concerts and carnivals. But that was over now. She was absolutely sure she was past all of that.

Still, Ruby couldn't help thinking that maybe now *was* the right time to find out once and for all. When she heard the sound of Ed's key in the lock, Ruby covered these things back over with the crumpled newspapers and fiddled with her bookcase, trying her best to look content.

★ ★ ★

On the first day she saw the leaves turn, the red ones had taken her by surprise. The last time she'd seen those leaves they'd been green as anything, and now, at just the right moment, they'd completely changed. She was driving to the lot to meet Jack and she'd been having a good driving day, had barely thought about the past at all for the five minutes or so she'd been behind the wheel. She was having a good day, and she smiled at the success in that.

Jack had on a pink sweater and khaki pants with a fraying hem. He'd been standing against his passenger side door, waiting for her.

He walked over to her passenger door, climbed in, hugged Ruby in the way he'd come to do in the last couple of lessons. And her heart warmed exactly as it had on the other occasions.

He sat back and buckled up.

"You got new glasses!" she said, noticing right away something different about him. They were tortoise shell and more squared than his previous pair had been.

"Yeah, well, I'm going to see my kids for Christmas. I didn't want to go out there looking like a cartoon character."

Ruby loved him with the tape on the glasses; she'd warmed to that detail of him. "I liked the way you looked in your old glasses, too," she said, smiling, backing out of the parking space.

"Why, thank you," he said, smiling big.

"Today we're going to take a drive to the automotive store and put together an emergency kit for you," he said. "And I'm going to show you how to change a tire. This way you'll know what to do in any situation."

They did just as he said, picked out flares and a fuzzy blanket, and outside, in the parking lot of the store, she learned to fit the jack in place, crank it up, remove the nuts along the hubcaps.

"Do you want to grab a burger?" Jack asked when they'd finished.

"Sure," Ruby said.

She drove them to Jones's. The place was full today—lots of guys in suits, as if a meeting had just broken up nearby. The guy in the little window yelled out "bacon double with fries" and "American cheeseburger with onion rings."

Ruby and Jack were just taking their first bites when Ruby heard someone ask, "Do you have any more mustard? You seem to be all out."

She swung around because she recognized the voice and the desperation regarding the mustard. And just as she did, she locked eyes with Ed. Her heart dropped all the way to her socks, and she worried because this pair had a hole at the third toe.

Ed was handed a yellow bottle and he pulled his burger from a paper bag, unfolded the foil paper, and squirted on an obnoxious amount of mustard. It was the kind of squirt meant to send a message, but Ruby wasn't ready to face the message. So when Ed came over, kissed her on the mouth, and then, with his hand on her shoulder, asked, "And who are you dining with here, Rube?" she simply answered, "Oh, Jack and I are volunteering together over at the . . . ummm, at the temple." She looked up to God and hoped he wouldn't smite her for this, but it was the only place she could think of that she would know and Ed wouldn't. "We're collecting cans," she said, shaking her head too vigorously.

Jack looked at Ruby questioningly, but God bless him, he kept up the ruse. "I'm Jack," he said. "So whaddya say, you got any peas you can donate?" he asked.

"Not much for peas," Ed said, unsure of it all, it appeared. "What do we have, Ruby?" he craned his head around to face her, his eyes searching.

"White beans?" she asked, though this was nothing like what he was looking for, though this was nothing at all really.

He waited a second longer, searching her in that way—his eyes darting back and forth over her features as if he could see through them. Her fingers were numb, grabbing onto her own thigh, her tongue was bone dry.

"Well, it was nice meeting you, Jack." He raised his white paper lunch bag up; a small oil spot had grown in the front of it. "I gotta get back so I can eat this," he said. Ed leaned down and kissed Ruby softly.

She hoped this meant he loved her—whether or not he believed this scenario—and so she said, "Have a good afternoon. I'll see you later."

When Ed had pulled out of the lot and down the main street, Ruby let out a huge sigh.

"You haven't told him?" Jack asked.

"I'm going to. It's just, it's never been the right time."

Jack breathed big. "Do you mind if I'm blunt here?" he asked.

"Please," she said.

"There's never going to be a right time to talk about the really difficult things. But if you can't open up to him, if you can't lean on him about the things you really need his support for, then what will your relationship be based on? Marriage is not an easy thing, Ruby. But communication is the key to it."

"I know. You're right. I'm going to do it. Soon," she said, convincing no one so much as herself, "I'm going to tell him everything."

While the leaves fell and fell, Ruby tried in the ways she knew how, to make her apartment into a home. After she'd emptied the boxes, she fashioned candleholders and napkin rings, napkin dispensers, and door stoppers from silver until their place looked like a trinket shop. "This place looks awesome," Ed said with sincerity one day when he came home, his back no longer edging a towering wall of boxes. It was nice that he'd said that, instead of the truth, which was it looked very cluttered and not very practical, what with these things getting knocked over every other time either one of them turned around. He twisted an invisible cigar between his fingers, double-raised his eyebrows, and said, "You should do this for a living."

As far as her jewelry, she'd been making things and making

things. She was still doing food—a Hershey's Kiss, a Bibb Lettuce, a Grape Tomato—mainly flat, two-dimensional pieces with generous proportions meant to hang on long chains. She'd forced herself to head back and forth to the caster every other week now, to take the long ride and dare herself to not head back up to Middleville.

She always found her way back somehow, and this enabled her to convince herself that she was doing something about the problem of facing her fears, when really she was just stuck in the same step over and over again, like an alcoholic who keeps apologizing to people because he's afraid to start the next step—continuing to set right any *new* mistakes as he goes along.

Despite the large inventory she'd accumulated, she hadn't had the nerve to sell any of it, afraid what someone might say of her identity now that things were supposed to be looking up. Ruby understood it was probably not the healthiest way for an adult to conduct herself—relying on accessory magazine reviews for the status of her mental state—but she was swayed by this idea all the same.

One night, just before Ed would be getting home, Ruby plunked the last package of chicken into the pot. Now she was getting good at browning the skin—at rubbing it with a pat of butter first and turning up the temperature real high so it crisped nicely—and then turning the flame down, letting it cook slow, until all the pink was gone and the blood drained. Now she could tell from looking at it just when it was done.

They weren't eating out on the patio anymore—it was too cold for that now. In the morning, webs of frost covered the window corners and the sliders stuck from the ice. It was cold and didn't show signs of letting up.

When the chicken was done, she swished the juices around with a wire whisk and sprinkled flour into it for gravy, made it into just the sort of thing you bought in a can for seventy-five cents. She smiled at that, and with the tongs she'd unpacked, squeezed a leg and a breast onto a plate for Ed. She pinched some string beans onto the plate, brought it to the table, and then did the same for herself.

"We gotta go shopping," Ed announced. "I'm low on the old ice-o cream-o." His words were flashes of light, upbeats.

She'd just been reading the supermarket circular. "Alfalfa sprouts are on sale, sixty-nine cents for the large size," she reported.

"Alfalfa this," he said, twisting in his seat, grabbing his butt like he meant it, which he didn't.

They both smiled halfheartedly and finished eating in silence. A tree branch scraped against the window.

Ruby was thinking about grocery shopping. It was true Ruby had grown up poor. From the things people had said about her clothes and binders, she knew she'd grown up wearing poor clothes and carrying poor binders, which she had tried to pin down as the reason for all the misfitting she'd done.

But it wasn't her mother who'd attracted Ruby to poverty grocery shopping. She didn't believe in off-brands and packaged fruit that was on its way out if someone didn't buy it in a four pack for seventy five percent cheaper that very morning. Her mother liked to splurge, liked to come home, drop her keys on the table that was always by their door, no matter the state, and declare, "We're going out!" her shirt shimmying around her giant chest like mad. It was Ruby who'd look down at her chicken cordon bleu, its cheese bubbling out at the sides and think, *This could be a sweatshirt!* She'd think it over and over and over until the food tasted leathery and heavy on her tongue.

Now she was facing things, though, Ruby was going to give everything she had to paying full price and not looking back. Look how much she'd spent her first time at the Stop & Shop; sure she had been wasting time so that she wouldn't have to drive home, but it showed she had it in her to splurge. She would try to look away as the checkout boy passed the items over the scanner, read a magazine or inspect a new brand of gum, not even minding if he might make a mistake or two, possibly double-scan or enter an endive as radicchio. Because she could afford it.

An hour later, she dodged around the Super Stop & Shop, stopping to appear too interested in a head of cauliflower, asking "can you believe the size of this?" She lingered over a certain type of potato chip, saying to Ed, "What exactly is the difference between ruffles and ridges?" But she couldn't dodge the outrage rising in her cheekbones like bits of lead stuck there. Had Ed really chosen the rolls that cost two dollars and fifty cents more than the ones right next to them? Was that ice cream truly selling for seven dollars and eighty cents? By the time they reached the deli counter, Ruby was beside herself. Ed was ordering individually wrapped hotdogs. And they cost eight dollars for six of them. She thought of saying something wry such as, "I think they have the coordinating twenty-dollar buns back in the last aisle, should I go grab them?" but she restrained herself. She'd barely put anything of her own in the basket for fear of sending the bill sailing even further out of control. All this and she was peeking around the aisles like a spy, trying to avoid Richard.

At the end of aisle nine, she tried to ignore the six-dollar boxes of cereal Ed was eyeballing. She looked down at her black slipper flats, considering their tiny leather rosebuds, and looked up to see Richard standing not ten inches from her, in front of a shelf of granola sacks.

"Well, hello there," Richard sang.

The fluorescent lights had taken a toll on her vision, and the overpopulated aisles had caused some anxiety on top of that. But she looked into his face for a few seconds, noting that the facial hair had grown longer and mangy, with some sickly looking bald spots here and there. There was a whitehead beneath his right nostril. He was shorter and thinner than she'd built him up to be. It occurred to Ruby that this moment was important, that it was imperative that she look this in the face. She swallowed big, spoke slowly, the way she'd been advised in the third grade. "Well, hello, Richard."

She longed to say something mean-spirited, something denigrating his ability to grow a beard properly, but that didn't seem to be the way to go.

And as if the universe were congratulating her on making the right decision, on looking at him right in the face like that, he replied, "I'm sorry about the other day. I'm sorry I said that about you being homeless. It wasn't right."

"Yeah," she said haughtily, although it seemed there was no reason for that tone now. "You should be."

Ed was coming up from behind now, and she heard the squeak of the wagon, saw Ed nod at Richard, looking a little confused.

"Thanks for that," Ruby said by way of good-bye as they turned toward the checkout.

Richard said, "See you around," as if looking to Ruby for approval, as if, perhaps, he'd dreaded seeing her as much as she'd dreaded seeing him.

At the car, Ruby let out a long breath of relief. The last time she'd been here she couldn't even drive herself home. But look at her now. Just look at her now.

They packed the paper-in-plastic bags into the trunk. Ed said, "I'm gonna make me one mean sundae. You want one?"

"Sure," she said. She wasn't going to say a thing about the eight-dollar hotdogs. In fact, she was feeling rather celebratory. She might even eat one.

Twelve

Driving is both a privilege and a responsibility.

—Connecticut Department of Motor Vehicles Driver's Manual

On a Thursday in the last week in October, Ruby woke up at 6:45 a.m. to notice it was still dark outside. This time of the year didn't depress her like it did most people. She always thought she looked far better in the dark, plus it was much easier to hide in the shadows; it required less makeup and sleight of hand.

She fixed herself a coffee, loaded it with sugar and milk, and sat before the kitchen slider to watch the sun come up, wrapped in an old afghan. So much had happened to her this year and at a time like this, with so much beauty, it was impossible not to see the good in it all.

The coffee soothed as it went down and Ruby pulled her knees up into her chest and wrapped the blanket a little tighter around her, poking her fingers through its large loops. The sky was grayish but a hint of pink blazed in between the peaks of the hills across. Ed came in to join her. He took a seat next to her in a matching chair from the kitchen set they'd purchased at the Home Depot. A few months ago, she never thought she'd utter any sentence containing the words "Home Depot," yet here she was.

"Good morning, baby," he said, smiling.

"Good morning back atcha," Ruby said. She handed her mug to him in case he wanted a couple of sips.

"Mmmmm," he sighed after a long sip.

"I wish I could come with you today," he said.

She was going to a local farm to pick pumpkins and apples with Ed's mom. "Yeah, well someone's gotta work around here," she said, joking. She'd been working overtime, firing off so many pieces, pretty soon she'd have to go start selling. She told herself in a week or so she'd be ready to do it, feel confident enough to face the possibility of rejection. For now, it was enough just to love the pieces herself.

"I know. Just imagine what might happen if someone didn't investigate insurance claims for one afternoon. I think the world would come to a screeching halt." He fluttered his lips.

The sun was gaining strength now, breaking rays of color and clarity through the gray. "Looks like it's gonna be a beautiful day," she said, taking the mug back as Ed passed it to her.

The Country Farm was huge—acres and acres of hilly pasture, trees as far as the eye could see. Suzanne was driving the Mercedes. "I've been coming here since I was a little girl, believe it or not." She had Yanni playing on the cassette deck.

That was a nice thing to think. Tradition. Stability. Ruby couldn't imagine something more grounding than that. She couldn't help but compare her own mother to Suzanne. Her own momma despised routine. If she went to a Chinese restaurant two times she swore she'd never go back. They'd drive around and around, Ruby's stomach growling as she thought sadly about the pretty swirls of egg drop at Chef Wong. Eventually they'd find some greasy place with torn red vinyl chairs, and Momma would let Ruby circle the items she wanted on the long paper menu. "Chef Wong's was better," her mother would whisper with a mouth full of egg roll confetti, leaving Ruby to wonder why, then, they hadn't just gone there in the first place.

"For Halloween, I always used to dress like a ghost—I'd cut out eye and mouth holes in a sheet and that would be that. My momma said every year she'd ask what I wanted to be and every year I'd say a ghost." Ruby didn't remember that so much as remembered her momma retelling the story each year. It did seem like something she'd do. Sometimes it felt she had erased parts of her life altogether— she'd forgotten so much of it. She thought of the way her one friend, Derek in Las Vegas, had recorded home videos, with loud, fuzzy blanks between the scenes.

"Ed always wanted to be the Incredible Hulk. Even when it wasn't Halloween."

"I could see that," Ruby joked. Skinny, lanky Ed must have made some Hulk.

"He just loved the Hulk. He had the poster, the blanket, the Underoos. At one point, we were in the middle of dinner and he announced, 'From now on, everyone call me the Hulk.' His father and I tried to encourage his individuality and so we did it for six whole months until he was over it."

Suzanne drove in a jerky manner, sitting perfectly straight, so close to the steering wheel her chest touched. What a difference from her momma's wild, casual driving style that made Ruby think the world simply stepped aside for her momma to cross. Nothing scared her, it seemed.

They drove past pretty trees dressed sparsely in red, orange, and golden leaves, and colonial houses done up with hay bales, bloody-mouthed zombies and blank-faced scarecrows. Inside, the car smelled of a green pine air freshener, from which Suzanne had carefully removed the top of the plastic wrapper so that just the right amount of scent wafted around. There was a Post-it note on the dash in front of Ruby that said, "Dry cleaning!!!" Ruby channeled a joke her momma often made in the face of excessive exclamation points, "Your dry cleaning must have behaved pretty badly to deserve three exclamation points." But Suzanne looked confused, her tidy lightened brows in a jumble. So Ruby changed the topic, immediately feeling her sense of humor inadequate.

"Do you know somewhere good to get dry cleaning done?" she asked, though she'd worn only knits and jeans since she'd moved.

Mrs. Robbins went on about the relative merits and drawbacks of about five different dry cleaners before they came to the parking lot.

They parked at the peak of a hill where there was a dusty graveled area cleared for that purpose. A couple of families with small children were scattered around the pumpkin patch.

"So, you want to look for a very orange color—no yellow pumpkins that aren't fully matured." They walked along a row of pumpkins, their huge leaves poked with holes, the long vines of them sweeping all around. "Look for a green stem and pick the pumpkin up and check for any mold."

The pumpkins came in all shapes—not just the super perfect round ones Ruby was used to from the corner stores and supermarkets where she'd picked her pumpkins from before. There were curvy ones and tall, skinny ones and pumpkins that looked like someone had stepped on them with a very heavy foot. She couldn't get over how she plucked hers—a twisty, misshapen one she had a soft spot for—directly from the vine. It seemed to her a reminder that she was connected to the earth, just like other people were—not just alone on it, as she had often felt before.

Suzanne chose two small pumpkins—one a tiny bit larger than the other—to stack on her front stairs, and then they picked too many apples and walked their spoils up to the tiny wooden shack to join the line of people waiting to pay. Suzanne insisted on paying for Ruby's. "It was so much fun to see someone enjoy this for the first time, I should be paying you," she said.

Ruby fidgeted but smiled immensely, feeling connected to this woman. "Thanks," she managed without garbling a syllable.

After, they headed to Suzanne's house, a small colonial that Mr.

and Mrs. Robbins lived in since they were first married. Inside the cozy kitchen, with its oak cabinets, tin ceiling, and backsplash, Suzanne handed Ruby a spare apron—an old fashioned ruffled model that Ruby loved for its kitsch appeal. Ruby and Suzanne peeled, cored, and sliced apples until their fingers ached. And then they mixed the wedges with sugar and nutmeg and a pinch of salt. While they waited for the juices to render from the apple mixture, they spoke about the Hulk and paged through some bridal magazines to get an idea of dresses Ruby liked.

As the sun set outside her future in-laws' front window, beyond the lacquer piano and above the hills and trees, Ruby thought it was as cozy a day as she could remember.

When she arrived home again, Ruby twisted her key in the lock, pushed the door open with one hand, and held her two apple pies in the other. "You home, Hulk?" she asked when she heard the sounds of the television.

"What did you call me?" he asked, his feet sliding from where they'd rested on the table they'd built.

"Ummm, nothing." She balanced a pie and her pumpkin and he stood to help her now, sniffing grandly.

"Yeah, that's what I thought," he said, with some good-natured bravado, his head pecking *Saturday Night Fever*–style. "I like the way you look with my mom's pie plate in your hand like that," he said. "It really brings out the color of your eyes."

They went to their kitchen and sat at their quaint kitchenette, the refrigerator humming, and laughed over the mangled pumpkin Ruby had picked, Ed calling her a bleeding heart, and ate apple pie until their stomachs ached. It was so close to perfect that Ruby could literally taste it—and it tasted just like sugary apples dancing on her tongue; it was the way she'd always imagined.

Thirteen

Make sure that there are no loose objects in the vehicle that could hit someone in the event of a sudden stop or crash.

—Connecticut Department of Motor Vehicles Driver's Manual

On a surprisingly cheery November day, rather than drive home from her lesson, Ruby decided to turn left to go to a store, Yore, that she'd spotted a while back. It was just the type of local place to start selling her designs to—a task she'd managed to put off since the bad reviews. Sure, she'd made some things she thought could signal her comeback, but selling them was altogether different.

Maybe she was riding a high from the elation of the lesson, from being on the way, for being closer to the truth. She pulled into the turn lane, holding onto her necklace like it really could give her some bravery, like it could be a magic talisman. They had those in that game she played as a child, too. *Pick up the magic talisman*, you could type. *Put it in your sack.* Now she wanted to type, *Turn Left. Park car. Walk into shop.* But in order to do so, she'd have to forget what had been written about her, or at least stop caring about it. She'd have to face the fact that maybe the driving lessons hadn't solved it all, that it had just been one step. But that was just too much for then.

At the turn lane, Ruby froze. Her hands tightened up on the wheel like eagle talons, but she didn't know it. Wasn't she past this by now?

HONNNNNNNNNNK! The light had changed without Ruby realizing. There were normal things alongside the road: a McDonald's with a colorful plastic playscape and a hardware store featuring a giant blow-up ladder on the patch of lawn out front, but in this car, nothing was normal. Her fingers were numb and jumpy. Her neck was hot, sweating.

Okay, she thought. *I'll just go now. I'll just go.* But it wasn't as easy as it sounded. She couldn't do it. She thought through the motions in her head, what she'd have to do—take her foot off the brake, place it gently on the gas—and it sounded easy, it really did. A monkey could do it! But her foot had turned to stone. Behind her the one honk had turned to two, three, ten, maybe one thousand honks now. People started screaming, "Get off the road!" "What the hell is wrong with you?"

Finally, the cars started going around her, some even onto the sidewalk, others into oncoming traffic on the wrong side of the road. Her hands were stone now, too, and they wouldn't move from ten and two o'clock, spots which she'd just read about in the driver's manual. All the rules of the road went running through her mind and seemed to be mocking her. The more control she lost over her body, the more lucid it seemed her thoughts became. *You're not moving forward.*

Finally, a police officer appeared in her rearview. He turned his siren on and instructed her over his speaker. "Pull over into the parking lot, ma'am," his voice screamed over the street with an electric crackle. "Pull over," he repeated. But she couldn't move. He turned the siren on for another cycle in case this would persuade her. Finally, he pulled the patrol car up next to her. Cars were still honking like mad. "Learn how to drive!" someone screamed and gave her the finger.

The police officer was out of his car then. "Watch it," was all he said to the fluffy-haired guy passing. The guy's own features turned stoney as he faced forward again and drove past. "Ma'am, do you think you can turn into that parking lot?" He spoke loud enough so that she could hear through the glass.

He pointed just where she'd wanted to go.

She shook her head.

In the end, he drove his own car and then hers into that parking lot. "All right, miss. What's going on here? You don't look like you're on drugs or anything." He had very dark hair buzzed short and a way of straight talking that had an edge of lightheartedness to it.

Against her car, the gleaming in-your-face shine of it, she crossed her arms like armor, and then let them fall to her sides and said, "I don't know what happened. I just froze up." Her words were chopped by sharp breaths that brought on tears that poured onto her hands—which were moving double-time. She couldn't face it if she went to this jewelry store and it turned out she still didn't know the real Ruby after everything she'd done.

He waited a long moment; cars whizzed by behind his back, making him appear stable, unmovable, permanent. And then he considered his lower lip with a hooked pointer finger, back and forth, back and forth. He let out a sigh. "Listen. You cannot hesitate when you are driving. You have to act swiftly, make a decision and follow through. When you don't, you put yourself and everyone on the road in danger."

The officer asked for her license and after he'd been in his car a long while, he came back. Ruby was cold, but barely aware of that, her long sleeved shirt weighing on her, trapping her against the car like a metal blanket she couldn't shimmy out from under. "I could give you a ticket for not having a Connecticut license," he said.

She met his eyes briefly, but couldn't hold it. She considered her own toes as he said, "I wrote you a warning for an improper lane change. But, Ms. Reynolds, I want you to have some faith in yourself. If you're not confident in yourself you can get into really dangerous situations."

She knew he was talking about driving, but it was funny to hear it like that, a command from a police official, in uniform, telling her to have some confidence. It could be the punch line to some joke. Later, she'd lose the ha-ha sense of it, be left with something different, poignant. She turned briefly to look at that shop behind her before she drove on—finally, now, when she'd been forced to. Under that YORE sign that had spoken to her so sweetly earlier, she now saw a woman emerge. She must have been the shopkeeper, since she was carrying a broom in her hand. Ruby hated to think that woman had seen her like that. If they all thought she'd lost her sense of self before . . . she could just think what they'd say now!

The officer waited for Ruby to turn out of the parking lot.

She waited for the right moment, and instinctively knew when to move her foot over to the gas pedal, how hard to press down, how to hand over hand her wheel to the left. There was a confident rhythm to it, and that came from her . . . somehow it had come from her. Now all she had to do was tap into that part of herself and she'd be just fine. The officer followed her through the twists and turns of the back way to her subdivision. If only he could show her the path to her confidence, to the thing that would click and have her yell "aha!" But he left her at the driveway, where she turned and he continued straight, raising his palm into a brick wall of good-bye.

Even as she heard the skin sizzling in the pan a couple of hours later, Ruby knew it was ridiculous to eat chicken again for dinner. Now they'd gone to the supermarket and bought pork chops and hotdogs and turkey burgers and a couple of steaks; they didn't have to eat the chicken. But the thing was, Ruby could *do* chicken. She was good at it. And it came out right, perfect even, every single time—the same. She used to eat out, take-in, but she'd never cooked. It was exhausting, how self-sufficient she had to be living out in the country.

"Oh, chicken!" Ed said, with his fingers splayed on his cheeks, and his mouth a big O. He said it funny, and sweet, and he didn't ask why. And they ate dinner with the lights off and a couple of candles on the windowsill. Ruby scooped some couscous onto Ed's plate, and some onto her own. "You didn't tell me there'd be couscous!" he exclaimed, and leaned over to her face and kissed Ruby right on her nose. A grain of couscous stuck there and that made them laugh and laugh.

Ruby was going to tell Ed about what had happened in the car earlier, about the driving lessons and all of that. But as the night stretched out and the laughter layered over and over itself, it just didn't seem right to spoil it, to risk it, either.

When Ruby met Jack for her lesson the next day she pretended yesterday never happened. The wind was strong, but the leaves were all gone now, so all you got were empty, nubby branches moving a couple inches one way, and then the other. She concentrated on successes. During the weeks, she'd practiced driving. She'd gone a little further and a little further. She'd taken herself to Brooklyn over and over again. She'd explored Connecticut, too. She'd gone to a jewelry supplier about an hour away. There was a sandwich shop next door and she'd eaten a cheese sandwich piled high with vegetables and told herself she wasn't lonely, just adjusting—and that was different. She told herself she'd draw up designs—all the designs swimming around in her head—but it was impossible to hold the pencil and eat the sandwich at the same time. Next time, she'd bring a book. At one point it seemed a woman in three braids was coming to chat. Ruby decided she could look past the three braids, but it turned out the woman was only collecting the salt and pepper shaker from Ruby's table, so she could refill it. OK, she was lonely again.

Jack drove up, slowly, obeying all the traffic regulations as a good example.

She smiled when she saw him. She liked his camel wool jacket and his front pleat pants.

"You ready to 'drive for life'?" Jack asked her when he buckled himself into the seat alongside her.

Ruby smiled. Jack was a friend. Back in New York, Ruby and Dina would've thought a slogan like his was lame. But, the word "hokey" was falling out of her vocabulary. She didn't know why she'd been so averse to it before. By definition it pointed to things that are simple, ordinary. And deep down that's all she'd ever wanted to be. It was even starting to dawn on her that this new Last Leaf piece was better because it had come from someone she really was, and not the person she'd tried to be in Manhattan. But she wasn't going to say that editor had been right—not yet, anyway. And not only because this person she was now sat alone most days at the lunch table.

It was wild how Jack could tell her what to do and have her do it— like a snake charmer or a magician. Ruby wondered if there wasn't something more to it than that. He was a father and she always read too much into that.

"Why, hello there," he said, a familiar face, a real friend, she thought. They made a left and at the stop sign, another left. They drove and drove, and Ruby didn't think she'd ever seen this part of town before. There was a white post fence and horses galloping inside—horses that could jump right over that fence, but never did, just stayed put because that is what they were told to do. Past the horses the landscape went wild with tall grasses, and then deep woods and, finally, an industrial shopping plaza and then across the street, a sign for 91 North.

"Go ahead," Jack said, and dipped his head a bit. In the silence between them, it didn't seem impossible that Ruby felt some real pride coming from Jack. His face hadn't changed and he hadn't gestured in any way, but there was something there between the silver eyebrows, the S curves of them, waving wildly themselves, like they could have gone off if they'd wanted, just might at any moment. Maybe Jack had been tamed once.

"Have you toured around Hartford at all yet?" Jack asked, that harsh striation in his voice again. He cleared his throat with his hand grasping it and then raised and lowered his eyes with a great big breath. Ruby thought he looked thoughtful that way.

"Not really, no. Not, well . . ." She knew her words were minced, but she didn't mind it so much with Jack. And when she didn't mind it so much, it tended to taper off.

"Great! I know this fabulous place for yucca fries!"

It was funny that Jack suggested just the sort of thing she'd been wanting—something different, something exotic, something not cheeseburgers or chicken.

She drove for a while in the direction of Hartford. She noticed that when she was driving, the weight and release of it, the rearview and sideview and neck twist of it, Ruby was someone she'd been only briefly—a girl she barely remembered from inside a worn-out bomber jacket in Las Vegas who'd just passed her driving test. "This is your ticket, Ruby Booby, I'm telling you—your ticket." Her mother had lifted a pebbled glass the size of a flower vase and drew a long sip of Pepsi in her daughter's honor. They were at Pizza Hut, and Ruby had loved Pizza Hut—the hot cheese, the sweet sauce, the crunchy, thin flowers of green pepper—in every state, the same. She'd thought it was true then, that having a license would free her from her mother's tether, that from that moment she could've done just what she'd wanted. Only later would she go to that party and realize the truth—that there was an emotional pull, too, and that was just as strong as anything physical—a license, a car, any of it.

But now she felt that initial surge of freedom again. And no matter what happened with the rest of her life, she was not going to give up on this, toss in the towel and stop driving this time around. Ruby parked a couple of spaces away from the entrance and Jack dropped some change for the meter into her palm.

"Thanks," Ruby said. "I never have any of that." At the bottom of her purse were only ever pennies and softened paper bits, old Tic Tacs.

Inside, they were South of the Border—either Cuba or Mexico. There were piñatas and the distinct smell of tequila pervaded. At the brightly tiled table, Jack ordered the pork tacos and Ruby followed suit. The yucca was crisped on the outside but a little mealy on the inside, with a great aromatic spice; the strings of pork were smoky, sweet.

"So tell me about Drive for Life," Ruby said, wiping some salt from her hands onto a napkin. A fire truck roared by, and then it was silent again.

"You're lookin' at him." Jack shimmied straight up in his seat and bobbled his head around for effect.

The waitress refilled their water glasses, removed the paper straw wrappers.

"You mean, you're the only person there?" Ruby didn't know whether this undercut the depth of her experience somehow, having an epiphany with a small beans company.

"Yep. Well, sure there used to be a lot more—as many as fifty at one point."

"What happened?" Ruby thought Jack must be a good father. She saw he didn't wear a wedding ring, though, and wondered about that. In her experience, men did the wrong thing, they were failures and disappointments, I'm telling you. Otherwise you failed and disappointed them. Sometimes, it could go either way.

"What happened?" He sighed and then repeated himself. "What happened? Well, I'll tell you a story, Ruby." There was some adjustment of his glasses.

She smiled at the way he said that, kind of joking, but in a way that you knew it would be something big.

"Young Jack Christianson was quite a looker." He winked at Ruby, who found this endearing and then turned shyly to her yucca. "And it wasn't but two minutes until the woman running the driving school gave me a job. She could barely look me in the face!" He cleared his throat, smiled at that long gone day somewhere up in the ceiling, with its twisted paper streamers. "I made coffee. I answered the phone, 'Driving School!'. . . That was the name of it then. Only the most senior people got to actually drive in the cars—two huge boat-like things with double steering wheels. And at first I'd get annoyed, sitting there like a receptionist, filling out papers—by hand, mind you—and offering people coffee or tea or hot water with lemon." Jack looked twenty-five years younger as he traveled back there, and something about that made you want to cry and cry.

"Well, everybody's gotta start some . . ." Ruby's voice trailed, but it seemed Jack got the drift.

"Exactly!" he perked up and his own voice cracked, went silent at the end while he punched at the air, snagging his shirt on a mush of bean so that it hung now from his elbow. "Those people, drinking their tea as if it was a magic elixir, they would talk to me. You see, Ruby, like you, those people were scared! They were scared out of their minds. And I would go home to my wife—oh, she wouldn't understand it at all, she'd say, 'Jack, why don't you get a real job?'" Jack smiled at it now, but it was apparent this wasn't funny, wasn't something small. He continued, "I would try to explain to her—that fear they had, it was never about the driving. It was always something more. It was what it would mean, it was that they were scared, unhappy, that they'd never wanted to face their choices, to face that they'd had choices, that they'd *chosen* to stay put. But driving!" He stopped for effect.

The waitress cleared their plates, slapped a check at the end of the table.

They both regarded the paper briefly in the silence.

"But. Driving." He let her sit with that for a second, though he didn't need to. She knew. "I know that *you* know what I mean, Ruby. You are a fantastic driver. A natural. As a matter of fact, I think you're cured."

Ruby was afraid of herself getting onto that old tack of hers, wondering ridiculous things . . . *could* he be my father? And so she tried to steer him off somewhere lighter. "Jack tell me . . . what do you think of—" But he cut her off.

"Ah, I let you do that once," he said.

She was surprised. She liked that he didn't let her fall into her old patterns—because she would and she would. Ruby often thought that with some real discipline she could have been much, much more.

She tried desperately not to look for her own traits in his. Ruby could convince herself of a lot. *It only takes one.* It didn't seem so strange if she thought about it that way. It could be. Really, the whole thing could be a huge setup—Drive for Life, this teacher and his big personality, Ed even could be in on it. In fact, it was a little crazy that he hadn't picked up on what was going on—maybe he had but that was part of his role, he wasn't allowed to say anything.

She could see it all unfold, like a grand finale: the waitress would shuttle Ed out with a finger over her mouth. *Ssssshhh!* She'd tell him that before they'd pop out from the back room and yell, "Surprise! This is your father, Ruby! You are the heiress to a driving school!" If you drew enough lines, if you decoded enough similarities, counted up the number of vowels and divided them by the consonants, it didn't seem so impossible.

At her car, back in the blank light that she was learning was a New England winter, she felt miserable. No one had jumped out, no one had yelled surprise. And even worse, she wasn't going to see Jack again. It was their last lesson and she'd just be one of thousands of lost souls he taught to drive.

"Hey, Ruby, I'd love to stay in touch," he said.

Her heart soared. She twisted the cold steel knob on the parking meter back and forth.

"Yes. That would be very nice. I'd love that." She scratched at her nose while she said it.

"Well, we're friends, aren't we?"

"Friends, yes. Definitely," she said, shaking her head sharply. Ruby promised herself she wouldn't make too much of it, that she wouldn't imagine that maybe they were all waiting for a better time to spring the surprise ending on her.

Fourteen

Remember that there are other road users such as motorcycles, bicycles, and pedestrians that are harder to see than are cars and trucks.

—Connecticut Department of Motor Vehicles Driver's Manual

It was snowing now, but Ruby didn't let that put a damper on her driving. She could drive in the snow! She could drive any day, anywhere, and she would. She would go in the kitchen to make a hot cocoa and realize she didn't have any left. She would pile on tank tops and T-shirts and sweatshirts and coats until she couldn't recognize herself, sit in the car for a while with the radio working, and finally when the car was warm—drive the twisty street to the main street and make a right into the parking lot of the supermarket. She and the yellow lines were familiar with each other now. You could go and come back, she told herself each time.

She would see Richard, and he would wave with a tight smile now. Probably, he felt more stupid than she did. And now there was the checkout girl, Gloria, with her frizzy short curls and quiet way. And she wanted to know, "How are you?" She was friendly and seemed to really mean it. And the bag boy, Thomas, would hold the can up and remark with one pinched eye, "Swiss Miss, huh?" like a

philosopher of food. And Ruby could come back with snappy re-
marks the way she could with Dina. She'd say very seriously things
like, "Oh, no, I'm from New Jersey."

One such snowy day in December, Ruby left her apartment to
drive to a couple of boutiques in Fairfield, in hopes of selling her
new pieces. The Hot Wheels girl yelled from her patio. "Hey." Her
voice was a dare, her eyes slits.

Ruby turned around, her head tilted awkwardly with the heft of
hat and scarf. "Hey." Ruby nodded.

The girl had one hell of a strong gaze. Despite the weather she
had only a light corduroy jacket on, and it was unbuttoned.

Ruby was balancing her case, purse, keys, and a travel coffee mug
only a few feet from her car.

"Boy, you are really driving these days." The girl in the wheelchair crossed her arms. Her blond hair was up and blowing in all directions, and lent her a mystical quality. She released her brake and
wheeled herself carefully down the slight drop from patio to grass
and then over to Ruby's parking space.

"Are you the driving police or something?" Ruby asked, opening her back door, throwing her case inside.

"Are you the wheelchair police?" The girl stared Ruby down.

So she knew Ruby had been watching. Her heart went cold
with it.

"It's no big deal. I don't give a crap." The girl was striking. Her
eyes were gray, her cheeks red circles of vitality. "Freaks take an interest in each other."

Ruby was taken by her audacity. Though she was trying to seem
tough, the girl was more than that. You could see it. "Whaddyou
want?" Ruby asked the girl, matching her tone.

"Can I come with you?"

"You don't even know where I'm going."

"Anywhere's better than here."

"Don't you have to ask your mom first?"

"I already told her."

Ruby didn't know what to think. "Pretty presumptuous, but fine," she said. The girl intrigued her.

The girl wheeled herself to the passenger side of the car. She pulled herself up and into the seat. From there she folded her chair up. She didn't ask Ruby to put it in the back so much as look quickly at her and then toward the rear of the car.

Ruby walked around, picked up the chair, and slid it into the floor space between the back and front seats. The girl finagled herself into the passenger seat by holding on very firmly to the top of the door frame.

"So, where are we going?" The girl asked once settled.

Ruby turned the car on. "Maybe you'd like to tell me your name first? And please put your seatbelt on."

"Sammie. Nice to meet you, Ruby Reynolds."

Jeez! This girl was something else. Had she sifted through their mailbox?

"How old are you anyway?" Ruby asked.

"Seventeen."

"Did you graduate?" she asked and shifted into reverse as if it were nothing. She wouldn't let Sammie see her sweat.

They were on their way before Sammie answered. "Yeah. Whaddyou think, just because I'm in a wheelchair I'm stupid?"

"No. No, I didn't mean that at all," Ruby said. "C'mon, don't be like that," she softened her voice. It was difficult to concentrate on the road with this kind of tension. Why had she agreed to take this girl with her? Because she was a bleeding heart was why. Because she hadn't seen this girl with a father. Because her heart broke when she heard her chair smacking into the doorframes. Because maybe in this girl, she saw a little bit of herself.

"Are you going to college?" Ruby asked, turning to her at a red light.

Sammie turned her face to the window. She made it clear she wasn't going to answer. Ruby didn't press.

They drove in silence until they were on the Merritt Parkway, on their way to Fairfield. "I'm going to sell some of my jewelry to the shops on the Boston Post Road in Fairfield," Ruby said.

"You make jewelry?" Sammie perked up.

"Yup."

"You know, I wouldn't mind learning something like that," Sammie said. "Is it hard?"

Ruby thought about it. It wasn't exactly hard to use the tools or to learn the techniques. What was hard was getting really good, refining your eye, your tastes. But that was something you had to learn yourself, as you went along. That isn't the kind of thing you want to tell a beginner, though. That's the kind of thing that would deter someone from trying in the first place. "No, not really," Ruby said.

The girl was quiet again for a while. And then her voice softened when she asked, "Do you think you might show me?"

Ruby tried not to think how this girl was going to get to her second floor apartment. "Sure," she said.

Outside the first store, Ruby was getting herself prepared to present her designs. She was taking a few deep breaths, straightening her shoulders, mumbling some catchphrases while she took Sammie's chair out of the back and then her own belongings.

"What the hell are you doing?" Sammie asked.

Ruby lowered her eyes, twisted her mouth tight. Ruby could remember wanting to appear that tough and never quite getting there. "I'm preparing."

"Whatever," Sammie said, rolling her eyes at Ruby. "It's a little weird."

Maybe being alone wasn't so bad, Ruby was thinking. Why did she have to go and rescue every wounded bird?

At the counter, there was a woman sitting on a stool. She wore big glasses with jeweled frames. Over the top, was how Ruby would describe the woman. Her sweater was fuchsia with beads sewn along the neckline, her pants a Palm Beach seascape complete with flamingos. "Can I help you?" Her words were quick knife dices. Neil Diamond played on the sound system.

"I'd love to show you my jewelry designs," Ruby said. She took in the space around her, tried to gauge which styles this woman would warm to.

"So go ahead," the woman said, her glasses slipping slowly down her nose. You were never wanted in this industry. That is, until you were wanted.

Ruby opened her case.

"Oh my God!" Sammie said. "I didn't realize you were, like, a *real* designer."

Ruby and the woman behind the counter shook their heads in unison. Their gestures said *teenagers*.

With her sausage fingers, the woman went right for Ruby's bigger pieces—the Last Leaf on a long wraparound chain. Another one she'd created for the collection: Fallen Leaf, this one on wild Chinese silks tied and woven just past choker length. She pulled her glasses off and laid them on the glass counter, which encased ten similar pairs.

Sammie was at the Bravery piece, and then the Pocket Change necklace, feeling lightly with her tiny hands, her rough cuticles and chewn nails giving away so much. "Ruby, do you think I could have one of these?" she asked.

"You think you could be a little nicer, maybe, if I give you one?" Ruby never thought she'd be the type of parent to buy her kids off, but now she wasn't so sure. It seemed like a decent idea if it worked.

"Oh, I could be a whole lot nicer."

Again the shop attendant and Ruby shook their heads.

"This is some sales team you've got here," the woman finally said.

"I'm Ruby and this is Sammie, and believe it or not, we are completely unrehearsed."

"Do you think I should choose this one or this one?" Sammie asked, holding them both up.

"The larger one looks stunning on you," the attendant said. "I'm Mrs. Katz." She held her hand out to Sammie and then Ruby.

"I don't do well with the understated crap," Mrs. Katz said. "But I'll take three of these Chinese silk pieces if you can do a fifty-percent discount."

"Deal," Ruby said.

The next store was called Sweetheart and inside it was bubblegum pink and gold with hearts everywhere. When Ruby opened her trunk, again Sammie said, "Oh my god! I didn't realize you were, like, a *real* designer."

Ruby smiled tightly.

"Do you think I could have one?" Sammie tried again.

"No," Ruby said.

"You must be sisters," the woman at the counter said.

"Nah," Sammie said. "Just friends." But her smile was unmistakable.

Ruby smiled. The woman ordered two each of Pocket Change and the yoga necklaces.

"You hungry?" Ruby asked Sammie after one rejection and another sale.

"Duh. I'm, like, starving," Sammie said, holding her hair back from her face.

"Like burgers?" Ruby asked.

"Yeah, but I seriously can't stand those places that put mustard on them," she said. "Yuck."

"I think we're gonna get along just fine," Ruby said.

She took Sammie to Jones's. The cook shot her a knowing smile as she walked up to the window to place their order. They ate a burger and fries apiece. "That's really weird what you do with the ketchup," Sammie yelled.

"Oh well, I'm weird, what are you gonna do?" she asked and shrugged her shoulders.

"Hang out with you more," Sammie offered with a lopsided smile. And that's just what they did.

A few days later, Ruby carried Sammie up the stairs to her apartment to show her the workbench, how the tiny plates of metal came, the scale with its penny weight measurements. She showed her how to use the saw, tightened a goggle strap over her pretty blonde hair. They started with something simple—a plain square—which Sammie completed with relative ease.

Afterward, Sammie and Ruby sat at the kitchen table drinking hot chocolate with mini marshmallows, and the extra marshmallows Ruby liked to float on top.

"Don't you wanna know what happened to me?" Sammie asked, setting her spoon on the table.

Ruby shook her head, pulled her knee up on her chair.

"I wasn't always like this," Sammie said. "I could walk. I barely remember that now, but I could. One day I had a horrible headache. I was about eleven years old and my mother fed me children's Tylenol. I took nearly the whole box, but my head was pounding and pounding. I threw up a bunch of times all at once. And this went on for almost five minutes until I blacked out. When I woke up I was in the hospital. It turns out I've got AVM, which stands for Arteriovenous Malformation. The pain was actually an aneurysm, which left me with one side of my face drooping; I couldn't even talk. But I was lucky to have gotten that stuff back pretty quickly."

Ruby swallowed big; her heart was doing the conga. She couldn't believe the things Sammie had survived. And here she was, so very brave. "Oh my God," she whispered. She wouldn't cry; Sammie wouldn't like it.

Sammie shook her head slowly. It was awful, her look said.

"This hope kept me going for so long, I was sure I'd get my legs back. I had the surgeries so I don't have any more aneurysms, but for now, the damage hasn't corrected itself in three years, and so I haven't been able to walk again. It doesn't mean I never will, but for now, I'm trying to take a break from hoping. I just can't take it anymore—waking up, wishing this will be the day. It's exhausting, all consuming."

Ruby tried with every ounce of her will to keep it together. And though her chest had never felt so empty and cold, she somehow managed to find the strength to. Here was this brave, wonderful girl, her friend.

When she called Jack next, it was the following week.

"Drive for Life!" He was too eager, and her heart went out to him for that, for trying too hard. She pictured him in an empty cinder block room with an institutional clock that hadn't changed since 1971.

"Jack, it's Ruby."

"Ruby!" The warmth in his voice made her smile big.

"Hey, Jack, would you want to go to this store in New Haven I heard about? I'd like to see if they'll buy my jewelry."

There was a glimmer of something in his voice, and Ruby tried hard not to think it that special brand of pride she was always looking for. She tried to think it was anything but that.

They took I-91, and this time it looked more familiar. This time, when the trucks went screaming by, she didn't tighten her hands so rigidly around the wheel that her knuckles turned white.

The boutique was called Ripe. It was nestled in a line of adorable boutiques housed in brick, and the area looked a lot like the West Village. She really took to it, the Yale students darting around, bundled up in wooly scarves and pom-pom hats, their ski jackets puffed around them.

Jack came into the shop with her, standing back a bit, like he wasn't sure exactly where to be. He removed his leather gloves and took a while pulling the empty fingers of each straight, and then rolled them carefully into a ball. He looked dreamy there in that old-fashioned shop—its rolling brocades, draped every which way, tassels and footstools and curvy upholstered wing chairs, tiny racks of delicate garments hung here and there. It was apparent Jack had a romantic side, the soldier of bravery that he was. Within seconds, he was poking through a trunk of vintage fabrics, ostensibly holding an opinion of each—his head shaking or twisting with vigor.

Ruby had made herself a great carrying case for her pieces a year or so ago. She'd made it from old tin ceiling tiles and she'd poked grosgrain ribbon through holes she'd drilled here and there—so many holes, so many ribbons, all yellow, big and small and shiny and matte. The ribbons were bow tied and knotted and crimped and shredded. It was something to look at. It was something that made you curious to see what might be inside.

Ruby hated selling herself, she could barely introduce herself; there wasn't a way in hell she was going to master the subtle unsubtlety of the sale. You had to be able to tick off your accomplishments like a class roll call, gesture dramatically, and at the end of it all, pull out a form and say, "So how many should I put you down for?"

She'd learned to let her work sell itself. This case was a great step in that direction. She could be just who she wanted to be with that case, with those necklaces—an Alex Trebek of accessories sales, if you will. After all, when things got tense in a business situation, you couldn't go off drawing Goofy or talking about fast-food condiments.

"I'm intrigued," the woman behind the counter said when Ruby placed the case in front of her. She smoothed down the back of her chocolate pixie haircut with a manicured hand.

"I'm Ruby," Ruby said and stuck out her hand. She looked back at Jack, who was now looking at a couple of modish plush parrots with an X stitch for an eye. "And this is Jack, my . . ." Oh, what was she going to say now? Why had she said, my? Why? "My . . ."

"Driving instructor," Jack said, smiling at the shop girl and then at Ruby.

The truth? Ruby wouldn't have thought of it. In fact, she would have stuffed it down, down, down, like the trash in an overflowing can, so she'd never have to empty it. Ruby looked at her boots, turned her toe in, out, and then ventured her gaze up again.

"Nice to meet you both. I'm Selma," she said. And then, "Driving instructor, huh?"

Ruby shrugged her shoulders, attempted a silly-me smirk, but Jack was having a moment. He reached into his pocket and took out a neat stack of business cards, stamped with his logo, secured with a rubber band. "Here, take a few. We've got sixty years of experience," Jack said. The zipper on his coat was swinging wildly with his giant move up to the counter.

Ruby tried to do the math. Jack was about seventy-eight then, if he'd started his job at eighteen. That was too old for him to possibly be her father. She partially opened the door to the truth with a thud.

"I'll put them out on that desk over there," Selma said, pointing to an antique roll-top that was stacked with business cards and postcards; in between each, a beaded white porcelain bud vase held a white rose. She pulled at the rubber band and then let it go gently, without a sound.

Ruby opened her case. She stood back and let Selma hold the pieces, try them on at the long mirror behind her.

"Ruby, I didn't realize you were so accomplished," Jack said. His lines were all stretched horizontal; he leaned into the depths of the case. "I'd love to buy one for my daughter."

Ruby's chest went hot with envy, longing.

He found the loose change bracelet, clinked the coins together as he held it up high. "This one," he said, shaking his head at something this meant to him.

"Jack, you're quite right," Selma said. "She's extremely accomplished. She's not at all washed up." Selma referred to an *Accessories* magazine article from last year. "In fact, she's knee-deep in a renaissance."

"What's this renaissance business?" A bigger woman's voice boomed from the door, which she'd just jingled through.

"Ah, Merry," Selma said. "I saw her first."

Ruby recognized the woman instantly as she came closer and

Ruby's tongue swelled, her nose hairs trapped her breath from coming; her coat was strangling her.

"Oh, no, no. I definitely saw her first. I saw her at my very own shop." She touched Ruby lightly on the back like an object on a shelf.

She had! This was the woman from Yore. And she'd seen Ruby freeze up like a worthless girl, afraid of her own shadow, her silver car like an alien craft drawing a crowd. A police officer pulling her over for this, making it all official, signing away her pride at the dotted line. And just now here she was, when Ruby was on the verge of some success—both personal and financial! Her laundry was flapping in the breeze, the whole neighborhood watching it from below. Could it be that no matter where you drove that you were always in the same place? That running or not, you couldn't escape who you were?

Ruby looked to Jack, but he couldn't have put it all together. Ruby could try; still whenever she opened her mouth, *Fooby* was going to come out. But maybe that wasn't as bad as she'd once thought. After all, there was Jack all the same, as if she weren't a raving freak and just a friend, like anyone else.

The women were trying on the necklaces, helping each other with the clasps, noticing nothing so much as each other, sort of forgetting Ruby and Jack were there at all. Ruby thought about what Jack said. She thought that he did know her very well. *One may have friends all over the world, but very few will truly know your heart.* Her momma loved that one. She loved to say it when Ruby felt melancholy on an empty Friday night in a new town, a long evening of avoiding thoughts of the party she wasn't invited to ahead of her. Her momma always told Ruby she liked those nights, just the two of them playing spades at a rickety table they'd picked up at some yard sale.

Sure, they'd laughed a lot, drinking hot cocoa or mint iced tea, depending on the season, but couldn't they have done this wherever they'd lived before? Did they have to be so isolated from everyone?

She'd felt honored then, before she was old enough to know any better, that despite all the people her mother left behind, she always wanted to be with Ruby . . . even if it often seemed that no one else did.

Now, in this dreamy shop, Ruby imagined it was the literary quality of the saying that appealed to her mother's sensibilities—the way she sounded bookish when she said it. Her momma loved to tick off sayings. But only Ruby knew they came from Bartlett's. While they'd drive, her momma would sometimes ask her to check them off: "*Energy and persistence conquer all things.* Benjamin Franklin." She'd sing it over and over again until it stuck. Once she'd committed it to memory, she'd say, "Check it off, Ruby," When her Momma had enough to busy herself remembering, she'd say, "That's enough," and Ruby would replace the green Sharpie pen they used as a placeholder.

Though her momma had liked that saying so much, she hadn't followed those words, had she? The truth of this hit her then, like a stack of cement blocks.

"I'm Jack, the driving instructor," Jack said. He was her friend because she hadn't given up . . . wasn't that true?

The woman, Merry, stood for a second, her brown eyes ping pong balls until she'd made the connection in a grand, "Ohhhhhhh." Her wild, light brown hair, the color of the golden fries at Jones's, bounced as she shook her head up and down, finally. It was obvious she remembered Ruby vividly—her red hair had always made her stick out, just as she wanted to fade away.

Ruby hoped she wouldn't laugh.

"Ha!" the woman said anyway.

"Ha!" Ruby tried this out, master of speech that she was. Besides, it didn't seem the woman meant it in a mean-spirited way.

"Ha!" Jack echoed.

"You know," Merry said, her finger at her bottom lip, "I thought about you a lot after I saw you that day. I thought about you in that car and then walking across the street toward my store with your head hung so low. I wanted to come out to you, to say something. But I guess I was scared to. You looked so . . . embarrassed. I didn't want to make it worse."

Ruby's cheeks burned. Without realizing, her nails had dug into her palms, and she tried to unfurl them now, her skin stinging slightly. It didn't seem fair that Merry could know so much about her. Ruby didn't *want* to be embarrassed, she didn't want to be afraid, she didn't want to be afraid of being afraid. But how did she go about saying that?

"She *was* embarrassed," Jack said, defending.

Ruby turned around; her jaw smacked to her chest. "I wa . . ."

"That's why I helped her. She didn't know how to drive. Or I should say, actually, she is a fantastic driver. She was just scared was all. She didn't know where she might go once she started."

"Ain't that the truth?" Merry said, as if she thought the very same thing every single day.

Selma shook her head in agreement, curled her lips, looked far out to the accuracy of the statement, somewhere past the cloth bust draped with a tea-colored, lace-trimmed dress and long, long pearls. "I swear to God, I was just thinking that, just thinking it yesterday. I was done here and my ex had Amanda—my daughter—and I don't know what I was thinking, I drove right to our old house and sat across the street for over an hour! I watched the family—my family!—in there eating dinner through an opening in the curtains—my curtains!—and I wished that could have been us again. I wished it was us. I know that's a useless, pitiful way to spend your time, but I couldn't help it. That's all I wanted to do. I can't do takeout. I don't know how to cook for one. The meat always comes in two-pound packages. The meat only comes in two-freaking-pound packages."

She was quiet for a second, and Ruby thought of Richard, of the guy putting those two pounders together. He'd never have thought of Selma and her problem.

Selma continued. "And then I got in the car and just started driving. Didn't get home until two in the morning. There were moments when the window was open, and the long grasses along the road were swaying, when I could have left it all, given up completely, I really could have." She breathed out big after she was done speaking, like she'd lost ten pounds just by saying that.

Ruby's eye was tearing. It was the kind of thing she didn't think people were supposed to tell you right away, if ever. They never told anyone their predicaments, Ruby and her momma. They kept their history to themselves, and sometimes didn't even venture to share with each other. Mostly when Ruby asked about her father, her momma acted as if she hadn't heard. She'd say, "Shall we make pork for dinner? Or would you rather chicken, Ruby Booby?"

She'd tried crying, screaming, even once she'd held her mother down on the sofa, her legs straddled on either side, her foot straight down between the cushions. "JUST TELL ME!" She'd screamed and screamed until her voice hurt her and she couldn't breathe, until her mother had had to push Ruby's head down between her knees to stop the jumping gasps. While Ruby's momma rubbed her daughter's back in the intricate series of tiny circles that she liked to have it rubbed in, she screamed at the only person who knew such a thing about her, "I ABSOLUTELY HATE YOU!" She'd said that out loud for the first time. Oh, she'd thought it. She'd thought it and thought it. She'd thought of all the evil people in history and read their biographies and circled what she found as parallels—Attila the Hun, Vlad the Impaler, Adolf Hitler. She screamed it and screamed it, until her throat burned. And after she finished, her mother smacked her—one loud sting on the cheek. And then she'd said, "I only love you, Ruby."

Ruby moved aside. She hadn't wanted to hear those words. She just wanted them to be separate so she could just break off, like she'd read California might do some day. She could picture herself as the *H* in the Hollywood sign, floating in the Pacific Ocean, not a worry in the world.

Her mother got up off the couch. "You can fight who you are all you want to Ruby. You can try, believe me. But in the end, you are my child. And you and I, Ruby, we aren't like all the rest of them. We're not going to settle for lives like the rest of them." For all that talk, she'd always encouraged Ruby to become an accountant, something secure and stable. How much more like the rest of them could she possibly be?

But this was nice, this sharing she was doing in this charming shop, with its buzzing stained-glass lamps sitting on elegantly worn bureaus, hand knotted blankets poking out over the drawers.

Merry went over to her friend and put a hand to her arm, rubbed up and down and up and down. "Aw, Selma."

Her own eye was tearing now.

Selma was stroking Ruby's Bravery piece. She felt the smaller medallion's smooth surface, just the way Ruby did when she wore it herself.

Looking around the store now, in light of what she'd just learned about Selma, everything looked different. When you knew the filter all of these selections had passed through, it gave them a new significance, a unique luster that you didn't see every day. The huge pink peonies, weeping over the blue glass vase spoke to you intimately. The old wine crates, with their foreign writing had mystical qualities, they said to Ruby that in your mind you can travel wherever you like. This store, it was obvious now, *was* its owner.

"You've got talent Ruby. It's got to come from somewhere," Selma said. And now that meant something real to Ruby. It didn't just pass over her like most compliments did. It seemed a tangible thing—a compliment from this woman who wasn't afraid to be who she was. "Maybe Jack here has inspired you. You've really come a long way from these earlier pieces in your book."

Jack liked the idea of that. Ruby saw what it meant to him. She said, "Jack is a w-wonderful man. He's changing my life here, that's what he's doing." Her stupid problem had evoked so much just then. She saw something like power in it. What a strange idea! The weakness she devoted her life to painting over in broad, black strokes was accomplishing something for these four people. It had a purpose. And it was quite clear that something profound had happened here—between the group.

"She's a great student," Jack said. "A great student." He reached for a handkerchief in his pocket and handed it to Ruby, and she thought her heart would bust.

By the time Ruby and Jack zipped up, replaced their gloves and hats to leave, they were hugging good-bye—old friends who didn't want to part ways. Merry and Selma ordered ten pieces total. The four of them had lunch plans for the day after tomorrow.

Two days later, Ruby and Jack met Selma and Merry for lunch at a spot called Hot Tomatoes. Everywhere you looked there were pictures of tomatoes—a Rodin statue holding up a tomato, a pop art tomato soup can, a tomato husband and wife.

"How'd your daughter like that bracelet?" Selma asked Jack when they'd all ordered.

"Oh, she didn't say," he said.

"Well, did she get it?" Merry asked. "Because you can track that kind of thing nowadays."

"Oh, she got it." Jack sipped at his Coke through a straw. "She's just busy, you know. She's an actress . . . in Hollywood." He sat up straight. He was too proud to say anything might be wrong.

But you could get it out of him. "Wow," Selma said. "That's exciting, isn't it? What's she been in?"

"Right now, she's in a commercial for those socks you heat up in the microwave to help with muscle aches."

"Oh, you mean Hot Socks?" Merry asked. She yanked up the sleeve of her green sweater.

"That's it! Hot Socks. Yes, exactly."

"Just . . . heat up your Hot Socks!" they both sang in unison and set the group giggling.

"That's some dinner conversation," Ruby said. She looked around, took in the manner and dress of the neighboring diners, mostly in suits with ties, briefcases resting at the foot of the table. It was an old New York habit—people watching—and a way to blend into her environment, feel a part of it all. She'd just had her hair trimmed, with some shorter layers cut in around her face and it had given her a boost while she dressed in a pale purple blouse and jeans for lunch.

"Well, it is lunch," offered Merry.

"Right." Ruby rolled her eyes at herself.

"Ruby, how's the driving going?" Merry asked.

"You know, it's actually going really well," Ruby said. "I pretty much drive everywhere now. I'm pretty much over it. In fact, I've already driven to Brooklyn and Manhattan a bunch of times."

Everyone's eyes grew wide as they took in what she'd said.

"Really?" Selma asked her. "I, myself, have never done it! I always take the train."

"She's got it all down," Jack said. He patted her shoulder and looked her hard in the eye. "This woman, she can do anything she puts her mind to."

"That's nice of you, Jack," Ruby said. She tried to be nonchalant. She tried not to grab onto him and hug him until his ribs compacted. That look, it was the kind of thing she'd stayed up nights dreaming of. And here it was—meant just for her.

"It's not nice. It's true!"

They all turned to the waitress, who was balancing all four plates beautifully.

"All right: mozzarella and tomato sandwich! Fusilli with sun-dried tomatoes! Tomato and artichoke salad! Eggplant parm!"

"That woman's got a lot of energy," Ruby said. There was a freedom in being yourself. It was much easier than keeping tabs on your revelations, planning your words. It was you, but better. And here she was, doing just that.

"So, Ruby, those two necklaces you brought me sold out.

Everyone loved them. I can't wait to get the others in. I was thinking, with the holidays and everything, why don't you double my order?" Selma said.

"Double? Are you sure?" Ruby asked.

"You really are the worst salesperson in the world," Merry said.

They all got a kick out of that. Because they were starting to
know her. And they knew it was true. Ruby shrugged.

"I think it's her best quality," Selma said.

"I personally like the 'fear of driving' the best. I wanted to know
you right away that day when I saw you almost getting arrested,"
Merry said.

Ruby stabbed at a grape tomato half, unsure. She liked what she
was hearing. She found it hard to believe, still she really liked it. And
beyond that, she liked who she *was* just then. "Oh yeah, that's my favorite part," Ruby said, rolling her eyes. But it had been a turning
point, hadn't it?

"Well, if it wasn't for that," Jack said. He didn't have to finish.
Ruby knew what he meant. And so did Selma and Merry. They
shook heads in agreement, a breathy sigh shared between them.

"So what's up with your daughter, Jack?" Merry pushed after a
couple of minutes.

He put his sandwich down—just the corner, which apparently
he didn't feel like eating. "Well, Merry, when my wife passed on
three years ago my son and daughter moved out to California."

"That sucks," Merry said.

Jack laughed an unfunny laugh. "It does suck, Merry. But you
know what? They were gone long before that. You just don't get a
lot of respect for being a driving teacher."

"But that's crazy!" Ruby said it too loud. She lowered her voice
and cleared her throat before continuing. "I mean, you really help
people! How could anyone not respect that?" Ruby would have
given the world for Jack to be her father, to know that her father was
such a wonderful man.

"Well, there's more to it. I couldn't afford to send them to college."

"There are scholarships for that!" Merry seemed personally offended. She let her fork fall with a klink. She needed her hands to emphasize her point.

"And they didn't ever have nice clothes. Or a car to drive to school."

"Lots of kids don't have that!" Ruby was horrified to recognize the pain with which Jack was delivering this information.

"My wife tried to tell me." Still he defended his children, tried to do the right thing. "She told me many times. But I just wouldn't listen." He shook his head, like he'd take it all back if he could.

She didn't even want that daughter wearing her bracelet! In the world of deserving and undeserving, where was the balance? How did this girl retain that kind of attention, after so many years, after so clearly showing her disinterest in Jack? You could lose days, weeks thinking such thoughts. She knew this firsthand.

"The weird thing is," Jack said, leaning back against the booth, "When my wife died, I got this huge life insurance policy settlement. She'd have loved the life I have now."

"Life is back-ass like that sometimes," Merry said. And then she said just what Ruby had been thinking. "You know, I'm really glad we met you both. I'm really glad."

Ruby was caught up in the emotions, in the closeness—that tangible feeling she was always in search of. She got carried away in the moment. And then Ruby did something very uncharacteristic. She put her own arm around Jack, and gave him a squeeze.

Fifteen

Conflicts from other areas of our lives distract us while driving, such as: family issues, marital problems, resentments from the job, difficulties with authority, and feeling controlled by others.

—Connecticut Department of Motor Vehicles Driver's Manual

Ruby's mom was going to Florida for Christmas. She didn't like the way Christmas had become the official American December holiday. She was Jewish. "We're a nomadic people, Ruby Booby," she liked to say. More than once her momma had compared herself to Deborah, arguably the strongest woman in the Old Testament, leading Ruby on to battle, with never-ending strength. But who had they been fighting? And what for?

At Christmastime, their battle became clear enough: Santa was evil. So was the color red, the color green, and anything with silver stars. There was no such thing as a Chanukah bush, a Chanukah Harry, and don't even get her started with the spelling "Hannukah," which was completely blasphemous, Americanized bullshit, as far as she was concerned. She became outraged at the sales and claimed she'd prefer to pay full price; she despised the commercials, the music, and once was taken away in a squad car because she'd tossed a can of pumpkin into a holly-ringed candy cane display at the supermarket.

★ ★ ★

But Ruby hated to pull the window shade slats apart and see the distrusting faces of the carolers when her mother didn't answer the door. She'd have loved to get into the holiday spirit, let the harmonious voices commingle in her face, even if the group were dressed in Bermuda shorts and tank tops.

In Florida, Ruby's momma liked to act like it was any other day of the year. The absence of snow, she felt, made this an easier task. They'd wake up on Christmas Day and drive around and her momma would always say the same thing. "I just don't understand why everything's closed," she'd say.

Ruby thought of her today, driving Louis around, saying the same thing. In comparison, Ruby looked around her own apartment and felt proud. This year, she was celebrating the part of her that wasn't a nomadic people, whoever the father she'd inherited that from might be. This year, she'd gone to all the shops carrying seasonal goods and stocked up. She'd purchased jingle bell doorknob covers and a berry-branch garland, and cinnamon scented candles. There was a pine wreath on their front door and a ten foot tree in their living room. Ed taught her how to pinch and toss the sparkly, weightless silver tinsel up and over the branches so the strands looked like snow, delicately shimmering in the light. They strung lights and tried not to worry about the lead poisoning warning on the box. They drank egg nog and officially decided they didn't care for it. There was Christmas music on the radio, and that got them festive. Because she got caught up in the mood, Ruby wound up giving her gift to Ed early.

While it wasn't the truth—wrapped up in a beautiful bow and tucked inside the envelope—it was something that indicated a future, something that she could look at and say, hey look, we'll be together long enough to do this. She'd considered matching denture travel cases, sterling silver hearing aids, a lifetime supply of extra large cotton briefs, but none of those seemed exactly right.

She passed him the envelope while John Lennon sang, "Happy Christmas, War is Over."

"Now are you *sure* you want me to open this up early?" He was dangling it back and forth like a ringing bell.

Ruby grabbed for it. "Nah, nevermind." She sat on it so he couldn't take it back.

"What?" Ed stared at her, bug-eyed. "Are you serious?" he asked, puffing his bottom lip out in a pout.

She stared him down, her eyes slits. "Nah," she finally said. "I'm just kidding." Ruby made a show of lifting her butt up on one side, pulling out the envelope, and holding it out to him.

Ed swiped it, shaking his head at her. This time he ripped into the envelope before she could react. His eyes traveled over the lines of text on the small paper.

It was a gift certificate to the Captain's Inn in Kennebunkport, Maine. The reservation was for June. On the enclosed postcard, the room they'd be staying in was pictured. It was called "Cactus," and was papered in buttery yellow and white stripes. A huge gilt frame showcased a painting of birds on a few flowering branches. A fireplace glowed red in the foreground.

"That's an awesome gift," he said softly, pulling her face toward his. "So thoughtful."

"Yeah, well, that's the kind of gal I am," Ruby said. But how much of the gift was a test for herself? A test that she'd tell him by the time they went to the inn? "So can I have mine?" She smiled, trying.

"Nope."

Thankfully, waiting was something she was getting good at.

Christmas morning, though, seemed to speed toward them. They barely left a square inch of tree empty. The next morning they hit the mall. Even at 9 a.m. the parking lot was jammed. As she approached the doorway, the familiar Salvation Army bell sang out—*ding, dong, ding, dong*—and Ruby dropped a dollar into the red bucket.

She did it to be charitable, but also because her momma was against the Salvation Army altogether, as it was founded by a

Methodist minister as an evangelical group with a mission to convert "unchurched" people. Ruby had tried to tell her mother the group now reached out to AIDS victims, the homeless, and battered women, but she said, "So do plenty of other people."

If Ruby sat around counting the chips on her mother's shoulders, she'd have enough for dozens of chocolate chip cookies.

"Merry Christmas," the Salvation Army soldier offered. He didn't look like an anti-Semite to her.

"I love those guys," Ed said. "It just feels like Christmas when you see them."

He pulled out two singles and said, "I see your dollar and raise you a dollar."

She shook her head in mock irritation and pushed the door to the vestibule open with both hands. She shooed Ed through in a grand gesture.

Once through the second set of doors, they were two of millions holding onto their bundled coats, overheating and getting itchy under all that winter wool, or so it seemed, the mall bursting out of its steel and neon seams. Sale signs smacked them every which way and Ruby felt melancholy for Fifth Avenue at this time of year—the scent of honey-roasted peanuts, and a hot coffee in her mittened hands. She missed the street performers at their peak season, their money plates overflowing with crumpled dollars and silver change. She felt the loss of the biggest snowfalls, when Central Park was a new, wondrous place with everything hidden under white, crunching snow and the attention-starved dusted off their skis for a cross-country run from Eighty-sixth Street down to Sixtieth.

But she felt, even as they turned into a record store to browse through the CDs, that if she'd made it in New York, New York, she could make it anywhere. The trick was to believe that.

Back in the corridor, the mall music was turned up a few notches, everywhere Ruby turned she was faced with prehistoric-size silver bells and sleighs dangling. Santa was on the lower level at Nord-strom's children's department, or so said a giant poster featuring Santa and two of his elves, children on either knee.

Ruby had picked out the retro red sweater set with the holly sprig at the right shoulder because it was festive. She'd always liked the way women looked festively dressed for Christmas. She chose a plaid wool pencil skirt and kitten heels to match. She was on the fence about the brooch—a set of jingle bells that ding-donged whenever you moved. She told herself she was in a hokey phase and this was her final exam.

"Ooooh!" Ed cooed behind her in the full-length. "Festive!" She turned around to face him standing alongside their unmade bed. He was wearing jeans and a faded T-shirt with the words "Yeah, right" over his chest.

"You mean you don't wear red or green on Christmas?"

"No, not since I was five," he deadpanned.

"Oh, this is all wrong, isn't it?" Ruby surprised herself with tears. Why was she crying over her outfit? So what if she looked like her fourth-grade school librarian?

"Rube! You look beautiful! I think it's adorable that you want to get into the spirit of the holiday. Please don't change."

"But I look like a giant ornament compared to you!"

"Okay, how about I wear a red button-down?"

"Would you?" She thought that would work.

"Sure!" He tossed his shirt on the floor, next to two other shirts, a pair of khakis he'd worn to work the previous day, and two pairs of white briefs—one lying perfectly flat as if someone had pulled the corners taut and the other crumpled into a puffy lump.

Ed disappeared inside the large walk-in closet all these new apart-ments came with. She could hear him slide his own hangers along the plastic-coated wire rod, atop which he'd allowed his piles of sweaters, T-shirts, and workout pants to degenerate into a population of semi-folded, classless clothes that didn't care a bit if shirts hung out with pants and vice versa.

When he emerged, he was wearing the red shirt, unbuttoned, and nothing else. She tried not to think that his collar was badly in need of ironing. He scooped Ruby up and onto the bed like a pile of freshly cleaned towels. Tenderly, they made love like two sexed-up Christmas ornaments. He wore the shirt the whole time. Ed kept ringing her bell pin and saying, "Oh, I'm gonna ring your bell all right . . ."

Ruby's hair was rumpled on the left side. But she didn't mind it all that much. It wasn't that kind of day. She felt something and dared to think that possibly this feeling could be happiness.

On the drive over to Ed's parents' house, Ed played Christmas music on the car radio. *Santa Baby* . . . It was freezing, cold air seeping through the poorly sealed window edges. They both shivered in surprised, violent bouts every few moments.

"What do you normally do on Christmas?" Ed wanted to know at a red light, in front of a giant lumber shop where long wood boards, as high as their second floor apartment, leaned against the place haphazardly.

Scurry down the chimney tonight.

Ed had spoken with Ruby's mother twice, in quick, contained circumstances where Ruby could monitor her momma to whatever degree she could be monitored. Where her momma was concerned, Ruby had enforced a strict don't ask/don't tell policy. You're not just gaining a wife, you know . . . she figured the less he knew, the better.

The one memory that sprung to mind wasn't the kind she felt like sharing: last year, in a swell of hope that somehow things might be different, Ruby had accompanied her momma to Florida for the holidays. She'd managed a few years off from making the trip, using her part-time job and then her full-time one as an excuse, but she'd always been a glutton for punishment where her momma was concerned, so she accepted the invitation.

Dina thought it was funny, how Ruby felt about her momma and that yet, now faced with the choice of freedom, she ran back all the same. "Maybe there's just something chemical about mothers and daughters," Dina said. Her own mother drove her nuts; she often said she felt like a foreign movie her parents watched without the subtitles. She could do a great impression. "Al, could you pass me the popcorn?" she'd yell. "I think the girl is excited about something . . . or it could just be gas."

Ruby didn't think her momma misunderstood her as much as misused her, unapologetically filled her with fears and hang-ups, robbed her of the possibility of happiness over and over and over again.

All the same, she'd gone to Boca, where the Christmas Eve drive of outrage was as depressing as ever. Worse, her mother was getting old but hadn't realized. So, when she was flirty with waiters and hosts, snapping horrifying come-ons like, "Sure, I'd like a cherry on you, I mean that, doll," they would be repulsed instead of responsive like they'd been all through Ruby's mortifying childhood. This forced Ruby to feel bad for her mother, and she wasn't sure which scenario was worse.

At a southwestern restaurant called Cattle Rancho they'd eaten at the day after Christmas, Ruby'd acted like she had to go to the bathroom. But instead of turning left to the restroom hallway, she'd turned right to where the coffee pots and soda fountains were kept and sought out the slim, blond waiter with his condescending air. She tapped him on the shoulder of his denim shirt and he turned, his steel-tip cowboy boots poking toward her. Now she'd got him she saw it had been a mistake, it wasn't this smug college kid whose opinion bothered her; it was her own. All the same she was there, so she said it. "My mother is a beautiful woman, you know." She hadn't known what else to say and so she'd come out with something she'd heard her momma say often. "When she was in college the men lined up, I'm telling you." She hadn't recognized her own voice.

"Oh, that's wonderful," was all the guy said, offering a dazzling smile that made Ruby want to scream.

"Oh, we went to Florida. My mother is always in Florida at Christmas." She said this to Ed by way of a safe response, looking toward the Wal-Mart, the Home Depot, Circuit City, so he might not notice her tone.

"Yeah, but what did you guys *do* there?"

They turned off the main drag onto a residential street, where wire Christmas trees were strung over the streets from telephone polls.

"You know," she said for lack of anything better.

But he didn't know. That was becoming increasingly clear. And pretty soon he'd stop asking. And what kind of place would Ruby be in then?

She'd seen Ed's family pretty regularly since she moved to Middleville. They liked to stage gatherings for birthdays or Arbor Days or Sundays. She liked them but often felt like a half-woman, half-snake circus freak in their presence. They smiled too much. They didn't like to complain or talk about other family members behind their backs. It was a take on family that she wasn't intimately acquainted with. And though it was the kind of thing she'd always thought she wanted, now she was here, Ruby didn't know her role, wasn't sure of the pacing, the modes of communication. Though she was right there with them all, she didn't feel like the family was hers; she felt lonely, as if she weren't a part of things at all.

The dinner was nearly ready when they arrived, a turkey scenting the whole house.

"Hello!" Suzanne and Randolph Robbins sang, coming to the door with smiles, the way, Ruby assumed, normal people did on the holidays, when they were concentrating on enjoying what they had, rather than running from it. Suzanne wore one of her signature aprons, a dainty ruffle scalloped along the edge, and Randolph had a spot of gravy on his pink shirt sleeve. Sure, she knew that pink spotted shirts and smiles didn't necessarily mean someone had a perfect life, but those who couldn't lay claim to such things, she was pretty sure they were at a loss somehow.

Could it be that not only had she missed out all along, but, that once given the chance, Ruby wouldn't be able to embrace a normal life ever? Was she spoiled goods that had come so far only to turn around and drive back? Like mother, like daughter, she couldn't help but think.

Ed and Ruby were put to work chopping vegetables for a salad at the kitchen island, in front of a giant cutting block and two sharpened chef's knives. Inside a Polish pottery bowl, painted with tiny yellow flowers on a blue background, there sat a tomato, giant green pepper, medium-sized cucumber, and a couple of bright celery stalks. Alongside, a fresh romaine lettuce flowered around a red rubber band.

"I thought this was my day off, Mom," Ed joked, tossing the tomato and pepper in the air, juggler style.

Feeling frisky from the impromptu sex and the excitement of a first Christmas, they kept nudging hips into each other, wiggling their feet together, palming the other's back.

"You guys are disgusting," Ed's brother, Stephen, said when he arrived, walking directly to the kitchen with his coat still on.

"And a merry Christmas to you," Ed replied. They accomplished an intricate handshake. Stephen kissed Ruby lightly on the cheek. "Shabbat Shalom," he said, bowing his head slowly.

"Baruch attah addonoi," Ruby replied. It was the only Hebrew she knew—the first words of nearly every prayer.

"Whatever, dude," Stephen said, winking.

Ann was Stephen's wife—a blonde with a very short haircut and a soft brow—and she came in after him, carrying two black garbage bags bulging with gifts.

"I like the separation of power in your family," Ed said.

"Merry Christmas," Ann sang, breathy from carrying the gifts in, rolling her eyes at her husband.

Ed's sister, Caroline, was the last to arrive. Her two boys were ages three and five. They spent most of the dinner under the table. After dinner, there were a lot of grounding traditions: stringing cranberries, opening gifts, frosting cakes. The boys stayed under there through most of the traditions, sometimes poking a head or stockinged foot out from beneath the white cloth.

During the cake frosting, Suzanne snuck sips of her chardonnay as if she were cheating on a test. She glided behind Ruby in her pink wool suit, gently touched her arm and then reached for a knife and a rubber scraper. Her cheeks were growing flushed.

This, Ruby thought, is Christmas. Then why did she keep picturing her momma, growing more and more irritated with Louis, her voice rising until finally she closed herself off and decided she was better off talking to no one at all? Ruby thought maybe it was the wine she herself had drunk, and so she slid her glass over to the far side of the island, out of her reach. Her momma's idea of a Chanukah gift was a joke—she chose books she'd enjoyed and tied them with some utility twine, not bothering to straighten out their used paper covers or to gift wrap them. Sure, Ruby had enjoyed the books well enough, but did everything she ever got have to be stamped with its cheapness right there on the top?

Ruby straightened her skirt with self-consciousness. Yes, maybe it did. Maybe, it did.

The cake was a Harvey Wallbanger and the frosting and spongy cake inside were green as a pistachio nut. Caroline's youngest boy, Alec, took a huge bite that left some frosting at the tip of his nose. Ruby laughed along with the other Robbins, enjoying the innocent humor of it, but something was missing. This was all too obvious now. After dessert, Ruby helped Suzanne wash up the Christmas china, shine up its border of shiny ornaments strung on garland.

Ruby was quiet when she felt Suzanne's eye on her face.

"I saw you with Alec. You're really good with kids. A natural."

Was she? "You think so?" The idea of having her own child shocked her. She thought of her legacy and feared what kind of a mother she'd be. She thought of that phrase for the second time of the day: *like mother, like daughter.* But hadn't she daydreamed about that very thing as a young child—dreamed of pushing her little girl on a swing, in back of a pretty white house not unlike this one? Hadn't she made lists of the nice things she'd tell her daughter to ensure her confidence, so that she'd know how beautiful and special she was? Where had the father been in those daydreams? Why hadn't she dreamed him into the fairy tale? Likely because she didn't know where he would fit, how a man could work into the in and out of every day. Sure, he could be off to the side in the dreams, fixing a car or mowing a lawn, but that was as far as her mind could travel. Whenever he tried to come under the table in a light storm, she'd always pushed him out.

"Maybe we'll have another place at our holiday table next year," Suzanne pressed on.

"We'll see," was all she said, gently laying the last dessert plate atop the rest. Still, the possibilities were so vivid there, under the soft light at the sink, drying to a shine the happy plates with their dreamy Christmas trees and angels and stacks of presents. Maybe there was a route from here to her dreams, a path that led under the table and inside her heart. And perhaps she was closer than she thought.

Next it was time for presents. Each family member took turns opening one gift, Randolph explained. First Ed opened one and then Ruby and then Stephen, and so on, until there was so much crumpled paper the room looked like the inside of a giant packing box. In the end, Ruby awkwardly, carefully slid open the paper wrapping on a gift certificate to Barnes and Noble, and a cookbook: *A Year of Chicken.* "Just what I wanted," Ruby tried to smile big, to show her thanks. She was always concerned with the conveyance of sincerity.

"Ed said you like to make chicken," his sister said about the cookbook.

"Finger lickin' good," Ed cackled.

For the first time she felt comfortable enough here to be herself. "The truth is, that's the only thing I know how to make." She shrugged, realizing how little she'd hesitated, how easy the words had sprung out after all.

Stephen said, "That's okay. When we got married, Ann only knew how to make hotdogs. But now things are much better, she can make burgers, too."

Ann shot him a look and then they both laughed—the little things that they knew about each other alive and jumping around them like the lights they'd just strung on the tree.

"Stephen only knew how to make a mess. But now . . ." She scratched her head with a finger like she'd just realized something. "Oh yeah, there's no 'but now.' He still only knows how to make a mess."

"Ha ha!" said Stephen. But it was too late, they all had a story about Stephen's messes.

"When Stephen was younger," Suzanne began, "I once thought he ran away because I couldn't find him with the clothes lying all over his room. He was right there under his blanket the whole entire time!"

"So that's where Ed gets it from," Ruby said.

"Yeah, see, I'm not the only one," Stephen defended himself. "Maybe it's really Mom who's at fault, since the both of us are such pigs."

"Well, I'm not a pig," Caroline chimed in.

"So how come I heard you oinking when you first came in?" Ed said.

She tossed a ball of gift wrap at him.

"Now children, settle down," Randolph said.

"Yeah, settle down," Ed told Caroline.

It wasn't difficult to picture them all twenty years younger, getting riled up in the backyard on a summer day, playing roles much like the ones they did now. She looked around the living room they sat in, Ed next to her on the smaller love seat, Stephen at Ann's feet by the recliner, and Caroline with the two kids next to Mr. and Mrs. Robbins. Judging by the flowered wallpaper and the gilded end tables, it didn't look like the place had changed much in years. With all of that steady security, Ruby wondered what it was Ed was looking for in her.

When it was time to go home, and they held shopping bags of gifts and leftovers in their hands, Ruby had the urge to pronounce, "I'll drive home."

"I'd be honored, little lady." Ed was John Wayne again and Ruby shook her head at the wonderful familiarity of that.

He reached in his pocket and held out a small box with a silver bow tied over the top. "You didn't think I forgot, did you?"

She smiled, reaching out for the box. She pulled at the bow and it came undone. She lifted the tiny lid, gently moved aside the tissue paper. And there, on a fluff of cotton, were two beautiful diamond earrings.

"They're for our wedding day," Ed said. "You'll have to save them for our wedding day."

"How will I wait?" she asked.

"All the best things in life are worth waiting for," he said softly, his tone pointed.

Ruby flushed.

He kissed her deeply, passionately.

"Now are you going to take me home or what?" he said, squeezing her hand.

"You've got a deal," she said.

The highway was empty, like an alien had zoomed by and sucked up all the cars. She drove close to the jersey barrier to show herself she wasn't afraid. Ed lounged back, going over the night in the John

Wayne voice. "It sucked that Caroline's husband had to work. I think she was pretty upset about it," Ed said.

"What does he do again?" she asked.

"News production for channel 8. He's always working holidays."

"That really is hard," she said. "Holidays are about being with your family," Ruby said, though hers was miles away—her momma in Florida and her father God knows where.

It was exactly then, with their turnoff just a few feet ahead, that Ruby was struck with a thought, like a bolt of lightening. Why couldn't she hire a professional—a private investigator—to find her father? She'd hired a professional to teach her to drive and that had worked well enough.

The idea fizzled through her, brought brand-new hope to the old wound. The street reflectors, the swishing trees, they all looked different now, they looked bright with potential. They seemed to echo her excitement, this new loophole she'd not yet explored, this new view of things that could just be the very thing she'd hoped for. She could find one of these great Dick Tracy types who would really throw his heart into the job, call her at odd hours with leads and such.

"You're an excellent driver, little lady," Ed said as she turned off onto their street. "It must be in your blood."

Well, it was on the one side. But what about the other side? She was going to find out. She was definitely going to try to find out.

Sixteen

If you do not have emergency flares or other warning devices, stand by the side of the road where you are safe from traffic and wave traffic around your vehicle. Use a white cloth if you have one.

—Connecticut Department of Motor Vehicles Driver's Manual

The week after Christmas crawled along at a slow pace with nowhere to be and nothing on the agenda. Dina was with her family on Long Island. Ruby knew her friend considered that the last stop before hell. But Dina had a funny way of liking Long Island without wanting to. She had a favorite pizza parlor and a favorite stop for super egg bagels. She liked to watch the sunset at a certain strip of beach and despite jabs at each of them, frequented the same old parking lots and bars where she knew she'd run into her former classmates.

"Merry Christmas, bitch," she said via telephone on Christmas morning.

"Right back atcha," Ruby said.

"I got a cookbook!" Dina complained. "You think they're trying to tell me something?" She loved to be outraged at the intention of gifts.

"I got a cookbook, too," Ruby tried. Ed was in the shower, but that's not why she didn't complain. She didn't mind the cookbook. She'd been leafing through it, getting excited about béchamel sauce and buttermilk gravy.

"What kind is yours?" Dina asked. "Mine's French."

"Mine's chicken."

"Chicken? Who wants to know how to make chicken? That's like the only thing everyone *knows* how to make."

"Do you?"

"No. But, jeez. If you weren't my stupid lesbian lover at that wedding you'd be right here with me and maybe you could have taught me. Would it help if I told you that Ed was wanted in four states?"

"Nah." Ruby was looking at a fresh dropping of Ed's little bunny socks. This time, their message didn't go unheard. She heard what they said loud and clear: you'd better share *your* problems now, they said. And they had a kind of nasty tone. When she snapped back to the conversation she wondered, would she be with Dina if she wasn't here with Ed? Or would she have gotten sucked into going with her momma to Florida—creeping back to that one person she seemed to both hate and still manage to think about more than anyone else in the entire world?

"Great. I've lost another one folks." She had a bitter tone. Ruby imagined her addressing her childhood unicorn collection and garish Formica furnishings the way she'd seen her do before. "Being alone bites." Dina rarely complained. It was strange to hear the words in her voice. Sure, she ripped her dates apart and grew irate, but she never got into her feelings. "You don't know what you have, Ruby." She sounded incredibly melancholy. There seemed to be something else in her voice, something Ruby couldn't place.

Ruby wanted to console her friend, find out what was really going on. But you couldn't push with Dina. She never responded to that. "Yeah, well, nothing's as perfect as it looks, you know that Dina . . ." With Ed in the apartment, she couldn't say anything about the secret, that she was going to hire a private eye. She'd longed to get Dina's input on it, to see what she thought of the idea. But she hadn't gotten a chance to be alone since Ed came home from work that last day before the holiday.

"Well, don't screw it up, Ruby. I don't want you spending next Christmas with me on Planet Long Island with the unicorns."

Holidays were the worst when you were alone. Ruby could re-member before she'd met Dina, going to Macy's in Herald Square and crying into a grand display of men's red sweaters. Her mother had been in Florida hating everything with Ricardo, the bookshop keeper. She hadn't gotten a Chanukah card from anyone and she was already feeling like she should leave New York City, though she'd sworn up and down she never would.

She hadn't made any friends and the only thing she had going for her was the ton of jewelry she was churning out as a result of the pain she was feeling—long days with her torch and the delicate blade of her jeweler's saw, turning sheets of metal into the shapes of endangered animals: the slender Vicuña—the smallest member of the camel family—with its sad eyes and pointed ears, the knowing look of the Red Wolf, its leathery black nose and striped fur and de-fensive stance. She'd come across them in a used book at the giant Strand bookstore's sale table. Ruby was immediately taken by their devastating plights—rich Spaniards shot the animals dead for coats—and found solace in saving them this way. She'd donated a portion of the proceeds to the National Wildlife Fund and though the pieces were only sold at one shop, the press ate it all up, shooting up her popularity for the very first time, and bringing in orders from across the country, even internationally.

They were tiny, fragile things that looked drippy and melancholy—she was using lots of old pieces from antiques fairs, things people had cast off, to dangle from the animals, drape over their elegant necks, to give them this new identity. She thought she understood about becoming extinct, the end of a species, to have your well-being stolen from your hands.

She had just broken things off with Eric the law student for no good reason at all. They'd met in a local dive bar that Ruby liked because they played old Bruce Springsteen songs on the jukebox. She'd been drinking a Michelob because it was on sale for two dollars, and it was the last two dollars she had, as the profits she'd made so far were slower to come in than she'd expected, and when they arrived it was necessary to reinvest in producing more pieces for incoming orders. She'd been sitting there, with a magazine in front of her, opened to an article called "What Men *Really* Want," to cloak her from the obviousness of being alone. It wasn't quite cold yet, and she was wearing a fitted T-shirt and old jeans with flat sandals, one of her Endangered designs around her neck, the Ivory-Billed Woodpecker, with its extraordinary, long, narrow beak and angled head crests.

"Hey, you know, I've always been wanting to know that myself . . . what *do* men really want?"

She'd looked up, suspicious of the type of guy who'd look over her shoulder and try something like that and pull it off. As expected, he was gorgeous—crystal blue eyes, dark hair, muscular in a lean way—almost too gorgeous. They'd spent the whole night drinking Michelobs, and then the night after that. On the third night, when he walked her home, she let him up, and then he'd come there every night. One day, Ruby thought she saw something detached in his face when he said, "Should we order a pizza?" and when he called the next day she simply didn't answer. Eventually he'd gotten the hint.

She'd hated herself in Macy's Herald Square that day because she knew that if she hadn't been so afraid she might have just asked, "Hey, is something bothering you?" And then he could have said, "You know, yes. I had a really bad torts class today. I was called on and completely fumbled it," and then they would've enjoyed the pizza and she'd be spending Christmas with him instead of among the men's sweaters at Macy's.

Ruby wasn't sure if Dina's sadness was something like that, or if there was more to it. Either way, Dina had pulled her up more than once, and she was going to return the favor.

"Well, you know I wouldn't mind coming out there in a couple of days. I always liked unicorns." She'd been to Dina's parents' home plenty of times. Their house was a jumbo split-level stuck in the eighties. Dina went nuts about the clutter, the half-empty bottles of shampoo all over the tub rim. She complained about the mildew in the basement and the off-brand cheese. But Ruby liked the worn, lived-in look of the place. The steady, consistent pace of Dina's parents, Al and Trudy, was exactly to Ruby's taste. When she walked up the faded blacktop driveway, *she* even got the feeling she was coming home.

"Yeah, well no wonder your line is getting panned. There's no accounting for taste."

"Ha ha. Very funny." Ruby knew Dina only tossed out lines that good when she was really upset about something.

"All right, yeah. Do that. When will you come, Mario Andretti?"

"I'll come out on Thursday, when Ed goes back to work. Hey, do you think your mom can make those brownies?" They were Ruby's favorite—just your traditional Duncan Heinz, but with added walnuts and some M&M's sprinkled over the top.

"Whatever, loser," Dina said.

"Love you, too." She made a loud kissing noise and hung up the telephone.

Ed still had two days off after Christmas. Mostly the two of them sat around and watched movies on television, whined over the commercial breaks, and ate too much salt on their popcorn. They also had sex. It was the ideal break from life, its expectations and disappointments, confusions, and distractions. She had thought of the private investigator on a more concrete level, choosing an exact day she would begin her search for one and just exactly what she would say. Ruby decided on the budget she'd allot for the project. She'd done everything short of doing something about it.

On Thursday morning before she headed out to Dina, she sat at her workbench. And with only one broken jeweler's saw blade, which she couldn't find anywhere until she saw it had stuck into the ceiling, she cut a new piece. She hadn't had a specific plan when she started, but the holiday got her fired up. She hadn't wanted to, but she'd pictured Momma driving down Worth Avenue blaspheming anything red or green while Louis asked what they were going to do today; if they could maybe go out to eat. Louis wouldn't understand that *this* is what they were doing today. Ruby decided on a beautiful 18-karat gold, and pulled out a sheet of metal to sculpt the model: a huge palm tree charm and a tiny wreath charm, both of which she'd string on a heavy 1980s-style extended-length chain. She called it "Christmas in Miami."

She rushed through the metal working, trying to get all the details in while she could envision them in her head—the branches of the palm, the ornaments along the wreath. Now her ideas were out, ready to bring to the caster on the way back from Dina's. She'd never trust her designs again to the post office. Ruby smiled at how impossible the idea of the trip had been to her not so long ago, how she'd shuddered at the idea of traveling the highways herself, the impossible distance she'd seen between herself and her destination.

There was one detail between now and then that hadn't changed very much, and that was the fact that she'd not gone to Ed, that she'd not opened up to him and asked for his help. She knew, even as she began this long, champion trip, that she was still in the danger zone as far as her relationship was concerned, that all the pretty invitation fonts in the world weren't enough to fill in the negative spaces she'd left in their relationship. Sure, she'd made their metaphorical sprue, poured the plaster of paris, but she hadn't melted the silver grains, hadn't shot them through the mold that was there, waiting to be filled. But she knew life wasn't as simple as making jewelry. And come to think of it, making jewelry wasn't that simple in the first place; it was laborious, back-breaking work. And with real life being that much more difficult, the fact was, she might not succeed, though to all appearances it looked as if she should. These days, Ruby was learning more and more that nothing in this world was black and white.

The roads to Long Island were empty. There were long stretches when she didn't pass even one car. The temperature was frigid. Even in the car, her breath clouded in the cold. Despite herself, on the long drive, her mind went to the ways she'd often passed time on the road.

"Solitude lies at the lowest depth of the human condition. Man is the only being who feels himself to be alone and the only one who is searching for the Other."   —*Octavio Paz*

"Scared cows make the tastiest hamburger."   —*Abbie Hoffman*

She entertained herself with these bits of wisdom she owned, though she'd always chided this pastime of her momma's. She remembered the story of Bartlett, how he'd always kept notes on his readings. A lifetime book-man, beginning as apprentice and ending as owner, he had indulged in many, and his ownership of information had made him as ubiquitous and useful as silverware.

Her momma loved to tell her that story, and Ruby wondered what she'd have to do to make *herself* useful, if the secret message was that her lack of usefulness had been the reason she'd failed at becoming ubiquitous, becoming anyone but her momma's daughter. And also she wondered, was this a warning? If she ceased to be useful to her momma, a person to comb the knots from her hair at night, rub her palms over her shoulders after a long drive, laugh at her jokes, would she eventually be left by her, too? Why should she care? Ruby didn't have the answer to why, but the painful truth remained: she did care, despite the very great price, she couldn't help but care.

"'In the future,'" Ruby said aloud to the humming heater,

" 'Everyone will be world-famous for fifteen minutes.' Andy Warhol." She'd always liked that one, figured that if it was true, she'd have a good chance to be discovered by her father, or, conversely, to discover him.

Within two hours, Ruby was in Massapequa, Long Island, where the frantic streets were white instead of blacktop, and she turned into Al and Trudy's driveway. The deep brown facade of the home, with its row of high hedges sprinkled with festive berries, looked dated next to the lighter gray and white neighboring homes.

"Ruby! Let's see the ring, dear." Trudy embraced her in a gigantic hug and then grabbed for her palm. Her frosted hair was chopped softly at shoulder length and it sprawled down over Ruby's shoulder, soft as silk. "Al!" She yelled up the stairs in her gravelly voice, "Ruby's here with her rock!"

"The game's in the final quarter. Ruby, so glad to see you. I'll be down in half an hour." His voice traveled warmly down the stairs.

Trudy shook her head with a knowing smile. "Forget him," she said.

"Don't I get a hug? She's *my* friend, you know," Dina said coming in from the living room.

Hugging Dina felt wonderful. She'd just washed her hair and it was still damp. There were moist circles from where the ends had brushed at the shoulders of her high school T-shirt. Dina always wore that here. Every graduate of Massapequa High School 1994 had signed it. "I'm so proud of you for driving here," she said when they'd pulled apart, making their way into the kitchen. Ruby pulled a worn seat up to the big wooden table and rested her elbows on the checked rubber placemat in front of her. "Ah, you know," Ruby joked.

"Ruby that is quite an accomplishment—driving, marriage, moving out to the country. Wow! You girls today . . . you really do have it all. I can't believe how successful the both of you are. Did Dina tell you she got a promotion? She is now officially the director of the dining out editorial pages in *New York Life* magazine . . . the boss of ten writers."

Dina grimaced as she sat next to Ruby.

Ruby nudged Dina. "How come you didn't tell me? That is awesome!" But even as she said it, she could tell Dina was distracted by something else, and it must have been something unbelievably disturbing. Otherwise this promotion would have been a huge, gigantic deal to her. She'd always wanted that spot . . . and here she'd achieved it, at only thirty years old. There had to be something terrible going on for her to react with so little emotion.

The three women had some coffee and brownies and then Al came downstairs. "What a game! Can you believe those Islanders won in triple overtime with a two to one win?"

"Dad, you're the only guy in the entire world who still roots for the Islanders!"

"That's not true. You love them don't you, Ruby?" He kissed her lightly on the cheek and winked their solidarity on this point. He had a generous nose with a flattened tip, and the lines that formed when he smiled just then made him look unbelievably friendly. He grabbed a brownie from the plate and took a huge bite, tumbling crumbs onto the green linoleum floor.

"Jeez the whiz! Use a plate, would you?" Trudy shook her head and interjected, "Nothing changes around here!"

Ruby smiled. That was just why she loved it.

"Oh yeah. I'm a *huge* football fan."

They all laughed comfortably. That was Ruby's role in this family—the "daughter" who was clueless at sports.

"All right, I'm gonna take Ruby up to my room so she can get settled."

Dina's room hadn't changed a bit. It was a capsule of 1994, with hints of her post-Massapequa life sprinkled around. There was a bright pink paddle from her sorority, a luau princess award, pictures of Dina with her college boyfriend, Troy. Ruby thought how appropriate that Troy's picture was last in the row of snapshots, as so many things had stopped at Troy. Dina had thought they'd marry, have two boys and a Suburban, go to soccer practice, and vacation in Aruba, watching the boys from two lounge chairs.

And when Troy left Dina because he wanted to "live a little" before he settled down, Dina left that fairy-tale outlook behind for a cynical bitter one. The fact that she'd never changed her room, though, always struck Ruby. It seemed to her that Dina would take up that old outlook again if she could. The unicorns, the sorority paraphernalia—they wouldn't still be there if Dina had given up entirely on her old self.

Ruby picked up a plush unicorn now. "It's been too long, My Little Pony . . ."

Dina plopped on her bed with a squeak from the old mattress springs and tossed a much larger unicorn at Ruby's butt.

Ruby turned to her friend and saw that she looked just as tired and worn as she'd sounded on the phone. "Are you gonna tell me what's going on, or am I gonna have to beat it out of you with this unicorn's horn?"

Dina looked her square in the eye and said, "You can't beat a pregnant woman. It's dangerous."

It took several seconds for the sense of it to sink in. But when Ruby's eyebrows disappeared up behind her bangs, Dina's expression was confounding. It was as if she was holding back both a smile and tears; like she wasn't sure how to react until she saw Ruby's reaction.

Ruby couldn't help but smile. Sure, she was about to hear a complicated, in all likelihood sad, story. But she knew how Dina felt about children—it was the one and only thing she had never become cynical about. How many times had Ruby caught Dina looking dreamy at a little girl in a booster seat mushing up a buttered roll into a wet paste? "Dina! I think that is wonderful!" She held her friend so tight it hurt.

"Be careful there, would you, Aunt Ruby . . . you don't want to hurt your little niece." The words brought tears to Ruby's own eyes. This here was her family in a funny way, wasn't it? She wouldn't have been capable of such a rush of emotion if it weren't. And she experienced such joy at her "sister's" joy now, she couldn't believe she hadn't put it in those terms before.

She thought of a quotation from Tolstoy's *Anna Karenina*: "Happy families are all alike; every unhappy family is unhappy in its own way." In all likelihood she wouldn't have forged this unique relationship with Dina, this "family" of theirs, had she not experienced all the hurt she had.

Dina began to explain. "Now comes the crappy part. . . . You remember that guy from the building, with the thing?"

"Oh no! He's not the father, is he?"

Dina leaned back against the wall; already she instinctively brought her hand to her belly, rubbed it in gentle circles. "No. Thank God! But after that awful no show date, I went out to MeKong the next night and ordered a *huge* plate of pad thai, which was delicious—as you know. I devoured the entire thing in about ten minutes. And when I looked up, there was this adorable guy. He was a little older, and he was still dressed for work in a suit. 'Boy, you've got some appetite,' he said, just like that. He had a deep Boston accent. And then Jason smiled and his whole face lit up. We drank plum wine for about five hours and then I went back to his apartment!"

"Ooooh!" Ruby interposed. "You did it . . . didn't you?"

Even then, worried as she was, Dina couldn't help the smile from spreading across her entire face.

When she didn't answer, Ruby prodded further. "Tell me! You better tell me!" She giggled with anticipation.

"Yes! I'm a big whore! I slept with him! And it was awesome! Oh my God! I haven't felt like that since . . ."

She didn't have to finish. Her eyes traveled to the picture of Troy—he'd been voted the prince of the luau and there was a laurel around his long, swingy cornsilk curls.

"I can't believe you didn't tell me any of this!" Ruby really was shocked. She usually got the play-by-play—even the details she wouldn't want to hear.

"Well, the thing is, Ruby, it was *so* amazing that I couldn't even believe it. I was afraid to jinx it. I thought if I changed one element—telling you, or going to my apartment instead of his, wearing a different perfume—that the whole thing would be ruined!"

"So, you haven't told him because you don't want anything to change?"

"Bingo! Give the girl a lifetime's supply of Rice-a-Roni!" Now she let out a deep breath and her face turned miserable, reflecting the end to the story; she let her head sink into the pile of pillows against the headboard.

"If things are that good, I'm sure he'll be happy just like you are!"

"But what if he isn't?"

"You can't wait forever, Dina. You're gonna have to tell him at some point. Fathers should know their children." Ruby felt her own friend's pain at her chest. She shook with the full impact of what she'd said. Here was a chance to right that wrong, to come full circle from the father her own mother had pulled her from. And yet, on the other end of it, she could understand Dina's quandary; she'd found with Jason what she'd missed for so long after Troy and now there was the possibility that doing the right thing might cause him to slip between her fingers. She knew Dina well enough to understand she'd rather hold out for the possibility of happiness than have her heart crushed for sure.

Didn't Ruby feel that very same way about Ed? Wasn't she just waiting and waiting to share her deepest, darkest secrets, fearing that when she did he might go running scared? Wasn't she keeping on the very, very back burner the possibility that she might never have to tell him? That if, in the end, she couldn't bring herself to tell him something that might make him leave her, she could pack her things up and go . . . if not to New York, then to somewhere else? Was it possible that we were all more alike than she wanted to admit?

Dina had never gotten over Troy and the bitter disappointment of that. And now she had found someone she could really love, after all this time; of course she was deathly afraid of a repeat ending—not only that she could lose Jason, but that doing so might springboard a lifetime of loneliness because in her mind, no one could ever come close to comparing to him.

She sat down next to Dina and pulled her in close, with an arm over her shoulder. She rubbed tenderly. "I'm here with you, no matter what happens," she said, her own tears falling onto Dina's shoulder. "But I'm learning something now, Dina—you have more control over the way things turn out than you think you do. Despite how it looks, you can have the life you always wanted if you just know how to look for it." She knew it was true. She also knew it was one of life's most difficult challenges.

"When did you get so hopeful?" Dina's tone was sarcastic, but her smile gave her away. "I just hope you're right. I hope you're right. I guess somewhere deep down I know I have to tell him, but I just don't know if I can do it. Not yet anyway."

It occurred to Ruby how useful she could be to her friend without even struggling to be. She could be useful, and somehow, it could be the most natural thing in the world.

They spent all night talking, reminiscing. Together they went over all the possible scenarios of Dina's situation.

The next day at the mall they couldn't help but dive into the more comforting side of the situation: meandering through the tiny outfits, with their smiling dinosaurs and kittens printed on one hundred percent cotton, hung on miniature hangers.

Dina seemed to enjoy plucking through the plush doggies and kitties, handling the new vernacular that would soon become her everyday speak: "Oooh, look at this widdle duckie." Ruby thought she'd outgrown the baby talk, but what she hadn't realized was that everything in life cycled back on you.

With weightless shopping bags at their feet holding the airy baby things, the girls sat in the food court, neon adding a strange tenor to their faces. "Do you think I'll be a good mother?" Dina asked.

Ruby was forking through a particularly greasy bowl of pork fried rice. How had this happened, that the daughters were becoming the mothers? "I know you will be," she said. But how could they know these things? They couldn't. They just had to go along and give it their best shot.

On the way home, she stopped off at Leonard's. Later that afternoon, Ruby drove through the midtown tunnel, barely holding her breath, as she barreled toward Manhattan.

She followed the FDR up to a place where she liked to eat chicken salad sandwiches. Ruby sat in the window with a newspaper, flipping the pages, taking bites of the sandwich. She'd come with the hope she might look at this place differently after what she'd just learned with Dina; she'd hoped that she was freed from her momma's point of view, that now that she was a woman she could have her own, profoundly different perspective. She sat at the big booth eating her chicken salad sandwich, drinking two Cokes. But the only epiphany that came to her was that this sandwich wasn't nearly as good as she'd remembered it.

When she got in the car, turned the key and felt the music vibrate the dashboard, Ruby had a chill at the realization that she felt oddly at home.

Seventeen

On cold, wet days shady spots can be icy. These areas freeze first and dry out last.

On cold, wet days shady spots can be icy. These areas freeze first and dry out last.

—Connecticut Department of Motor Vehicles Driver's Manual

During the snow storms that punctuated the days, Ruby. She side-stepped the real slushy spots, watched for icy patches and—breathy—reached her car. She pushed off snow drifts from the windshield and used the defroster to clear the view ahead and behind. Some days she met Jack. Some days she met Ed's mom, Suzanne, to choose flowers, photographers, or a band. One day they'd gone to the castle to see someone else's wedding reception from afar.

"Plenty of people get married during the week now . . . it's cheaper," the saleswoman had told them when she'd escorted them out to the green where an arch of beautiful flowers was set under a heated tent. Cheaper. This was the way Ruby had once lived. She still half expected Suzanne to mimic her vision of herself, to say, "Oh, well, why don't we switch to a weekday, then?" But she didn't.

Suzanne grabbed her hand when the bride walked down the aisle, all the attendees standing at attention. "You're going to be a beautiful bride," she said. Tenderly, she touched Ruby's red head with her own frosty blond one.

Like that, they watched a couple's life change forever and then they went out for tea and pie down in Middleville's Main Street area, talking seriously of tulle versus silk, hand embroidery, long and short veils. At night, Ruby felt satisfied. She baked cookies while she spoke to Dina on the telephone. She asked every night if Dina had told Jason yet. Finally, one night she had.

"We were at a new restaurant down on Allen Street and Jason was like, 'Would you like a glass of wine?' and I said, 'I can't drink wine.' He looked very confused and then scrunched and then smoothed out in a matter of seconds. And then he felt for my hand over the tiny carafe of olive oil and asked, 'Are you going to have my baby?'"

"What an awesome way to say it!" Ruby's breath had caught in her throat the whole time, but now she could breathe free. There were tears of happiness at her eyes.

"I know it! And so, I answered, 'Yes.'"

"And? Hello, you're killing me!" Ruby could just picture her friend smiling in that way she loved to see her best.

"And he came over to my side of the table, stood me up and spun me around and told me, 'You just made me the happiest guy in the world.' Ruby, if you could have seen the way he looked at me!"

"Woah! This is so exciting!"

"Just wait! Then he took me to Tiffany, picked out a beautiful ring, and asked me to marry him!"

"Oh wow! It's like a movie. It really is. So have you thought at all about what kind of wedding you'll be having?"

"Well, we're just gonna have a small wedding at my parents' place. Family only. And I'd love it if you could be my maid of honor, Rube."

"I'd be honored to return the favor," she'd said, thinking how strange life could turn out, how the most surprising, wonderful things could happen.

The women made plans for Ruby to come into Manhattan, choose bridesmaid dresses together, and have Ruby meet Jason.

Her collection was growing. She worked and worked until Ed yelled into her studio, "That's it! I'm calling workaholics anonymous." He took a seat in the corner, with a can of root beer in his hand, and watched her soldering tiny stars onto her newest Americana pieces, playing around with her extra pair of goggles, pulling them up over his butt. "You can never be too careful," he said, making them both laugh.

A reporter for *Bazaar* had been at the caster's when Leonard was working on one of her pieces and wanted to include it in an upcoming story. Ruby hoped that when the article came out, she could brag about it to the stores that used to stock her stuff and get them to reorder. It seemed everything around her was settling into all the places she'd carved early on, as she hoped they would.

In the meanwhile, she stuffed the doubt as far down as she could, twisting the words of that police officer in her head so that they backed her up: *You've got to have confidence in yourself.* She remembered all the present details, considered what she had now, rather than worry about losing it all; she remembered there were smaller boutiques to sell to locally. It wasn't just New York and L.A., she'd learned. There was a whole country out there, and selling was selling. With this perspective, she sold, and she sold. Sam was with her; she was learning the trade—in the leaps and bounds way a passionate beginner can. Ruby loved the hope in Sammie's face, the anticipation she shared waving Ruby off to Leonard with one of her own designs.

And the shop owners gasped, "Ooooh, this is amazing," and "I'll take ten for Valentine's Day." She put together mailings with color photos and price sheets for the New York and California stores, and she was receiving orders. And for the first time in a long time, Ruby was crossing off items on her list with the tenacity of a pup on a chew toy.

She'd created her own rhythm here—work in the mornings, calls in the afternoon, shop visits, and then more work after that. In between, she lunched with Jack and met with Selma and Merry. She planned her wedding with Suzanne. She was comfortable in a way she'd never been in New York, where she'd done things the way she supposed they ought to be done—the way she saw everyone else do them.

She'd found a yoga studio. Inside the lofty studio, with its neutral walls and rich woods, large, leafy green plants hanging down from the ceiling, she liked the relaxed way they came at the practice—less competition, less aggression. She liked the way her instructor told her, "Envision a bubble around you. There are no winners or losers here." Ruby had even spied an opportunity at the adorable boutique in the studio—she inquired about selling a few designs. She worked quickly, and then offered a set of three pieces—tiny, strong but deceivingly delicate-looking things, just like the practice of yoga itself, that could even be worn during class. They were Sanskrit symbols that spoke to her—those of Peace, Harmony, and Balance—mixed in with other everyday items that offered to her the same feelings, such as a coffee mug and the scraggly bare tree outside her window she'd grown fond of. They incorporated opposing materials—leather and lace, gold and silver, pearl with chain—braided, knotted into one.

She'd slowed down time, altered it to fit in nearly everything she wanted. And she looked out to the empty trees and the humps of hills beyond and didn't see barren, dead things as she used to in the winter. But when you slowed down, when there was more time, she found you couldn't escape yourself in quite the same way you used to. You couldn't go grab a drink rather than think about why you weren't doing something. Instead, you had to face things, no matter how hard you tried to push them off.

Every time you turned around, there you were—in your rearview mirror, in your side view, too. She just hoped that time would remain on her side where it really counted, that she hadn't already used too much of it. She prayed that Ed was patient enough to wait for whenever she was ready to open up to him.

Eighteen

━━━

A poorly running engine may lose power that is needed for normal driving and emergencies, may not start, gets poor fuel economy, and pollutes the air. It could also die on you when you are on the road, causing you and other drivers around you a problem.

—Connecticut Department of Motor Vehicles Driver's Manual

In April, Ed took her on a surprise trip.

"Are we there yet?" She kept asking this, as if it were a hysterical question, after every fifth road sign they passed. After the second time, Ed stopped laughing. After the third time he opened his eyes like Susan B. Anthony coins, or that child in *Home Alone*, and screamed like a madman until there was no more breath in his lungs. Then, he breathed in and out ultra-theatrically, his torso heaving, never once switching his gaze from the road.

"It's a lot funnier in my head," she said, by way of explanation. The trees were bare, but the snow that had settled on their limbs gave them a pleasant look, like the pretty black and white prints of Central Park often sold by street vendors in New York City.

A little into the trip, Ed played an old Tesla CD she hadn't thought about in years. Not since Rob Lerner, who'd come after Thomas Scully. He'd come right up to her in the food court at the Meadows Mall in Las Vegas, where she worked at the Maclevaney's

Muffins, and asked, "Can I butter your muffins?" Sure, that doesn't sound like someone you'd want to date. And that pretty much summed up Rob Lerner.

He played Tesla like nobody's business—"Signs, signs, everywhere are signs." He artlessly tried to learn the guitar riff. It really meant something to him. Therefore, by association, it had meant something to Ruby. After so much leaving and losing, what else had she to call her own but the things that people who condescended to include her in their lives had?

For the next few miles Ruby thought of Rob Lerner, his frizzy long hair, his not-quite-clean skin. What was it she'd liked about him? Likely the fact that no one else liked him. She didn't like anyone to be disliked. Plus, her mother hated him. Double plus, he had a real stutter, and so, next to him, Ruby spoke like an elocution instructor. She'd enunciate and say without fear, "We would like two cheeseburgers—no mustard—two orders of fries, and two Cokes, please." She hated that this made her feel like Nadia Comaneci standing atop that Olympic winner trinity—her arms hyperextended over her head—but it had. And so, it was even more pathetic when Rob broke up with *her*.

Tesla was not as good as she remembered. But Ed seemed to like it well enough. In fact, he knew every word. Maybe, "He said you look like a pine upstanding young van, I think you'll do," didn't sound quite right, but for the most part, he was thoroughly familiar.

They passed houses and farms with silos and red, peeling barns. She watched the black and white cows wander aimlessly around the newly green fields. The road winded, rose and fell, but the lines continued to wherever it was they were going.

"You know," Ed said, putting the CD on pause before the next track, turning slightly to her, "this next song is about Thomas Edison—about how he stole the glory for the idea of alternating current electric power, you know the AC system we use for freaking everything—from Nikola Tesla. It was just because Edison was a better businessman that he became famous for it in the end . . . he wouldn't even give Tesla a twenty-five-dollar-a-week raise, and the guy wound up digging ditches after that kind of work."

Ruby shifted in her seat to face him more fully. She tucked her left leg up to create a triangle with her right on the worn out sheepskin seat cover. She liked the way Ed's arm rested on the window frame, how his shape shown through his gray sweater. She liked his gold cross, small and simple, hanging on the inside of the sweater, and the faith she knew it to represent. There was something admirable in maintaining faith, something brave and solid. There was something admirable about cheering for the little guy, the underdog, that should have inspired her to share her own trials.

But she let herself get wrapped up in the details of this story of two men who were no longer alive. It was so much easier and more pleasant. Besides, Ruby always liked a good story. And Ed was a good storyteller, explaining all the details of the story in a way that made it come to life before Ruby's eyes, the windshield her movie screen, playing out the events he described. He had a head for facts, dates, details, and this enabled him to recount a full, fleshed-out story.

At the sign to Chicopee, Massachusetts, Ruby croaked once more, "Are we there yet?" This time she twisted around her hair as if she were five. There were no more jokes to make about the pilgrim's hat on the Massachusetts Turnpike sign. In fact, the ones she'd come up with hadn't been that good to begin with.

Ed turned to her, craned his neck, and pressed his lips soundlessly at her left eye. When he returned to the wheel he felt for her hand and held it on top of her thigh. "I love you, Ruby," he said.

Now he'd said that, it dawned on Ruby that maybe this was significant—the two of them driving away together.

"I wanted to tell you something," Ruby said.

Ed turned his eyes from the road, he squeezed her hand.

"I've had just enough Tesla for one day," she said, uncomfortable with what she was supposed to have revealed, the idea that she still hadn't been one hundred percent honest with him weighed on her chest. She'd had all that time, yet hadn't made a move one way—by telling Ed—or the other—by calling the P.I.

"Well, fine," he said and pressed a couple of buttons to switch to the radio.

Where they were going was to Gloucester, the home of the Gorton's Fisherman. When they turned off the exit, the town was a little depressed looking, with faded pastel sided A-frame houses in pinks, peaches, and pistachio green. "It's the town where *The Perfect Storm* was filmed," Ed said, pointing out the famous statue of the fisherman in the mackintosh when they approached. He parked and locked the car door behind Ruby.

He took her hand and held it lightly, cottony. "We're gonna go whale watching." Ed revealed his plan, looking right in her eyes, nose to nose. And then his face turned into a big smile.

The double-decker, shiny white boat, with the words CAPTAIN JAMES stenciled in red on the side, held 120 people. A lot of them were families, bearing soft-pack coolers and children with bumpy ankles and gangly arms and purple scabbed knees, riding on shoulders or at chest level or in big blue strollers bearing unidentifiable stains.

Ruby had recently bought her first pair of loafers and she was glad to have the practical shoes now. In fact, in her nautical stripes and relaxed denim, Ruby looked just like everyone else. And that was okay with her.

The woman on the PA system had an easygoing voice. She started out with a lighthearted welcome. "Hello, folks. I'm Sandy, and on behalf of all of us at Captain James Whale Watching Tours, I'd like to welcome you aboard and say we are thrilled you could join us today—the largest whale watching fleet on the East Coast, with seven boats serving Massachussettes, Cape Cod, Block Island, and Maine. All right, folks, give yourselves a round of applause for choosing the best whale watching vessel around."

Everyone clapped. There was a hoot or two.

"Rowdy crowd today I guess. Just our style, folks . . . Anyways, this boat we are on today is our flagship vessel, the *Captain James*, and it is a stunning fifty feet long by fourteen feet wide. Once we settle on our way, we will have Jimmy open the refreshment stand, where you'll be able to purchase hotdogs and hamburgers as well as an assortment of chips, candy, and refreshments."

There was some smiling and laughing and whining as visions of sugarplums danced in the children's heads.

"Would you want one of those one day, do you think?" Ed whispered in Ruby's ear, tenderly brushing her hair with his fingertips.

She smiled, moved in even closer, took his hand, and whispered back, "Not that one over there," pointing discreetly to a sandy-haired boy with curls who was yelling, "I want candy NOW!"

"Okay, so how about that one?" Ed said, smiling and pointing to a sleeping baby, cuddled into his mother's chest.

"I'll take two," Ruby said.

The boat was not very rocky as it slowly left the wharf and gained speed toward deeper water. But it was windy, and even with her hair tied back and a baseball hat on, Ruby's hair was smacking her in the face.

They were out a good forty minutes before the first sighting, Sandy pointing out the long pointed beak of the great blue heron and the fluffy piping plovers, who, she explained, have had their nests disturbed by beachgoers over the years. When they came upon a common sighting spot, Sandy told them to be very quiet, that this was where they often saw Britney Spears, who got her name from markings on the broadest part of her that looked like the letters *B* and *S* and because she was a rare humpback whale, which is sometimes referred to as a "singing whale" because of the oft-studied sounds or "songs" they sing.

"There are only about fifteen thousand humpbacks left in the world because they are slow swimmers and therefore often the target of hunters. When Britney jumps, notice her lumpy dorsal, or rear, fin," she said. "It just so happens that Britney, like many of the whales you'll see today, travel to the Caribbean and back to this very spot every single year." There was some static over the speakers and then Sandy's voice became excited. "Oh, here she comes over on the left," she said.

All the passengers scrambled, squealing, a parade of red, blue, and yellow slickers and hats, little kids wobbling with high pitched shrieks, over to that side, so that Ruby didn't get a peek. "Did you see her?" Ruby asked Ed.

"Just the tail," he said. "I mean, the dorsal fin." Then he took her hand, "Com'ere," he said. "This is the spot to see from." They stood, looking over the opposite edge of the boat, behind them the slowest in the group still huffing toward the other side. One kid said, "Mom, is that *really* Britney Spears? I didn't see her."

Ed and Ruby laughed silently, facing each other. Ruby was struck with the connection between them. Never had she been so close to the real thing—to sharing the kind of love that meant something. Ed wasn't worthless, he wouldn't disappoint her. By now, she had to know this. If that was true, then why hadn't she shared her darkest secrets with him? Why had she left him out of that? She kissed him at his ear a couple of times, overcome with her feelings for him.

"That tickles," Ed said, and tickled her back at her kneecap. She jumped, and at that same second she saw the water stir a bit. There was Britney Spears, soaring up from the water, in a perfect arc. Finally, her tail surfaced, bumpy just as Sandy had described, massive and white, rimmed with black, and then she was out of sight.

The boat was pure chaos. Everyone who'd been gathered on the other side of the boat mobbed Ed and Ruby, trying to get a picture, a video. "Did you see her?" "Did you see her?" they all wanted to know.

"Boy, she really *does* look different in person," Ed said to Ruby. Everyone surrounding laughed. Ruby beamed.

Sandy was back on the PA. "It looks like we've got a lot of action today. Tony's gonna drive us over about one hundred feet west where we saw a couple of our blue whales, or balaenoptera musculus, yesterday around this time."

While they scooted around slowly, waiting for a glimpse, Sandy filled them in on more whale trivia. "The blue whale has been measured at more than a hundred feet in length and is considered the largest, heaviest mammal to ever exist, though they survive on a diet comprised only of euphausiids, which are basically small crustaceans that look a lot like shrimp."

"Ewwww, gross," called the same boy who'd been in such dire need of candy earlier, the remnants of a chocolate bar smeared over his face.

"This whale population has shrunk to ten thousand," informed Sandy.

Why was it that such large, strong animals couldn't cheat their destinies? She pictured them all, desperately scrambling to get back to where they'd come from, searching for their homes, only to fail, be speared by a fatal blow. What made her think she'd make it? "I wonder how they know how to come back to the very same spot like that every year," Ruby said aloud.

"Home is where the heart is," Ed said.

The simplest of phrases, her mother often noted, contain the greatest truths.

One after the other, the whale watchers saw Lil' Kim, the ironically giant blue whale, and Luke Perry and Farrah Fawcett—the sei whales. It was addicting, getting a glimpse of them. You wanted it to last much longer than it did. Just when you thought you'd really got a look at one of them, they were gone, out of sight and you couldn't get the picture back in your head. Like many of the best things in the world, Ruby could see that this experience was fleeting.

In the meanwhile, out there, in the middle of the ocean it was easy to forget about everything else. There was just this boat, these kids in miniature striped polo shirts wanting to know if there was a gift shop. Ruby thought, it was the ultimate in surrendering control—putting your fate in the hands of Sandy and Tony, two faceless voices from somewhere above. It was a light, easy way to be—letting the tide coerce the boat here and there, wherever the wind happened to go, having faith in the unknown. She thought about the idea of this surrendering, giving into the truth of life—its constant movement, its spinning surface, its lack of guarantees and imperfect routines, traffic jams and speeders, tickets and pile-ups, its going out on limbs, and sharing the truth of yourself from the bottom of the trash bag—and having the courage to try anyhow. She was so close she could taste it.

After their boat ride, Ruby was buoyant. Her emotions had been jogged up and down, as their boat had been; they had hit high speeds, and now slowed down to a more manageable hum of activity.

"Nice do," Ed said, feeling the fluff of Ruby's hair at least five inches from her head. She pulled down the mirror over the passenger seat.

"Whoa, that is not a good look."

It was nice, how his deep belly laugh mingled with her higher pitched wail, creating their own song.

She pulled the hat off, smoothed down as much as she could manage, and twisted her hair into a fat braid. Ed drove them to a seafood restaurant where they had to wait a little while for a table. The place was jammed with senior citizens, and most of them had abandoned their tables to dance to Neil Diamond on a tiny wooden dance floor.

"Wanna dance?" Ed asked.

Normally Ruby would be too embarrassed, too afraid of looking stupid, of being too caught up in the moment and jutting her hips too hard or snapping her fingers with too much emphasis. But the day at sea made those risks seem minuscule. The whole earth was turning! What did it matter if Ruby snapped wildly or out of beat?

Still, compared to the couples surrounding, with their dips and their singing along, Ed and Ruby were reserved. It was a slower song, and they were swinging side to side, their hands clasped at either side of their faces. "This brings back some memories," Ed said, recalling the night they'd met.

"Yeah," Ruby said, glad she'd danced and not said no, happy that they'd meandered to that memory of their first meeting at the wedding. "That was kind of amazing, wasn't it?"

What was equally amazing was how far she'd come, that she was going to drive them home later, that she'd made so many real friends, that she'd managed to invigorate herself for the first time, really.

"And so is this," Ed said.

"Wooohoooo," the couple to their left hooted when Ed and Ruby became involved in a long, passionate surprise kiss.

"How long have you been married?" the couple asked.

Ed and Ruby smiled at each other. "Twelve years," Ed said.

Ruby pinched his butt under his untucked shirt.

The couple seemed unfazed. "We beat you. We've been together for fifty," the husband said, a Boston accent cutting sharp edges to the statement.

"Fifty years today," the woman said.

"What's the secret?" Ruby asked, her hand still at Ed's shoulder, with his fingers pressing around it.

"Happiness," the man said. "If you're not happy, you'll never be happy with someone else." They looked to each other, not exactly smiling, but knowing—knowing each others happiness with or without its trademark.

You could bury your problems, but eventually you had to drive out to the dump and take out the trash. She hadn't meant to drive out to the dump. But she had all the same. And now it seemed she was nearly done emptying it all out. But there were a couple of bags still in the corner, and they were starting to smell bad.

"Ed, party of two!" rang out over the loudspeaker.

After dinner, which was composed of shrimp and lobster and scallops broiled to perfection, Ruby drove the couple of hours home. At the wheel, she realized there was not only danger at the wheel, but that there was control, too. There was the ability to choose where you'd like to be, not only to run away. There was the chance to help others or to help yourself.

They arrived home exhausted, barely able to climb the two flights to their apartment. They shed their clothes in heaps on either side of the bed and crawled in, heating each other with the warmth of their bodies. They made love sweetly.

When, rather quickly after, she drifted off, Ruby dreamt of her father. She'd driven herself and Ed to see him and now she looked at him, sitting in a corner, looking down at the floor. His face was not visible.

"C-c-c-can I help you?" he finally asked, stuttering as Ruby sometimes did, spittle at one corner of his mouth. It looked as if the words sucked the life out of him. His skin was gray, sick looking.

Ruby ran to him, Ed trying to hold her back. "Dad! It's me! Ruby! Remember?" The man faced the wall still, a couple of over-grown wiry black hairs sticking out above his left ear. "It can't be Ruby. I've looked all over the world for her but she doesn't exist, obviously."

Ed was looking at both of them—Ruby and her father—back and forth like he couldn't believe it. "What's that he's saying, Rube?" Ed wanted to know. It was as if he couldn't comprehend what her father said, though to Ruby it was clear as day.

"I knew you wanted me," she said. "I just knew it." In the dream a giant weight had been lifted, as if Ruby could float right up to the clouds. But just as soon, she turned to find her father gone, vanished into thin air.

Nineteen

———

Do not take your eyes off the road ahead for more than an instant. Traffic ahead of you could stop suddenly while you are checking traffic to the sides, the rear, or over your shoulder.

—Connecticut Department of Motor Vehicles Driver's Manual

The start of all the upheaval could probably be traced back to the following day, when Ruby met Robert Cohen for the first time. It was also the same day she took Sammie to the University of Connecticut for a campus tour. When she'd look at it later, it would seem slightly poetic: an end and a beginning—though neither appeared so at the time.

When she woke, the dream was heavy on her eyes, forcing her to press the snooze alarm five times until Ed said, "You going to get up Ruby, or are you sleep sprinting?"

"I'm sleep sprinting," she said, and turned over once more, burrowed her head under the lighter cover they were finally able to switch to after the long, cold winter. Under there, her breath beginning to stifle her, it became clear she wasn't going to get back to sleep again this morning.

The dream had forced her to wonder: why had she waited so long to call the private investigator? Was it because the idea had been ridiculous? She recalled the initial surge of excitement when she'd first thought of it. Why had that waned?

She knew why. She'd been afraid of what she might find. There was a voice in the back of her head that said: why wake sleeping giants? That was her momma's voice, and she wondered if maybe it wasn't right. Everything was going well. She was taking her time in opening up to Ed, but she was close. They seemed to be getting closer every day, she had a whole new family of friends here, she'd found a stand-in father in Jack—and though it likely wasn't the healthiest relationship in the world, it was enjoyable and rewarding. She was getting her career back on track and nearly done planning her wedding.

All the same, she pretended to sleep while Ed showered, combed his hair, buttoned up his shirt, and knotted his tie. She kept the ruse up when he leaned over to kiss her good-bye. The second she heard the door click shut, Ruby tossed the covers off, jumped up, and ran down the short hallway to her office. Inside her "Ideas" scrapbox, where she always tossed bits of paper from magazines and photos, brochures and the like, Ruby dug down to the bottom to unearth the folded yellow "P" page from the telephone book, which she'd torn out all those months ago.

At 12:30 p.m. Ruby met Sammie at the Civic. Sammie hauled herself up and into the front seat. Ruby folded the chair and slid it into the back. She settled into the driver's side and passed the directions to Sammie. Today Sammie had one side of her shiny hair pulled back in a mother of pearl clip; the ends fell in a perfect waterfall over her shoulder. She wanted to look special somehow. At her neck was the necklace Ruby had given her. There were two dots of rouge at her cheek apples.

"Exit the parking lot." Sammie read step one from the directions Ruby had printed out on the computer.

Ruby looked over dramatically, rolled her eyes.

"Make a right and take 91 South to New Haven, State Street

exit. Turn a quick right at the first stop sign. 325 is on your left."
Now Sammie read all of the directions at once.

"I thought you were a good navigator. Apparently I was wrong."
She yanked the sheet out of Sammie's hand and tucked it between
her seat and the console. Winter was gone just in time—only days
ago it had looked like there was nothing left for the cold to ravage.
Now each day was warmer—enough so that Ruby could swap out
her parka for a corduroy waist-tie jacket she liked to wear in-
between seasons—still most everything was dry enough to look like
a forest fire had swept through. She swerved to avoid huge broken
branches that had cracked off and now littered the road.

Sammie shrugged her ski coat off and apathetically threw it in
the back. It slunk from the seat onto the floor. The radio station was
playing a Frank Sinatra marathon.

Sammie hadn't complained.

"You like this music?" Ruby asked her.

She inched her shoulders up slightly, listlessly, as if she could take
it or leave it.

They were silent, considering the music for a bit.

"So, a private investigator," Sammie said. "How'd you find this
guy?" They were turning onto 91 now, approaching the same spot
where Ruby's heart had raced over and over again. Now she accel-
erated naturally, nonchalantly glanced in her rearview and over her
shoulder like it was absolutely nothing at all.

"In the phone book," she said. It hadn't been difficult. You could
just look for a private investigator in the yellow pages, the same way
you could find a piano tuner. Ruby flipped to "P" and then scanned
for the most Jewish-sounding names. It was the same way she se-
lected physicians. Sure, she'd chided her momma for suggesting such
methods, but her instincts pointed her in the very same direction all
the same.

"In the *phone book*?" Sammie threw the words back to her with
disgust.

"What's so bad about that?" she asked, turning quickly to look at Sammie and then returning her gaze to the road.

"Well, it's not exactly thorough research, is it?"

"Sometimes you just have to do things, just jump in and accomplish them."

"I guess," Sammie said.

But Ruby wondered about that advice. Was this true? And what did she know of it? Should she have advised that? She couldn't help but think of Dina, of the way she'd be forced to say such questionable things to her own child over and over again when she had nothing better to offer. Was this parenting, on the whole?

Private Investigator Robert Cohen's office smelled of maple syrup. There was a veiny brown leather couch with nail heads. Stacks of papers rose like precarious, twisting skyscrapers on just about every inch of linoleum surrounding. There might have been a desk beneath it all. It looked like Robert Cohen watched too many private eye movies.

Sammie wheeled herself over to the desk. Ruby took the seat alongside.

"So. What can we do for you, Miss . . . Ruby Reynolds, is it?" His skin was porous and had a shine to it, so that in the beam of the overhead lamp he looked extremely important and a little bit like Swiss cheese.

"Yes. Well . . . I'd . . . ummm—" Ruby felt her back hunch over to its edge. She could have rested her head on her lap from that position.

"She wants to find her dad," Sammie said. "And we're not gonna get ripped off and pay for you to go to strip clubs or anything, so don't even think about it."

Ruby and Robert Cohen were struck speechless. He shuffled some papers, and then smoothed down his scratchy sweater. Ruby cleared her throat.

"So," Robert Cohen tried again, "we're talking about a paternity case here."

"Yes," Ruby said. She clapped a palm over Sammie's mouth. Sammie pulled it off.

"And is this your . . ."

"I'm her best friend," Sammie said.

Ruby was surprised to hear Sammie say something so affectionate. It hit her warmly and seemed to go straight to her eyes where tears were poised and ready to fall. But she wouldn't show that. She already knew Sammie would say something like, "Don't be lame." She thought of Jack and Ed and Merry and Selma. Was she ungrateful, to have all of that and still be sitting here, looking for something more?

Ruby crossed and recrossed her legs so that her patterned black tights whirred from the movement. She shimmied her skirt down a bit, folded her hands over her chest, and cleared her throat.

"Right up front, I'd like to tell you that digging up the past is a pretty huge undertaking. Cost aside, when people disappear, there's always a reason."

Ruby's stomach convulsed. Her ears throbbed. Just to grab onto something, she pulled her hair back into a bunch behind her head.

"Do you have any idea why your father disappeared?" Robert Cohen came in closer, sucked his teeth as if something were stuck between them.

Though she'd piled up enough possibilities to rival the population of China, there wasn't one she could actually say aloud. She wasn't going to say the things that only sounded pathetic to her ears now, such as he left because everyone leaves Ruby, just look at her. She didn't need Sammie to tell her to get a life. She was more than aware that she was in need of one. "No," she lied instead, and quickly darted her eyes down at the desk.

Sammie leaned in closer. "Do you think maybe he killed someone?"

"Most likely no. It's usually nothing extreme like that. Ah, the ways of the heart." Robert Cohen sighed deeply, crossed his legs up on the desk like a hero in a black and white movie. His foot kicked a copy of *The Heart Is a Lonely Hunter*. It slid off the top of a pile of papers soundlessly. "Usually it's a much more subtle thing, what drives a person to do something. It's an internal struggle, it's the coals of desire, shifting to create an intolerable heat. The human heart, my girls, is a strange and amazing thing."

The girls exchanged glances, but Robert Cohen didn't know it, looking dreamily up at the ceiling. "So where will you start?" Ruby wanted to know.

"The morgues?" Sammie offered.

Ruby glared at her.

"What? That's what they do on television—the morgues, the police department, the fire department . . . right, Robert?" Sammie looked for reinforcement.

"Please, call me Detective Cohen," he said.

Sammie looked confounded. Likely people didn't challenge her that way because they were afraid to treat her normally.

"Well, sometimes, yes. But don't you girls worry about that. Let Detective Cohen worry about that. Ruby, you worry about why you really want to have this information. Because, believe me, you think it's going to just change your life, one-two-three! But it won't! It never does! Whatever crap was lying on your desk before, it'll still be there after I tell you your father is Joe Schmoe from Nowheresville. And we'll start with an hourly rate of eighty-five ninety-nine plus expenses."

"He's weird," Sammie insisted when they were in the car once again. Judging from her reaction, she was a little young to understand what Detective Cohen meant in there. But it hit Ruby like the toppling facade of a cement building. Her hand was trembling if she didn't concentrate hard on stopping it. Weren't those her own fears he'd just confirmed? And if so, why had she gone ahead and signed the contract anyhow?

"Jeez. Whaddyou think was up with all the mumbo jumbo?" Sammie buckled her seatbelt.

"Hey, Sammie, do you mind if we drive to UCONN in silence?" She didn't mean to sound so harsh. But the idea of speaking just then was impossible.

If she'd only known, if she'd only known. It was the excuse she used for everything. She'd held onto it for dear life and now she might lose it. When she was just starting her senior year of high school, a brand-new Massachusetts resident—Westfield, town of 41,500—Ruby had lost fourteen fathers. Some years back, she'd taken to writing down the possible reasons why. She wrote and wrote and filled that notebook nearly to the end. But on the ride to Massachusetts from Las Vegas, which was long as could be, Ruby realized that she'd never know the answer.

At a rest stop she took the book from her knapsack and threw it in the trash. It disappeared under paper towels. She thought she was over it. But then Fifteen left, right in the middle of a heat wave, and when the sky darkened and the thunder cracked, she was right back under the kitchen table. She wouldn't act like that if she knew her real father. If she just knew he was out there and that he'd had a very good reason for leaving, like maybe going off to war or devoting his life to the fight against AIDS in Africa, then she could face it all, she'd have the same courage that everyone else had.

UCONN was laid out on a rather large campus, known for major snow storms and major keg parties. The first never stood in the way of the second. There were modern science facilities, the Connecticut Repertory Theatre, and plant growth facilities that housed over 3,500 individual plants. But what was it that Sammie was interested in? Ruby didn't know.

"Are you here for the tour?" the charismatic young man in horn-rimmed glasses and a plaid button-up shirt at the front desk asked. Over his head, a sign was magic markered with the words SPRING IS A STATE OF MIND.

College and its snarky, droll attitude sprang fresh in her mind.

She'd liked that about it. Ruby had liked that lots of students at Kingsborough were from somewhere else. There wasn't just her, standing in front of the blackboard being asked about the road that had taken her here. This point had buoyed her somewhat in her first semester of college, when she'd hoped things could change for her among talk of Kant and Heidegger, Nietzsche and Karl Marx, where it seemed no one had answers, where it seemed she wasn't the only one with impossible questions.

But it was Ruby who had to answer now. Sammie, who'd been so direct at every other place Ruby had ever seen her, had taken to slouching and shrugging. "Yes, we are," Ruby said.

"The tour meets in fifteen minutes at that big oak tree out there," he said, passing leaflets to both Ruby and Sammie. And then he pointed with enthusiasm in the direction of a cafeteria, beyond open double doors below a neon sign that blinked EATS, where lots of kids were shuffling, loaded down with backpacks and stacks of books, earphones sprouting. "You can grab a Coke or a snack over there to your left. Have a fabulous day," he said, having spent his allotted energy on them, apparently, and turned back to his text book.

"Want a drink?" Ruby asked Sammie when they were coming upon the cafeteria.

"Nah. You can go. I'll wait out there." She wheeled herself off before Ruby had a chance to disagree, her head at an angle that wasn't going to attract many friends.

Ruby figured she'd give Sammie a couple of minutes out in the courtyard. But when she reached the entrance to the cafeteria and turned back to look out at her, she looked so tiny—a sole wheelchair shining in the sun while people strode back and forth politely ignoring her or offering sympathetic smiles, which Sammie would no doubt anger at.

Ruby choked up at the refrigerated drink section. A gentle voice said, "Here," and poked a tissue at her nose. The boy wore metal glasses with lenses that weren't exactly clean. He offered a twisted smile. What could she say? Being picked up at a weak moment by a guy about twelve years her junior made her feel better. She thought there were good people and surely this had to be a sign for Sammie. She settled on a jazzy bottled green iced tea and bag of Doritos. She could see the boy with the tissue walk right past Sammie in the courtyard, as she forked over two twenty-five at the register, and this angered her for some reason. "Thanks," she said to the cashier.

Back outside, Ruby twisted off the iced tea cap and took a sip. It wasn't actually that good. "Dorito?" she offered.

"Okay," Sammie's voice was still small. It required some watering. Ample sunlight.

Ruby pulled open the brochure the guy inside had given to them. She leafed through the pages, not noticing much. "What do you think you might major in?" Ruby asked.

"I don't know. Teaching?"

Yes, Ruby could see that. She was definitely bossy. But beyond the jokes, she knew it could work. Sammie could do that very well. "I think you'd be an excellent teacher."

"Yeah? Why?" Sammie asked this without her usual edge, as if the answer really mattered to her.

"Because you have a natural curiosity about things, and a way of attracting people over to your side."

"Whatever," Sammie said, despite the spark Ruby had seen in her eye.

Ruby continued flipping through the brochure. "Oh, look, they have a Pizza Hut on campus."

"Woop-de-dooh." Sammy rolled her eyes.

People started to congregate around them for the tour. There was a couple swinging hands. A mother talked loudly to her son whose head was bent low. A pair of twins skipped over. A few others gathered. Some alone. One was apparently the guide. He introduced himself as Chris, then joked, "So you are the ones who think you want to come to UCONN, huh?"

A couple of chortles erupted. "If you can get him a scholarship," the loud mother yelled. The son's head sunk deeper.

Ruby widened her eyes in Sammie's direction.

"Well, luckily, I have this one scholarship right in my pocket," the guide said, digging his long arm way, way down in his pocket and pulling up nothing—a huge empty palm.

The son smiled and stood straight.

Nobody laughed.

"UCONN was founded in 1881, which makes the school one hundred and twenty-five years old. Over the years the university has grown big-time and now counts ten schools right here on the main campus in Storrs. We also have five campuses sprinkled throughout the state." He semi yelled these facts at them. "We started out as an agricultural school. As a matter of fact, to this day, you can get farm fresh ice cream any day you want it. My favorite is the chocolate— just saying." He was doing a great job, bringing everyone into the spirit of the place.

But when Ruby looked over to Sammie, who normally would eat this kind of thing up, she saw she still had that sullen, meek look on her face. She reached out to her with a hand on her hair. Sammie didn't pull away.

The guy continued on. "But—Mom, cover your ears—what you guys wanna know is, which is the party dorm, right?"

There was a "woop" and a few laughs.

"Fact is this dorm over to our left is known as the Jungle. It's one of the older dorms on campus, and it was built immediately following World War II, so that the returning GI's had a place to stay when they came home and went to school. And let me tell you, the place lives up to its name. Ever seen the movie *Animal House*? Well, those guys have nothing on the Jungle."

They followed obediently, now dreaming of college as portrayed in movieland, a place Ruby herself had never actually been. Now that he had them hooked on the fantasy, Chris began to walk them around to various points of interest on the campus. Sammie and Ruby held up the end of the line—possibly the only two who weren't going to hand their applications in directly following the tour.

"What's the teaching program like?" Ruby asked in front of the education building, hoping to get Sammie more excited.

"The Neag School of Ed has recently been awarded the Teachers for a New Era Grant from the Carnegie Corporation. They've got great programs for physical education and physical therapy as well. The programs are five years and integrate the master's degree— which all teachers must eventually get nowadays anyhow—with the undergraduate degree."

Sammie didn't say a word about that comment; she turned her head when Chris shifted his attention to her, and remained quiet throughout the tour. When it was over, Ruby asked, "Is there any- where you feel like looking . . . I mean while we're already here?"

"Nope. That was great." A person had never meant a thing less.

They made their way back to the parking lot. At the car, Sammie lifted herself into the front seat. Ruby folded her chair and placed it in back. They drove some time, passing identical light posts and trees, church spires and hills. It had been a long day. Sammie's de- flated mood hung over them like a thick fog.

"Do you think you'll go there?" Ruby asked, trying to thin it out somewhat.

Sammie shrugged.

It would be a titanic burden to go through life in a wheelchair. There wasn't much Ruby could say to change that fact. Even with- out such hindrances, Ruby found it hard to go through life. But, she considered, were their respective problems really all that different— in the way they both allowed themselves to be held back by them? And if they weren't that different, then what would Ruby wish for at a time like this, to make her feel better?

Once she figured it out, Ruby didn't hesitate. She laid her hand over Sammie's, rubbing her own fingers on top, finally weaving hers through Sammie's and holding on tight. Of all the trials and tribulations, it was one thing she'd always loved for her mother to do.

Twenty

Try to avoid panic stops by seeing events well in advance. By slowing down or changing lanes, you may not have to stop at all. If you do, you can make a more gradual and safer stop.

—Connecticut Department of Motor Vehicles Driver's Manual

It was strange, how Sammie came to go to New York City with Ruby. Ruby hadn't planned for it. She'd always thought it was important somehow, to go all by herself.

"I'm gonna miss you in New York City today," Ed said in bed, before he went into the shower.

"But I've gone a million times already, and besides I'll be home before you!" Ruby said.

"Still, I like to think about you here, with our things. It's, I don't know . . . better than not knowing where you are."

She wasn't sure what he meant by that, but she hoped her worst fears wouldn't be realized. Ruby told herself she was being paranoid and wrapped her robe around herself. "You're a dork," Ruby retorted, trying to cover up her anxiety. She tossed her pillow at him. When he caught it, he looked straight into her eyes, holding her gaze for a second and she wondered how much longer she'd be able to convince herself everything was fine. She'd carried it on for so long, and now it seemed that maybe her time was up.

"Takes one to know one," Ed said. He flipped her onto her back and leaned his full weight on her. Again, she thought his smile seemed forced. But she comforted herself in the thought that he still appeared invested and enamored.

"Aggh! You're killing me!" Ruby screamed. Was there a context behind all this or was it her imagination?

"Well, apologize then," Ed said, matter-of-factly.

"I'm sorry," Ruby said, more serious now. "And . . ."

"What? Were you going to say something?" Ed sat back, flopped on the bed, like he was expecting something.

A strike of lightening bolted through her. But she just shook her head. Shouldn't she wait until Robert Cohen gave her something to go on, something concrete she'd have to rely on, to show to Ed? It would be so much easier if she had that to inflate her.

This time she knew she wasn't crazy. Ed shook his head, squeezed his eyes shut. Still, he mustered a smile after, offered the smallest kiss on Ruby's lips.

After his shower, Ed smelled spicy—a mixture of deodorant and cologne that Ruby loved.

"Be careful today," he said, kissed her, this time long and lingering, as if he'd made peace with something in himself, and left.

Ruby tried her best to ignore the double entendres she could read into the exchange. She was busy doing everything she could to make things right on her end and pretty soon she'd know everything and be ready to talk with Ed about it.

She showered, gathered her things, stole out to the car, warmed it up, and was just about to switch into reverse when there was a knock at her window.

Ruby mouthed, *What?*

Sammie circled her fist to indicate Ruby should roll down the window.

"What's up?" Ruby asked. She was anxious to get on with the day and get back. That scene with Ed would not sit right, no matter which way she looked at it.

"I wanna come with you," Sammie said. "I've never been to New York."

There was something in her face, beneath the attitude, that spoke to Ruby—someone looking for an opportunity to control her own destiny. She sighed at the change in plans, but agreed.

The drive was uneventful until they reached the end of the Hutchinson River Parkway. It was something to go over a bridge the size of the Triborough and see Manhattan that way, from your very own car.

"Holy shit!" Sammie yelled.

"What?" Ruby felt panicked right away by the sound of Sammie's proclamation.

"Is that really New York City? It's . . . I don't know, surreal. It's beautiful."

Ruby turned her head quick, saw the water on all sides, and faced forward again. She was sort of freaked out now, though she'd done this all those times already. She tried to concentrate on the road. But what that meant was that she wasn't concentrating on the signs. And so she ended up going to Randall's Island. "Shit!" Ruby yelled.

She was lost and this was exactly what she had been afraid of.

"What are we gonna do now?" Sammie said.

"Turn around, I guess," Ruby said, realizing that it was really that simple. And this time she got it right. Along the lower parts of the FDR, Ruby watched her old home base flash by. She had such a strained relationship with it all now.

"I used to live over there," she said to Sammie.

"Oh yeah? What was it like?" Sammie asked, obviously enthralled by her proximity to Manhattan, the way Ruby had been the first time she'd stepped out of Grand Central Station with her mouth hanging open.

"It was very liberating to me," Ruby said. Sure, there had been the loneliness, but there was that, too—the independence—whether it was what she'd expected or not. Maybe it had been a necessary step to get to where she was now.

This seemed to strike something with Sammie, who shook her head as if she understood.

Though there were rushes of excitement over sharing these things, the biggest thrill came from seeing Dina.

"Look!" Dina pulled Ruby's hands down to her belly. She was already wearing a maternity shirt, and she'd started to show. "I've got a baby growing in there!"

Sammie looked surprised. "Can I feel?" she asked, though they'd only just been introduced.

"Sure," Dina said. It was apparent the pregnancy was softening her demeanor.

They were at the corner Italian place. How long had Ruby thought of this spot? How long had she pictured the waiter welcoming her with a hug, a great big "How have you been?"

The waiter didn't give her a second glance. Obviously, he'd completely forgotten her. After he tossed a couple of menus on their table, he went over to the next table and hugged the woman who'd sat down there. "How have you been?" he asked with vigor. It was strange to be forgotten, yet Ruby wasn't that hurt by it. She had new haunts, new people to yell "Hello!" when she came back.

"Let me get this straight. You're both getting married? What—did you plan it or something?" Sammie was twirling spaghetti around her fork.

"Where did you pick this girl up?" Dina said, her face revealing her lightheartedness.

"Maybe we should be asking the same thing about you," Sammie said.

"Touché," Dina said.

Ruby smiled. It appeared her friends were hitting it off . . . in their own way. The restaurant bustled in a purely New York way, cackling laughs and lots of "oh my god" exclamations and showy waiters. What was it that Ruby had loved about this place so much? She looked at it as an observer now and saw that in a way it was rather indistinct. It was a bland place that could have been anywhere in the world. Sure the food was decent, with big helpings of pasta and baskets of crusty garlic bread, but it wasn't the best. Had Ruby always sacrificed quality for comfort? Had she been looking for conformity over distinction? Was *this* what people meant when they'd panned her collection?

"It's so great to have you here," Dina said.

Ruby turned to her wide-eyed. Sammie was looking around in wonder.

"How was the drive?" Dina asked.

Sammie turned her attention back to the conversation and grimaced. "She drove really well. Well, except for when we went to Randall's Island by mistake." Sammie smoothed her hair down in the back with both hands. Was Ruby crazy, or was Sammie proud of the transformation in her?

"Oh, she's always getting lost," Dina said, seeming to have enjoyed Sammie's story. "You should see her. We'll get out of the subway on Forty-second Street and she'll be trying to figure out which way is west. She's the worst!"

It was going to be a long day. "You guys, don't mind me, really. Speak your mind." Ruby chomped into a warm slice of garlic bread.

She saw a missed call on her cell phone after the salad course. She scrolled through the numbers. It was Robert Cohen. Her heart sped up. "I'll be right back," Ruby said.

She escaped to the bathroom, leaned against the paper towel dispenser. She dialed her voicemail and waited, hoping there was something, anything he'd said that she could grab hold of. But there were no messages. She considered that he'd left a message on her home telephone and she dialed that number next. Ruby waited impatiently through her own outgoing message, pressed the pound key, and entered her code.

"You have no new messages."

She felt her heart plummet to her knees.

She dialed Robert Cohen's number. There was no answer. She left a message. "When you get this message can you please call me with an update?" she asked, trying her best to sound calm. She returned to the table.

"She's waiting to see what her private investigator has to say about her dad," Sammie correctly guessed, in the "dare me" tone that sometimes made Ruby want to smack her.

"Why don't you just stop now?" Dina asked. "It's not too late."

"I just can't. I need to know. I'm not a complete person until I find out, and the thing is I can't go forward without feeling complete."

"That's pure shit," Dina said.

"No, you know, sometimes people need to be ready before they can accomplish difficult things." Sammie was young; it was a child's perspective, but Ruby allowed herself to believe that there was a certain amount of experience that might lend it more significance.

"Hey, let's not worry about this now," Ruby said. "Today is about fun stuff, weddings and dresses and friends."

"Okay, but when this all comes and bites you in the ass, don't say I didn't warn you," Dina said.

"Deal," Ruby agreed, though the words rang through her ears and down to her heart.

With the air cleared, they sat for a long, enjoyable lunch, indulging in tiramisu for dessert. After, they went to get their hair cut at a bustling, utilitarian salon in Chinatown.

The day was warm, though not terribly sunny, a light gray blanket poking out from the building spires. The three women traveled far west to the bridal shop. The bridal boutique was carpeted in a white Berber, woven with a wedding bell pattern. Ruby was in love with midnight blue and had clipped out a dress from a magazine that she'd particularly liked for her bridesmaids. It was long and cut deep at the neckline.

At two o'clock, they sat, waiting for the saleswoman to bring out a rack of maternity bridesmaid dresses for Dina to try.

When she came back with the dresses, Ruby said, "And now, I'm gonna need to get fitted as a bridesmaid for my friend Dina's wedding, too."

The girl twisted her high ponytail, looking confused, like they'd all gone off and joined some married-with-children cult.

Sammie interjected. "They're both getting married! Isn't that so cool?"

"Oh! Okay. I get it now. Do you know your color?" She asked Dina.

"I've always really liked yellow," Dina said, as if it had just hit her.

"No!" Ruby said. "You're just saying that because you know I look terrible in yellow!"

"I wish I could deny that, but it's true. It really is. You know how you'd live to torture your sister if you had one?"

"No . . . no, I don't know anything about that." Ruby pursed her lips.

"Oh, I know exactly what you mean," Sammie said.

"Why am I not surprised?" Ruby asked, smiling big. She couldn't help but think how comfortable she felt with both of these women. She'd never had close friends, much less friends that felt so much like family. How many times had she sat watching sisters— shopping at the mall, having coffee—and wished to be just like them? And yes, the so-close-you-can-be-catty-and-laugh-about-it part of it had come into her own dreams, too. This came so close to those dreams, her heart bubbled over.

The woman went to gather another round of dresses from the back room and Dina ducked into the dressing room. "So you live in Ruby's building?" Dina asked Sammie through the slatted door.

"Yeah. I live with my mother . . . which sucks."

"Give me a kid who lives with her mom and I'll give you a kid who thinks it sucks," Dina was speaking from experience. She'd commuted to Manhattan from her parents' Long Island home for a year after college. To quote her, it made her "want to poke her own eyes out." Ruby wasn't so sure that was true. She knew Dina, and if she'd wanted to leave, she would've—period.

"But it's worse since I'm in a chair. She treats me like I can't do a frickin' thing. It's always, 'Sammie, be careful,' and 'Sammie, let me help you with that.' She's just not cool like you guys are. She'd never let me come to Manhattan."

Dina had just emerged in a satin strapless A-line dress that looked pretty nice, and she and Ruby exchanged raised eyebrows. "You mean your mother doesn't know you're here?" Ruby asked.

"Not exactly," Sammie admitted; she let her back sink into her chair with a thump.

"You better call her right now!" Ruby felt like a mother, or a pissed-off big sister, maybe. How had she gotten this involved? Already she cared so much for Sammie she felt compelled to speak with her mother. It was impossible not to. The girl was just bubbling over, wanting to experience life all over the place. Ruby wanted to explore all the options with her—she knew it was possible to rig a car so that Sammie could drive; there was no reason she couldn't have a fulfilling life just like anyone else could.

"All right, all right." Sammie took her cell phone out and dialed.

"Hi Mom, I'm in New York City." She said that and then smacked her phone shut. "She wasn't there," Sammie said.

"Is there somewhere she thinks you are?" Ruby asked.

"Home, probably."

"Good luck with that," Dina said, turning her back so Ruby could unzip her.

Ruby got the feeling this could turn out badly. But they were here now, and there wasn't much to be done about it. She told as much to Sammie, who didn't seem the least bit concerned.

"Honestly," Sammie said. "I could have gone to the Super Stop

& Shop and be in just as much trouble as I am now. I'm not allowed to do anything. If I want to do something, I have to sneak. She'll be mad, but it's the only way with her."

Why was it that mothers never seemed to understand their daughters? Did they simply pass down their own hang-ups blindly, without bothering to realize they hadn't given birth to themselves? Ruby thought it just might be a national epidemic. "We'll work it out, Sammie."

The saleswoman was approaching the three of them now, with a whole rack of yellow dresses for Ruby. And from the woman's vantage point, they were likely an odd group, all in fresh, matching Chinatown haircuts blown out glossy. Dina with her chestnut hair, a few inches shorter than Ruby, but looking much more flashy—even pregnant—in stiletto boots and rhinestoned jeans. Sammie's blond bob gleamed over her Abercrombie sweatshirt and loose cargo pants. Pink pumas peaked out from the hems. And Ruby, well, it was funny to admit it, but she was dressed more like Sammie than Dina—she had on a fleece pullover and army green pants with navy blue sneakers. Earlier, Dina had called the outfit "ghastly." Ruby didn't think it was ghastly. But she definitely looked like an out-of-towner. And funnily enough, that was okay.

Dina jumped up at the sight of the rack and began pulling through the various yellow dresses. "Ruby, wow, you have to try this one!" It was by far the largest dress, with a thick, scratchy crinoline underlay that pushed it out several feet on all sides.

"Gee, hmmm," she propped her chin up with her finger as if pondering that idea. "Remember when you said your dress better be navy . . . or else. Well, I agreed. I'm not wearing that dress . . . or else!"

"Ha!" Sammie laughed. "You guys are hysterical. You're not going to truly make Ruby wear that dress, are you?" Sammie wheeled herself over to it and made a sour face at the feel of it between her fingers.

Dina said, "Well, she owes me *at least* that much. If it wasn't for me, she wouldn't have even met Ed in the first place." She disappeared behind the fitting room curtain to try on the second navy dress.

"Is that true?" Sammie asked.

She told her the whole story.

"Wow. That's pretty cool," Sammie said. "So who else are you having as a bridesmaid?"

"Just Dina," Ruby shrugged. It was a little embarrassing, but that was it. She didn't have a family with sisters and cousins and little nieces to sprinkle flowers down the aisle. There was her grandmother, whom she used to cherish—despite the fact that her mother had only taken her to visit twice—but she died five years ago. At the funeral, Ruby couldn't get over the fact that she barely recognized her own grandmother. But when she'd been alive she knew her grandmother mainly the same way she did now—from the very old sepia-toned photo she had in her possession. She could spend hours comparing the traits of Ruby and her momma against her grandmother's snapshot, looking for similarities, tracing the blood that joined her grandmother to her momma and then to Ruby.

She'd spoken to her on the telephone a couple of times. She had a thick accent from Hungary. Her grandmother said, "Pitzka!" and then she asked with a sing-song, "S-oooo-ah, how you like-a school?" She'd allowed her grandmother's musical voice to crest and cadence while she shut her eyes under the blanket of it.

"Ma, we gotta go," Ruby's momma had pulled the phone from her. "Yeah yeah yeah," she said into it and then hung up.

What had driven her mother that far from her family? Ruby didn't know. She just didn't know.

"There's no one else you'd want in your bridal party?" Sammie had a bridal magazine open on her lap.

Ruby shook her head.

"No one?" Sammie seemed to be hinting at something.

"Nope." Ruby wondered what exactly Sammie was thinking.

"What about me? I've never been a bridesmaid. And we've got something special you and me. You're like the sister I never had. I . . . well, I haven't had this much fun in . . . well, ever."

Ruby felt her cheeks flush with the idea of that. It was funny how she'd always wished for a sister, sitting in the front seat of her mother's car and praying that the next time she turned around a sister would be sitting back there braiding a doll's hair and saying "me, too" when her momma asked for a Coke.

"You know what? I would be honored to have you for a bridesmaid." Ruby embraced her new little sister in a big, warm hug—the kind she'd always wished her momma would wrap her in, rather than those skimpy back pats she went for when sentimentality was in order. "Now get in there and try on some dresses."

The saleswoman looked at them like this was going to be the hardest she ever worked. "Let me guess, you want a whole other rack of dresses now?"

All three girls laughed and answered in unison, "Yup."

Dina came out in the second blue dress—it had a straight neckline and cap sleeves, with a lightly embroidered empire waist and a plain mid-calf skirt with ample room to puff up when big bellies required it. It looked perfect, and Ruby said so. "Yeah, but I'm sure in four months I'll look like a cow," Dina said.

"Yeah, you probably will," Sammie agreed and couldn't help from giggling.

"Boy, it's like you were always part of the group," Dina said. "And I don't mean that in a good way."

"Which is a good thing," Ruby explained.

"I got it," Sammie said.

"Hey, Dina, little sister Sammie here is gonna be bridesmaid number two," Ruby said.

"Well, just remember I'm number one," Dina said with a wink. "Now get in that room and try on some of those dresses for me." The saleswoman was just coming back with Sammie's.

"Perfect!" Dina agreed.

"So I don't have to wear yellow?" Ruby tried, although Dina had settled on a yellow one already.

"Over my dead body." Dina smiled too big.

"That could be arranged," Ruby joked.

"Shit, I look awesome," Dina said of her next dress, ignoring Ruby.

"So do I," Sammie said when she emerged in her first dress.

Dina retreated back inside her dressing room, and Sammie stayed a moment before the mirror to consider the spaghetti-strap slip dress she had on.

A couple of seconds later, a chilling scream unleashed from Dina's stall.

She ran over, yelling, "What? What is it? Are you okay, Dina?" Her hands clenched into nervous fists as she approached.

When she pulled the curtain aside, Dina was huddled in a lump on the tiny bench, looking more pained and vulnerable than Ruby had ever seen her.

"I think something's wrong with the baby," she said, tears beginning to spring from her eyes.

"Someone call 911, please! Now!" Ruby yelled. She forced her own tears to stay in place. She would not let Dina lose this child.

"I've got it," Sammie said. She'd already fished Ruby's cell phone from her purse and began plucking at the numbers.

"I promise you, everything is going to be okay. You just close your eyes and breathe," Ruby found herself saying. She was calm and composed and she rubbed Dina's hair like she used to do for her momma when she asked.

Her cell phone rang in Sammie's hands. "It's Robert Cohen," Sammie said, looking at the tiny screen. Her heart thumped, but Ruby's own fate would have to wait.

"Later," Ruby said.

The paramedics had arrived and they gently encouraged Ruby

and Sammie to the side. They placed a breathing mask over Dina's face once they'd laid her out on the stretcher.

Ruby and Sammie accompanied Dina in the ambulance. They were incredibly silent as Dina moaned and groaned and the siren screamed a pathway for them down to Saint Vincent's Hospital.

Amazingly, Dina didn't have to wait long. Right away, the emergency room physician, Dr. Wadman, ordered a blood test. "This will test for the pregnancy hormone as well as the progesterone levels so that we can ensure that everything is okay. We'll have the results in four hours," he said.

A little while later, Ruby and Sammie were ushered out of Dina's area again, her curtain drawn up for privacy, so the GYN could perform an examination.

When they were allowed back in, Dina still looked very nervous and pale. She explained, "She wanted to make sure the cervix wasn't dilating, which would have meant a miscarriage."

She was so teary and shaky that Ruby worried over what Dina would say next.

"It wasn't. She said that was excellent news."

Ruby let out a huge sigh. "Thank God."

"Now we just wait for the blood tests," Dina said, only allowing herself to be partially relieved until she had all the information.

Ruby grabbed for her hand and held it tight, stroking Dina's forearm in what she hoped was a comforting way.

In a few minutes, Jason met them.

He looked green and slightly sweaty, like he'd run here all the way from his downtown office. When he saw Dina lying there, his eyes became wet, and Ruby's heart went out to this man she'd never even met before. A father; he was going to be the father of Dina's child, and from the looks of it, he was a gentle, caring man.

"Hey," Dina said sweetly, and kissed him, her hand soft at the back of his head. Jason was tall and very good looking, with an athletic build. He had deep brown eyes, sprinkled with light specks, and his cheeks were nicely sculpted. There were gold-toned wire-rimmed glasses resting on his pointed nose.

"So, what are they saying now? Is our child okay?" He took her hand in two of his own, the tears springing now, his face contorting.

"Hey, we're just going to wait outside," Ruby said, her hand at Sammie's shoulder, thinking she'd officially meet Jason later.

"No, no, you stay," Jason said. "I know Dina wants you here."

Now her own eyes moistened. They didn't have the final word yet; now was the worst part—the waiting.

Dina shook her head, her hands now moving to her tiny bump, holding it instinctively, the way mothers do, as she explained all the details to Jason.

"Ruby, the famous Ruby," Jason said, a few moments later. He turned to her and Ruby stuck her hand out for him to shake.

"And this is Sammie." Ruby introduced them.

"Hi," Sammie said, without offering a hand.

Finally the GYN, Dr. Kerry, knocked softly on the door and entered in a white jacket over a navy flowered dress, a stethoscope around her neck, a chart in her hand.

"How are we doing, Miss Davila?" The doctor had a warm, staid tone, like an informed friend.

"Okay," Dina said. She looked as if she would cry again. Her chin quivered.

Please God, Ruby begged, *let her be okay. Let her have this. She deserves it more than anyone.* She was surprised to realize she was wringing her hands, and let them fall softly to her sides now. She tried her best for a hopeful look.

"Looks like you've got a healthy child coming, folks."

They all smiled uncontrollably through the tears. "So what happened?" Dina asked, her words hard to find.

"It looks like the cramps are the product of the fetus implanting itself into your uterus. This is not completely uncommon, and can sometimes happen after intercourse. So, my only advice to you would be to take it easy, decrease your activity, take a break from intercourse for a little bit. Other than that, just go for a follow-up with your own doctor in a week or so."

They stayed long enough to watch Dina eat her rigid slice of meatloaf and a tiny cup of Jell-O, and when Ruby was sure her friend would be okay without her, Ruby and Sammie said their good-byes and took a taxi back to the car.

"You have a really amazing friendship with your friend Dina," Sammie said once they were settled on the FDR North, right before she fell asleep.

In the silence, the road changed from winding with low-income housing alongside to more deeply winding with only woods aside, and Ruby worked out all the things that had happened. One second they'd been having a great time, messing around like kids, and the next they were all forced into being adults, scrambling to do the right thing in a terrifying situation. It was so abrupt, the way things could just flip that way. Ruby felt queasy from the motion sickness.

Did she have it in her to telephone Robert Cohen after all this commotion? Was she ready to hear what he had to say?

She remembered the strength she'd mustered for Dina earlier and dialed Robert Cohen's number, Sammie fast asleep beside her. "Robert Cohen here," he answered. "We find your guy."

"Hi, Robert. It's Ruby," she said as softly as she could speak into her earpiece. Every time she called, Ruby couldn't help but feel wracked with anxiety.

"Ruby. Oh yeah. I just wanted to tell you that we didn't get too far in Florida. Looks like all the current residents on the block didn't know you guys. There was one pediatrician who had you on his chart for a case of strep throat back in 1980, but he didn't have any paternal records. So, I'm off to Bayonne, New Jersey, tomorrow, to see what the deal is over there." Should she be with Robert Cohen, investigating her past where it had unfolded, flipping through records that proved she existed? The whole conversation left her feeling odd, especially in light of the terrifying events of the afternoon. Was this a dangerous business she was dabbling in—getting involved in the essence of her being again? Would it ever be enough that she was here, now, at this one place in time? She thought about the road she'd wandered down, until she turned into the parking lot of her apartment complex.

When they arrived, police sirens were flashing like a July fourth spectacle. Ruby was glad they were done with their own sirens and emergencies for the day, but did wonder what was going on.

As they approached, Ruby realized the squad cars were right alongside her spot. Up above, on their terrace, Ed stood in his droopy pajama pants and a T-shirt with a tear beneath his left underarm. Her stomach cramped up again as anxiety gripped her. The possibilities cruised through her mind like a video on fast-forward and she could barely pull herself into the spot and shift the car into park.

"What the?" Ruby roused Sammie by shaking her shoulder.

"Oh shit," Sammie said.

"What? What is it?" Ruby asked, as it seemed Sammie recognized what was going on immediately.

Within seconds, Sammie's mother was rushing the car, that thick, dark hair in a high ponytail that swished as she ran. She screamed, "My baby, my baby!" Her hair came undone, and seemed to engulf Sammie's entire head as she tore the door open and grabbed her.

Ruby watched in shock. She hadn't spoken with Sammie's mother, had only seen her from afar a couple of times. But now she could see that Sammie hadn't been exaggerating about her reaction to Sammie going to New York. The police officers were approaching, the pair of them moving in tandem, as if Ruby were some dangerous criminal. They needn't have worried, she couldn't have moved if she tried.

Up above, Ruby could see Ed, wide-eyed, at their terrace. He regarded her with the look of someone he barely knew, as if he'd been living with her all this time and just realized she was actually leading a double life: with another husband and two children and a golden retriever named Barker. Sure, this was her take on it, but the truth was, this assessment probably wasn't so far off. It hit her so hard just then: she'd shared her fears with everyone but Ed. Sure, it wasn't meant to hurt him, but by default it would. It absolutely would. When she looked up at him again he'd disappeared. She assumed he was on his way down—concerned for her.

"Get out of the car with your hands up," one of the policemen yelled.

Her heart thumped. Only in nightmares and Bruce Willis movies did these things happen. She operated somehow, was able to twist her body, stand up straight, and raise her arms up over her head. On the other side of the car, Sammie's mother was grabbing her daughter to a standing position in a frantic way, one of Sammie's useless feet dragging on the concrete. She leaned Sammie awkwardly against the car and then leaned in to pull her chair from the back, huffing and puffing, banging it along the door frame and the side of the car.

Sammie was trying to grab onto the roof, hold herself up. Ruby knew Sammie hated to be a part of a spectacle just as much as she did and her sympathy went out to her, to the burning that must be at her cheeks, the anger heavy in her chest. She remembered the pain of powerlessness, of having to do what your mother said because there was no other choice.

And Sammie's mother wasn't making it any easier. She was apparently oblivious to her daughter's personality altogether. She called into the dark night, the stars above so ignorant to this all, "This is the girl who kidnapped my daughter! We saw her watching us a few months ago. She must have been planning this for a long time. It was . . . it was premeditated."

"Mom! Mom!" Sammie was screaming. But the police officers were already at Ruby. One of them was blond, forceful. But the other one Ruby recognized. He was was the officer from her driving incident outside of Merry's shop. He stood back a little, as if trying to place her. Finally he said, "I know you." They pulled her around to face them again, not painfully, but quickly and tightly.

"No, I don't think you do," Ruby said. Ed was just approaching the scene and she looked to him, mortified. What could he possibly be thinking?

"We're gonna have to cuff you," the blond one said. Her world turned watery. Confusion, mortification, and anger shadowed the movements, where she'd put her keys, purse. And then she heard him—a voice clear above the confusion.

"What are you doing?" Ed asked the more aggressive police officer. "You are gonna have a serious suit on your hands if you don't have a reason for cuffing my fiancée."

"This fiancée of yours has been accused of kidnapping this poor handicapped girl." He slivered his eyes.

"But she just took me to Manhattan. We ate Italian food and tried on dresses! I'm gonna be her bridesmaid! And I'm not a poor handicapped girl! Did you ever hear of being politically correct?"

Sammie's mother smacked the chair against Ruby's car as she pushed Sammie into it. There was a loud bang.

"Just listen to me! Please! Mom! I *asked* Ruby to take me! She did me a favor. She took me somewhere—somewhere you're too afraid to let me go. And I think I'm going to move to New York, go to college, become a jewelry designer. I actually felt . . . good there. But you wouldn't understand a thing about it!" Sammie was shaking with the force of her own voice, with the pain the words came from. It was obvious Sammie had waited too long to say something herself, and now it was coming out all wrong.

It was becoming slowly, eerily clear to all that this was some sort of major misunderstanding. The officers tried to clarify. "So, is everything okay here?" the blond one asked. The other officer looked at Ruby. "Oh, yeah, I remember you now! *You* drove to Manhattan? That is really awesome. Looks like you're doing really well. I remember you were afraid to make a left turn."

Everyone looked to Ruby. She couldn't bring herself to respond.

She hadn't waited all this time so that she'd be forced to tell him this way!

She remembered what that older couple at the restaurant, after their whale-watching excursion, had said about being happy with themselves, that this was the secret to a happy relationship. It wasn't until just this second that the full weight of that statement hit her. Yes, yes, she'd thought it was important before, but she'd pushed it off casually all the same, waiting for the right time and turning her attention to easier things like china and place cards. She'd existed as if this secret weren't the most important thing. But now she knew, it was the most important thing—most important of all. She had to share it all with him. *You have to be happy with yourself first.* And the very reason she hadn't shared was that after all this time she still had no confidence in herself, she still worried that her collection of quirks, of bruises and scrapes, would make her undesirable, and in the end, would send Ed away.

With that same businesslike tone laced with warmth, the officer continued, "I remember you were so terrified to drive that day. You choked me up, honestly."

Ed was white, like the life had been kicked from him.

Sammie was proud of Ruby, and that's why she also said too much now, not realizing how Ed would react to the surprising realization that everyone knew Ruby better that her own fiancé. "But you don't even know what a big deal it is that she's accomplished this—seriously. She had a lot of issues about driving because of her childhood and stuff. You wouldn't believe some of her stories. She doesn't even know who her father is—we've hired a private investigator to find him."

Ruby could feel her eyes shoot open wide. Had Sammie just said that in front of Ed, or was this another nightmare? She looked to Ed. She knew it was a bad sign that he hadn't yet touched her. He wouldn't say anything there, in front of everyone. But there would be some difficult words ahead. She only prayed she hadn't ruined it all. There was only one hope she could hold onto: if he could love her, unwavering in the midst of this—whatever he imagined it might have been—well then, he could love her. That was clear enough.

"Good job," the officer said, shaking his head. Then he turned to the blond officer. "Tony, I think we're done here."

"Well, I guess it's all right if you go," Sammie's mother said, more quiet, likely embarrassed now. The parking lot was still and the ground was damp, the lights on each building weren't usually bright enough to block out the stars, but when Ruby looked up at them this evening, she couldn't see more than a handful.

"Thanks, Ruby. I'm glad Dina is okay," Sammie said before rolling her way to the door.

"Mom!" she yelled now when her mother banged her chair. Ruby guessed it was self-consciousness that had her so riled up.

"I'm sorry for the confusion," Tony said, with obvious regret. Some fuzz came across his radio. "We got a car theft over on 217," it squawked.

As they were walking off, Tony asked his partner, "So what happened with that girl the last time?"

Ruby watched, holding onto her car like a life preserver, as the two cop cars executed K-turns and drove out of the parking lot, making their way to the street beyond. She watched them until they disappeared completely from view, not wanting to face Ed yet. The sound of their cars faded, and then there was only silence.

"Ruby, what the hell happened here just now?" His jaw tightened and it appeared he'd run out of the patience he'd maintained in front of everyone.

Where did she start? How did she find the words? "Why don't we go upstairs and talk about it?" She bought herself a few minutes, took the two flights slowly, waiting for the sentences to crystallize in her head.

Inside, the apartment was set for a very different scenario. Ed had made dinner for them. There were candles set out on the table—standing in the two sticks she'd made for them—and two complete sets of their china pattern on either end of the table. They must have arrived in the mail today—a gift for their wedding; their first gift. She looked at the pretty place setting; it was much more beautiful than she remembered, delicate with its elegant flower in the middle—bowl, small plate, dinner plate, teacup, and saucer. Perhaps it was she who'd softened her view of things, now saw shades between black and white, good and bad, happy and sad, fear and strength. She wanted so much to tell Ed about all of it.

"You made dinner?" she asked.

"Chicken . . . I know it's your favorite."

She laughed at the irony. She'd been afraid so long even to share that tiny detail. She'd thought it was a breakthrough when on Christmas she shared that she didn't know how to make anything else. But she saw now that she'd been too slow to work up to the larger, more important parts of the story. And even then, she hadn't explained that she'd been afraid to go back and face Richard, that she'd had trouble asking a simple question about how much to buy. She hadn't said a word about the insecurity that had spurred it all.

Ed screwed up his face tight, as if she'd just smacked him.

"I don't get you, Ruby. I really don't." He shook his head, looking at her hard, like this might help him to get a better view.

"How could you?" she said. She'd meant it as an opening, a way to say, "I haven't let you." But nothing came out after, and hanging by itself those three words sounded harsh, accusatory, as if he wasn't capable.

"Ruby, why don't I know anything about you? Why does that girl downstairs, that cop, for chrissakes, know more than I do?" He looked defeated, all hopeless curves; there was a hole in his sock exposing a purple bruise on his second toenail.

She still had her jacket on, and her clothes felt stuck to her, like she'd have to peel them off after everything she'd been through with them on today. And she just stood there—not knowing how to explain the answer to that, knowing he'd been patient, waited and probably suspected she'd needed time, realizing she'd run out of it now, that this was make or break. She felt the back of her engagement ring with her thumb. She was so close. She'd come so close. All she had to do was start: *I was scared you would leave me.* He would understand. It was obvious in his every look, every touch, that he would understand. But this wasn't enough of an assurance for Ruby. "You do know me," she said pathetically.

He shook his head, some imaginary line having been crossed. "How can you just stand there and lie to me?" He rummaged around in his pants pocket and pulled out Robert Cohen's contract with her. "I found this in your jeans when I was cleaning up earlier, trying to do something nice for us, something that might encourage you to open up to me. A private investigator, Ruby? How could you go off and do something like this and not even talk to me about it? I swear if feels like you are living a double life—that you just don't trust me enough to be part of the really important things. I'm sick of rummaging around for clues, Ruby. I feel too desperate, scrambling after you like this."

Her limbs went cold with the reality of it all. She'd been caught. She'd been found out. And worse was what she hadn't accounted for, how hurt and angry Ed would be. Her face burned. *They'll only disappoint you, Ruby Booby.* Had her mother gotten that the wrong way around? "I . . ." But the word faded to nothing. She felt her mind turn to its familiar excuses—if only she could have had a little longer, if she'd gotten the truth from Robert Cohen, she would have come to Ed—but she could see the emptiness, the untruth of this now. It would never have been enough to make her stay, to unpack every little last bit and trust someone for real. Her worst fears had been true all along. She was exactly like her momma.

"You'll tell a freaking stranger your entire life's story and you won't tell me a goddamned thing. Do you really think this is going to work out?"

"Ed, I'm sorry," she said, her throat impossibly tight. He was right about all of it. Still, the words she searched for were somehow kept hostage atop a giant mountain, and she couldn't find the path to even start the climb. She didn't have the right shoes, the right build, the know-how, one of those heavy-looking backpacks.

She watched, powerless, as he pulled a bag from the top of the hall closet, made his way to the bedroom and loaded it with shirts and pants, ties, underwear, old pilled socks he still had because she hadn't even been able to find the words to advise him to get new ones, she hadn't even been capable of communicating a tiny thing like that.

Finally, he pulled his own jacket on—the tan fabric skimmed his shape so nicely—and said, "I'm going to stay at my brother's place for a little while."

Unbelievably, she watched him turn, close the door behind him, heard his footsteps down the stairs. She moved to the window, saw him walk away from her—a painfully familiar sight, a recurring nightmare that she now saw for what it was: a self-fulfilling prophecy—and she couldn't stop the tears from coming now, even if she'd tried.

Ruby found herself lying on the bed, face down, trying to block reality out, willing herself back to a time when she could have had more time to work it all out, to peel back some of her onion skins. This was a childish endeavor, and she knew it even while she dug her fists in beneath her pillow, locking herself in like she once had when her momma decided to move from Northern California to Southern California, though she'd made such terrible claims against it, though she'd already warned Ruby that she didn't have a big enough chest to be let through the dividing line. Still, she had to indulge a little in the tempting, though unrealistic, possibility of it.

She pictured herself in turquoise (in many of her imaginings, Ruby pictured herself in turquoise, since it never seemed to look nice in real life and this exercise made her feel at least she got some use of the color), at an expensive seafood restaurant they'd once eaten at in West Hartford. In front of a giant pane of mirror, beneath a gigantic circle-over-circle chandelier, Ruby would have said, "Listen, Ed. There's something you don't know about me. I'm afraid to drive. I'm afraid of men walking out on me. I haven't got much confidence. I've never gotten over the fact that I don't know my father, even though I make cavalier jokes about my childhood. I'm afraid if I tell you all these things, you'll see there really wasn't much to love in the first place."

But it wouldn't take. She couldn't say those things. Maybe it was best that he left. Easier. Now she'd never have to go through the pain of it. She was doing better with her business now, so maybe that could keep her busy. She'd managed to convince the public that she knew who she was, even if she couldn't convey that to Ed, or herself, for that matter.

After a couple of hours, Ruby got up and made herself some tea. She sat on one of the four kitchen chairs and waited for the water to boil. It was incredibly quiet. The refrigerator compressor kicked on for a moment to fill up the silence, but then that quit and the nothingness was even more apparent. The kettle seemed to take forever to boil. Looking around the kitchen, she noticed suddenly that Ed had cleaned up in there. She walked through the whole apartment and realized he'd cleaned every room. He'd picked up the socks, the underwear, the undershirts and ties. Everything was in its place; all the things that had become intolerable to her were completely corrected and now she realized they hadn't meant a fucking thing. Ed was gone and she'd let him empty all the drawers onto the floor, hers, too, if he'd just come back.

The water was boiling furiously when she returned to the kitchen. She pulled a mug down from the cabinet. It was from Ed's company: American Insurance. She was reminded of the way he answered his extension at the office. "Ed, American Insurance," he said.

"Oh," she'd said once. "I was looking for Venezuelan Insurance. I must have the wrong number."

"Hilarious," he'd said. "Wanna have lunch?" She'd had all those chances to share—lunches and dinners, long car rides. All those times she saw the expectation in his eyes, she'd convinced herself it wasn't there, that it was all in her imagination.

She blamed her momma, sure she did. It was impossible not to. But her momma wasn't here now; she hadn't done this to Ruby. Ruby'd done it all herself.

Ruby sat with that idea, watching the clock until it was midnight. She dialed her momma twice, but hung up before the call went through. Once she'd waited to hear her voice on the other end before cutting the connection.

She couldn't bother Dina, who needed rest, who had bigger worries then. Jack would have been sleeping for five hours already. Sammie had her own problems. But then she thought of it: Selma and Merry. She knew they'd come.

"Can I ask you something?" Selma said, now occupying one of the kitchen chairs at 1 a.m., next to Merry—both in pajamas pants and T-shirts, sipping tea.

"Sure," Ruby said. Her eyes were puffed, but she didn't hide it now. It was too late for that, and she knew it.

"Why did you open up to us, fill *us* in on all of your demons, but not Ed?"

It was an excellent, fair question. "I guess it's because there didn't seem to be as much of a risk."

"A risk of what?" Merry asked.

"Well, if you didn't like what you saw, if you decided I wasn't for you, I guess . . ." She didn't guess. She knew. She had that part memorized, her brain was branded with it, like a number on a cow's ass.

Selma shook her head, her eyes glistening. "Listen, I've got skeletons in my closet. I've got things people wouldn't like to know."

Merry took Selma's hand then, as her tears were coming quicker. "I'm . . ." Selma paused, looked from Merry—who shook her head in encouragement—to Ruby, and continued, "I'm an alcoholic. Five times off the wagon in the past nine years alone. And that's why I don't have custody of my own kids, of my own house. I've done some things that would make your momma look like a saint."

Ruby was shocked. Here was this beautiful person she'd come to know, and she felt, from the second the words came out of Selma's mouth, that she could forgive anything she'd done, no questions asked. Then why was she so angry at her own momma, so relentlessly unforgiving? "Selma, I'm so sorry. Hey, I forgive you—" She covered her mouth after she'd said it, thinking how strange a thing it was to say. "I mean, I would never hold that against you."

"You've got to tell him," Merry said to Ruby. "It's the only thing. Somehow, you've got to find a way to tell him, and hope to God it isn't too late."

They embraced—the three of them—crying into their tea, propping each other up. Like a family, Ruby thought. This was just what she'd always pictured a family to be.

The next few days were long and empty. Ruby found, when she tried to work, she made ugly things: a long tooth with twisted roots and a cavity; a snail crawling out of its shell; a half-eaten sandwich. She dressed on the third day, wore a green sweatshirt with a zipper and dark jeans with sneakers. She sat on the grass staring at her car. She'd given so much power to the car, but had it been displaced power? Had she been mistaken about it?

Ruby saw very clearly the best way to explore the answer to that question. She was going to take a road trip.

She went back upstairs to pack a few things. She checked in with Robert Cohen.

"I've been talking to people in all the areas where you lived, and I actually found a woman who worked with your mother over at Salamander Books who remembered your mother talking about a guy who was your father. I can't say more than that right now, and nothing has been substantiated, but we're getting somewhere."

Ruby's heart beat the Pachanga. Could she be close? Despite where she'd ended up, how she'd held out for this information in order to feel ready for Ed, being this close did bolster her now. If she could get this information and then come to Ed with that behind her, she'd be stronger, more prepared to face him. She'd have the strength of her father behind her. And she imagined this to be a great, mysterious strength that could solve all kinds of ills.

She'd find out soon. But for now, she was compelled back to the little silver car that had somehow become connected to her, this thing that slept outside her window, no matter the weather, this thing that was always there when she went out to it in the morning. Where was she going? She wasn't sure. She was just going to drive. She drove to the Mobil station first and bought a map. It was the first map she'd ever owned all by herself, not sharing it with her momma. Ruby opened up the entire thing—let the mass of it drape over the steering wheel and well over onto the passenger seat. She ran her finger from where she was up north and slightly to the east. Boston. Why not? She hadn't been there in years.

It occurred to her that her momma lived forty minutes outside of Boston, but this hadn't played a part in her decision, had it? Ruby told herself it was mere coincidence, backed up out of the parking space, and made her way to interstate 91. She followed that to the little pilgrim signs for the Massachusetts Turnpike, remembering the day on the whale-watching excursion. It had seemed she'd made some kind of breakthrough that day, hadn't it? Thinking back, she hadn't really. She'd just felt closer. But now she saw that this thing wasn't like horseshoes—close didn't count for anything. You had to give a relationship everything or it just didn't work out. Sure, she could complain that she didn't know about marriage, hadn't had an example to follow, but by now she knew what had to be done. She only had herself to blame.

Ruby drove, listening to the Supremes, feeling down but somehow stronger, the road out before her, and behind her, the choice of which way to go, it seemed was completely her own.

She followed the signs to Boston, the route clear and simple to follow. This was in her genes after all. And maybe that wasn't as horrible a thing as she'd once imagined.

Ruby parked in an underground lot by Fanueil Hall and walked to the enormous food court. She zeroed in on the nearest clam chowder vendor, ordered a large and a diet soda, and took her orange plastic tray to a corner table to watch the people come and go.

The soup wasn't all that different from the kinds she'd had at home, and this made her think that nothing was ever as good as it was cracked up to be. Halfway through her second to last mouthful she was really hit with the full sense of this sentiment. Would another life have been so much better for Ruby than the one she'd had? She thought of her friends—Dina and Merry, Selma and Jack, Sammie's snarky attitude—and she knew she wouldn't have wound up along this particular road if even one thing in her life had been different. She didn't have to love her past, but she did have to face this one fact: her mother had made her who she was. And there was a point when she had to accept this. And that point was right now. She didn't have to love everything about herself, but she did have to make peace with who she was and how she got here. And she didn't need to know who her father was to share this revelation with Ed. She could do it right now. And she would.

Ruby tossed her tray and ran to her car, wanting to do this now, before she lost the nerve. She moved in jerked, furious movements, her heart racing, her palms sweating along the wheel.

It was dark out, the sky a thick navy blue, by the time she pulled up at the Patriot Rest Stop, nearly three quarters of the way home. Her phone started to ring. She looked down at it, inside the tiny plastic tray in the center console, and saw it was Selma calling.

"You're my one person," she said, the connection perfectly clear, as if Selma were sitting right next to her, even if the sentiment wasn't.

"What's that, Selma?" Ruby asked.

"I've been arrested, and I'm allowed to call one person, and I called you."

Ruby could barely believe this was real. She'd never known anyone who was arrested before. She remembered what Selma had told her the other night about her alcoholism, but hoped this didn't have anything to do with it. However, she didn't ask. Selma was her friend, and more, and this meant she'd be there for her the same way Selma had for Ruby. "I'll be there," she said.

"Okay, well, if you could bring five hundred in cash, that would also be helpful," she said.

"Okay," Ruby said.

Her reconciliation with Ed would have to wait. She just hoped it could.

Twenty-one

You must always share the road with others.

—Connecticut Department of Motor Vehicles Driver's Manual

By the time Ruby reached the police station in New Haven, Selma had just finished all the paperwork and she was going to be released, with Ruby's five hundred dollars and a promise to appear in court. She was quiet in a way Ruby hadn't seen her before. It was evident even with Selma's deeply tanned natural coloring that she was embarrassed, that it had cost her plenty to call Ruby and to prove this terrible thing about herself.

But Ruby felt only sympathy for her friend. She took her out to an all-night diner, complete with neon, on the main strip in Middleville to go over everything that had happened.

They sat in a large booth, ordered a coffee and a hamburger apiece, and settled in.

"So tell me what happened," Ruby said.

"Well, first, after work I met up with two women who own the shops near Ripe—Esther and Patricia—and we went to grab a bite at this Mexican place around the corner. We had a nice time, ate some gooey cheese and beans and crap, drank a margarita each. But then the girls wanted to leave. I didn't really want to go home, because I was feeling pretty down and didn't think it would be a good idea to be alone. So I stayed. And I had four more margaritas."

Ruby's palm cupped her mouth. "You didn't."

Selma shook her head. "Oh, but I did. And when they closed the place up, I walked around and went to another place, and had a couple of gin and tonics. And then I walked to my car and thought, *Well, I have to get home.* I can't exactly stay here all night. It seemed like a good idea at the time. But, now, it's pretty obvious that was only because I was loaded, which was only because I'd called my daughter Becky earlier to see if she'd done well on her Spanish test and she told me what did I care? It's not like I was involved in her life the way Jonathan's new wife, Cindy, is. I swear though, I didn't think about a thing all day but that Spanish test. At one point I felt like I was in that classroom with the girl, taking the damned test. And she tells me what do I care?"

The waitress brought their coffees, and a saucer filled with sealed creamer cups. They each dumped a creamer and a couple of sugar packets into their coffee. Ruby let her fringe bangs fall over her eyes so Selma wouldn't see the tears.

"That had to have been awful for you to hear," she managed to get out.

"Come on, Ruby, you've got to resent a thing like that, having the kind of mom who couldn't find her way yourself. Maybe she didn't drink, but she made you pay for her mistakes all the same."

Ruby shook her head. "No, I don't resent what you did, Selma. You give me the other side. And I think that's important—to see the other side. It's much easier to be black and white about things, but going through these things with you kind of tears down those boundaries."

Selma was quiet, sipping her coffee. "You're a lot smarter than you look," she said, finally.

"That's not the first time I've been told that," Ruby said. "So

why don't you tell me how the police wound up getting involved?"
She hooked her arm over the back of the yellow vinyl booth.

"I was driving and heard the siren and then noticed the lights behind me. I pulled over onto the shoulder and the cop walked up to
the car.

" 'Good evening, ma'am,' the guy says. 'Where are you coming
from?' And I say, 'Oh, I had dinner with my girlfriends,' but it must
have been obvious from my speech or eyes or something because he
goes, 'You have anything to drink tonight?' And I say, 'No, I didn't.'
So he asks for my license and registration and then he tells me to get
out of the car and tells me he's gonna give me a couple of tests because he smells al—"

Selma got stopped up on account of the tears. "I'm sorry, it's
just, I don't think I'll ever be out of this cycle. It feels like I'll always
be screwing everything up, getting just that close and then fucking it
all up again. Don't feel bad for me, Ruby. I do this all to myself. All
of it."

"No, I know. We all do. We all do." She repeated it because the
truth of it hit so deeply.

They were silent for a second, in the sober truth of that. Then
Selma shook herself out, and the burgers arrived. "Anything else,
ladies?" the waitress asked, and when they shook their heads, she
tore their check from her pad and placed it face down on the table.

"So now he says he smells alcohol on my breath. He takes me to
walk along the white line on the side of the highway, puts me at one
end of it, stands a few feet away from me, and tells me to walk in a
straight line toward him, heel to toe and then to turn around and
walk back. Of course I can't make it halfway to him without trip-
ping over my own goddamned foot."

"And what happened after that?" Ruby felt all her limbs tense.
She hated to think of Selma going through all of this, what it would
mean to her children, to her relationship with them. If there was a
way for her to undo it, she would. She certainly would.

"Well, the guy makes me sit there for about another twenty-five minutes, just waiting while all the time I've gotta pee. He makes me sit there and wait and finally he looks at his watch and says, 'All right, now we're gonna do another test.' He tells me to lift one leg up while I touch my nose. It's ridiculous and my limbs won't obey at all. I was sure I'd failed. He tells me he's going to test my eyes now, and takes a pen and runs it past my eye to one side and then the other. He says he can tell from this test, which is called a horizontal something or another, that I'm intoxicated and that he's going to have to place me under arrest."

"You must have been terrified," Ruby said. For once, she could barely eat her hamburger.

Selma hesitated for a second, as if she were going to say something but thought better of it. "Yeah," she finally said.

Selma stayed the night at the apartment and by morning Ruby had narrowed down her attorney list to two. "What do you think of these two?" Ruby asked. She passed the pages she'd printed out over to Selma.

"J. Thomas Pecorina or T. James Romano—what is this, a joke? You give me dueling cheeses to choose from?"

"I thought they sounded like names you could trust," Ruby said, pouring out some coffee for Selma and herself. The truth was that their websites had impressed her most. She hadn't haphazardly scanned for Jewish-sounding names; she'd carefully researched the best candidates, and these fit the bill. It wasn't that Ruby had purposely tried to do things in the opposite way that her momma would. It was that she'd listened to her own voice alone—and this was where it had directed her.

"All right, let's go with Pecorina, then, since that part comes first; it sounds more important."

"They both specialize in DUI, it says right there on the websites, so I think we can trust him," Ruby tried to sound confident. "Plus, I remember Ed mentioning these guys. He'd had a couple of claims with them and he said they're pretty good." It felt strange to say his name. Since he'd been gone she tried not to utter it.

"Ed, huh? Are you going to talk to him?"

Ruby wasn't going to let Selma think she'd stood in the way of anything. But the truth was, she'd lost that nerve she'd had the night before, had no idea how to grab hold of it again. She checked her phone but there were no messages, the same went for email, the mailbox. She couldn't help but wonder how he'd fared these two evenings without her? Had he been missing her? Or had their distance reinforced the idea that maybe they shouldn't be together after all? "Hopefully," she said, her nose wet from the tears before she knew it.

"Oh, Ruby, you've got to talk to him. I'm sure he's missing you like crazy, just sitting there waiting for you to call."

Ruby shook her head. She couldn't talk about it anymore just then. She was back to waiting things out, and no one was going to convince her otherwise.

After a lunch of tuna salad sandwiches on white toast, Ruby drove Selma home to shower and change and then to the attorney's office. The office was housed in a small brick building across from the library, where Ruby and Ed had watched the fantastic singer and danced with such freedom, the world at their fingertips. She pulled into a spot facing the pretty library. "You ready for this?" she asked Selma.

"Ready as I'll ever be," she said. She had dressed conservatively, more so than she usually did—in a navy pantsuit—and Ruby thought how much more like a mother she appeared, her idea of them, or what they should be rather, fluctuating always.

Ruby squeezed her hand, shook her head in what she hoped was an affirmative manner. Together they walked into the cold building, found the placard for J. Thomas Pecorina, Attorney at Law, and walked the steel staircase up two flights. Ruby pushed the door open, and at the reception window announced, "Selma Torano, for Attorney Pecorina."

"He'll be right with you," the woman with her giant eyeglasses and shellacked updo announced.

"Thanks." They took seats on either side of an occasional table, stacked with issues of *Time*, *Life*, and *People*. There was one other person waiting—a young man in khaki pants and a sweater, and he was bouncing his crossed leg up and down, as if he were as nervous as Ruby and Selma were.

"Selma Torano," the receptionist called, this time emerging from behind a door, holding it open for them.

They both stood and followed the woman down the hallway to the last white door, past a handful of others. Inside the room was rather sterile: Berber carpeting, a long wooden table, six leather chairs, a couple of windows looking over the branches beyond—which Ruby noticed now were in full bloom. How strange that time could go on, as if everything were as it had been, as if she and Ed weren't apart.

J. Thomas Pecorina entered, in a navy suit and a tie designed with a world map down the front. "Now which one of you is Selma?" he said. Selma stuck her hand up, as if she were a schoolgirl and scared as hell. "And this is my friend Ruby."

He shook her hand, in a caring way, long and firmly, and then did the same for Ruby. "Ladies, would you like some tea or coffee?"

They both shook their heads no; Ruby imagined that Selma wanted to be out of there as quickly as possible.

"Now, let me confirm all your info first," he said, opening a file containing about five computer-printed pages. He took her date of birth, social security number, and contact information and wrote it on a yellow legal pad. "Have you ever had any trouble with the law before?"

Selma turned to Ruby, her mouth sagging to the floor. She answered facing her like that. "I had another DUI five years ago and I went through the program."

Ruby screwed her face up. She had no idea Selma was in such a bad way. It must have been treacherous, all of her darkest secrets coming to light this way. But in a way Ruby felt closer to Selma than she ever had before, to be on the other side of her—the side people didn't ever get to see.

"Unfortunately, you can only use that safe-driving program once in ten years to avoid jail time or community service, so we might be looking at some other penalties, but why don't we start from the beginning and see exactly what we're looking at here. Why don't you walk me through your version of the events," he said, sitting up straighter, his pen poised to take notes down.

She went through the whole story, flushing as red now as she had the previous night. Ruby wished she could let Selma go home and do all of this for her. It was terrible to see someone you cared about suffer so much, especially when you knew they were already angry as hell at themselves for it all.

When Selma got to the part about sitting in the car for twenty-five minutes, Attorney Pecorina stopped her. "You're sure it wasn't thirty minutes?" he asked.

She shook her head yes.

"If that's true, you might be in some serious luck, because the law clearly states that the second test must be administered no less than thirty minutes after the first one. And if that time is inconsistent, by even as little as two minutes, then the entire testing process is legally invalid."

Selma looked slightly hopeful. "Now that would be lucky, since this is your second offense, and as I said you wouldn't be able to get off on what they call the criminal phase with just the program this time around. If you plead guilty, you could be looking at six months of jail time. For the second phase, which they call the administrative phase, you could get at least a ninety-day license suspension—and up to a year.

"Now the good thing is," he continued, smoothing down his tie, "that you chose to go with someone who's got experience with this system. So it's my job to educate you and guide you through it all. For the jail time, we can often substitute one hundred hours of community service. But if this is true, about the tests not being a half hour apart, chances are you can walk away on a technicality."

Attorney Pecorina directed Selma to call him the second her court appearance notice came in the mail. If they missed this date, all the penalties could be much worse, he advised. She promised to do so, and for now, Selma could breathe a little better, with the tiniest inkling of hope.

"Would you mind driving me to work?" Selma asked. "I feel like such a loser, I can't even drive myself to work; can't even pick up my own kids." Finally, in Ruby's passenger seat, looking out at that pretty old library, Selma let it all go.

Ruby spent some time at her apartment, cleaning incessantly, rather than call Ed and face things. She went out for a walk with Sammie, listened to the excitement in her voice about going to Hunter College. "You've done this for me, Ruby. You treated me like a regular person; not like a cripple," she said. It warmed Ruby's heart; and when Sammie asked if it was raining, because of the tears flowing down onto Sammie's hair, she didn't lie. She said, "No, you made me cry, you pain in the ass." She couldn't help but hope that one day she'd have this kind of close relationship with her own daughter. And if her own daughter was half as wonderful as Sammie was, she'd be the happiest mother in the world.

After the walk, the afternoon dragged out long before her, and Ruby found herself falling into childhood patterns—looking toward her books, longing to dive into their worlds for companionship. But then something hit her. She didn't have to retreat into those make-believe places for camaraderie. Ruby had people that cared about her now. Was this lesson so hard learned that she'd have to lose Ed permanently to have gained it, though?

She put on a floppy brown hat with a leather strap around the base, grabbed her keys from the pretty bowl, and looked at herself in the mirror beside the door. They'd bought the ornate gold thing at a garage sale right when they'd moved in. It had been so much easier to take someone else's old belonging into this place and hang it up, so much easier than diving into her own things and everything that came along with that.

She gazed at herself in the oval mirror. There was something different. And it wasn't just the hat. Ruby was standing taller, there was a steadiness to her gaze that hadn't been there before. Here she was, with a bunch of wedding plans and no groom to be, and she was still standing strong.

She smiled at herself. There were horrendous mistakes she'd made, but Ruby had a hunch that girl in the mirror could fix them.

She locked the door behind her. The day was sunny, not a cloud in the sky—just miles and miles of bright blue open to the possibility of anything, open to the interpretations of anyone who happened to look up at it. So many things had happened, but one thing had remained unchanged. She could climb into her car and go where she wanted. And now she pulled up to Jack's office, where so much of it had begun.

The front door of Drive for Life was all glass, and when she came near, she could see Jack sitting at his desk, staring up at the ceiling. There were two empty desks off to the side, and Ruby knew they hadn't been used in years. On top of both of them stood wood-look file boxes, two of them open, with neat manila file folders standing upright inside.

Jack looked like a person going through the motions, waking up and getting dressed and driving to work, far after the time had come for a change.

He'd done a poor job shaving; a tiny tissue stuck to his chin; probably his vision wasn't what it once was and the fact that no one had reminded him to pull it off hit her hard. She couldn't help but think that same thing that got her every time—how could life be so unfair? The people who got fathers didn't even appreciate them, and the ones who'd give anything to have one couldn't even track them down with the help of a private investigator.

She shook herself from such thoughts, knowing they wouldn't do her a bit of good, and shifted her hat down in the back. Ruby pushed the door open.

"Is this the best driving school in the country? Because someone told me that it was," she said, by way of greeting, and went around the desk to hug Jack. He looked like he needed a hug; she sure as hell did.

"It's always a pleasure to see you," he said. "I was just thinking about you, actually." He stood, pulled the guest chair from the front of the desk over to the side of it, close to his own chair, and motioned for her to sit.

To hear him say that about her! Ruby realized he didn't have to be her father for that to feel good. It just felt good to have her friend, Jack, say it. His foam hat was off to the other side of the desk, and his hair was thin—see-through—and she could see a few darker spots on the skin above his ears on either side. "Good things, I hope," she said.

"Yes, good things. But I was also a little worried. I haven't talked to you in a couple of days and I hoped you were okay."

The idea that he cared for her well-being swelled up inside of her. It made her feel like she could do anything. It was becoming clearer: she just needed to jump in and say to Ed all the things she hadn't. There was no other way.

She told Jack what had happened—with Dina and Sammie, and finally, how Ed had left her. How she'd never told Ed that Jack wasn't someone she knew from volunteering at a canned food drive.

Jack shook his head. "I'm so sorry, honey," he said. The sound of him saying those things brought a stream running from her eyes, wetting down her neck and inside her shirt. "All I know, Ruby, is this one thing. There are a lot of things that people never say to the person they love because they are afraid of what might happen if they do. But the truth is, if those things send that person away, then they never really loved you in the first place. And it would be a lot better to know that kind of a thing up front, than to go through forty years of marriage only to find yourself old and no longer attractive, and to find it out then."

It was solid advice that only experience could inspire. And that's what made it so heartbreaking. "Jack, you are *very* attractive. Hey, if I wasn't in love with Ed . . ."

He waved her comment off with a grin. "I'm old enough to be your father," he joked.

And this time, when he voiced such a thing, it didn't hurt nearly as much as she would have expected. "Hey, you wanna grab some lunch?" she asked.

"What'd you have in mind?" he asked, shrugging on the light canvas jacket that hung over the chair back.

Just then, Ruby felt the vibration of her cell phone in her coat pocket. She lifted it out. The screen showed the call was from Robert Cohen, the PI. Her heart plunged. She wasn't sure what she was about to hear, but she couldn't wait unnecessarily. "Hey, sorry, Jack, I have to be rude and take this call."

He waved her on encouragingly, to show he didn't mind at all. Jack turned to lock the door while she walked the few feet to her car.

"Robert!" Ruby was surprised at the rapid pace of her heart. All this time, she'd been alternating between hoping and then forcing herself not to hope so much. Now she couldn't help but again feel that too much was riding on this. Was this just another roadblock she'd stuck in her path?

"Ruby! How are you?" He sounded far off; there was the sound of traffic honking and groaning on his end.

"Okay. Do you have something?"

"Well, as a matter of fact, I do. I'm here in Jersey, and I've been following around a Gregory Jameson born in Bayonne, New Jersey in '53. Haven't been able to confirm one hundred percent yet, but I've got a strong hunch this might be our guy." She heard a car door slam and the noise on his end settled down somewhat.

Ruby's breath caught. Could it be? "Jameson?" She was puzzled.

The name was new to her. The tears were not. She said the name over and over again, pulling apart the syllables, attaching her name to it: *Ruby Jameson.*

"I checked the records in the hospital where you were born, in New Jersey, and that showed nothing. So I did some snooping with the neighbors over there."

New Jersey! That was so close. Could it really have been that her father was here, right under her nose, all this time? She tried to remember more about her neighbors, the places they'd lived. She did recall that they'd lived in two different spots in Bayonne—an apartment over someone's garage with bold brown and green flowered carpeting that Ruby would pretend was a garden she had to care for, and a tiny house behind the pet shop, where Ruby was permitted to play with the dogs in the fenced-in area in front of her house. "So how do we find out for sure?"

"That's where things get tricky. But I'm working on it, Ruby. Robert Cohen always gets his man."

"All right. Well, call me as soon as you know anything." Ruby felt like the truth must be so close, she could top the hamburger she was about to eat with it. *Was this it? Had she been right to pursue it, to hold out for this last bit to make her whole?*

"Will do."

Ruby snapped her phone shut and zipped it back inside her coat pocket. *Gregory Jameson. Gregory Jameson. Gregory Jameson.*

"What the heck was that all about?" Jack asked. He had climbed inside the passenger seat, but hadn't closed the door, so he must have caught the gist of the conversation.

"Do you really want to know?" Ruby asked as she climbed in, turned to him.

"Yeah. You can tell me anything, Ruby."

"Well, I went and hired a private eye to find my dad."

Jack removed his hat, placed it in his lap. His finger edged the rim. "Are you sure that's what you want to do?"

Ruby wasn't sure. Just when she thought she was, she'd flip-flop and think this was a terrible idea. Already her stomach was whirling with anxiety over what seconds ago she'd been thrilled beyond comprehension about. "Well, no. But I just feel like this is something I need to do."

"Do you know *why* you need to do it?"

She thought about this before answering, grabbed onto the steering wheel, sliding her hands left and then right on the locked wheel. "Because then I can finally be comfortable and move on with my life."

"Ruby, I hate to point this out, but you said the same thing when you came to see me for your driving lessons. Honestly, do you know how many times I started a sentence with 'When I . . .'? Thing is, there's always something that'll stand in your way if you let it. And if you're always looking for that one thing you're missing, you'll never see what you've got right in front of you. You'll never be happy. For you, it's your dad. For my wife, it was wealth. And look where it got her."

They sat there, exploring the planes of each other's faces, and the truth of what he'd just said. Inside the compact car there was a world of experience between them.

For all their experiences, though, they were both in this same place, Ruby thought. She hoped it wasn't true that finding her father wouldn't help things. Despite the strength she'd tried to have, she couldn't bear, after all this time, if that were true. It was accurate to say that not long ago, she thought learning to drive would allow her to be comfortable and that this would change her life. And it had been a good start, but here she was again, that same aching, unsettled-until-this-is-done feeling in her gut. Maybe the Reynolds women just weren't cut out for marriage. Maybe her momma had been right all along.

Jack zipped up his coat higher—all the way to his chin. "Hey, why don't we get out of here?" He put his hand on Ruby's and looked at her seriously. "I wish I could tell you this and you would take it to heart and not allow yourself to make these mistakes, to get hurt by them. But I am a father, and I know that children have to make their own mistakes, and no matter how hard you wish otherwise, they'll never learn from someone else's experiences. It has to be done by them; it's the hard way or no way at all for most of life's important lessons."

"Thanks, Jack," she said. So many times she'd dreamed of this kind of tender advice, the kind of caring that was so apparent in Jack's eyes then. And as she turned the car on, the car he'd taught her to drive, she realized that in a way, her dream had already come true.

They shared a nice dinner. Afterward, Ruby picked Selma up from the shop and dropped her off at her home. When she turned the key and pushed the door of her own dark, empty apartment open, she still wished she'd find Ed there, even though his parking spot had been empty. But it was all blackness in there, and she stumbled for the light switch. Suddenly the telephone began ringing.

She dropped her keys into the bowl and ran for it, hoping, praying it was Robert Cohen with the big news. Her breath came shallow, like she couldn't gulp enough air to prepare her for this.

"Hello?" Ruby asked, the old-fashioned telephone cradled between her cheek and shoulder. She wrung her hands.

Her heart dropped as soon as she heard the sing-song voice clearly. Even through the miles, her momma's words boomed. "*Ruby Booby*, guess who's coming for a visit?"

Twenty-two

The rules and commonsense suggestions can also help refresh the memories of parents and others who have been behind the wheel for many years.

—Connecticut Department of Motor Vehicles Driver's Manual

First there was a triple knock at the door that Ruby would recognize anywhere. Then she heard the sing-song voice clearly through the door, "Ruby Booby, aren't you gonna let your momma *in*?"

Even before she opened the door, just sixteen hours after her momma had called, Ruby felt the air, the normally rigid lines of the floor, walls, and ceiling wave up under her momma's spell. She was bigger than anything, it seemed to Ruby. No matter the time, her momma could come crashing into Ruby's life and create havoc.

As a child and teenager, Ruby would burn up with embarrassment when her momma paraded her around to the delicatessen, the mall, restaurants, announcing personal things, such as, "Ruby just got her first bra today! Smaller than a doll's, I'm telling you!" She'd squirm, fidget with a sliver of paper in her jeans pocket, wishing she was old enough to leave.

"Ruby!" Her momma threw her bags onto the carpet dramatically. Her red hair, unarguably the source of Ruby's red hair, was wild—not soft like Ruby's but more like a brillo pad that had been frayed to an unrecognizable shape. It was still long and still in a ponytail with a puffy elastic at the base of her skull. "Let me look at you!" Momma stood in the doorway, so Ruby couldn't close the door. Ruby looked out into the dim light streaming from the sconces along the hallway walls and hated the idea that the other tenants on her floor could possibly hear this.

"Did you gain a little weight?" Momma asked. Had she? She hadn't thought about it. But, since she wouldn't have to worry about fitting into a wedding dress any longer, it didn't seem to matter much. In a huff of self-pity, Ruby wished she'd gain a hundred pounds, a thousand pounds, just to show her momma, yes! My life is screwed up and it's all your fault; this is why I am the size of a Macy's Parade Woody Woodpecker! But she wouldn't.

On the other hand, Momma certainly had put on a few pounds herself. She'd never been thin, but now she was thicker around the middle, so that her jeans bumped out below the waistline. She wore the same kind of long, plain shirts she'd always been fond of—this one a hunter green with three buttons at the neckline. The shirt made her chest appear enormous and gave her no shape whatsoever. Ruby never understood the look. Why couldn't her momma just tuck her shirt in? She caught herself caring about this ridiculous thing, the same kind of thing she always fell into around her momma and made a conscious effort to stop. What did she care about her momma's shirt when her entire life was falling apart?

There were more important things happening here for her to concentrate on. And the first of them was: she was not going to tell her momma about Ed leaving. No matter what, she would not let her know that things hadn't worked out, that she was just like her.

"Momma, why don't you come in and sit down and I'll make you some tea?"

"Do I look like some old lady to you? I don't need to rest, Ruby. I'm here to help you!"

Momma showed herself into the apartment, nearly trampling over Ruby. "Please, follow me," Ruby mumbled at her back. Sixty seconds and already she'd retreated back to childhood.

"It looks . . . interesting in here. Whaddyou call this?" She was fingering a frame Ruby had made from a couple of pieces of driftwood that she and Ed found at a tiny beach he liked in Rhode Island. When she'd presented it to him, he'd nearly cried, he was so touched that she'd done that with a memory of theirs. Inside was a picture of the two of them in front of their Christmas tree.

Looking at it now, it was nearly impossible to keep the guise up, to act like everything was okay. The pain ripped through Ruby like a jackknife. There they were—right in front of her; couldn't they just get back there? It seemed so simple, and yet Ruby knew that picture only told half the story.

"It's a frame, Momma."

"But what is it made from? Looks like trash or something."

She wasn't going to bother explaining. She picked up her momma's bag and brought it into her studio. There was a pull-out sofa for her momma to stay on in there.

"I hope this is not a photo of you in front of your own Christmas tree, Ruby." Apparently her momma wasn't ready to move onto another subject. Her voice rang out strong down the hall to Ruby.

She tried to ignore her comments. If she engaged, it would only be worse. She knew that and tried to resist.

"You know how I feel about Christmas trees, Ruby! They stand for everything that is wrong in this world. Everything covetous and ignorant and competitive."

Already Ruby felt herself being sucked in. Her momma was bigger, it seemed, than all of the changes Ruby had made, all the accomplishments she'd piled up. On the tip of her tongue was the name she thought could save her from it all: Gregory Jameson. He probably loved Christmas, waited for it all year like Ruby did. Ruby felt a small pang of power at the idea that her momma didn't know about her search for Gregory Jameson.

"It's not ours," she lied. Sometimes that was easier.

"Oh," Momma said. The conversation had centered around Ruby for about as long as her momma could ever stand and so she steered it around to herself. "So that's it with Louis. I told him I wasn't coming back from this trip."

Though she wasn't along for the ride this time, Ruby felt the familiar terror creep through her limbs, the slippery slope of moving on. "Where will you go?" she asked, sitting back on her own sofa, with its perfect, matching cushions—the same ones she'd had in New York City, the same ones she'd had for six years by now—as if it were a life preserver that could save her from the deluge.

"I'm just gonna drive and see where the wind takes me," she said.

Oh, how Ruby hated that saying! She'd been just four years old the first time she heard it! She couldn't remember much about living in Bayonne, New Jersey, but she remembered her momma saying that, sleep still at Ruby's eyes, warm at her chest and back, as she carried her daughter into the front seat. Ruby hadn't known what was going on. "I'm just gonna drive and see where the wind takes me," she vaguely heard her momma say. Ruby drifted off to sleep dreaming about that cute little poodle she'd played with all week. Wherever Ruby threw the chewed-up orange ball, that dog would run and grab it, bring it back to Ruby. When she woke, they were already way upstate in New York. She told herself the puppy never left, that unlike the other dogs he got to stay just where he was, unchanged, so at least she would know how exactly to miss him.

But she wasn't part of that now. Now she was living in Connecticut, and she hadn't run away when a problem had presented itself. She hadn't exactly solved it yet, but there were many facets to it all—just like the pretty diamond on her hand—and there were successes she could count among them. She had a family of friends, even fatherly Jack, and she wouldn't be sucked into the black hole that was her momma.

"So what do you want to do?" Ruby asked.

"I want to go get your dress, of course."

"You want to go get my wedding dress," Ruby repeated it. Her heart went cold with it; she couldn't possibly go through the motions of trying on a dress. She'd never get through it without her momma knowing Ed was gone.

"Yes. I'm your momma," she said.

But Ruby understood it was more about Suzanne *not* getting the dress. Ruby's momma couldn't stand to think someone else would be there for those kinds of things. Suddenly Ruby was reminded of another thing she hated for her momma to do; she hated when she said, "*My* Ruby painted this!" or "*My* Ruby baked this entire cake!" She'd say it like it was something she herself had done, like none of the bad things she'd done mattered at all, as if the fact that Ruby could paint a turkey by tracing her palm and blobbing it in with brown tempera color made her a fabulous mother.

"You really think this place is going to give us an appointment today just because we want to go? People wait weeks to get these appointments."

Ruby knew that today was a Wednesday, and it wouldn't be nearly as difficult to get an appointment as if it were a Saturday, but she hated her momma's self-importance—as if everyone should step out of the way; Eleanor was coming. It had always been this way: she'd walk into a supermarket as if she owned the place, waving at the security person, the deli workers like she was Miss America, parading Ruby around like her crown. "*My* Ruby here grew four inches this year!" she'd say to the man Ruby couldn't pick out of a lineup, her momma passing her a slice of Swiss cheese to snack on while the guy ran it through the blade extra thick, so her momma could run through it real quick, like she did with everything. She never knew how to make anything last. Ruby would stand over the cart, hunching until her face was barely visible, wishing she could be one of those Swiss cheese holes, or her own kind of cheese: Muenster or Gouda, milder choices that were more like her, that didn't have anything to do with her momma.

"Just give me the number, Ruby. I'll take care of it."

Ruby had no doubt she would. She was a saleswoman and she was excellent at it.

Five minutes later, they were all set for an appointment in three hours at Stella's Bridal Shop. Suzanne had mentioned it as a place to check out. She'd asked Ruby if she wanted to go plenty of times, but she'd always declined. As pathetic as it seemed, the feeling kept popping up: she wanted to be with her momma when she chose her dress. How could she hold so much anger and yet, somehow, be drawn to her momma in such an instinctive way? Momma showered and changed into a nearly identical outfit.

"Well, we might as well get going. I made a lunch reservation while you were in the shower," Ruby said. "I'll drive," she insisted; somehow this seemed important.

"That's cute," her momma said, like she didn't want to take Ruby seriously.

They walked the staircase down to the main level, pushed the door open and walked across the lot. Finally, they approached Ruby's car. For some reason, Ruby had built this moment up in her mind, as if something monumental would happen. As if her momma would see the car and recognize how far Ruby had come, how difficult the road to here had been. "Here it is," she said, waiting, somehow requiring her momma's approval. She walked around to the passenger side to open the door for her momma.

But she should have known better than to build that kind of expectation.

"Well, this must have been expensive," her Momma said, dragging a finger along the roof. She only ever bought beat-up cars, great big things with banquette seats that guzzled gas and sent noxious fumes up into the air. Ruby thought of them then—through time they'd all merged into one dented, cracked, stained image. This was their familiar ground in a way, strange as it was. It was where Ruby had grown up, on the road.

"Please use your seatbelt, Momma," Ruby said. She tried to hide her disappointment, but it festered the way it always did. This tiny point of contention would spur the growth: Ruby knew that she never used seatbelts in her own car. Always they were tangled and unusable, stuck or completely slack. Soon Ruby would blow up; it was the only way she communicated with her momma.

"Oh, come on! That's silly. I've never used a seatbelt in my life. What the heck do I need to start using one now for?"

"Because it's my car, Momma. I like to feel safe and know that everyone in it is safe." And the tension grew; that tug at her jaw doubled in intensity.

Her momma rolled her eyes, like that was the most ridiculous thing she ever heard. She clucked her tongue while she felt for the belt and clicked it into place. "I don't know when you got so ordinary, Ruby. I don't know when you got to sticking to so many rules. I always told you, we're not like them." And this was how her momma could get to her. She didn't know why she should feel the sting of her momma calling her "ordinary"; it was all Ruby had ever wanted to be. But she knew her momma used the word as an insult, and she hated the way she felt at the sound of it.

Ruby was trying her best, but her momma was pushing her. Why? She wanted to know why they couldn't just be like everyone else! Why had her momma always said that? Had Gregory Jameson been too ordinary? Maybe he liked to wear seatbelts or save driftwood from the beach and her momma just thought that was too plain for them. It took every ounce of self control she could muster to keep Ruby from accusing her mother of just that, of begging her to tell the truth once and for all. But she had Robert Cohen for that. Soon enough she'd know. Right now she had to concentrate on keeping up appearances.

"Ed should be home the day after tomorrow," Ruby said. She figured her momma would be gone by then. "He had to go to Houston. He's going to be so upset that he missed you." In all this time, they hadn't met. They'd spoken on the telephone a couple of times, while Ruby worried over what her momma was saying, what kind of mortifying thing she'd revealed.

"She reminds me of you," Ed said. "The way she laughs." This comment had sent Ruby into a bad direction, though she hadn't shown it. But what would have been the harm?

Ruby was taking her to the most elegant restaurant in the county. Ruby had sat at her laptop computer while her momma showered, searching restaurant reviews online. Finally she'd called Selma to get a recommendation.

"Oh, your mother will love this place," Selma had exclaimed. "But, dear, can I ask you a question?" she'd asked.

"Okay," Ruby said. She was sitting on a kitchen chair and leaned into the back of it then. Her back felt tense. Her entire body did.

"Why all the pressure to impress your mother?" Her voice was kind. She'd come to look forward to hearing it.

"Selma . . . she's . . . sort of hard to please."

"Aren't they all, dear?"

"You're not," Ruby offered, her left shoulder popping up slightly.

"No, not with you. But with mothers and daughters it's different. Mothers want to protect you from the world—no matter how badly they fuck up trying. They want to save you from everything they suffered, even if half the time they wind up dragging you down with them in the process. Unfortunately, you guys don't come with instruction manuals, and we don't get tested before we are allowed to take you home."

Ruby knew the words had come out at a great expense for her friend. "You're going to work everything out, Selma. And I know you'll find a way to make your children know that you love and care for them. There isn't a person in the world who couldn't love you," she said. But even as she did, Ruby knew things weren't that simple. She understood that a hurt child could be very unforgiving, could easily fall in love with a step-parent just to hurt you back. Ruby thought of her hunt for her father with questioning shadows moving in. Why was this so important to her?

"Is Merry driving you tonight and tomorrow, too?" Ruby asked.

They'd worked out a schedule, but she wanted to be sure that Selma knew Ruby was there if she needed her.

"Yes, she is. Don't you worry about me. Maybe you should be worrying about trying on wedding dresses rather than telling your momma the truth."

Ruby breathed heavily. "I know, I know." Even after all of the problems this behavior had started, why was Ruby still hiding the truth to keep up appearances?

As she took the long, curvy road to the restaurant, past quaint farm houses and fields of grazing cows, Ruby stole glances at her momma in her own passenger seat. She didn't look very comfortable there. She'd shifted her old brown leather bag a half-dozen times, applied her berry lipstick, pulled her sleeves up and then down again. It would be the right thing to tell her the truth; Ruby loved to think she'd be compassionate, say the right things. But she wouldn't. And this was why Ruby couldn't tell her. She'd smell Ruby's self-doubt like a shark sniffs out blood, and who knew where Ruby would wind up then?

Despite everything, there it was, their resemblance. In her momma's profile, she could pick out so many pieces of her own—the tiny ears with the translucent skin, the faint eyebrows, the long, but sparse lashes. Sometimes it broke her heart that the only person she could see herself in could have used her so poorly, could have denied her the one thing she'd wanted her entire lifetime, and now, could be contented with only sporadic phone calls and surprise visits.

"We're here," Ruby said, tearing her gaze from her momma, her mind from those thoughts, and back to this moment, surviving this.

"Farm," Momma said, as if the word on the restaurant sign were a sexually transmitted disease.

Of course, Ruby thought. She hadn't picked it.

The restaurant was an old shabby chic barn with wide wooden planks on the floor and walls, and came to a high peak at the middle of the lofty ceiling.

"Ruby, party of two," Ruby said to the hostess—dressed not

unlike Holly Hobby, in an old bonnet and period dress, in keeping with the theme of the place.

"Ah yes, we've got a fabulous table overlooking the hills. And it's a very clear day," the hostess said as they followed her. How funny they must have looked behind her, two pouting redheads behind this old-fashioned girl, walking all the way across the room to a large round table painted white with the edges rubbed for an old look. With the wall of wood frame windows and the hills beyond, Ruby thought the place was utterly charming, wished they could be a happy mother and daughter enjoying such a place.

When the hostess handed them menus, Ruby's momma said real loud, "They had a place kind of like this up in Sonoma. Remember, Ruby? You loved the baked potatoes." She turned to the hostess. "We would just order two baked potatoes and a Coke. You were always crazy for Coke." The hostess stood awkwardly, unsure whether she had to stay for the rest of the information about Ruby's relationship with Coke, until she finally smiled nervously and headed back to the front of the restaurant.

Is that how her momma remembered it, all cozy like that? Ruby pulled the menu up over her face and tried to steady herself. All she could think was how much easier this would be if Ed were here. But she'd never have been herself enough to let him help her through it. Could she now? Hadn't she learned how to feel comfortable enough by this point? She tried to refocus, regain the perspective she'd had at Fanueil Hall, the confidence that had sent her racing home, just before Selma had phoned her.

Ruby remained composed throughout the salad course. She was hell-bent on getting through this, in keeping up the guise. She was maintaining an excellent score, reigning her momma in. And Ruby could tell it was annoying her momma. She didn't like to be reigned in. She liked to make all the rules.

When the check came, mother and daughter grabbed for it. Ruby conceded and allowed her momma to pay for it. Ruby supposed it would make her feel good to do this thing for Ruby. But when she opened the leather folder, she exclaimed, "Wow! This place is expensive. I guess I'll put off my retirement."

"Shall I pay, Momma?" Ruby asked.

"No, no," she said. "I will pay." But the words weren't meant to comfort Ruby. Her momma had so often spent money foolishly, but if it wasn't her own idea, it was never a good one. Ruby sipped her Coke, thinking this would be over before long. She'd get through it.

They drove to the bridal boutique after, and Ruby thought, stealing looks at her momma again, that at least the day was half over. "So how long will you be staying, Momma?" Ruby asked, keeping her eyes on the road as she spoke.

"Oh, I haven't thought about it yet." That's what she always did; this way she had all the control and Ruby was left squirming around, wondering what was going on and when. She might have every intention of leaving tomorrow, but she wouldn't dare say it.

"You're a good driver, Ruby. You always were. I have no idea why you were so afraid of it. I didn't raise you to be afraid of things."

Ruby let the comment pass. If she said one word, she was afraid she would blow. All this time and effort, all the pain and the fears she'd built up in Ruby, and *this* cavalier comment was all she could come up with? It was no wonder Ruby was such a mess. What had her momma been trying to teach her with all this running? It was how she'd learned to be afraid, of this Ruby was certain.

And yet, she knew her momma thought of herself as brave, a soldier of uniqueness, a woman who didn't settle for the ordinary. What a worthwhile cause! Ruby couldn't shake the anger now. It had taken hold of her and wasn't going to let go. Nothing would change between them. No matter where she went, she'd always be the daughter of Eleanor Reynolds and Nobody. She would always be powerless in her desperation to know herself better.

Courage wasn't exactly the word that came to mind. Her idea of teaching courage had been to repeat that horrible phrase: *Don't look back, Ruby Booby; remember Lot's wife. Nobody's got any use for salt these days.* She'd turn it into a joke, even at the worst times, when solid ground was once again behind them, shrinking and shrinking. Ruby looked behind her now, and saw a lost chance to tell the truth to someone who ought to hear it. Where had Ruby gathered her particular set of priorities? She'd learned them in defense, as a way to protect herself, to polish herself off despite how she felt, the fear that burned through her, so at the next stop she'd have a chance to be someone people wanted to know. What better thing than to be the kind of person that someone wanted? It was all crawling up her ankles now, twisting like vines over her kneecaps and around her thighs. And she knew her attempt at hiding it all had been futile. This thing had its own life force, and no matter how many times she hacked it down it would sprout up this way, reminding her who she was.

There was only one parking space open at the bridal shop, and in her frustration, Ruby had a difficult time rocking her car back and forth into it. "I've never been great at parking either," her momma said.

Inside Stella's Bridal Shop, a person like Ruby could almost believe things would be okay. It was an ethereal kind of place—all charm and antiques, sparkly rhinestones and pointy satin shoes. Rows of colorful bridesmaid dresses lined the walls like a candy box of dreams come true.

"Ruby Reynolds is here for her bridal appointment," her momma said to the prim woman behind the glass case, with its unfamiliar, dreamy wares: silk bags to hold gifts, lacy garters, and crystal headpieces.

Ruby sat on a toile slipper chair a few feet away. The entire room was walled with mirrors—framed mirrors, small face-only mirrors, long beveled edge floor-to-ceiling mirrors, and mirrors opposite where Ruby could get a look at the backs of the dresses. The effect was that she couldn't seem to escape herself; she couldn't get into character of the girl planning her dream wedding. This time she didn't think she'd be able to pull it off. She was reminded of something she'd learned in philosophy, something that had scared the crap out of her: the monads—who live without windows and doors, according to Leibniz, because they are isolated and outside. He'd said that the monads are not at home, that no homes exist *for* them. Was this, finally, her fate? Here she was in Connecticut, where she'd come to build a life with Ed that was now broken. And here was the only living blood relative she could claim and this woman was again without a place for Ruby to come to when she needed one. The result was less communication, less trust. Would it end with Ruby alone, with no ties, despite the roots she'd created here with Jack and Sammie, Selma and Merry?

Through the raucous noise in her head, Ruby understood someone was speaking with her. "I'm Stacey, and I'm going to help you to find the dress of your dreams," she said. She was a tiny, delicate woman in a waist-tie dress and slender tan boots.

She asked Ruby what she'd like, but Ruby didn't have the answers. Stacey ticked off a list of possible wants: a tight bodice, a defined waistline, a long sweeping train. And Ruby shook her head to each of them, without the will for anything more. What did it matter which dress she chose?

"Aren't you too tall for that type of dress?" Momma asked suspiciously.

"Oh, no!" Stacey exclaimed in her exclamations-only tone of voice. "You'd be surprised at the options! I'm sure we'll find something for Ruby!" Her rolling curls bounced with the force of her words.

Ruby kept her lips tight, communicated through nods and eye movements.

"Well," Momma said miserably and rearranged her coat on her lap.

Stacey went to the dress room to pull out some options for Ruby, and the two of them were left alone again. Momma never felt the burden of conversation. That was another tactic of hers. She'd let people feel awkward first, that way when she spoke, she had both hands on the wheel of the conversation.

After a few moments, Momma said, "Well, how much do you

think those dresses are gonna cost you?" She looked angry, suspicious, as if Ruby was having a traditional wedding just to spite her.

"About two thousand dollars," said Ruby.

"Well, I was going to offer to pay for it, but not at a price like that!"

Oh, how Ruby was instantly thirteen again! On the way to buy school clothes, her momma would talk grandly about the nice things she would wear to her new school. And then when she'd pick up a tag and see a complete outfit went for twenty bucks at least, she'd say that was too much, and let's go to the Salvation Army where people are sensible.

But Ruby *had* two thousand dollars! She'd spend double that just to piss her momma off if she really wanted to. But really, all she wanted at that moment was to stop trying on dresses, to get out of this place.

Stacey came back with a great froth of dresses, and instructed Ruby to remove her clothes. There she was, with her hands over her breasts, a Little Bo Peep petticoat tied tight around her waist, her stockinged feet sticking out with the gangly toes, when finally she began to cry.

Stacey unhooked, unzipped, and unbuttoned and didn't notice. Ruby didn't look up; she knew if she looked at her momma, she wouldn't go through with it.

"Ruby always hated to wear white," her momma said to Stacey, also unaware. "She said it made her look pale, which it did."

"Momma," Ruby said, her gaze still steady at her feet, her eyes watering them plentifully. But the word wasn't audible obviously, because both women kept on.

She wanted to tell Stacey to stop, but it was too late, she was lowering a huge embroidered princess dress over Ruby's head.

She could feel her chin quiver. She must look ridiculous, she knew.

Stacey crouched down to the floor next to Ruby and tried to fasten the ankle strap of the high-heeled shoe. But it was stuck somewhere in the hemline. She was gently attempting to unhook the gauzy material from the right shoe when she must have felt Ruby's tears on her head, because she looked right up at Ruby and whispered, "People get stuck in these things all the time! Really! These dresses have nothing to do with real life! They're fairy-tale dresses! And fairy tales are very impractical!"

But Ruby couldn't keep it up any longer. "Momma." She said it louder now.

Her momma's face was drained of color, the way Ruby had seen it only once, when she'd fallen from the rope climb in school, all the way from the top, where she'd promised herself she'd go to impress her classmates this time. They'd rushed her to the hospital and Ruby's momma had a pen stuck through the top of her hair when she arrived, this same yellowish pallor to her skin. "What is it, Ruby?"

Even then, Ruby hated the spike of worth she felt when her momma's reaction showed her she cared. "Ed left me."

"Jesus Christ," her momma said.

"I'll leave you two for a second," Stacey said, excusing herself.

This didn't have to be a fairy tale. But it had to be something real at least.

"What did I tell you, Ruby? You never listened to me. No matter what kinds of things I learned the hard way so you wouldn't have to, you just wouldn't learn from my mistakes."

Ruby went cold with the familiarity of that sentiment. It was precisely what Selma had said to her.

"Momma, how could I learn? How? I don't even know who I am. I'll never know who I am." She couldn't keep the tears back now. She knew her momma wouldn't tell her. Tears didn't work with her. She hated what they meant: that Ruby was having a weak moment. There was nothing worse than a weak moment. Soon enough, her momma would leave. She couldn't be around this kind of thing.

"You know exactly who you are, Ruby. You've never changed. You're precisely the same as the day you were born. You were always such a fragile thing, so open to hurt, to pain caused by others."

Her momma's features hardened, a change from whatever softness she'd allowed them in the past few hours. There was that look that Ruby couldn't stand: Momma was disappointed.

Why should she care what her momma thought? How could she not? Here she was in that cycle again. Ruby sat down on the floor, the dress blooming around her like a giant Thanksgiving Parade float. And she was stuck in the middle. She let her head tip back against the wall. Even without her momma, Ruby had managed to lose another person, to have Ed drop right out of her life as if he had never been there in the first place. There was one way out, but Ruby apparently didn't have it in her to go after it. "If I was so fragile, then why in hell would you drag me all around the world, over and over and over? Do you know what that did to me? Do you know how little I care for myself? That's why this didn't work out, that's why nothing will ever work out! Even the critics in my industry say it! Everyone knows Ruby Reynolds has no sense of self, Momma. And that is *your* fault. *You* did this to me."

Momma sat back down on the chair, drew a huge breath and let it out again. "Ruby, when you were a baby, I once gave you three blocks. You picked one up, and then looked at me. You put that one down and exchanged it for the second one, and then you did the same thing with the third. You didn't trust that you knew which block was the right one to pick. This is who you are, darling. I tried to show you over and over again how special you were, I told you every day that we're not like everyone else, we're not ordinary. But the more I said it, the shyer you got. I don't know what else to say about it."

This is why she'd said those things? This was more than her momma had revealed to her before. When she thought of this intimate thing her momma knew about her, this baby Ruby she had in her head to this day, it reminded Ruby what they were: mother and daughter. It was undeniable. There wasn't a thing she could do about that. No matter what she did to reject it, Ruby would be connected to her momma until the day she died. And even then, they'd share histories that go on and on. Her momma would never change;

she'd never be the kind of mother Ruby wanted her to be. She'd never apologize or settle down, and even if she did, it could never change the past.

But there was one thing that Ruby could do to help herself now. She could let go of all that anger, which she could see now was holding her back so fiercely. She could try and let it go and forgive her momma, not in words, which her momma would bat down, but in her heart, where it really mattered most.

With that thought, Ruby felt lighter already. Stacey came in and silently removed the dress. There wasn't anything to say. Ruby slipped her jeans and top back on, plugged her feet into her slip-on flats. She'd been stuck under a five-hundred-pound bodybuilder's weight, and she'd finally found the strength to lift it off herself. She didn't feel good exactly; it wasn't the outcome she'd hoped for her whole life, there wasn't the great embrace, the warm words, the apology, but she saw now this was the best she could hope for. *Fairy tales are very impractical.* But here was something that wasn't. Here was something concrete she could work with, build up from. If she could forgive her momma, she could stop worrying about becoming her, she could concentrate on who she was, and maybe, one day, feel comfortable with whatever that might be.

It had been a long day, and they were both exhausted. Still, when they drove past a used bookstore, Ruby turned around and pulled into the parking lot. Here, among these dime-priced paperbacks, there was something they shared. Here they could pick through the wire shelves and ask, "Did you read this one?" like two people who understood each other very well.

Their conversation was restrained, but not so very much more than normal, since the bridal shop. They had Chinese takeout for dinner, which Momma still compared to Chef Wong after all these years. And Ruby's momma was all settled in the pull-out bed, watching 1960s sitcoms on Nick at Nite, when Robert Cohen called.

She grabbed at the phone jerkily when she saw who it was. She ran into her bedroom and slammed the door shut. If her momma knew about this!

"You're not gonna like what I have to say, Ruby."

Her chest heaved. She sat down on the bed, her legs bent out on either side of her as if she were a leggy calf. After a giant gulp, she asked, "What? What is it, Robert?" She grabbed at the skin on her leg absentmindedly.

"I hit a wall, Ruby. Gregory Jameson isn't your dad. He was just someone your momma was dating out in Bayonne. The woman who told me she remembered him as your dad just had it wrong was all. There aren't any more leads. I really believe this is the end for this search."

She wished he'd never told her that name. She wished she hadn't known the syllables of it, thought whether he'd gone by Greg, hadn't tried her name with his—Ruby Jameson—and liked it so much. *You were always so fragile.*

Despite the forgiveness she was working toward, she'd wanted to tell her momma, "Look! I met him and he loves me and he's going to give me away at my wedding and this time there is nothing you can do about it!" But now there wasn't a single part of that sentence she could utter.

Everything was a disaster. She'd gone from bad to worse. She'd had it all, and now she saw, she'd gone and sabotaged it for herself. There was a long, lonely ride ahead of her if she continued down this road, but she hadn't the map for another destination, she didn't know where to find such a thing. She'd tried to find her own way and wound up getting very, very lost. She thought perhaps she was headed for Bayonne, but now, her heart crashed with the truth of the matter: she wasn't. She wanted to pump her fists in the air and turn blue and scare her mother half to death and finally after all these years have some kind of revenge, closure—something. But she had to remember what she'd felt earlier. Somewhere there was still truth in that, still a better way, though her vision of it was clouded over now.

"Aw, Rube," Ed would have said. But he wasn't here. So, she cried as silently as she could into the place where his chest would have been, so her mother wouldn't hear it over Dick Van Dyke. And finally she fell asleep.

In the morning, Ruby brought her momma a cup of chamomile tea with one sugar cube in a huge mug. Ruby sat down on the open sofa bed and looked at her momma, sleeping soundlessly beneath the soft Egyptian cotton duvet. She could only imagine what her momma would say about the cost of that!

The steam rose and warmed Ruby's face and she really gave her momma a good look. She'd been wearing those flowered floor-length nightgowns since Ruby could remember. They were all flammable polyester and drove Ruby nuts. Couldn't her momma look glamorous, like Marilyn Monroe or Lana Turner? She'd always wanted her to be more like that. Maybe if she'd been more like that, her father wouldn't have left. Maybe if her momma wore more makeup than the swipe of berry lipstick she'd always worn, done something more with her long hair than wear it in a ponytail. After all these years, it was the very same length!

But there were changes. If Ruby inspected around her momma's eyes, she could see a greenish pallor. She could see that she had some brownish freckling at her nose that didn't used to be there. Her hand, balled up loosely over the cover, bore an intricate ladder of deep creases, even in that position. There was a frail quality to her thin arm, the sharp angle of her elbow. What Ruby would give to know the truth inside of that body!

Could one woman truly be deserving of so much resentment? Could she be as huge a force as Ruby felt her to be? Inside her head were answers, but Ruby wouldn't ever know them. She'd failed at finding her father, and it had seemed last night that this would be her ultimate undoing, but now Ruby was more on par with what she'd felt at the bridal shop. Could it be that letting this go, too, had been the best road all along? What could she have gained from knowing this other thing about herself? Would it really change who she was? Would it magically make her life fit together like a ten piece puzzle?

With a start, her mother woke. For a quick second she smiled at Ruby, looking down at her. Then her face took on a mocking demeanor and she asked, "Are you gonna give me that tea cup or am I just supposed to lie here and stare at it?"

Her momma propped herself up on a couple of pillows against the back of the sofa. Ruby handed her the mug and she chipped away at the sugar cube with her spoon.

"Just the way I like it," she said, finally taking a sip. Her glance shifted around the room. "You're doing some beautiful work here," she said. "I think maybe it's your best yet. There's a real sense of . . . well, I guess it's a sense of you," she said.

"Think so?" Ruby asked, trying to seem unfazed though her heart ballooned with those words. Was this her momma's way of apologizing? Despite everything, she couldn't help but care what her momma thought. Once, Ruby had endured a terrible day at school in Massachusetts. She'd decided to go out for the dancing team. But when she arrived at the gym after school, the group of five popular girls in her grade had laughed wildly and then shouted, "I don't think so! Ruby Reynolds, dancing?" She'd stood there, far too long, while the girls got more and more girls laughing. Some of the girls Ruby had actually spoken with from time to time, worked on group projects with. But now with everyone wanting to make the team, they figured they'd better follow suit. She'd sustained her stance, just inside the double doors of the gymnasium, until Mrs. Waxman emerged from the locker room and yelled, "That's quite enough now."

She'd run home the ten blocks she normally rode on the bus, the anger, the frustration with always being new, always being a misfit, high in her chest, drowning her heart. Her momma must have seen Ruby coming from the end of the block because when she reached the house, her momma folded Ruby in the tightest hug, lifting her feet off the ground, kissing her on the ear several times with loud smacking sounds.

"Screw those girls!" she told Ruby after she'd babbled it all out in sobs.

Ruby had been drawn to the power in her momma's voice when she'd said that. She'd tried to zero in on it, scrape a bit of it off to call her own. They went out for fried clams at the Howard Johnson and her momma said that same thing she always did, "We're not like them, Ruby Booby." Just then, the idea of it had seemed like a wonderful, empowering thing, like she was part of something those girls could never be. When she'd gone to school the next day, at least for a while, she'd kept that with her.

It had been some time since Ruby remembered her momma like that, wanting to be connected to her, rather than fearing the worst. "Momma, can I ask you something?"

"Sure," her momma said, blowing at the tea.

"Do you think I'll ever be happy?"

Her momma shook her head, her lips tight. "I do," she said. "You have a spark in you, Ruby; I always told you. There's something special inside of you. But you have to see it. Only you can ignite it."

They were quiet in the echoes of that idea, the empty apartment so big just then.

Momma sighed. "Ruby, it's time for me to go. I need you to drive me to the airport. I'll have my car shipped to me when I settle in back in California." Cars being driven by trucks, finding their way without drivers, finding their way as Ruby couldn't. She felt empty—a sagging balloon descending to the ground; one tiny pinhole could be her final undoing. She'd be alone again.

"Fine." Ruby turned on her heels and got ready to drive her mother into Hartford. Rather than closure, Ruby felt sliced wide open. But on the way home, her hand on the wheel, not like her momma's but in her own way, the way she'd come to recognize these many months, she drove along the three lane road, her car keeping pace with all the others, and she remembered something. She wasn't like the rest of them. And because of that, she'd found others who were just as unique: she'd found Sammie and Jack, Selma and Merry and Dina. She may not have Gregory Jameson, or the kind of mother who would wait it all out with her, encourage her without fail, but she'd had Ed. And she knew exactly what she had to do to get him back.

Twenty-three

Turn on your emergency flashers to show you are having trouble.

—Connecticut Department of Motor Vehicles Driver's Manual

Ruby knew if she didn't do it in person, she wasn't going to do it. And so, directly from the airport, she drove to Ed's brother's house and sat outside wating for Ed's car to drive up. She stared at the little canary yellow ranch house until it became unreal in her mind, until she couldn't be sure if she were even at the right house.

However, Ed's truck finally came chugging up the steepest point of the block, right to the top where Ruby sat waiting, and tugged right at her heart. Seeing him was just like the feeling she'd always imagined love to be like. The slightly off-kilter line of his nose, the angle at which his teeth touched his bottom lip—it all came flying back at her as familiar as details about herself.

When his car pulled into the spot in front of the house, it was on the opposite side of the street from Ruby's car. When he opened the door to climb out, his head turned and he saw her there, her car facing in the opposite direction.

She opened her door, stood up, then walked around, closed the door behind her. The sun was just dipping down behind the hills and shooting a pink light around everything. Her limbs shook violently, but she knew she had to move forward. It was now or never. Somehow she made it across the street.

"What do you want?" he asked. He looked hurt, somehow bruised. His voice was hollow as she'd never heard it. It had been five days since he left. And he hadn't heard from her. Of course he would be angry, hurt.

She took in his scent: soap and aftershave. His hand went to his hair and she wanted to grab it, to kiss him and tell him that way, the way they'd never had trouble communicating. This was uncharted territory, the terrifying unknown. "Do you have time to talk?" she asked. A car zoomed by past them, its free-spirited speed having the effect of further emphasizing the gravity of Ruby's situation. She could keep driving, keep running, or she could face this, accept who she was. This moment was do or die, and she knew it.

He sighed. And she could see the way her hang-ups had hurt him; the great wake of her weaknesses. It wasn't just her own future at stake now. *Will you marry me, Ruby?*

She took his hand and pulled him toward her car. She drove them, in silence, looking over to him every once and again, to that same pond he'd taken her to when he'd brought her naan bread and chutney. It was there she'd seen the beautiful ducks, how complete they'd looked, gliding over the water together.

They sat on that same bench and Ruby turned to Ed, took his hand in both of hers. "Ruby, I'm not going to go through this again. I gave you so many chances. I . . . I can't do this without all of you."

She had hurt him, but she had to show him that she wouldn't do that now. "Ed, look. I know what I did was wrong. I knew it all along, but I let my fear dictate my actions. I didn't know how to trust myself. What I need you to understand is that it wasn't you I didn't trust." She knew this was the most important thing. He'd tried so hard to show her that he was patient and kind, and that whoever it was that had hurt her before, he was nothing like them.

He looked at her, his eyes wet, his jaw set. This wasn't going to be easy. "Do you know how much it hurt to see you share yourself with strangers, rather than with me? Do you know how low I sunk, rummaging for scraps of clues about you in your jeans pockets when you weren't looking?" It was obvious that these images of himself were haunting him.

Her chest froze over. "I do. I understand. Believe me. I hate to think I did that to you. It was the same . . ." She had to pause in order to get the words out. The sobs were nearly uncontrollable now. "It was the same way my mother had treated me." She'd only just drawn the parallel.

"Tell me, Ruby, please." These words marked a change in his tone. He'd shown his cards; despite the front he'd put up, Ed still wanted to make things right with Ruby. And this gave her the courage to go on.

She told him everything—about the way she'd never known her father, what this had done to her, the way she'd really felt at each of her new schools, the way she'd majored in philosophy to find a meaning behind it all, and had only come out more terrified in the end. She explained her tenuous relationship with her momma, about her yellow-page searches, her failed relationships, the private eye, and how terrified she'd really been to drive and exactly why.

Ruby gave Ed a snapshot of her life. She told him about how she'd allowed herself to settle in just once, in Lake Okeechobee, Florida. Ruby had tried the word out cautiously at first, because they'd been there two years with Jeff. She'd said it slow and timid, only when her momma wasn't there; when he'd tuck her in at night she'd whisper nervously, "Good night, Dad." She told Ed how she'd noticed his mouth turn up at the corners when she did that. How at school she'd made a Father's Day ashtray, a clay and tempera paint monstrosity, for Jeff. And so when her mother started to stay out late and later still, she'd sit at her window and watch for her car lights on the driveway. Ruby had dreamed up a dramatic scene, where her momma would have their stuff in the car and reach into Ruby's bed to scoop her up to go. But Jeff's arm would be tight at her shoulder. "She's my daughter and she's not going anywhere," he'd say.

But in actuality it hadn't gone down that way. Ruby had woken up and they were off to Southern California, where she'd go on to ignore Hank, jumble her name and image, getting closer to high school, closing herself off tighter still. Now she'd never hear Jeff say again, the way he had once, "You know, Rube (he often called her Rube), your daddy was a fool to leave a special girl like you." By the time she'd settled in Orange County she wasn't even sure he *had* actually said that.

"Do you think you can survive the rest of your life without knowing who he is, Rube?"

The fact that Ed had handled her name that way, shaped it into something loving once again, touched her deeply.

"Ed, I have never wanted anything more in my life. I have a crazy person's collection of telephone books circled with possible matches. I have clipped out photos from magazines and made composite images." Her greatest fears were revealed, and here was Ed, looking at her lovingly, possibly more lovingly than he had before. She was further encouraged to go on. "And now, I have to find a way to forget because it's only going to hurt me in the end, hold me back from this life I have now." She couldn't believe how much like her momma's words these—her own words—were.

"I can't even imagine what it must be like to not know. And I can only guess what it cost you to say that." He looked at her long, deeply, his hand at her hairline, sweeping down to her mouth, before he kissed her, bringing on the tingle not only of attraction, but of this being the real thing, the enduring kind of love her road had finally taken her to.

She looked to the sky, stretched her spine up tall, and then grabbed for her purse, a few inches from where she sat.

He moved next to her on the bench, dragged her hair back from her face with both hands, and kissed her softly.

Could it be a good-bye kiss? After she'd come so far and accomplished so much?

He pulled her into his chest, which smelled of a different detergent, a sign they'd been apart. His old T-shirt felt soft on her cheek. It was the safest she'd ever felt and she would do anything to make sure she held onto this. The possibility of losing him made her limbs go numb.

"Ruby," he spoke into the top of her head, the wind of the word on her scalp. "I would never leave you because of all that. I think you're the bravest girl I know. What's crazy is that your *momma* wouldn't want you to know your father or even tell you why. And then on top of that she dragged you all around the country until you didn't even know who you were anymore! I can't even believe the things she's done!"

But hearing the very words she'd thought countless times come back at her, Ruby couldn't help but feel—after the past couple of days she'd spent with her momma—that maybe there was more to it than just that black and white version. She was reminded of the weekend before she'd left to start her life in New York. Her momma had bought her a washed silk dress and a printed scarf. It was the kind of elegant thing Ruby had always pined over in her secondhand, ill fitting, unstylish clothing. Why, then, had her mother presented her with a gift like that? When Ruby pulled the top off the garment box, she was shocked.

"Why now?" she'd asked, thinking of all the odd jobs she'd pursued just to get the right pair of sneakers.

"Because you are going to start your life now. You are not going to go backwards and wonder. You are going to be someone new in New York City." She'd looked far off when she said it. And it was then that Ruby glimpsed for the first time that her momma might have been weak and afraid, too—though of what, she didn't know. Something had happened to her, Ruby thought then; but she'd never tell what it was.

It had been difficult over the years to remember this hurt she'd seen in her momma, and to remain sympathetic about it, since she never shared, actually shared, any of the details with Ruby. Ruby had shut Ed out in the same way; even so, he'd continued to be considerate when his own needs weren't being met, though he'd felt like a complete stranger in his own home.

Sure, she hadn't been afraid to drive, her momma, but she had other vehicles for her fears, and Ruby had just been an ignorant bystander, wailing and turning blue from holding her breath at each stop. But Ruby didn't have to treat Ed that way. She had a choice. And it would require letting go to take that sort of action. Could she? She was going to try. For now, it was the best she could do.

"Rube, I wish you'd told me all that before. It kills me that you thought that any of that would affect the way I feel about you. But I'm glad we have it all out there now. We are going to make a beautiful life and nothing is going to stand in the way of that."

Ruby was buoyant as she'd ever been there, with all her secrets out. She was ready to run a marathon, conquer the world, zoom around all night long.

Twenty-four

Warning signs: These signs are usually yellow with black lettering or symbols; most are diamond-shaped. These signs warn you to slow down and be prepared to stop if necessary. They warn you that a special situation or a hazard is ahead.

—Connecticut Department of Motor Vehicles Driver's Manual

"Don't you think we might go somewhere different today?" Jack asked. They were over at Jones's again. She'd been there with Sammie just yesterday. Just as Ruby had bit into her cheeseburger, Sammie had exclaimed, "Okay, so I'm definitely going to Hunter!"

"Really!" Ruby couldn't believe it.

"Yup." Sammie bit into a fry.

"Can I ask what brought on the change of heart about school?" Ruby had asked.

"After my mom accused you of kidnapping me, we had a very long talk. And she said the reason she was always shielding me from everything was because every time she took me somewhere I acted terrified."

"Is that true?" Ruby had asked. It had definitely been true at UCONN, but in New York City, Sammie seemed to truly shine.

"As much as I'd like to blame my mom one hundred percent, yes, I freak out when people look at me. I hate that they think I'm slow or stupid or a baby just because I'm in a wheelchair. But you and your friend Dina . . . you guys don't treat me like that at all." She'd said it before, but it must have meant even more than Ruby had assumed.

"I'm glad. I really am. But what do you think gave you the courage now?"

"Well, Ruby, remember when you were terrified to drive?"

"Do I ever!"

"Well, I was thinking a lot about how . . . you did it anyhow. I mean, it took you forever, but look at you now. And I thought I should try the same tactic."

Ruby couldn't help thinking about the chain reaction, now that she was at the same table with Jack. If it hadn't been for him, she wouldn't have learned to drive, Sammie wouldn't have been influenced by that . . . it was fatherly work Jack did, helping people to face things, live life fully, and yet his own family scorned him.

There were things, she was realizing, that would never make sense. It wasn't that you had to stay put to fix them, like she'd thought. It was just the opposite: you had to find a way to move on anyhow. The thing was not to run away.

"What a day, huh?" Ruby said to Jack, taking in the breadth of spring—all the blossoms, the green everywhere. It was possible to forget the dead winter completely in the glory of it all. It was important to let it go for a while, she knew.

"Number twenty-five!" the cook yelled, although Jack and Ruby were standing right there, the only patrons. He slid the two plates, heaped with French fries, in their direction. They resumed their seats at the same table they always sat at, although they had their pick. As they did, one other patron approached the order window—a dark-haired man in a flannel shirt with cut-off sleeves.

"How's the driving school going?" Ruby asked.

"Well, spring is a little slow. In fact, I'm thinking of maybe downsizing." Jack removed the top of his bun and squirted some ketchup on top of the onion and thick tomato slice. He replaced the bun and lifted the burger to his mouth to take a huge bite. "Yum." He shook his head with satisfaction. He'd had his hair cut very short, so that he looked nearly bald.

"What do you mean downsizing? You're the only person there." Ruby took the plastic ketchup bottle and started squeezing her design on the ruffled edges of the paper plate. She worried that Jack meant he'd close the place down. She thought of him, the way he described himself—a young man with Brylcreem greasing his hair down, charming all the ladies who came in.

Jack shook his head, smiling. Some similar memory must have sparked in his head. "I'm real glad I got to know you, Ruby Reynolds," he said. "The thing is, I'm old. And I want to be closer to my kids—they don't need to think I'm a hero. I'm fine with them not getting it. I just want to have them, however I can."

Ruby couldn't help her tears at the sound of his loving, gentle desire.

He put his burger down, straightened out his features. "Spending this time with you . . . it's helped me to realize that," he said.

It was the closest she'd get to having the kind of relationship with him she used to irrationally wish for. And though she hadn't thought like that for some time now, the sound of it moved her greatly, touched her deep down. She took his hand in her own, squeezed it tightly to show this. "Well, gee whiz," she said. She was going to turn it into a joke, make light of everything, as she was prone to do. But then Ruby thought better of it. "That really means a lot, Jack. I'm real glad I got to know you, too."

In a few years they probably wouldn't see each other very much, wouldn't remember everything they'd said or how many hamburgers they'd shared. But they'd have this, if they ever wanted to go back to it.

"I was going to head over to Selma's shop and show her a new design. You want to come along?" Ruby re-looped her scarf over her neck.

"Sure," Jack said.

Ruby hated to think he felt useless. A person like Jack needed to feel useful. He closed himself inside the passenger seat, buckled up. The road was slick with the rain that had fallen in black spots you could see only when they glimmered in the sun. Ruby did her best to avoid those.

At Selma's shop, Billie Holiday was playing . . . a little too loudly. And the recording was scratchy, like an old record can sound. Selma was working on a new window display. Huge patchwork flowers seemed to spring from the base of the window. They were extraordinary in their colors and detail, silk greenery braided around their wire stems.

"Hey there!" she yelled in her big voice, a huge red dress and her rosy cheeks, flushed from working hard in the window, giving her the appearance of Santa Claus.

Jack helped Selma down; his loose skin, Ruby knew, was surprisingly soft. "Working hard, huh?" Jack asked.

"Yup, gotta get the kids into college somehow." She walked over to the register, bent behind, and picked up a patchwork quilt embroidered with letters of floral, gingham, and paisley. It read WHAT'S LOVE GOT TO DO WITH IT?

"That's awesome," Ruby said, unzipping her coat. There were all the traditional quilt colors—reds, blues, greens, and lots of white. The letters were artfully uneven and there were broken hearts quilted all over it. In New York City something handmade like that could sell for over seven hundred dollars, easily.

"Well, this fabulous quilter I know made it for me for only a hundred dollars."

"Wow. That's a steal." Ruby ran her fingers over the intricate quilting.

"I know; she says it's real hard to get business around here. It's not like Manhattan or Boston where you've got shops on every corner."

"So how are you doing?" Ruby asked.

Selma reached underneath the counter, pulled out a small coin. "Seven days sober," she said.

This was hard-won, Ruby was sure of that. Soon enough, Selma would have to go to court, face the music, possibly jail time. "I'm so proud of you," Ruby said. And she felt it deep in her heart, the way you do only when someone in your family achieves something, something you understand the value of—because you know them for their best and worst.

"Oh yeah, and Jonathan's new wife has got them calling her Mom."

"Oh, that's gotta be awful," Ruby said.

She fiddled with a glitter-on-paper sun, twisting it into a cone and letting it snap back.

Ruby showed Selma her Ugly on the Inside collection: the long tooth with twisted roots and a cavity, the snail, and the half-eaten sandwich. Selma shook her head. "I'm blown away," she said. "You've really got it, you know." She ordered them all. The last collection she'd stocked had gotten mentioned in the *Hartford Courant* and in the Connecticut section of the *New York Times*. She'd sold out . . . not to mention the foot traffic and extra purchases that came along with it all.

On the way home, Jack was silent for a good while, staring outside the passenger window. Finally he spoke, turning to her, the jersey barrier whizzing by. "I actually wanted to ask your opinion on something about Drive for Life. I was approached by some huge corporation. They want to buy the property from me and turn it into an Outback Steakhouse," he said. "They're willing to give me a load of money for it, but I don't know if that would be selling out, if I should wait and look for someone to continue the business instead."

"What?" Ruby was shocked. "No, you have to do it if that's

what you want. If people are ready to help themselves, they'll find a way to do it. You can't help everyone," she said. It cost her dearly to deliver the words she knew would persuade him to move far, far away, but it was the right thing and she knew it. The big company would pay well and Jack would be able to enjoy retirement comfortably.

In the rearview, she could see a white truck speeding up the on-ramp.

"Ah, well, I guess you're right . . . I just don't have the same business as I used to. Everyone goes to the big driving schools. I get a couple of clients a week . . . they need me, so I've kept it going all this time while business tapered off. But it just doesn't make sense anymore is all."

Ruby switched into the right lane, because that truck had merged behind her directly into the left, and looked determined to drive way faster than the speed limit, despite the wet road. She'd checked her mirrors and craned her neck first and everything looked clear.

"Do it. Go out to your kids, Jack. It's the right thing for—" Without her realizing, the truck had gained even more speed and was now switching into this slow lane that she wasn't even all the way in yet. Even Jack didn't see the truck until it was too late. When her whole front end and most of her back end were in front of it, she saw the truck speeding like crazy right into her rear!

Rather than slam on the brakes, like her instincts told her, Ruby turned her wheel fiercely to pull aside into the left lane and sped up. They were both silent in the slow motion terror of the movement. Finally they cleared the truck by mere inches—Ruby's car half in both lanes—as it hurtled by and far out of the danger zone.

In the aftermath, her hands shook uncontrollably. Her heart pounded in her ears, at her jaw. It seemed her entire head was pulsing.

"That was close!" Jack breathed big. "Are you okay?" He laid a hand on her shoulder as Ruby stared straight ahead in shock, her foot on autopilot over the gas pedal.

"Yes. Yes, I am okay." And as she said it, she realized she'd been very close to disaster, but she'd made it. She was now safe, and so was Jack.

"You did a fantastic job reacting to that. That was pure survival instinct. Now, the trick is not to let that scare you off the road. Near misses, accidents even, are all part of driving. The road is unpredictable. But unfortunately, it's the best thing we've got." Jack's serious advice took on a tender note, the way he pushed his glasses back over his nose adding to his empathetic look.

Twenty-five

When a vehicle is struck from the side, it will move sideways. Everything in the vehicle that is not fastened down, including the passengers, will slide toward the point of crash, not away from it.

—Connecticut Department of Motor Vehicles Driver's Manual

A couple of days before her wedding, Ruby had a to-do list longer than that book of rejects she'd dated and tossed in what felt like another life. She had to pick up the key rings to loop through the Two Peas in a Pod charm she'd created for the favors. There was a final payment to drop off at the bakery. She had to pick up her dress, the veil, her shoes from the shoemaker. There was makeup to purchase at the mall and lingerie to buy. All of this on her list, and yet the whole day something felt off. She went through everything and she couldn't imagine what it was.

At any rate, Ruby was zooming along 191 North. She should have felt better about it all than she did. It seemed the closer she got to the wedding day, the more she thought about her father. This time she shared her feelings with Ed, and this made a great difference, but it didn't close up the hole that she was starting to see would always be there.

A few raindrops gently descended, melted into the windshield.

Quickly, one became two, two became four, and then Ruby needed the wipers to see. Just as rapidly, even that wasn't doing enough to clear her view. Her heartbeat picked up, she touched the brake lightly, concentrated on picking out the yellow line as best she could in the sheet of water clouding her view. *Okay, don't get nervous Ruby, you can do this.*

Ruby's mobile telephone rang, startling her slightly. When she realized it was just the phone, the earpiece of which was already snuggly over her lobe, she went to grab for the handset, rooted around in the center console for it, and shifted her eyes for just a single second to see the number, irrationally thinking it could have been Robert Cohen, still hoping despite herself, despite the fact that he'd closed the case long ago.

In that one second she missed the chance to swerve to the right, onto the shoulder, where the eighteen wheeler that had lost control, jackknifing across three lanes, would have missed her. There was unbelievable noise, harsh and scraping, sparks, a fiery burst, and then slow, dull pain. And then, just as quickly, the feeling subsided to numbness; she didn't feel nearly as bad. She couldn't see, but in her head, Ruby sensed the darkness of the stormy sky brighten up. It was a gigantic relief somehow.

She floated off on a huge, round inner tube, mild water beneath her and the sun high above. She floated far, far . . . to the end of the earth it seemed, where she could see over the edge. And then the earth moved, hurling her into a deep, steep fall, and she sat up with a start, realizing she wasn't floating at all.

She was in bed, and her momma was there, nearly sitting on top of her. She looked nervous in a way she never had before.

"What happened to you?" Ruby asked, her momma's face worrying her.

"Do you remember anything?" Momma answered with a question.

"I remember rain, and then a big yellow tube, like the one our neighbor in Orange County had . . . I think I was in the Caribbean

Sea, maybe." Ruby began to realize the crazy sense of what she'd just said, but wasn't clear on why she'd said it.

Ruby's momma smiled. "That's so like you, Ruby, to forget the pain."

"What do you mean?" Ruby had an itch on her face and realized she couldn't move her right arm to scratch it. She couldn't move her left arm either. Panic overtook her. "What happened to me?" Tears welled up as her breath and heart sped.

"Shhhhh, shaaaaaa baby," Ruby's momma said. Now she could remember her momma saying that when Ruby was sick with strep throat, all her limbs weak and achy. Her momma rubbed her arm, she could feel that slightly.

"Don't stop, momma. Please, don't stop."

Ruby drifted back to that sea, gave herself over to the warmth of the sun above her, floating low and lower.

When she woke again, there was some pain at her chest. Her momma hadn't moved from her perch on the bed, rubbing her arm gently still. She looked as if she'd been crying.

"Go ahead, Momma. Tell me. What happened?" She had to concentrate very hard to focus on her momma's face, so that it didn't separate off into thousands of little swirls, moving all over the place.

As soon as she started to speak, her face twisted, her words sobbed a little here and there. "You were driving to have your nails done. You were getting married." Her lips pulled in, her eyes squeezed in tight.

Ed! Oh, she remembered Ed. Longed to see him, as if she were Dorothy, returning to Kansas, and hadn't seen him in far too long.

"They think you reached for your cell phone. A tractor trailer skidded out right into you. And for ten seconds, Ruby, you . . ." She seemed to be unable to go on.

"What, Momma?" she asked, her mouth feeling droopy and raw.

"You had died. For ten seconds, I had lost you forever." Her momma leaned into her now, her tears falling over Ruby's cheeks.

The moment hardly seemed real—or as real as her tube ride on the Caribbean Sea had been. It definitely didn't feel as if this was her they were speaking about. Ruby had died? The idea was detached from her, floating up above them, something she wouldn't work out for some time. And because of that, there was a heavy, steady calm in her voice when she spoke. "But I'm okay now?" Ruby checked.

Her momma looked at all of Ruby, from her feet to her head. Ruby shifted her gaze to see what her momma had seen. Most of her was covered in white bandages. This couldn't possibly be her own body she saw. She couldn't place what had happened, and through the haze, a wave of terror washed briefly over her.

"You've got quite a few broken bones. And you're gonna be here for a while, but . . . yes . . . you are going to be fine."

That, at least, was a wild relief.

"Am I still getting married?" She wasn't sure which memories were real and which weren't just then. She thought of Ed walking away, as she watched him from the window above, as unable to move as she was right now in this hospital room. Was she ready for the answer to that?

"You're not getting married tomorrow, that's for sure, but the castle said they have a date open in the fall if you'd like it." Another huge wave of relief went over her.

"Ruby, there's something else I'd like to talk with you about, before I chicken out."

"Yes?" In her haze, she hadn't the slightest idea what her momma might say next.

"While you were gone, I . . . I realized that you were right about something. I should have told you about your father." She looked to the ceiling, to the walls, and finally to Ruby.

Just then Ruby thought all the broken bones in the world would be worth it if her father was going to walk right through that door now. Her eyes went crazy, blinking and twitching, wild with anticipation.

Her momma held a piece of paper out in front of Ruby's face.

In her momma's all caps handwriting, its rigid, straight lines and unforgiving, sharp *N*s and *T*s, the paper read: *GERRY RICHARDS, CLEMMONS, NORTH CAROLINA*. She repeated the words out loud, and they clashed and echoed with the words and pains in her head.

"Is he coming here now?" Ruby couldn't contain her excitement. The calm had broken and a shot of pain stabbed at her left leg. Tears moistened her pillow. The overhead florescent light seemed to burn her skin.

"No. I haven't spoken to your father since we left him."

Ruby was horrified. She'd wasted all these years just because her momma had wanted to move on!

"But why?"

Her momma looked up to the ceiling, nearly bending her neck in half. And just like that, she opened up to say the words Ruby had thought she'd waited a lifetime to hear. "Your daddy was a terrible drunk, Ruby. And when you were just seven months old, with your tiny little fingers and toes, your daddy . . ."

Your daddy! The words were too much to bear. It sounded so wonderful. She could forgive him for being a drunk! Surely she could. She pictured her curling her baby fingers around his one big finger.

"What, Momma?"

"Your daddy picked you up when he came back from a night at McDylan's, drunk as a skunk."

She thought maybe now that she heard it she could remember something about this. Yes, he was reading her a story, maybe the one with the rabbit on the cover. It stung, the way her breath raced through her cracked ribs. She urged her momma to move along, "Please finish, Momma."

"And . . . well, you started to cry. Of course you did, he woke you up right after I'd just got you down again, and he smelled like the inside of a gin bottle. And he told you to shut up! He said it eight or ten times over and over."

That was a little odd, maybe. But in a certain light, maybe it could be a little goofy, or sarcastic, as if a baby would know what that meant!

"I came in and tried to take you out of his hands, I was so scared he'd drop you; your blanket was dangling so close to the floor. I'll never forget that, it was almost touching the floor. But when I came close, he swatted me out of the way. He was cursing up a storm about how he could take care of his own baby and who the hell was I, just like his own momma. And I yelled, 'Give me the baby! Give me my Ruby!' And he knocked me to the ground with a swift arm. And all the while I watched your face, you had that tiny tuft of red hair and it was blowing from the force of his words. And he looked at you and then smacked you so hard you started to scream."

Ruby was shocked, stunned. What were these words? What was this thing her momma was trying to tell her?

"And then when you wouldn't stop crying. I kept grabbing for you . . ." Her momma covered her mouth, looked briefly at Ruby and then at the plasma drip alongside. "And he just . . . he just threw you right onto the floor." Her momma cried and cried after she got that out, great heaving wails that brought the bed to shake, that made Ruby's body jostle painfully.

She sniffled and then continued. "I scrambled to the floor, grabbed you, soothed you to stop crying. It was a miracle, Ruby, that you had nothing but a cut on your hand. I stayed up all night waking you, worrying you had a concussion. I paced back and forth in our crappy little living room with the shag carpeting. And when I saw you hold on to your little rabbit, so glad you were okay, so innocent and helpless you were, I said to myself, I'd be damned if I was going to let that man hurt my Ruby again. By the time he woke up, I had us hiding at another house. And when, a few years later, it looked like he found us, I moved us to Florida—so you'd be safe."

Ruby didn't want to believe this. She couldn't have waited her whole life just to hear this awful tale. "No. That can't be true!" she yelled though her head seared with burning pains. "I saw his notes in your drawer, Momma, when we lived in California. You saved them; they said, 'Dear Beautiful Girls.' There's no way someone who wrote those things could do something like that." The sting was throbbing and Ruby tried to bring her hand to her head, but it only moved a couple of inches before she couldn't stand the pain.

Her momma looked sympathetic—an emotion she didn't normally do.

A nurse came in for a moment and looked at Ruby's chart, went to grab for the stethoscope around her neck, but then saw the tears in her momma's eyes and said instead, "I'm glad to see you're awake. I'll come back in a little bit to check on you."

Ruby was glad for the moment of silence. This was so much to take in. When the nurse closed them inside the room again, Ruby's momma stood up to pour a cup of water for Ruby from the tiny plastic yellow pitcher. She brought it over to her daughter's lips and gently lifted the back of Ruby's head so she could drink without dribbling. It was strange to have her care for her this way. Her momma sighed. And then she sat down again, rubbing Ruby's head the way she used to when Ruby was very little and couldn't sleep.

Ruby closed her eyes and listened to what her momma said very carefully.

"Baby, he *was* that man from the notes. He was the gentlest, most wonderful man you ever want to meet. That's why I fell in love with him, got married to him. We had such a fabulous time together, walking on the beach at the shore, watching the waves, dancing at the clubs at Jenkinson's beach. You've got his gray eyes, you know. It was what first made me love him, the way his eyes looked out in the moonlight, the way they glittered so brightly—huge, deep things—just like yours."

It was obvious that these memories hit her momma hard. She was always saying not to look back, but here she was doing just that. And she was doing it for Ruby.

Ruby grabbed her momma's hand. She'd never felt so connected to her. It was an unbelievable thing to know how your parents met, how they'd danced at Jenkinson's beach, how her momma had saved her like that.

"He loved Bruce Springsteen." She nearly laughed when she said that, evoked something from before it had all gone horribly wrong. Maybe back then, she'd thought she could have a fairy-tale life, make it everything she wanted it to be.

Despite the pain, the casts, Ruby thought it was all worth it to hear these words now.

"We were going to get married right there on the beach . . . But when he fell back to drinking, he was someone altogether different. He was a fragile man and right before you were born, he lost his own momma. She had cancer and he went and stayed with her in the hospital every day when he got out of work. Two weeks he spent like that, and when he got there on that last night, she was gone already. And then I didn't see him for two days. He came back a different man." That was the end of it, Ruby guessed, from the way her momma's voice trailed off.

She wasn't sure what to do with it all, but an amazing calm came over Ruby. Now she knew. No matter what happened now, she knew.

Ed tried very hard not to cry when he finally saw Ruby awake for the first time, white plaster on nearly every limb, her hair hidden up under twists of bandages. He'd fallen asleep in the hallway after staying up next to Ruby all night, and her momma woke him to tell him Ruby was now awake. His gulp shone at his Adam's apple and Ruby felt her own tears well up at the sight of that.

"Ruby!" He kissed her long and gentle. Her mother excused herself to the cafeteria.

"Mom," Ruby called as she approached the door.

She turned around, looking exhausted, ashen.

"Thanks." She smiled a great, big smile, tears still falling.

Her momma shook her head like she understood.

For a while Ed and Ruby sat, just loving each other, happy that they were okay.

"How long have you been here?" she asked him.

"As soon as they brought you in. You know what they said, Ruby? They said, 'Boy, that is one lucky girl.' They said it about a hundred times, Ruby. They said, you . . . you could have . . ." He didn't finish.

"Shhhh . . . shaaaaa baby," she said. Her one free hand moved a little more now. And with it, she rubbed Ed's hair, comforting him. Ruby had almost died! It would have been unbelievable that she might have died behind the wheel of a car! Miserably ironic. And then she saw it all very, very differently. "You know," she whispered, "I think that crash was something I've been leading up to my whole life. It sounds crazy, I know. But now, I don't feel afraid of crashing, losing everything. I know that I've missed so much in my life because I didn't know how to see things."

"I'm never going to let a thing happen to you, Ruby Reynolds. I'm going to make you the happiest girl in the world."

"Well, it's too late for that, Ed Robbins. I already am. I already am."

A half hour later, Ruby's hospital room door opened to reveal Merry, Selma, Jack, Sammie, Dina, Jason, Ed's entire family, and Ruby's momma.

"If you wanted me to come and visit, Ruby, well, you could've just asked," Dina said. Jason was on her arm and she looked fabulous, despite the worry at her brow. Her belly was showing more now and she had on an adorable fitted shirt that gave her bumped middle a lively look. They both leaned in to kiss her.

Her friends and family had all introduced themselves in the hours since the accident. They'd bonded and exchanged stories and worries. Sammie rolled herself over to Ruby's side. "You know I wouldn't have let you go anywhere," Sammie said, tearing despite the tightness she tried to maintain from brow to chin. "You have to help me with my jewelry. I need a role model, you know."

"Don't forget about all that money you put down on your bridesmaid's dress!" Dina reminded Sammie.

"How you feeling, darling?" Jack had his head cocked to one side, his thinning brows furrowed in worry.

"You know what, I've never been happier. I really haven't."

"Yup, she's one weird girl," Selma said, kissing her cheek.

"Well, that's what we love about her," Merry agreed, laying down a bouquet of flowers at Ruby's side table.

"And she makes a mean chicken in the pot." Ed smiled, sitting next to his fiancée, this thing that had once served as a symbol of how little she'd shared with him now a private joke that meant just the opposite.

"That's my recipe." Ruby's momma beamed, maybe not aware of all the things that made her daughter click, but trying in the ways she could.

And for once, Ruby wasn't going to deny that connection. "That's absolutely right, Momma, absolutely right."

Twenty-Six

"Dum dum deeee dum," Dina hummed as she draped the veil over
Ruby's head. Her belly was so big, her blue dress looked like a tent.
But she was happy as hell. That was obvious. "You look beautiful,"
she said.

The scar in the middle of Ruby's forehead wasn't going to fade,
the doctor told her. "You could go to a plastic surgeon, though, and
he can get rid of it, no problem."

But Ruby didn't want to get rid of that scar. Like the other
things she'd experienced in her life, she now saw the accident as
something unique that had made her into the person she was today.
And that scar, over the long months of agonizing pain and physical
and emotional therapy, the learning to get back on the road again,
had served as a reminder of that fact. She now considered it her
most striking feature. It was something that made her different. And
that, she needed to remember, was okay.

Rather than wear bangs to cover it, as the hairstylist had suggested,

Ruby swept all her hair up and away, showing off every bit of that scar. All the people at her wedding, the people who loved her, would know just why she'd done that.

"Oh! You look georgous!" Sammie said. She'd just come rolling back into the bridal suite after leaving for the fifth time.

"We know you keep going out there to smooch that Ronnie guy!" Dina teased.

Sammie blushed, but she was no wallflower. "Yeah, so?" She'd changed so much since she'd gone off to school, Ruby could barely recognize her. She was so bold, beautiful. Jack had rigged her car so that she could drive with her hands, had taught her all the rules of the road before he himself had packed up and left for his new life.

The door opened once more, and Ruby's momma walked through, in a frothy sheath, in the same blue as the bridesmaid dresses. "Rube! You look absolutely beautiful! This whole place, the wedding, it's perfect."

Ruby doubted if her momma really approved of the place, the money, the whole thing. But this was a new level in their relation-ship . . . sometimes, when they disapproved of each other, they just lied. Amazingly, it was bringing them closer. After all the difficult truths they'd shared after that accident, the lying was a nice, easy thing. Her momma was trying out a new part of California—San Diego—for the moment. She'd met someone new, James—a teacher of social studies—and Ruby welcomed him warmly the day before, at the rehearsal dinner. After all, he wasn't her father . . . and she didn't need him to be.

The wedding was the very fairy tale that Suzanne had promised. And it was obvious she enjoyed stirring this kind of magic for Ed and Ruby.

Just before they walked down the aisle, Jack handed Ruby a tiny box.

"What's this?" she asked.

"It's your something blue," he said. "Go ahead, open it."

Inside the box was a pretty antique brooch. Jack pinned it to her dress and it looked exquisite, as if the dress had been waiting for something just like it.

When Jack walked Ruby down the aisle, his smile lit up the whole room.

And two weeks later, Ruby would have a similar look on her own face.

"What?" Ed would tickle her, on their fluffy hotel room bed, as she sat down next to him, freshly showered and ready to hit a restaurant for dinner.

"Looks like you're going to be a father," she'd say, smiling.

Ed would kiss Ruby one hundred times, all over her face and on her belly. And then he would say, "Well, I hope it's a girl. I've always wanted to have a daughter."

Ruby had the strangest feeling that it would be. Mothers, she'd learn one day, could sense these kinds of things.

And as the sun would set, they would take the long way to the restaurant they'd grown to love in Maui, stopping to take pictures in front of palm trees, so they could one day show their little girl how she was born out of so much love.